African Trio

Georges Simenon

African Trio

Talatala

Tropic Moon

Aboard the *Aquitaine*

A Helen and Kurt Wolff Book

Harcourt Brace Jovanovich

New York and London

Printed in the United States of America

Library of Congress Cataloging in Publication Data

Simenon, Georges, 1903–
  African trio: Talatala, Tropic moon, Aboard the Aquitaine.

  Translation of Le Blanc à lunettes, Coup de lune, and 45° à l'ombre.
  "A Helen and Kurt Wolff book."
  1. Africa—Fiction.
  I. Title.
PZ3.S5892Ah 1979 [PQ2637.I53]   843'.9'12   78–22272
ISBN 0-15-103955-0

First edition

B C D E

Contents

Preface, vii

Talatala, 3

Tropic Moon, 119

Aboard the Aquitaine, *231*

Preface

When we asked Georges Simenon to write an introduction for African
Trio, *he suggested that we use extracts from a reportage on Africa he
did for the magazine* Voilà *in the early thirties. The following excerpts
sum up his impressions of colonialism and his intimations about
Africa's future.*

I intended, in my reportage, to give an overall view of the African
continent, but there is no such thing as one Africa: there is an infinite
variety of Africas. There is the colonial bureaucracy, consisting of
people sent over with three-year contracts, stationed in coastal cities or
in the towns of the interior, confined to their offices, wearing a tie at all
times and temperatures, dealing with Africans only in the shape of
office clerks and women in colorful costumes. This is the Africa of red
tape, of interminable reports and supplementary reports.

There is the Africa of the timber companies, of men who travel by
river into the interior, who build villages for one or two hundred native
woodcutters, and who consider themselves true colonial settlers.

There is the Africa of the virgin forest, of the pygmies who live in its
depth, the Africa at the end of the railroads that young engineers have
built with ruthless disregard for their own and the railroad men's lives.

There is the Africa of the native villagers who buy their wives and
bicker, endlessly and patiently, over the goats and hoes of the dowry.
. . . There is the Africa of those who practice the art of poisoning and
witchcraft.

Living in Africa, the white men sweat, complain, succumb to apathy,
and end up hating the world and themselves. Once able to go back to
France, they swear never to return to Africa again. But they do return,
and not because they can't obtain employment elsewhere. They return
for a multitude of reasons, chiefly an ambience they no longer can do
without.

But the time of colonial Africa is running out. We are living in the transition period between adolescence and maturity. Tomorrow the black who has today bought a fuchsia-colored suit at a French department store will be dressed in impeccable black and take his seat at international meetings, dignified and unbending. The native lieutenant of today, proud of his stripes and the prizes won on the range, may become a general. Not in a foreign army—in his own.

What kind of recollection will the African have of us white colonists? Will he remember gratefully the railroads paid for with the life of one laborer for each tie beam? The banks that gave him paper money, knowing full well that paper wouldn't last in the humidity of the huts and that the blacks would have to exchange it for coins at a rate of five francs for three? Will we be remembered as benefactors because we introduced the Africans to spirits much higher in alcoholic content and much more expensive than their native palm wine? Or for having sown the countryside with small beings of mixed color?

All these questions I put to an old-time colonist who had "gone native," with a hut in every village. Here is the answer:

"Our blacks in the villages can't count. They don't know how old they are. They have no notion of what goes on a hundred kilometers from where they live. But better than I they know what happened thirty or fifty years ago. Believe me, they keep a record, passed on from generation to generation, of all the rifle shots and whippings of which they were the target, and of many other things I prefer to keep quiet about."

My informant concluded his speech by saying:

"Believe me, the African's answer to us whites is *merde*, and right they are."

October, 1932

Talatala

Translated by Stuart Gilbert

One

"Do you hear, Georges?"

Her husband, who was just bringing a glass of beer to his lips, gave a slight start.

"What?"

"Ferdinand says that the only way to quench one's thirst out here is to drink tea—as hot as one can bear it."

"I know that."

"Then why do you drink beer?"

"Because I don't like tea."

"That's your fourth bottle today."

"Have I counted up the cigarettes you've smoked since breakfast?"

Trying to repress a smile, Ferdinand Graux looked away and met the eyes of the old Englishman from Nairobi; the twinkle in them told him that their owner understood French and was following the conversation.

Where was it taking place, this little conjugal squabble at the tea table? Already it was hard to realize what stage of the journey had been reached. Unless one made a mental effort, one had the impression that it had been going on for weeks and weeks, though in fact it had begun only on the previous day—at two in the morning, it is true.

The scene of this particular tiff was Aswan, but, Graux remembered, there had been a previous one in Cairo, over the tip.

"Do you hear, Georges?"

And her husband, as usual, seemed to be coming out of a dream when he barked out his:

"What?"

"Ferdinand says we needn't tip the waiter. Everything's included in the fare, hotels and board and tips as well."

As a matter of fact, Ferdinand Graux had first noticed this quaint little couple long before they took the airliner. In Marseilles, an hour before the steamer sailed, he had seen a small birdlike, excitable young woman dash on board, followed by a panting mother and a worthy-looking old fellow in his Sunday best, evidently her father.

At the time he hadn't noticed her husband, who was probably down in the purser's office, settling up for the voyage. The young woman, however, was very much in evidence; one kept running into her on deck and in the corridor, in saloons and smoking rooms, showing her parents around the ship.

All three shed tears when the time came to say good-bye. At first Graux had supposed the young woman was the wife of one of the colonial-army officers on board, whose rank entitled them to first-class passages.

Then came a gap. Graux had paid no more attention to her. His idea of an agreeable sea voyage was to be left in peace, and, following his invariable practice, he settled down with a book in his deck chair in a secluded corner of the boat deck. His first two days at sea were spent in the perusal of the three hundred pages of a book entitled *Statistics for an Economic Survey of the Postwar Decade*.

How had he happened to come in contact with the little birdlike woman? After some thought it came back to him. One afternoon, while he was reading, she'd planted herself beside his chair and stared, first at him, then at the book in his hand. Though they were in the western Mediterranean and the month was May, she was sporting a new and quite unnecessary sun helmet.

"Good lord! I understand why you look so glum if you always read stuff like that!" And noticing columns of figures, she added, "Are you an accountant?"

Graux shook his head.

"Then what's your job?"

"I'm a coffee planter."

"You don't mean it!"

He could picture her running up to her husband, who was playing cards on the bar terrace, and announcing:

"Do you know, Georges? That man who always keeps to himself—guess what he does!"

She was young, not more than twenty, and had the rather washed-out complexion of the city-bred girl. On board ship she seemed pathetically out of place and spent her days hunting around for congenial company. Her husband, who had already got into white drill suits, passed most of his time playing *belote*. The more select coterie on board took no notice of her and played bridge from morning till bedtime.

Obviously she resented being "out of it," and she paced the decks indefatigably, buttonholing stewards and ship's officers. On the fourth night out she badgered the purser into getting together an after-dinner dance on deck. When it began, Graux retreated to his cabin. On landing at Alexandria he supposed he had seen the last of them. Brushing aside the swarm of native porters milling around him in a cloud of dust, he walked straight to the Imperial Airways bus.

And whom should he find seated in it but the little woman and her husband!

"Taking our plane?" she cried at once.

He had a better right to call it "his" plane, considering that for the last six years he had been traveling on it, in both directions.

"You haven't met my husband yet, have you? Georges Bodet, Assistant Commissioner at Niangara, in the Belgian Congo."

"I've been there."

"What? You know Niangara? . . . Do you hear, Georges?"

That was the first time Graux heard that shrill "Do you hear, Georges?" of which he was to be so heartily sick before their journey's end.

The Airways bus halted outside a big hotel, and the little woman twittered:

"Say, let's sit at the same table. All the others are English and I won't understand a word. Do you speak English?"

"Yes."

That was enough to start her off again.

"Do you hear, Georges? . . . Didn't I keep telling you you should learn English?"

Poor Georges! Each time she addressed him in this way he winced, lowered his eyes, and kept silent.

A very fair young man of about twenty-five, he was already beginning to run to fat. He had done three years in the Congo civil service, at Matadi, and had used his first leave to get married.

"What! Drinking again, Georges?"

There was no question he drank rather heavily—but always beer, glass after glass of it, with the result that he usually seemed half asleep.

"What shall we do this evening? How about taking a look at the native town? It must be awfully quaint. Tell me, Monsieur Ferdinand . . ."

Only twenty-four hours had elapsed since then, but already she had dropped the "Monsieur" and was calling him "Ferdinand."

"And you must call me 'Yette.' My real name is Henriette, but that doesn't suit me a bit, does it? Much too prim and proper, and I'm not that sort at all. Folks have got to take me as they find me. I was born in Paris; my people live on Boulevard Beaumarchais, near the Bastille. Do you know it?"

Her expansiveness was almost embarrassing. She had told him all about her family in detail, and he knew now that her father was a department manager in the Magazins Réunis, that her mother was Belgian, and that she had made Bodet's acquaintance when visiting her grandmother at Charleroi in Belgium.

But though he knew all that, and felt vaguely sorry for her, he had refused to accompany the Bodets on a nocturnal jaunt around Alexandria. He had preferred to go to bed, while the young couple, escorted by a native guide, set out to explore haunts of more or less ill repute.

At two in the morning the hotel came to life again. The native servants started banging on bedroom doors, and soon a dozen people had gathered around the tables in the restaurant, where only half the lights had been turned on, over a breakfast of bacon and eggs and marmalade.

"Are all these people taking our plane?" Yette asked in shrill surprise. "Will there be room enough?"

She was pale and tired, and eyed the bacon and eggs with disgust. Even the *café au lait* displeased her.

"How horrid! It's condensed milk!"

Meanwhile the others, all English, were eating a hearty breakfast, in complete silence.

"I can't understand people stuffing themselves like that at two in the morning."

Convinced that these foreigners couldn't understand her, she didn't trouble to lower her voice.

It was pitch-dark when the Airways bus conveyed them to the airport.

"Try to get a seat in the middle of the cabin," Graux advised her. "Do you hear, Georges?"

She elbowed her way to the front and was the first to climb the steps. There was a faint glimmer of light in the eastern sky. The engine had not yet been started up.

"Oh, look, Georges! Do you see how Ferdinand's dressed?"

For her it was a revelation. Hitherto she had always seen him in gray suits, which, with his glasses and his quiet manner, made him look very ordinary. This morning, however, he was dressed like the Airways pilot: in khaki shorts that revealed his sinewy legs, a shirt cut on military lines, and a bush jacket.

"Why don't you wear clothes like that? They're much more sensible and wouldn't get dirty like those white ducks you always wear."

"Graux is his own master and can dress as he likes. I can't."

The last words were drowned in the roar of the engine, which had just started. The chocks were pulled away, and already Yette was clutching desperately the arms of her seat.

Meanwhile Ferdinand, as snugly ensconced in a corner as if he were in a railway carriage, was cutting the pages of another book, *Some Recent Theories of Production and Distribution.*

At six in the morning they landed on the Cairo airfield, after all the passengers had craned their necks toward the windows for a glimpse of the Pyramids. In a reinforced-concrete waiting room another breakfast was served and everyone provided with a lunch basket containing sandwiches, oranges, and a Thermos bottle of hot tea.

"You see, Georges—I wasn't sick after all!"

Graux knew that no one was ever sick on this part of the run. On the ground level it was beginning to warm up, and the glare off the sand made it necessary to wear dark glasses.

"Are you married?"

"No. Or, I should say, not yet. My fiancée will be coming out to join me in three months, when the rains are over. We shall get married in Niangara."

"Aren't you nervous about letting her travel all that way by herself? Georges would never dream of letting me do that; he's much too jealous."

The shrill, high-pitched voice was getting on everybody's nerves, and the British travelers were casting far-from-amiable glances in her direction. In any case, they had been traveling together all the way from London and already had a day's flight behind them—from Brindisi to Alexandria—and they had developed the usual clannish feeling toward newcomers. Moreover, owing to the presence of these three additional passengers, there were no spare seats on which to place their hand luggage.

The plane took off again and climbed to two thousand meters. Beneath them lay the Nile, a ribbon of silver on the drab monotony of the desert. After little more than a quarter of an hour, Yette began to show signs of discomfort.

Without a word Graux placed a little papier-mâché basin on her knees, and it was only just in time.

The heat was steadily increasing, and the roar of the engine made conversation impossible. Bodet, whose face had gone a livid green, was summoning up all his will power to keep himself from succumbing, and he managed to hold out till they landed in Aswan. There he hurried out of the plane and started looking desperately around him.

"It's behind the hangar!" Graux shouted to him.

The hangar was no more than a wooden shed dumped down in the desert. Of the town nothing could be seen except some minarets twinkling in the heat haze.

It was two in the afternoon, and the heat was telling on everyone. The sand was scorching underfoot. As at the other stops, a buffet was provided, and it was here that Graux informed Yette that the best way to quench one's thirst is to drink scalding-hot tea.

Which was followed by the inevitable "Do you hear, Georges?"

The old Englishman smiled. He was portly and silver-haired, and wore a well-cut light tweed suit. That was enough to place him. He was a businessman, Graux felt sure, on his way to Capetown.

It was equally easy to guess the destination of another Englishman, who,despite the high charge for excess luggage, had four rifles with him. He was going to Nairobi, big-game hunting. And the young army officers, laden with golf clubs and tennis rackets, were certainly bound for Khartoum.

Of the planter type there was only one representative: a thin, unkempt, middle-aged man accompanied by a woman in black, presumably his wife. Graux had heard him talking to the others about his apple orchard and cherry trees, which meant that he was on his way to Kenya, where the climate resembles that of Europe.

Yette was feeling better after her experience with the basin, and some cups of tea.

"Well, I must say I'll be glad to have a nice long sleep in Khartoum. When do we get there, Ferdinand?"

"We won't get there today."

"What? But the timetable says . . ."

"I know. But I've made this trip many times, and every time, because of the wind, or air pockets, or for some other reason, we've slept at Wadi Halfa."

"Do you hear, Georges? . . . Is there a hotel there, anyhow?"

"Yes, a very comfortable one."

That was so. When, at five in the evening, they landed in the midst of the desert, a van rolled up out of the blue and conveyed the travelers to a huge, immaculately clean building that looked more like a sanatorium than a hotel.

Set up by several pints of ice-cold beer, Georges Bodet developed an unwonted energy and proposed a "look around the town."

"There isn't any town, only a village a few miles from here. You'll have to take a taxi."

"Know what the fare is?"

"Two pounds."

"Oh!"

Graux could see him working out what that would come to in Belgian francs. The English passengers settled down to bridge, while Yette started shrilly grumbling about everything—the food, the drinks, and, above all, the fact that the native servants didn't know a word of French.

"Really, considering we pay like everybody else, it's up to them to understand us."

It got on her nerves, and her husband's, too, to see the Englishmen taking no notice whatever of them but keeping to themselves. That feeling of being "out of it" was more than she could stomach. Perhaps she also realized that the flimsy, rather gaudy dress she had had made specially for the journey was better suited for a picnic on the banks of a French river than for a desert outpost.

"Do you know the Commissioner at Niangara?" she asked Graux.

"I've met him once or twice. My plantation is only a hundred kilometers from Niangara."

"Do you have a car?"

"Yes, I couldn't do without one. It's waiting for me in Juba, where we leave the plane."

"Do you hear, Georges? And what's he like, the Commissioner? Is he married?"

"Yes. I understand his wife is going to have a baby."

"Then we'll get along together. I intend to have a baby, too, though Georges says it wouldn't be wise—because of the climate, you know."

Looking at her, Graux was inclined to agree with Georges. For all her vivacity, she was a delicate little creature, and he doubted if she could stand the climate, in any case.

"But I told Georges I'd made up my mind and he'd have to lump it. It's rotten enough for a woman out there, having nothing to do all day. If I don't have a child to keep me busy . . . Anyhow, I wouldn't mind betting there's one on the way." She began to go into details—Graux had the impression that she was deliberately out to scandalize him, or to display her modernity—while her husband frowned and lowered his eyes uncomfortably. She turned on him. "Why shouldn't I tell him if I feel like it? I daresay you think it's improper and all that, but I don't care. I believe in being natural."

The old Englishman was still smiling. His eyes met Graux's. And it was Graux who felt a trifle embarrassed. . . .

"You haven't told me yet. What's he like, the Commissioner?"

"You'll see."

"Is he young?"

"Thirtyish."

"Do you think he'll get along with my husband, and his wife will take to me? After all, we'll be the only Europeans there, won't we?"

And, cautious as usual, Graux replied again:

"You'll see."

"Is it a pretty place?"

How could one answer questions like that? She'd have to decide for herself, obviously.

"What did you say you grew on your plantation?"

"Coffee."

"Does it pay?"

"Well, not yet." So far he had laid out over four hundred thousand francs on it without return, for though coffee plants come into fruit in their third year, it takes five years before the yield suffices for a profit.

"Do you have any animals?"

"Yes, elephants."

"Well, I never! Did you hear that, Georges? Do you keep them as pets, or what?"

"No, I use them for clearing my land."

"How many do you have?"

"Three. There's one—Tom Thumb, his name is—who isn't even shackled, and comes to see me at breakfast every morning."

They were sitting near the two bridge tables. He was talking less for the benefit of the Bodets than for himself, and perhaps still more for the smiling old Englishman, who, every time he was dummy, quite openly listened in to the conversation that was going on in French. That old fellow, anyhow, knew Africa, Graux felt sure. For all his smiling ways there was little that escaped him, and, what was more, to judge from the expression on his face when Graux referred to his plantation, he probably knew a good deal about the coffee industry.

Graux decided he would like to have a talk with him, and after the Bodets had gone up to bed he lingered on, hoping that the bridge party would break up. But when he saw them cutting for another rubber, he, too, went upstairs.

Next morning they were called at three. At the early breakfast Yette still looked half asleep; her skin was shiny, she hadn't even washed or powdered her face.

"I'm sure I'll be sick again," she moaned.

Five of the passengers succumbed to airsickness that day, for the air was particularly bumpy, full of pockets, in crossing which the plane dropped abruptly hundreds of meters.

Then came Khartoum, and a big caravanserai in which once more no one knew a word of French. Yette was all the more exasperated when a number of pretty, well-dressed women invaded the hotel at teatime.

"Those women must be crazy, dressing like that in Africa!"

And she was even more furious at dinner, finding herself surrounded by ladies in low-necked dresses and men in dinner jackets.

The third morning came. It took an effort to realize that this was only the third day out. By now the nine English passengers were treating one another like old friends, and when Graux came down for breakfast, Yette, without thinking, said, "Good morning, honey."

None of them had much appetite that morning. Their eyes were aching. Bodet hadn't shaved.

They had transshipped into a hydroplane and were following the course of the White Nile, which here widened out into broad reaches of smooth water.

"I had no idea Africa was like this!" Yette exclaimed. "We've hardly seen any niggers."

"Don't worry. You'll see plenty soon."

"We'll be in Juba this evening, won't we?"

"So the timetable says. But usually something happens that obliges us to stop at Malakal. There we sleep in army barracks."

"All together?"

"No. You two will have a room to yourselves."

Bodet was showing signs of annoyance; after all, he, too, had lived in Africa, but for his wife apparently that didn't count. It was always to Graux that she applied for information, and after eliciting it she would turn to her husband with her irritating "Do you hear, Georges?"

It wasn't fair. Graux was his own master and had independent means. If he, Graux, had had to put in three years at Matadi as a junior civil servant, tied to his office, he'd have sung a different tune.

"I'd love to see his elephants. Do you know, he has a lion cub as well?"

Georges shrugged his shoulders and gave her a sour look.

There were two stops of half an hour for refueling; the passengers were given lunch and tea baskets, and the usual Thermos bottles of watery tea.

As Graux had predicted, they halted for the night at Malakal. During dinner Graux listened to what their pilot was telling the passengers at his table.

Yette noticed that they seemed excited and, turning to Graux, inquired:

"What's he saying?"

"Wait! . . . There's been an accident."

"Where?"

"Ssh!"

A few moments later he explained.

"It seems a plane crashed somewhere in the bush last night."

"One like ours—with passengers?"

"No, a private plane, owned by Lady Makinson. She was traveling in it with a friend, Captain Phelps. They left Cairo at about the same time as we did."

"Where were they going?"

"To the Upper Uele—about a hundred and fifty kilometers from my place. There's an elephant farm there, run by an Englishman, quite a character in his way. Lady Makinson was going to stay with him. The plane was due there yesterday evening, but it didn't turn up, and no news has come through."

"What did the woman want with a private plane?" said Yette disgustedly. "Swank, I call it!"

The English travelers seemed greatly distressed by the news, and one of them, who may have caught and understood her last remark, threw Yette a hostile glance.

Next day it was the usual round; they were called at three, drank some cups of tea, and stuffed wads of cotton wool into their ears to deaden the noise of the engine.

Gradually the desert became more level, and soon they were flying over a flat expanse of scrub jungle, toward which at one moment they made a sudden plunge from an altitude of two thousand meters.

Yette was terrified. Unable to make her hear, Graux tapped her on the shoulder and pointed to the window. They were hedgehopping across the bush just above an immense herd of giraffes and antelopes.

An hour later they stampeded a herd of elephants in the same way. Ferdinand hardly gave the animals a glance.

Yette was coming to admire him more and more. A strong, silent man! Just the sort she should have married. Behind the glasses his shortsighted eyes always looked so calm, so imperturbable.

"The blacks call me Mundele-na-Talatala," he had told her. "They'll give you a nickname, too. All the whites have one."

"What does yours mean?"

"The-white-man-with-the-spectacles."

"Do you hear, Georges? And what was their name for *you?*"

Incautiously he came out with it:

"The-white-man-with-the-thirst."

But Graux had not told the whole truth. Actually the blacks have two names for every European. One of these names is inoffensive and can be used in his presence. The other is used by them among themselves and represents their real idea of him.

Graux happened to know his "secret" nickname, which, as a matter of fact, was extremely difficult to translate. Roughly, it meant "the-white-man-who-is-a-man-only-when-he-has-his-glasses-on."

For the blacks are observant folk, despite their seeming stolidity. When he took off his glasses to clean them, the change in his face was amazing. All his self-assurance, serenity, and masterfulness seemed to vanish, and he looked no older than his real age, which was twenty-eight. Indeed, Yette might have found in him something of her husband's shyness—or, rather, lack of confidence.

When at last they reached Juba it was five in the afternoon. Juba proved to be an upcountry outpost of the usual type, with British officers in khaki and a group of half-naked blacks gathered on the airfield, and in the distance a few bungalows with red or gray roofs.

Here the travelers parted company, and Graux shook hands with the elderly Englishman, with whom he had not exchanged a dozen remarks.

"Has Lady Makinson been found?" he asked.

"No."

The Bodets were totally at sea. They had no idea what to do about their belongings, or how to get to Niangara, for this was the first time that Bodet had made the trip by plane. He and his wife had only their hand luggage with them; the rest was following by sea, and for the next two months they would have to make do with little more than what they stood in.

They were still wandering around Juba, discussing ways and means, when a touring car drew up beside them. Graux was at the wheel.

"Would it help you if I dropped you at the frontier of the Belgian Congo? I shall get there, with any luck, some time early in the night."

Yette insisted on sitting in front beside Graux, and Bodet, much to his disgust, had to squeeze in the back among the luggage. The road was fairly good, and every half hour or so they passed through native villages, where at last she could see the naked blacks she had heard so much about in Europe.

"Sometimes one comes across a lion on this road at night," Graux told her. "The headlights dazzle him, and he can't move."

"Isn't it dangerous?"

"No. After a while he slinks off, or else he gallops along in front of the car."

At last they reached Bodi, where the hotel was a wooden building of the bungalow type, set well back in a big parklike compound. They passed a frontier boundary post, but Graux did not stop the car.

"We'll fix things up with the authorities tomorrow morning."

Here the atmosphere was much less formal than in the English hotels. The owner of the hotel, a small dark man with graying hair, chatted with Graux familiarly about his plantation, his elephants, and their common friends. Bodet became quite cheerful now that he had Belgian cigarettes to smoke and Belgian beer to drink.

Just before going to their room, the Bodets showed signs of anxiety again.

"I'm afraid," Graux said, "that I can't offer you a lift, since I take a different road. But on Wednesday there's a bus to Niangara. It runs once a week."

"When shall we see you again?"

"Perhaps next week, perhaps in a year!"

Graux slept in a hut in the compound, the Bodets in an adjoining one. When, at six in the morning, he started out, he had a glimpse through the Bodets' window of someone sitting up behind the big double mosquito net.

From this point of his journey he was on thoroughly familiar ground. The headmen of the villages along his way greeted him as he went by. At the third village the headman signaled to him to stop and informed him in the native dialect that a "flying machine" had fallen in his plantation.

Obviously that must be Lady Makinson's plane.

With all their telegraphs and telephones the white men had not yet received the news; but thanks to their tom-toms the villagers along the road knew all about it.

Graux had some cubes of salt in his car, and he distributed them among the natives as one gives sweets to children.

He was really at home here, not merely in Africa, but in *his* Africa. And this Africa of his was very different from the great empty spaces flown over by Imperial Airways. Here were no hotels so white and scrupulously clean as to remind one of hospitals.

Like an exile coming home after a long sojourn in far lands, he recognized familiar landmarks, familiar faces, stopping now and then to pat the head of a child whom he had cured of fever, or to inquire after the health of an old man tottering under a load of firewood.

No longer Ferdinand Graux, he had become once more Mundele-na-Talatala, bespectacled and self-assured, and he drove faster and faster, thrilled by the joy of nearing home.

A hundred, sixty, forty kilometers to go . . .

A shower set in just as Graux turned off onto a side road that he had had cut across the bush by his own men. Under the drizzle the brick-dust-colored soil had turned a tawny red, and the foliage on either side, rustling faintly under the drops, glowed a more vivid green.

The sky hung low, like a vast pane of frosted glass suspended close overhead, and the ground here was almost level. It was as if one were moving in a two-dimensional world, scaled down to man's stature. Sometimes the tall grass bordering the roadside parted silently to frame the dark, still form of a watching black. At long intervals a lean and leafless tree, usually a silk-cotton tree, rose above the level green expanse. Rarely did one see a native hut; yet there were huts everywhere, twenty or thirty meters back, in the bush, the only tokens of their presence being clumps of bananas, with long pendent leaves like elephants' ears.

Graux knew that all along the way his passage was being signaled, that the green shadows of the wayside were full of watching eyes. The rhythm of the rain gradually quickened on the leaves and grass. A little black girl walked by, stark naked, sheltering her head with a big banana leaf. Evidently she felt the cold; he could see the brown silken skin quivering under the downpour.

And now, instead of hurrying on, Graux felt more inclined to linger on his way, and to steep himself in the elemental peace around him, a peace that actually seemed deepened by the presence of these simple folk living so near the soil.

Then a memory of his last homecoming brought a smile to his lips. At that time his assistant, Camille, a tall, lanky young man of yeoman stock, had been with him for only a year. In the contract Camille was described as his "factor," and the young man had taken this description seriously. He hadn't realized the difference between the still rather feudal-minded part of France he hailed from and the Congo.

So, when Graux came back from a short holiday in Europe, he had found all his native hands, over five hundred strong, massed in front of the brick bungalow, which was beflagged for the occasion. Chinese crackers, a native band, a troupe of dancers—nothing had been forgot-

ten, not even a speech of welcome recited by a nervous little pickaninny.

For almost the first time in his life Graux had really lost his
temper, had turned on the well-meaning young man with a stream of
abuse. So now, as he drove slowly through the market, the natives dared
not make any great show of welcome. There were about thirty of them
there, each sheltering his head under a banana-leaf umbrella as he
squatted beside his simple stock in trade: little mounds of yams,
batatas, and taros.

A dreamlike silence, punctuated by the soft patter of the rain.

Then, as a red brick wall came in sight, he saw two white men
approaching.

Two

The very way he introduced himself was characteristic of the man. In
the plane, for instance, not even the army officers from Khartoum
would have shown such perfect unconstraint when addressing a
stranger for the first time.

"I'm Phelps."

"I know . . ." was all Graux answered.

Because of the intruder, poor Camille couldn't greet his employer as
he'd have wished to.

"So you know about our accident? Can't think how you heard of it!
We haven't been able to get a word through to anyone. Your assistant's
motorcycle has broken down and . . ."

"A ball bearing gone," Camille ventured to interpose. "So I sent a
runner to Niangara. He should be there by now."

"In that case," Captain Phelps continued, "I expect you know that
Lady Makinson is with me and was injured in the crash. A dislocated
knee. I've done what I could, but . . ."

The three men walked slowly toward the terrace of the bungalow.
Camille was wearing a dark-brown homespun suit and leather gaiters,
the costume of a French farmer out for a day's rough shooting. Captain
Phelps was in a well-cut gray flannel suit.

"If you'll excuse me, I'll ask Lady Makinson if she can see you."

As Phelps ran up the steps into the house, Camille murmured uncomfortably:

"I had to let her have your room."

It was a big square building with a red-tiled roof, and a veranda running all around. Inside, the walls had been left in bare red brick, and their only ornaments were shotguns and rifles.

"Had a pleasant journey, sir?" asked Camille with a sigh; he was obviously distressed by the strange circumstances of this homecoming.

"Quite pleasant, thanks."

Graux was smiling. He had just heard a faint rustle at the back of the building, and, looking around quickly, he glimpsed the flutter of a white, blue-spotted dress.

It was Baligi, his housekeeper, hovering in the background, too timid to show herself.

"You saw it over there, didn't you?"

Yes, Graux had seen it. In front of the house the ground fell gently away toward a river. On the hillside beyond it was the coffee plantation. Here and there a tree broke the monotony of the straight rows of bushes, but something else, which was not a tree, now reared itself above the foliage: the tail of a plane.

"I thought they'd been killed. I was tuning up the motor when it happened."

Captain Phelps was still in the room occupied by Lady Makinson, and Graux patiently waited for him to reappear. He could see some twenty men at work around the fallen plane, and he cast a questioning glance at the young man beside him.

"I hope I did right, sir," said Camille uneasily. "We'd no sooner carried her here"—he gave a glance toward the closed door—"than she asked me to get the plane clear as quickly as I possibly could. Captain Phelps, who was only slightly bruised, went back to it at once. He wants us to clear a track up to the bungalow; it's the only place, he says, from which the plane can take off when it's been repaired. I explained that this would mean destroying at least three hundred five-year-old bushes. . . ."

Just then the door opened, and, smiling with that easy grace of which he had the secret, Phelps announced:

"Lady Makinson will be delighted to make your acquaintance, and to say how grateful she is. . . ."

Camille stayed outside. At first Graux couldn't find the bed; it had been moved to a new place, and the light was dim, for the windows had been hung with makeshift curtains.

"Come in, Monsieur Graux."

She spoke French without the slightest accent. Sitting up in bed, she was smoking a cigarette, and beside her lay a book that Graux recognized as one of his: *Captain Scott's Expeditions.*

"It must have been quite a shock for you finding us in possession like this, I'm afraid. . . . Jimmy, hand over your cigarettes."

"They're all we have left, you know."

"But I hope Monsieur Graux has brought a good supply with him."

"I'm afraid I don't smoke," he said awkwardly.

"Do you hear that, Jimmy? Which of us was right, in Cairo? I told you I wanted to bring a few thousand cigarettes, didn't I?"

"What about room for them?"

"Oh, you could easily have left behind one of your guns, or a spare suit. Do sit down, Monsieur Graux. I hate talking to people when they're standing. Your assistant has sent a runner to Niangara. Think he's there by now?"

"If he left the day before yesterday, he should have reached Niangara early this morning."

"So it'll be on the radio, won't it, that we're safe and sound?"

"Most likely. I expect Niangara telephoned Stanleyville, where there's a broadcasting station."

"Let's hope Ronald didn't start off at once," she said to Phelps, and hastened to explain to Graux: "My husband is military attaché at the Ankara embassy. At this time of year he's in Stamboul, with the children. . . . Jimmy, give me a light. And do sit down. You look so absurd towering over me like that when I'm in bed."

He was, in fact, a noticeably tall young man, broad in the shoulders, though otherwise sparely built. He had a very long face with a high, narrow forehead, and a small toothbrush mustache emphasized the whiteness of his teeth.

"I hope you're not too angry with me, Monsieur Graux, for having appropriated your bed. Really, we've been extraordinarily lucky—Captain Phelps and I, I mean. Do you know the elephant farm?"

"Yes, I've had dealings with Major Crosby."

"He's an old friend of ours. For years he's been asking us to come over for some big-game hunting. Since I'd just bought a new long-distance plane, I thought this was a good chance to try it out, and I took Captain Phelps, who's a first-class pilot, with me."

Meanwhile Camille, no doubt, was waiting patiently in the hall. Graux noticed on a table near the bed a bottle of whisky and a Thermos jug of ice water.

"We'd almost got there, on the afternoon of the day before yesterday, when suddenly we ran into a cloud bank. We were flying low, which made things worse, and it was getting on toward sunset. We cruised around for an hour, looking for a break in the clouds. Now and then we hedgehopped for a while to try to get our bearings. That was how we happened to notice your house. We circled around it for some time, trying to find a place to land. Finally we decided on that slope on the far side of the river. We came down as gently as we could, but, as bad luck would have it, we hit a tree and crashed."

"I hope you weren't seriously hurt," said Graux rather stiffly; for some reason, he was out of sorts.

"I put my knee out, that's all. But it won't keep us from starting off the moment the plane's repaired. Needless to say, we'll compensate you for all this inconvenience and the damage done to your plantation. . . . By the way, I suppose the people in Niangara will send the doctor at once?"

"Unless he's making his rounds upcountry, as he is half the time. Are you sure your knee is dislocated?"

"Quite sure. I started when I was a kid by breaking my shinbone, and ever since then I seldom get through the year without a sprain or two, if nothing worse. Oh, I know all about my legs, I assure you!"

Graux kept silent. And she, too, said nothing more—from which he concluded that the interview was over. Phelps moved toward the door, and Graux went out.

"See you later," said Phelps, who stayed behind in the room.

It was four in the afternoon. Camille, who had been waiting in the hall, took his pipe from his mouth and looked at Graux inquiringly.

The two men had known each other since childhood. Graux came from a well-to-do family; his father kept a large gunsmith's shop in Moulins and was a landowner in a small way. Camille was the son of one of his tenants, who worked a farm near Chevagnes. The boys were great friends in those days, and when Graux brought Camille back with him to the Congo, it was as much the young man's companionship he wanted as his services. But Camille had old-fashioned ideas and, for all his employer's affability, could never bring himself to talk to him on equal terms.

"What do you make of her?" Graux asked.

"All I know is that she's a leading light in London society. It seems her husband was aide-de-camp to the Prince of Wales for several years."

"I suppose the captain told you that, didn't he? What do you think is the situation between those two?"

"You've seen for yourself."

"No, I want your impression."

"Really, I couldn't say. He kisses her hand and treats her with the utmost respect. But she calls him Jimmy' and finishes up cigarettes that he has started. I've given him my room, by the way."

A good half of the bungalow consisted of a big hall that served as living room; behind it were only two bedrooms and a kitchen. Zinc tubs, which a boy filled with hot water brought in kerosene cans, replaced a bathroom.

"I've put my cot here," Camille added.

"I'd better do the same thing. Have mine brought out, too, please."

He smiled again; there had been a sound of someone moving in the kitchen—Baligi, no doubt, who must be wondering when her master was going to take some notice of her.

She was a fifteen-year-old Logo girl, already gracefully mature, the only native girl in these parts who wore more or less European dresses—though nothing underneath them.

Graux smiled because he had just recalled another "Do you hear, Georges?" Where had it been? Probably that evening in Khartoum, when they changed planes and had a longish wait. As usual, Yette was plying him with questions.

"You mean to say you've lived five years all by yourself in the Congo and been true to your fiancée all the time? Don't tell me you've never made love to one of those pretty little black girls I've heard so much about!"

To which he had replied quite coolly:

"I have a housekeeper—like everybody else."

"What does that mean, 'housekeeper'?"

"It means—everything!"

He should have caught on when he saw her cast a quick glance at her husband.

" 'Everything'? Do you mean you . . .?" For once she dropped her voice discreetly.

"Why not? In fact, it might be difficult to do otherwise."

"What about that girl you're engaged to?"

"She knows, of course. I've told her."

"And isn't she jealous?"

"There's nothing to be jealous about. When she comes out, my little housekeeper will get married to a native in another village."

It was then she had come out with her shrill "Do you hear, Georges?"

"Yes, I hear," Georges muttered sulkily.

"Ferdinand, anyhow, is frank, and I admire him for it. What a fool I was to believe you when you told me you'd never even looked at a native girl!"

Poor Georges! Poor Yette! By now they were arriving in Niangara and making the acquaintance of Costemans, the Commissioner.

His thoughts took a new turn.

"How are the elephants?"

"Fine. Tom Thumb was a bit off his feed last week, but he's got over it."

Graux checked his impulse to go and talk to Baligi at once. Better not show too much eagerness.

"Let's have a look around," he said, taking his riding whip from its peg.

Why, like the sky, was his mind overcast today? Always in the past on his return from Europe he had reveled in these first contacts and, like a child on the first day of vacation rolling ecstatically in the new-mown hay, had plunged himself wholeheartedly into the life of his plantation, its atmosphere of plenitude and peace.

Rain was still falling, the sun still hidden. Nevertheless Camille was wearing his old, battered sola topee, while Graux had on a terai felt hat with a double crown, which he had recently adopted as his headgear in the tropics.

There was a significance in this that had not been lost on the old Englishman in the plane, for instance. Of all the passengers, Graux was the only one who wore a double terai without the least romanticism or self-consciousness. For he was not a tourist, or even a settler; he was *at home* in Africa.

"How have the accumulators been doing?" he asked as they walked toward the river.

"One of the cells will have to be replaced; it won't hold the charge. . . . I've had the infirmary roof repaired."

It was on reaching the foot of the slope that one realized how little the bungalow mattered in Graux's life; his true interests lay elsewhere. As there was a six-meter waterfall nearby, he had installed a turbine and a small power plant. Just behind it was a brick kiln; then came a row of buildings—a storehouse, the forge, the carpenter's shed, the office, the infirmary—all in excellent repair, with numbered keys in every lock.

Of the village nothing could be seen but the peaks of some black cones in the bush.

"She doesn't seem to be in pain, anyhow," he suddenly remarked.

"Oh, she's been like that from the start. In fact, at first I couldn't believe it was anything at all serious. She never showed the slightest sign of distress, even when she was being carried on the stretcher. Of course, she says she's used to getting hurt. . . ."

"Who sees to her meals?"

"Captain Phelps. She won't eat anything that's been touched by a black woman."

Graux would have found it hard to say just how he felt. Had anyone asked Camille to give his impression of his employer's present mood, he would have replied, "He's in the dumps. Something must be worrying him."

As a matter of fact, however, it wasn't worried that he felt. His state of mind was, rather, as it used to be in Moulins when his sister said to him, smiling:

"A penny for your thoughts!"

And his mother never failed to add:

"The truth is, Ferdinand's bored stiff at home. He's eating his heart out to be back in his beloved Africa."

There was some truth in that. And yet everyone had welcomed him with open arms; they did their best to give him a good time. His sister and her husband, Dr. Farget, arranged little dinner parties to which all his old friends were invited.

"Is it very hot in the Congo?" someone would ask.

And it would send them into fits of laughter when he replied unthinkingly: "Very hot? I really couldn't say. That depends. . . ."

"Are the black girls pretty?"

"Not too bad."

"What do you do all day?"

That was a poser. All he knew was that there was enough to keep him busy from dawn till dusk. But to describe it was beyond him.

"Anyhow, you might tell us what your house is like."

"Oh, it's an ordinary brick bungalow," was all he found to say.

Again everybody laughed. And after a fortnight, though he had his fiancée's company, his one idea was to return to his plantation as soon as he decently could.

He would have made them laugh still more had he confessed that what he felt was, above all, a sense of insecurity, no less acute for being quite irrational.

This feeling was nothing new to him; he had known it even in his school days. The other boys had written him off as a grind because he stayed shut up in his room for hours on end. And indeed he did work hard and always had some awards handed him on prize days. But he didn't work for working's sake. He found in work an escape from the outside world, a pretext for remaining shut within four familiar walls, surrounded by things that never changed.

No sooner was he out of doors than he grew conscious of a strange uneasiness, for which he never could account. If someone spoke to him, his first impulse was to look away. "What a shy boy!" some said; others, less charitable, called him "sullen" or "conceited."

They were mistaken. He had the utmost admiration for his father, Evariste Graux, who was always to be seen, dressed in black, at the back of his big shop, or hobbling forward—he suffered from gout—as soon as someone entered. For, though he had three assistants, he believed in greeting customers himself.

"How are you, my dear Count? Were you at the Marquise's shoot yesterday?"

All the local gentry bought their guns and cartridges from him, and his son was much impressed by the judicious blend of deference and bonhomie with which he handled them.

With the farmers, too, he always struck the right note.

"Well, Lucas, how's that lawsuit of yours coming along? . . . I hear the rabbits have wiped out three of your lucerne fields. That's too bad!"

He was on friendly terms with the gamekeepers, to whom he allowed a discount, and with the poachers, too, who always told him of their lucky bags.

But somehow Ferdinand, much as he admired his father's ease of manner, could never bring himself to say "old boy" to anyone.

Talking of the dancers at the local cabaret, his friends always referred to them as "the tarts." But for Graux they were just girls like any others, whom he could never address otherwise than as "Mademoiselle." Even for his fiancée, though they had known each other since childhood, he had no pet name.

She was the daughter of a notary, Maître Tassin, who dined with Ferdinand's parents every Wednesday. In his fifteenth year Ferdinand had a habit of blushing every time he met Emilienne, who was then thirteen. Some time later it was rumored that she was going to marry an officer of the Moulins garrison, but years had passed and the marriage had not taken place.

During his first holiday at home, after three years in the Congo, Graux had been rather surprised to hear his mother say one morning:

"Why don't you run around and see Emilienne? She never let a mail go by without asking after you. And she's such a nice girl, isn't she?"

That was how it had come about. So now he was engaged, and Emilienne Tassin was to come out to join him when the monsoon ended.

A sensible young woman of twenty-seven, she was as placid as Graux himself, and all their friends agreed that they were "made for each other." He had given her a list of books dealing with coffee and vanilla growing, and his pet subject, political economy, too.

"Say, I hope you don't mind my having had those plants cut down?" Camille ventured to inquire.

The silence had lasted so long that Graux gave a start on hearing a voice beside him. They were still standing by the waterfall.

"Really, they as good as ordered me to do it," Camille explained ruefully, gazing at the broad red gash of naked earth that showed amid the greenery, a track that would serve once only—to extricate the plane. After a moment's pause he added, "Did you see my people?"

"Yes," Graux said. "I went to the farm. Your sister, Hortense, is going to have a baby."

"So soon! And how's my father?"

"Much as usual."

"Still drinking too much white wine, I suppose," sighed Camille.

"Yes, he hasn't changed. It's wiser not to contradict him in the evenings. But he's a grand old fellow, for all that."

His mind kept harking back to thoughts of that woman and the young Englishman in his bedroom, and he felt a sudden, unaccountable rush of anger. . . . All the same, he asked Camille:

"Did you tell them I know something about doctoring?"

"No, I didn't dare."

Graux had actually studied medicine for a while and during the last six years had been giving medical attention to his workers and their wives. He had helped many of the women through hard deliveries and once, when a black had had his arm mangled by a crocodile, had performed a successful amputation.

"By the way, is our old friend Potam still around?" His eyes strayed to the river, upstream.

For three years a hippopotamus had been living there, and they had come to regard him almost as a pet. He was not really dangerous, though he had a taste for practical jokes, such as upsetting native dugouts in midstream with a toss of his huge snout and watching the blacks floundering in the water.

"I imagine he's asleep by now. But you'll see him tomorrow morning."

Suddenly Graux made up his mind, strode quickly back to the bungalow, and knocked boldly on the bedroom door. Captain Phelps opened it.

"May I have a word with you?"

When Graux came to a swift decision, as he had just done, he always said what he had to say with an extreme, indeed excessive bluntness, due to the effort it cost him. The captain followed him onto the veranda.

"I want to talk to you about Lady Makinson. From what she said I gathered that she was expecting the doctor to be here at any moment. Not only is it most improbable he'll come, since he is almost always out on his rounds, but also she would do well not to have too much confidence in him."

He was conscious of speaking in a rather stilted manner and regretted it.

"Do you mean he's not a good doctor?"

"He may have been one in the past. But he's had too much to do with natives, and he drinks. . . . I don't have a medical degree, but I have a good deal of practical experience, for we have accidents here almost every day. If Lady Makinson feels she can trust my skill . . ."

"Just a moment, please."

Like an officer of the royal household given a commission, Phelps retired to the bedroom, and for the next quarter of an hour Graux could hear a conversation going on inside, in undertones. The lamps had been lit, since it was six o'clock, and Baligi was moving things around in the kitchen, hoping to attract her master's attention.

All this waiting was beginning to tell on Graux's nerves, and by now he was regretting his offer of assistance. Really, it was too absurd, hanging around outside his own bedroom door like someone soliciting an interview with a high official!

To while away the time he said to Camille, who had followed him:

"Go to the infirmary and fetch my first-aid kit. And a couple of ampules of Novocaine."

Obviously "they" couldn't make up their minds and were dubious about his competence. At last the door opened.

"Would you come in for a moment?"

Lady Makinson was smoking, as usual, sitting up in bed with her back propped against two pillows. Graux noticed that she was wearing flimsy silk pajamas that revealed the outlines of a slender body, small, tip-tilted breasts like a young girl's.

"Leave us, Jimmy."

She waited till the young man had shut the door behind him, then gave Graux a long, meditative look, blinking a little as the cigarette smoke got in her eyes, and said:

"Look away for a moment, please."

He heard a rustle of silk and guessed that she was slipping off the pajama bottoms.

"I'll see at once if I can have confidence in you. Come. . . ."

The sheet was drawn up nearly to her waist, uncovering two long, slim legs, one of them bandaged at the knee.

"Now, carry on. Wait! Give me a cigarette."

She smoked with little nervous puffs while he undid the bandage. Then, looking up, he said:

"I sent to the infirmary for some Novocaine. I intend to give you an injection."

"All right . . . But do hurry up!" she added fretfully.

He went to the door and shouted for some hot water.

"Perhaps the captain might give me a hand. . . ."

"No!" she said peremptorily, without adding any explanation.

"Very well."

She was smoking still more nervously and now and again gave a little sigh.

"Am I hurting you?"

"No."

She was thin, her skin tanned golden-brown, and the play of the long, lithe muscles could be seen beneath it.

"I'm afraid it may hurt a bit now—but only for a few seconds."

"Oh, hush!" she exclaimed impatiently.

She held out valiantly till he had finished. As he was fixing splints halfway up her thigh, he had to push back the sheet a little and thoughtlessly remarked:

"Excuse me!"

And blushed. His thoughts were out of control, and his one desire was to get it over with quickly. Then he heard her say:

"When do you expect to get the plane up here?"

"I'll put two elephants on the job. . . . I suppose it will be within three days at most."

"Be as quick about it as you can, please."

Which meant, presumably, that she was impatient to get away. He straightened up. She asked for a mirror and began settling her red-gold hair.

"And the comb, please. Thanks. No, wait a moment. Ask Captain Phelps to come."

As he approached the bed, Phelps threw her a questioning look, and she said at once:

"He's done a good job, I think."

Meanwhile Graux was hurriedly removing his paraphernalia: rolls of dressing, the hypodermic syringe, the empty ampule, the basin of hot water.

"Please let me know what you'd like to eat."

"Oh, Jimmy will take that up with you."

He must have cut a rather pathetic figure, seen from behind, when he was walking out of the room, for Lady Makinson called after him in a friendly tone:

"Thanks again, Monsieur Graux. Really, you did an awfully good job."

"She's crying," Camille said in a low tone from which he couldn't exclude a hint of reproach.

"Let her cry!"

They were dining together in the hall; the surroundings brought to mind a hunting lodge. Phelps had just gone by, carrying on a tray a can of jellied chicken and a bottle of Bordeaux.

"The English"—thus Camille always referred to them—were dining *tête-à-tête* in the bedroom, the door of which had a rather irritating habit of closing again the moment it was opened.

Phelps had grinned as he walked by with the tray.

"What do you think of the new butler?"

Their dinner began, as it always did, with soup, followed tonight by a fish netted that afternoon in the river. When they had finished the soup, Baligi did not come as usual to take away the plates and bring the next course, so Camille had to go to the kitchen.

It was on his return that he mentioned that Baligi was crying.

When Graux replied, "Let her cry!" he did something Camille had never seen him do before: he planted his elbows on the table. And when Baligi brought the soup, he merely grunted an absent-minded "Evening, Baligi," and the indifference of his tone cut her to the quick.

Now and again they heard a stifled sob, and Camille shot a timidly disapproving glance at his employer.

"No, it wouldn't do," Graux murmured, as if talking to himself.

"What wouldn't do?"

"They're English. They don't have the same ideas as we about such things."

"I don't follow."

"About Baligi, I mean. Try to explain to her, please. Anyhow, they won't be here for more than two or three days."

For some reason he was reluctant to go into the kitchen himself and explain things to his little "housekeeper." Camille could do it just as well. And of course it was out of the question to let her come and join him here in the hall during the coming night.

"Are all the English so damned prudish?" asked Camille, with a glance toward the closed door.

"Well, if they have dealings with native girls they keep it quiet."

"Just what you'd expect of them!" sneered Camille, making no effort now to conceal his ill humor.

For this upset to their domestic life was getting on his nerves as well. He had been hoping for some news about his people, and Graux had hardly mentioned them.

"By the way, didn't my sister give you a letter for me?"

"Yes, it's in my suitcase. I'll fish it out tomorrow."

Tomorrow! Under normal conditions they'd have got down to it at once and had a memorable evening opening suitcases, unpacking the odds and ends Graux had bought in Europe: presents for Baligi, for Camille, for old Uaraga, Baligi's father, who after three years' training had at last learned how to run the power plant.

And Graux hadn't even thought of telling Camille whether he had succeeded or not in getting the bounty that he had applied for on his coffee!

"What time do they go to bed?"

"I have no idea. All I know is that they stay together till midnight or one in the morning. And I can count myself lucky if they don't wake me two or three times in the night, to get them ice. Last night Phelps hauled me out of bed because there was a big spider on the ceiling. And they wouldn't let me kill it—I had to throw it out of the window—because Lady Makinson has some silly superstition about killing spiders."

Camille stopped abruptly, frowning; he had just heard another sob in the kitchen.

"Go and tell her."

"What shall I say? That because of 'the English' . . . ?"

"No, don't bother. I'll take care of it."

He rose and drew back the gray blanket on his cot.

"Are you turning in?" Camille asked. "Shall I put out the light?"

"Do, please."

The hall was plunged in darkness.

Graux called, "Bali!"—it was the pet name he had given her—in a low voice.

The joints of Camille's cot creaked as he stretched his lanky limbs. A dim form flitted through the gloom. There was a faint rustling, then silence fell, broken only by the sound of breathing, and all was darkness but for a thin ribbon of light beneath the bedroom door.

Three

Though Graux kept his eyes shut, sleep would not come to him. As clearly as if they were open, he saw, or seemed to see, that line of light under Lady Makinson's door. And then, quite suddenly, it went out.

He might easily have supposed that, without knowing, he had fallen asleep and dreamed this; but he was certain of the contrary and could even fix approximately the time when the light disappeared—eleven o'clock.

Now and again Camille, who was sleeping soundly at the other end of the hall, would heave himself over so ponderously that the cot seemed on the point of collapsing. Each time he made this movement he gave a snort, as if it cost him a prodigious effort.

As for Baligi, no one could have said whether she slept or not. Curled up in a ball, both feet pressed on her bedfellow's legs, she lay quite motionless; even her breathing was inaudible. But it was unlikely she was squandering such a rare, blissful hour as this on sleep.

Not long after the streak of light had vanished, Graux fell into a deep sleep. Suddenly he sat bolt upright in bed, staring in front of him with angry eyes.

"So sorry," murmured Captain Phelps. "I can't think how I came to do it."

What had happened was this. On leaving Lady Makinson's room— Graux saw the time on his wristwatch, ten to two—he had unthinkingly pressed the electric-light switch. And Graux, in starting up, had tossed the blanket aside, revealing the black girl snuggling up against him.

Hence Phelps's embarrassment and apologies.

Hastily switching the light off, he went across to his room, while Camille, who had not waked up, rolled heavily over with the usual grunt.

Baligi was certainly awake, but holding her breath, afraid to stir, dimly conscious that what had occurred was the last thing that should have occurred. And Graux, too, was the prey of disagreeable thoughts; he let her stay beside him for another quarter of an hour, and then, as she had been expecting, whispered:

"Go back to the kitchen."

For the mat on which she slept was on the kitchen floor, beside the kerosene stove.

Equatorial nights are all of the same length. From one year's end to the next the sun rises at six. By the time Camille woke, Graux was already up and about, on his way to the elephant shed. The rain had ceased. The sun showed as an orange-yellow ball behind a veil of fleecy clouds, the puddles shone with broken gleams of light.

There was one thing that Graux disapproved of about Camille, his disdain for cleanliness. He would go on wearing the same khaki shirt for days on end and frequently forgot to wash. He thought nothing of sleeping with his clothes on, then going straight out to his work after no more than a flick of his face with a damp towel.

When Camille entered the shed, he found Tom Thumb eating chunks of yam from his master's hand with every manifestation of delight. But Graux's thoughts were evidently elsewhere, for as soon as Camille came up he asked:

"Which runner did you send?"

"Maki. Last time he made the trip within twenty-four hours. I suppose he's waiting there to get a lift back with the doctor or the Commissioner."

At half past six the clanging of a bell assembled the blacks outside the buildings on the riverbank, and Camille held an inspection in true military style, while Graux remained in the background. Only when the workers were about to be dismissed to their various jobs did he intervene.

"Set them all to getting the plane clear. Let's get it over with!"

Still looking worried, he climbed the slope to the place where the plane had crashed; its nose was buried in the ground. Taking a pick from one of his men, he himself cleared away the earth around the propeller and soon discovered that it was broken. Shrugging his shoulders, he walked away, after casting a quick glance into the cabin, which was as elegant as the interior of a luxury car, with the seats upholstered in pale-green leather.

When he reached the bungalow, Captain Phelps, immaculately dressed as usual, accosted him at once.

"Really, I feel quite ashamed of myself," he said with less than his customary self-assurance, "making you sleep on a miserable cot. I hope . . ."

"Tell me," Graux cut in almost rudely, "where was that plane built?"

"Near London. There's only one other like it in existence, Amy Mollison's."

"Do you have another propeller?"

"No, of course not."

"In that case, will you kindly tell me how you intend to get her off again?" Though he tried to control it, there was a vicious edge to his voice.

"What! Do you mean to say the propeller's smashed?"

"It is. And I must say I'm surprised that though you've been here two days you haven't even troubled to inspect it."

The young man visibly wilted. Suddenly all his self-confidence had left him; for all his jauntiness, he was really rather shy and unsure of himself.

"I've just left Lady Makinson," he said rather quickly, "and I was coming to say she'd like to see you now, if it's convenient. She'd appreciate it very much. . . ."

Graux walked to the bedroom door, rapped on it, and walked in.

"Good morning, Monsieur Graux. I can't say how sorry I am for all the trouble we're giving you."

Was it an allusion to Phelps's blunder with the electric-light switch? Graux's expression was far from amiable as he stared at the woman who was sitting up in bed, with the remains of her breakfast on a tray beside her. She had already lit the inevitable cigarette.

"Do sit down," she said.

"I'm afraid I have very little time. What I'd really like to know is, what exactly are your plans?"

He remained standing, an obstinate look on his face, and she observed him with surprise.

"Sorry. I don't follow."

"I presume you know that your plane is out of action. The propeller's broken."

"No, really?" She smiled faintly and slowly added, giving a curious look, "In that case, I must wire to London for another one."

He had the impression that she was laughing at him up her sleeve. She had guessed that he was out to be disagreeable and was amusing herself by seeing how far he'd go.

"Provided, of course," she smiled, "they have one in stock. Let's see, now. It should be here within a week, shouldn't it, if they send it by Imperial Airways? . . . Do you know, you haven't asked me yet if I had a good night?"

He had the choice of two lines of conduct; he could give in—in other words, be his natural self again—or he could persist in his ungracious attitude. He elected the latter.

"I had no need to ask. Captain Phelps let me know already."

He glimpsed a little flash of anger in her eyes; for a moment she was on the brink of a sharp retort. Then she said quietly:

"Really, won't you sit down?"

The sound of a car horn outside saved the situation. Hurrying out, Graux saw the Commissioner's car pulled up by the steps. A black in brown and yellow—a convict, that is to say—was at the wheel. A plump young man in white ducks scrambled out of the car; to his surprise, Graux saw it was Georges Bodet.

"So they sent *you*, did they?"

Captain Phelps, who had just come up, introduced himself to the newcomer with his usual punctiliousness.

Bodet was in a bad temper.

"It's been a filthy journey. We've been on the road all night, and it's fairly swarming with wild animals; we could see their eyes glowing in front of the car at every turn. The nigger was almost more scared than I was, and he's a rotten driver at the best of times."

"Why didn't Costemans come himself?"

Bodet shrugged a contemptuous shoulder.

"You didn't tell me the man's half crazy. Would you believe it; yesterday, my first day, he insisted on my being at the office at six in the morning! When it was getting on toward eleven and I started taking off my coat and tie, he yapped at me in that dreadful Brussels accent he affects:

" 'Where do you think you are, young man? This isn't a tennis court—it's a government office.' "

Graux called through the doorway:

"Baligi! Bring some beer out onto the veranda."

Lady Makinson, who had no idea what was happening, called to Captain Phelps from her room.

"Is that the pilot?" Bodet pointed to the captain's receding figure, then shouted some orders in the native dialect to his driver, who handed him a briefcase bulging with documents.

"Here's luck! . . . This beer has saved my life! I was half dead of thirst."

And of heat. He was streaming with perspiration, puffing and blowing. He gulped down the beer—which made him sweat still more profusely.

"When your runner turned up . . ."

"By the way, where is he?"

"Oh, we dropped him at a village twenty kilometers from here. He said he had a brother there he wanted to see. As soon as we got your message, Costemans called Stanleyville. It seems that since the beginning of the year no one has applied for permission to fly over the Belgian Congo, and consequently no permit has been issued." He paused.

"Which means . . . ?"

"It means," said Bodet dolefully, "that I'm instructed to open an inquiry, and to keep the plane from taking off till further orders."

"That will be easy, anyhow. The propeller's smashed."

"I've been given a whole list of things to ask. I wonder if you can tell me whether Lady Makinson has a passport with the necessary visas? I've also got to ascertain if they have any firearms and, if so, whether they have been issued licenses to bring them into this country."

"How's your wife?"

"Fed up! Fed to the teeth! Yesterday she went to pay her duty call on Madame Costemans. And what do you think Madame Costemans did? She sent a message by the orderly to say she couldn't see her just then and would send an invitation when convenient—or something like that. You know what Yette's like. She was waiting on the veranda and could hear them whispering behind the door. Well, she flared up and shouted:

" 'No, my dear, you'll never see me here again, not on your life!' "

Gloomily Bodet poured himself out another glass of beer; after drinking it he rose with a sigh.

"Well, I suppose I'd better go and interview Lady Makinson."

Graux merely pointed to the bedroom door, then walked down to the little power plant by the river to inspect the dynamo and storage batteries.

He expected to be summoned back to the bungalow after a few minutes and was surprised at having to wait so long. For a good hour he tinkered with the dynamo, after which he whiled away the time standing at the window, watching the blacks clearing the track through the plantation. The sun had pierced the clouds at last, but it still had no brightness, and the light was more gray than golden.

He was in a mood that, though he couldn't have defined it, he knew only too well. Behind it lay a feeling of suspense; worse than suspense, a premonition of evil. An inner voice was warning him of impending catastrophe—in the meaning he gave to that word. For, to Graux, any disturbance of the even tenor of his life, any event that shattered his peace of mind, was nothing short of a catastrophe.

And on such occasions his nerves were apt to go to pieces, and he would say or do the most preposterous things. For instance, just now, what was it he'd said to Lady Makinson . . . ?

He pulled himself up. Why was he dawdling here, pretending to tune up the dynamo? Suppose Camille had chanced to come in? He'd have blushed for himself, for Camille knew quite well the dynamo was running perfectly.

"Hello!" The voice was one that invariably grated on him: Captain Phelps's.

Looking back to the bungalow, he saw Phelps making a speaking trumpet of his hands, bawling at the top of his voice:

"Hello! Hey there, Graux! Where have you got to?"

Without hurrying, Graux walked back to the bungalow. After a quick glance toward the bedroom door Phelps explained:

"Lady Makinson wants me to go into Niangara myself and send off some telegrams. This understrapper they've sent here has been given the most ridiculous instructions, and Lady Makinson is going to complain to London."

Looking crestfallen, Bodet came from the bedroom and motioned to Graux to come and talk with him at the far end of the hall.

"She's in a hell of a temper! It seems she's a big shot in London society. But what can I do about it? I've been given my orders. . . ."

"Listen! Have you seen Captain Phelps's passport?"

"Yes."

"What is he? An adventurer?"

"Not at all. He's the son of the chairman of Phelps & Phelps, the big New Zealand merchants and shipowners. We passed one of their boats in the Mediterranean. . . . Oh, am I glad that's over!"

He finished another large bottle of beer before leaving, accompanied by Phelps, who insisted on driving the car himself.

The bedroom door was ajar, and Lady Makinson could be heard calling:

"Monsieur Graux! Are you there, Monsieur Graux?"

An involuntary smile rose to his lips as he entered the room. To his surprise, he saw her seated on the edge of the bed, the leg in splints held stiffly out in front of her.

"What on earth are you up to?" he exclaimed.

"Come and help me. Call that young man of yours."

"First tell me what you intend to do."

"I intend to go and sit with you on the veranda. I've had enough of this stuffy room. Where's he got to, your assistant?"

Between them they carried her to a big folding armchair, and she lay back in it for some minutes without speaking, with closed eyes. Graux took the opportunity of studying her face attentively.

Again he had that disagreeable sensation of being thrown off balance. Yet he could look quite calmly at the grave beauty of the girl to whom he was engaged, or at his sister's merry, laughing face, or the faces of his girl cousins. . . . It was precisely for this reason—because he clung to preserving his mental balance and the thought of "losing his head" had always been repellent—that he had never indulged in flirtations. He had once explained it quite frankly to Emilienne when she asked him if he had had any love affairs before their engagement.

"No. I've had no love affairs. I've had dealings only with paid women."

For there was nothing to fear from women of that class.

Lady Makinson's eyelids were so finespun, so translucent, that he could see the eyeballs fluttering and even glimpse the pupils through them. Her nostrils, too, were quivering, whether because of the effort she had made or because she was in pain, he could not judge.

Though she was fragilely built, her fragility was not like that of the anemic girls he had sometimes seen in France. On the contrary, one could see at a glance that she was strong and marvelously fit; her skin, tanned by the sun, had the warm glow of a ripe fruit.

But what amazed him most was the combination of maturity and youthfulness he discerned in her. He knew she had two children, one of them a girl of eight, but motherhood had not left its mark on her, as it had done on the women of his family. And indeed he felt more than wonder; he was vaguely scandalized. Since his earliest days he had always regarded a woman who had had children as a being apart and sacrosanct, as if in becoming a mother she had ceased to be a woman.

And yet—last night hadn't he seen the light turned out in her bedroom, and Captain Phelps emerging some hours later? Naïvely he wondered if the dusky rings around her eyes might not be an aftereffect of those dark hours.

"Still angry with me?" she asked languidly, her eyes still closed, a faint smile on her lips. But before he could answer, she seemed suddenly to come out of a dream and, with a toss of her red-gold hair, opened her eyes. "Sorry! It's over now. I don't often lose my temper, but these wretched little bureaucrats with their red tape . . . But I won't talk about that; Phelps has gone to Niangara to fix things up. Tomorrow they'll be eating humble pie. . . . A cigarette, please."

She watched him as he brought the platinum cigarette case, so flat that it seemed incapable of containing even the thinnest cigarettes.

"Don't you ever smoke? No? And you don't drink, either, I suppose. I should say you don't have much indulgence for the failings of poor ordinary mortals. Of women especially. You loathe me, don't you? Out with it!"

"You're greatly mistaken, Lady Makinson."

"Oh, how serious you are! Sit down, won't you? And do try to stop being the model planter who can think of nothing but his precious coffee plants. Have you been here long?"

"Six years."

"Always by yourself?"

"There's Camille."

"He's a worthy young man, of course, but I shouldn't think his company's particularly inspiring. What do you do with yourself all day?"

He pointed to the plantation, to the elephants at work on the hillside, the row of sheds along the river.

"Only that?"

"I read a little."

"And are your books and your plantation enough to make you happy?"

"Yes."

He said it so simply and with such conviction that she looked at him with keener interest, in which was a shade of wonder.

"Do you really mean that? Really and truly?"

"Yes."

"And you don't want anything more of life?"

"Nothing."

"Love, for instance?"

"My fiancée will be coming out in three months, and we shall get married."

He would not meet her eyes, for fear she should see too deeply into his thoughts and feelings.

"Then it wasn't true, what you said just now. You *do* want something more."

He was on the brink of saying no but caught himself in time and stared at the red-tiled floor, puzzled and dismayed. For he had just realized that, had he said no, it would have been the truth.

What he sought above all was tranquillity, a stable course of life. For the moment he had been jolted out of his rut, but he knew he would settle into it again. If he was prepared to marry Emilienne, it was because he felt convinced she would fit in with his scheme of life. All the same, he ruefully admitted to himself, he felt no great desire to have her with him—now!

And it was worse when Lady Makinson added, after a short silence:
"I wouldn't mind betting she's a cousin, or a girl you've known all
your life."

A girl he'd known all his life, yes; indeed, almost a cousin, for their
families were connected.

"Why are you so sure of that?" he asked.

"Because that's how it was bound to be—with you."

"But why?"

"That's asking!" she said, smiling. "Another cigarette, please. I'm
sure the girl you're going to marry doesn't smoke. . . . Guess what
Camille would have found if he'd rummaged in the cabin after we
crashed! Two opium pipes and half a pound of opium. But of course all
that is outside your range. Yesterday, when you came in, Phelps and I
had just been smoking opium, and you didn't even recognize the
smell."

Something prompted him to ask:

"What's the point of smoking opium?"

She shrugged her shoulders.

"None whatever."

For the next five minutes they sat in silence, gazing at the red-and-
green expanse beyond the river, dotted with small black moving forms.
The coffee bushes in the distance looked no bigger than cabbages
aligned in orderly green rows upon the brick-red soil.

"Would you get me my bag, please? It's under the pillow."

It was in crocodile skin, with an emerald clasp and a monogram
topped with a coronet. She drew something from it.

"Look!"

Two children, a little girl of seven, a two-and-a-half-year-old boy,
standing naked on a sunlit beach.

"That was taken last year, in Therapia. The embassy is in Ankara in
the winter; in the summer we move to Therapia, near Stamboul. Know
it?"

"No."

Again they fell silent, while she went on holding the photograph as if
uncertain what to do with it. Finally she dropped it into her bag and
abruptly snapped it closed.

"I must say, you're a gloomy fellow!"

"I'm not, really."

"Then what are you?"

"Oh, nothing in particular!"

"Say, will you be offended if I ask you something rather indiscreet?"

"Ask away!"

"I'd like to see your little black girl."

Almost too hastily he rose to his feet and shouted, looking away from her:

"Baligi! Baligi!"

For some minutes there was not a sound. What could the girl be up to? Then, when they no longer expected it, they saw her standing shyly in the doorway, in her blue-spotted dress, the flimsy bodice of which was raised in front by her small pointed breasts. Baligi cast a piteous gaze at her master.

"Don't be frightened," he said in the native language. "You're a good little girl."

That set her smiling, and she even ventured a glance at the white woman.

"Does she speak French?" asked Lady Makinson.

Baligi herself answered the question.

"A little, madame."

"That's clever of you, Baligi! Now will you go and fetch the bottle of whisky and Thermos jug from my room?"

Graux had to confirm the order with a slight nod, and then the girl ran off the veranda almost dancing, though she had no idea why she felt so happy.

"A nice little thing," Lady Makinson remarked when she had gone. She poured herself out a whisky, and Baligi retreated to the kitchen.

"No use offering you one, I suppose?"

"No, thanks."

"What are you thinking about?"

"My plantation."

"That's a fib!"

"I assure you, I was thinking about the preferential tariff and the transport subsidies we've been promised. They're matters of vital importance for the planters in these parts."

"You'll be glad to see the last of us, won't you?"

"Naturally you'll stay here as long as necessary."

She uttered two or three words in a language unknown to him— Urdu, he suspected, remembering she had spent a good part of her childhood in India—and then asked:

"Phelps should be in Niangara by now, shouldn't he?"

"No, not for an hour or so. It's a bad road."

"Are there many Europeans there?"

"Four all told, and they're rarely there together. The Commissioner and his assistant—the young man who was here just now; the doctor, who's usually on his rounds; and the missionary, who spends most of his time on his motorcycle, visiting upcountry villages."

"Do you go there often?"

"Once a year at most."

"And how about the elephant farm? Do you ever visit Major Crosby?"

"Only when I want to buy an elephant, or get his advice about a sick one. I've been there three times in six years."

"Do you never see anyone from the outside world?"

"Oh, now and again—once or twice a year—somebody blows in."

"Nuisances like us, who turn you out of your bedroom?"

"That's nothing. I'm used to sleeping in a cot."

"Making much money?"

"So far I've sunk four hundred thousand francs in the plantation, but with luck I'll get them back in time."

"Are you keen on it?"

"On what?"

"On making money?"

"What I'm keenest on is selling my coffee. Especially if I can get it graded Standard B."

"Meaning?"

"Oh, it would take too long to explain. . . ."

"Thanks!"

"I mean, I'd be afraid of boring you."

Just then a bell rang. Lady Makinson gave a slight start.

"A visitor?"

"No, it's for lunch. Captain Phelps left before he'd had time to arrange your meal, so if you don't mind sharing ours, such as it is . . ."

She shot him a defiant glance and, without thinking of her leg, made as if to rise.

"Wait. We'll carry you in your chair to the table."

They could see Camille washing his hands at a tap, then damping a brush and running it over his unruly shock of hair.

"Give me a hand, Camille."

The table was covered with a red-and-white-checked cloth, in the center of which stood a soup tureen, enormous and ornate.

"To avoid using canned stuff we have soup twice a day. Will you try some?"

She observed two small white cases, each embroidered with an initial and containing a napkin. Camille tucked his napkin into his shirt collar. The spoons and forks, too, were marked with an initial.

It was almost cool in the central hall, surrounded as it was by the zone of shadow on the veranda, and the light was pleasantly subdued, tinged with a pink glow from the tiles and red brick walls.

"Were you your own architect?"

"Yes, and my own mason, plumber, and electrician, to a great extent. Have you had a look at my library?" There was a hint of irony in his voice. *"The Home Encyclopedia. Electricity Made Easy. Build Your Own Country House."*

She smiled. Camille knitted his brows, worried by a feeling that something more than he could fathom underlay this last remark.

"Do you have a radio set?"

"We have a receiving set, but we never use it. It's in one of the sheds down by the river, I believe, and I imagine the damp has finished it off."

"Do you get any newspapers?"

"Once every six weeks, when the mail comes. My sister sends me our local paper after she's read it. So I'm kept posted on the marriages and deaths in Moulins."

"This soup is really good. Did your black girl make it?"

"Yes."

And it was also Baligi who shyly served a dish of boiled fish, with melted butter and potatoes.

"If you like mangoes, they're in season. And I can get you some alligator pears. Do you know them?"

"I was brought up in India, I've lived in South America, Australia, and New Zealand. Ever been to New Zealand?"

"No."

"That's where Phelps hails from."

"I know."

He said "I know" so curtly that a silence followed, lasting several minutes, after which he spoke again.

"We'll have a visit from Major Crosby before the day is out."

"Why do you think that?"

"Because 'your' Captain Phelps will phone him from Niangara. Crosby will pick him up in his car and drive him here. He does a steady hundred kilometers an hour, whatever the state of the roads. And he never stops, unless he sees something to shoot at along the way."

The heat was steadily rising, and the stillness of high noon brooded on the jungle. Not a leaf stirred, and the only sound was a distant murmur of voices, women talking in a village hidden in the bush.

Camille had eaten less than half as much as usual. All were longing to have done with this dismal meal but lacked the energy to make a move. Baligi could be seen leaning against the jamb of the kitchen door, waiting for the order to clear away.

"Do you take coffee after lunch?"

"It would keep me awake, and I intend to have a siesta."

She made a movement, as if wanting to rise. Graux hurried to her side.

"Camille, come and help."

"I'm awfully sorry to give you so much trouble. I'll only ask you to carry me to my bed."

As they were carrying her into the bedroom, the injured leg brushed against the door. In fact, Camille was so clumsy that Graux called him to order with an unwonted sharpness:

"Can't you look where you're going?"

At last she was deposited on the bed, and Camille backed out of the room. Graux hesitated. Lines of dazzling light showed between the slats of the Venetian blinds.

"Couldn't you close them completely?" Lady Makinson asked fretfully. Graux had the impression that her nerves were stretched almost to breaking point.

He took longer than was needed to get the slats in line; after that, the only light in the room was a mere glimmer filtering through tiny chinks. A big mason bee was buzzing in the sultry gloom.

"Shall I kill it?" he asked.

His voice sounded so odd, his attitude was so quaintly woebegone, that Lady Makinson gave a nervous laugh.

Unthinkingly Camille had closed the door behind him. From beyond it came a faint tinkle of dishes; Baligi was gathering the plates and glasses on the checked tablecloth.

Four

February 26. There was a leopard roaming around the bungalow last night. The elephants were very nervous. Tom Thumb so much so that he wouldn't do a stroke of work today. Only a hundred and fifty kilos of salt left in store. A swarm of locusts passed south of the plantation at 5 P.M. In the distance they looked like a thundercloud.

February 27. The leopard came again. Camille is in one of his moods.

Each night since coming to Africa, Ferdinand Graux had thus recorded the principal happenings of the day. Every tenth day he sent the sheets to his mother in the guise of a letter. To dispatch it he had to travel forty kilometers in his car, to the junction between his private road and the main road, where he had nailed a mailbox to a tree. It had two keys; one of them he kept himself, and the other he had given to the busdriver, who carried the letter as far as Bodi. From there Smith, the proprietor of the hotel, took it to the Airways terminus in the Anglo-Egyptian Sudan, to which he went regularly once a week.

The envelope usually contained ten or twelve sheets closely covered with writing. To begin with, Graux had used ordinary notepaper; then his mother, pointing out that the letter sometimes cost as much as fifteen francs in stamps, had supplied him with a box of airmail paper.

Camille is in one of his moods.

One day when he was at home, he had tried to explain to his mother what this phrase—which recurred from time to time in his journal-letters—meant. For weeks on end Camille would be a model of docility, eager to anticipate his employer's wishes and spare him every trouble. Then suddenly one morning he would appear with a glum face, murmur a reluctant "Good morning," and stare at Graux with almost hostile eyes.

"Absurd as it sounds, I think he's suffering from jealousy when he gets like that," Graux had told his mother.

He and his mother had no secrets between them and understood each other perfectly. Indeed, in the small household in Moulins, they formed a clan apart. Like her son, Madame Graux never set foot in the shop, and she had built up around her in the big, dimly lit upstairs rooms an atmosphere of quietude and silence that strongly appealed to Ferdinand.

"But what on earth can he be jealous about?"

Just plain jealous, Graux explained, incredible as that might seem. It had begun with Maligbanga—a native girl, now married and the mother of several children, who, before her marriage, had been Graux's first housekeeper.

He had chosen her quite haphazardly, for her looks were not above average. Nevertheless, he soon discovered that Camille had taken a fancy to her. That he should have picked Maligbanga when there were far prettier girls available in the surrounding villages had puzzled Graux at first. But when Maligbanga got married and was replaced by Baligi, Camille promptly transferred to her his hopeless devotion.

Obviously it was more than mere coincidence. The truth was that Camille was incapable of choosing for himself; and also, Graux suspected, he got a romantic thrill from nursing a secret grief.

For weeks on end he hardly thought of it. Then suddenly his passion would blaze up again, and his distress was unconcealed . It was to such emotional crises that Graux referred when now and again he wrote in his diary, *Camille is in one of his moods.*

These sheets he had just found in his blotter were ones he had written during the week preceding his departure for Europe. There would have been no point in sending them, for he was due to arrive himself in France at the same time as the mail.

February 28. Shot the leopard at last! To tempt him within range I tied a dog under the veranda. Tried to save the skin, but the natives were so excited by their enemy's death that they slashed it to pieces with their spears.

The infirmary roof is leaking and needs repairs. While I am at it I think I shall put in a double roof.

His letters to Emilienne were shorter. He had told her once and for all that if she wanted "more details" she had only to apply to his mother.

More recently he had written:

There was a couple on the plane from Alexandria who made more noise than all the others put together. The man is a Belgian civil servant. He has been in the Congo only three years, but his liver is troubling him already. His wife—quite unintentionally, for she certainly means well—is going to lead him a dog's life, of which he had a foretaste on the way. In Africa one should be very careful whom one marries. Beside this couple, who drew everyone's attention to them, I must have seemed stolid as an Englishman!

And on another sheet:

May 18. I imagine you saw in the papers that two English aviators, Lady Makinson and Captain Phelps, had disappeared with their plane in the course of a flight over the Congo. I have just found them here, in occupation of my bungalow! Lady Makinson, whose knee is injured, has taken over my bed. They seem to find this arrangement quite natural!

May 19. You remember my telling you about the young couple on the plane, the Belgian civil servant and his exuberant little wife (who, by the way, rejoices in the name of "Yette" and hails from Boulevard Beaumarchais, Paris—which "places" her, as some of our snobbish friends in Moulins would say). She drank in every word I said and kept turning to her husband with a:

"Do you hear, Georges?"

He always scowled at her when she said it, but one felt that he, like her, was laboring under a sense of inferiority, because of his social background.

*Well, if Emilienne were here now, she might well take to saying to
me at every moment:*

"Do you see, Ferdinand?"

*For between myself on the one hand and Lady Makinson and her
young airman on the other there's much the same social difference as
that between the young Belgian couple and myself. It's a question of
upbringing, really (no reproach intended!). They're in my house, and
it's I who feel like an intruder. And I'm always being reminded of the
difference between us by absurd little details—like the glance she gave
those napkin cases Marie-Thérèse embroidered for me. I blushed as if
I'd been caught in some outrageous social solecism! (Please don't tell
Marie-Thérèse; she wouldn't understand.)*

*They even get on Camille's nerves. He spent ten years learning
English, and when he speaks it our guests don't understand a word.*

*Anyhow, I am hoping they will leave tomorrow. We are waiting for a
message from Niangara.*

On the last sheet he had written:

*Major Crosby, who runs the elephant farm, came to dine with us.
They asked me if they might talk English at dinner. It seems I speak it
without a trace of an accent. Lady Makinson will stay on till the new
propeller she has ordered from England turns up. So that I can have a
bedroom to sleep in, Phelps is moving to Major Crosby's place, and
Major Crosby is putting his car at his disposal. We are having a break
in the rains, which had only just begun, and the temperature is rising.*

As he wrote these last lines, in the bedroom Phelps had vacated, his
hands shook as if he were having an attack of fever. He had been in this
state all evening, so much so indeed that he had thought it best to
murmur something about malaria.

Major Crosby had turned up at five in his racing car, which in its
youth, fifteen years before, had made everybody turn and stare at it in
the streets of London. The whole body was of aluminum, it was shaped
exactly like a torpedo, and the roar of its engine could be heard a mile
away.

When it arrived, Graux was pacing the riverbank, trying to steady his
nerves. He had had a distant glimpse of Crosby in the driver's seat with
Phelps beside him and, instead of going back to the bungalow, had
walked a kilometer upstream, idly gazing at the river to see if the
friendly hippo was still in his old haunt.

He heard someone running up behind him and, looking around, saw
Camille.

"The major's here," he panted. "What do you want me to do?"

"Help Baligi get dinner ready for all of them."

"How about you?"

"I'll be back soon. Say I'm busy."

But Camille was too stupid to realize that the best thing he could do was to leave Graux in peace. He was worried by the look on his employer's face—the look of a man who had been shedding tears or is on the brink of them—and his flushed cheeks.

"What's wrong?"

"Oh, go away, damn you!"

Never before had he spoken in that tone to Camille. But his nerves were out of control; he'd go to almost any length just to be left in peace.

Yet, alone, he felt just as bad. Indeed, as Camille was going away he called him back.

"Camille! Have you seen her?"

"Who? Oh, Lady Makinson, you mean. Yes, I've just been helping Captain Phelps carry her to the hall."

"What did she say?"

"Nothing."

"How was she looking?"

"Oh, the same as usual."

"Go now."

He fell to wondering if he was feeling happy or depressed. Both at once, perhaps, but more depressed than happy. For though at this moment he was walking in familiar surroundings—surroundings that he, to a great extent, had personally created—he felt hopelessly estranged from them, as if some link had snapped between himself and his life's work.

He tried again to find the hippopotamus. Yes, there it was, lazily floundering in the muddy water, but now the sight gave him no pleasure. How absurd he had been, idling away whole evenings watching a stupid hippopotamus and making believe they were becoming friends!

"Old Potam!" He recalled a remark Emilienne had made to him:

"Do you know, I'm almost jealous of your 'dear old Potam.' You talk of him so sentimentally."

What craziness! To think that he, Ferdinand Graux, had let himself get into such a state! Yes, he must be really ill. Even the sight of the red roofs of his buildings in the distance filled him with disgust, a sort of nausea.

For he couldn't think of anything but her—and of *that*. Yes, *that!* A woman who, after all, was only a woman; an embrace that was an embrace like any other woman's. What sense was there in attributing so much importance to a mere incident, a momentary thrill? And in letting it play havoc with his peace of mind, fill him with thoughts for which he blushed, instead of taking it in his stride as any healthy-minded man would do?

There were moments when he actually imagined his whole life had been changed. No less than that. And changed by what? By an hour of blind passion, an ugly gesture.

He could have beaten his breast with rage against himself—but, no, at all costs he must steady his nerves, must become once more the rational, levelheaded man he used to be. And get things into perspective.

He had had an hour of "love" with Lady Makinson. Well and good. Now it was over and done with, all passion spent. How absurd it would be to suppose she attached any special importance to that act! For her it was an everyday event. Not only was she married, with two children, but she also had Phelps in constant attendance. No, probably it meant nothing to her.

Abruptly he turned on his heel and started back toward the bungalow. He had regained, or so he thought, his peace of mind and, as he strode quickly on, applied himself to thinking out the order to be given in Stanleyville for the repairs to the infirmary roof. Quite a lot of corrugated iron would be wanted, for one thing; there was practically none left in the warehouse. . . .

What was the sense of it? Was it any less absurd to be thinking about corrugated iron than about her? Looking back, he wondered what had been the use of sweating his soul out for six years, building up an enterprise that didn't bring in a sou; that was, on the contrary, a drain on his resources, and quite unsalable, since no one else would dream of settling in such a Godforsaken corner of the bush!

Most of all he was eager to find out if she, too, had changed. Just now, in his arms, she had shown a capacity for passion that amazed him. He had never conceived that a woman, especially a woman of her kind, could lose her self-control so utterly. At certain moments she had seemed like a little girl nestling to his breast, and he couldn't tell if she were whimpering or laughing. Now and again she had said some words, quite trivial words, but in a strange, faraway tone whose echoes haunted him still.

He took pains to walk at a steady pace, unhurrying, as he approached the bungalow, for he knew they could see him from the veranda. Crosby, a genial, hard-bitten, hard-drinking old Englishman, came down the path to greet him and slapped him on the back.

"Hello, Ferdinand, you old scoundrel! Had a good time on leave? You're a sly dog, keeping charming ladies hidden away in your bungalow. I'd never have thought it of you!"

She was smiling to him! He saw her reclining in the folding armchair, a cigarette between her lips, her eyes half shut because of the smoke curling up in front of them. A smile like that of a hostess welcoming an expected guest; no more. Ferdinand shot a sour glance at the young man seated at her side, who called to him:

"Your assistant has invited us to dinner, and I hear we're to have a jellied duck you brought with you from France. Very kind of you to let us have it!"

She said:

"Would you mind having a couple of eggs poached for me, Ferdinand? I never eat duck."

That "Ferdinand" came as a surprise, but she had said it in such a natural tone that no one, not even Phelps, noticed it.

A moment later she was talking about the plane, after excusing herself for speaking in English.

"I hope you don't mind. But the major speaks French with such an atrocious accent."

Phelps had brought a cable from her husband, which he read out loud:

HAVE BEEN MOST ANXIOUS. SEND NEWS DAILY. CHILDREN WELL. WIRE WHEN RETURNING. LOVE RONALD.

She showed no emotion but promptly started asking about the propeller. Phelps had to repeat word for word the cable he had sent to London, then give full details of the steps he had taken to get their passports in order.

Night was falling. The English members of the group had helped themselves to whisky; it was the major's third shot. All eyes were turned toward the hillside, over which a pale-blue mist was spreading, and the tall, tapering silk-cotton tree rising in lonely eminence above the undergrowth.

Now and again Lady Makinson turned to glance at Ferdinand, who tried in vain to find any special look in her eyes. She was just the same as usual and didn't even seem tired!

"Do you hear, Ferdinand?"

"Sorry. I wasn't listening."

"Up in the clouds, eh? . . . I was just saying that we really can't let you sleep any longer on a cot. Jimmy will go back with the major tonight."

Why "Jimmy," and not herself?

"If I'm not too much of a nuisance," she continued, "I'll stay on till my leg's a little better. Jimmy can use your car to come and see me, can't he, Major Crosby?"

He was totally confused. If this was a device of hers for being alone with him, why not make him understand it by a special look or intonation?

Baligi was setting the table, Camille hovering in the background, too shy to join the group. Ferdinand called him and turned to Crosby.

"I don't think you've met Camille yet. He's my assistant, and a very old friend."

"Does he speak English?"

"He understands it perfectly."

The question didn't have much point, for the three visitors proceeded to talk among themselves, ignoring their hosts. The two men ate the jellied duck, prepared by Madame Graux with her own hands, as if it were a *plat du jour* on a restaurant menu. The major continued drinking whisky, and Ferdinand was surprised to see Lady Makinson following suit.

"Heard anything of the colonel?"

They talked of things that interested them, people Graux had never heard of, mostly Indian-army officers and members of the diplomatic service.

"Have Jimmy's people cut him off yet?" the major asked.

"No, they've given me another three months' grace," grinned Phelps.

He was the heir apparent, so to speak, of the famous Phelps & Phelps, now in the hands of two strait-laced old brothers, one of whom had never married, while the other had only one son, the young man sitting at the table. He, however, flatly refused to have anything to do with commerce.

"Do they still pay your bills?"

"Some of them," Lady Makinson replied, and Ferdinand felt vaguely annoyed that she should know so much about Phelps's private affairs. But then she added: "I thought at first of registering my plane in his name, since I hadn't yet qualified as a pilot. Then someone was kind enough to warn me that if I did so, his creditors would promptly have it seized."

She seemed to treat that as a joke, and so did Phelps.

Camille was making desperate attempts to catch the drift of the conversation.

"Did you ever go back to Java?" the major asked. "And have you heard anything more of that quaint little Dutchman who made us laugh so much?"

"He sends me a picture postcard now and then."

"One of your victims, wasn't he?"

Ferdinand reddened. It had struck him that there might well be points in common between the comic Dutchman and himself. But had the Dutchman . . . ? Then he heard Lady Makinson speaking to him.

"What's wrong? Feeling bored by all our talk?"

"No. I think I have a touch of malaria."

"You'd better go to bed."

So that was how she felt about him! She packed him off to bed, the better to enjoy the company of these compatriots of hers, these people of her own social set, who probably regarded him as an outsider!

He could hardly believe that this was the same woman he had held in his arms only a few hours before, who, under his caresses, had seemed to lose all her sophistication and to become a queer little whimpering girl, pressing her moist eyes against her lover's breast.

"When are you going to look me up?" asked Major Crosby. "I have a first-class cow to sell you, if you want her. She's a marvel! When she's ready for it I just turn her loose in the bush, and last time she brought back with her two magnificent bulls who let themselves be shackled without giving us any trouble. I can let you have her for fifty thousand francs. What about it?"

"I'll think it over."

Crosby was in great form, discoursing with equal zest on big-game hunting, his financial coups, drinking parties, and society scandals of the Edwardian era. With his snow-white hair and plump, rubicund cheeks, he was the typical sportsman of an older generation. He smoked cigars banded with his initials and wore impeccably cut riding breeches of a discreetly original shade of brown.

Two or three times in the course of the evening, his eyes strayed deliberately from Lady Makinson to Ferdinand, who came to the conclusion that the major had guessed. . . .

"Well, well, I suppose we'd better get going," he said at last, glancing toward Phelps.

"Wait!" said Lady Makinson. "Will you help me into my room, Phelps, before you go? I'm still a poor helpless cripple, don't forget."

Ferdinand and Phelps carried her to the bed. As he was taking his leave, Phelps bent over her hand and kissed it ceremoniously.

"Will you come tomorrow?" she asked.

"Of course, if the major'll lend me his crate. That all right, Graux?"

"Of course."

"Good night. Pleasant dreams!"

"Good night."

Feeling somewhat at a loss, Ferdinand began to move toward the door, murmuring:

"Good night, Lady Makinson."

"Good night, Ferdinand."

It was preposterous, the way everything was happening, everybody behaving as if it were the close of a quite ordinary day. Before stepping into his car, Crosby lit another cigar, while Phelps called cheerily:

"Bye-bye! See you tomorrow."

In fact, it was the same kind of scene that may be witnessed any night at the front door of any country house in Europe after the breakup of a dinner party. The roar of the engine died in the darkness. As Camille followed Ferdinand back into the hall he was scowling, and something prompted him to say:

"I can't stand the English!"

"Ssh!"

Quite unnecessary; the door was closed, and she couldn't have heard.

"Are they going to stay here long?"

"I have no idea."

Camille may have had an inkling of something—or else he was putting out a feeler, for he had all the cunning of the French peasant in his blood; now he remarked with a casual air, as if announcing a trivial domestic event:

"Baligi was crying all afternoon."

"Why?"

No answer. Camille, who was to continue sleeping in the hall, was bending over his cot, straightening the pillow.

"Good night."

"Good night."

Graux hesitated for a while before entering the room where he was to sleep. It struck him he'd have done better to get Camille to sleep in one of the outbuildings—the infirmary, for instance, where there were no patients at the moment. For Camille's presence in the hall made it rather awkward going to Lady Makinson's room.

Nevertheless he walked boldly across the hall and knocked at her door. A voice asked:

"Who's there?"

His courage ebbed away, and he replied uncomfortably:

"I wanted to know if there's anything you require."

"Thanks . . . I don't need anything."

That was why his hand was shaking as, in his room, he recorded his impressions of that uncomfortable lunch party, and the "social difference" between himself and his guests of which he had become so distastefully aware.

He had spent some time trying to set his thoughts in order and finally had hit on no better explanation than that.

May 20. I am still convinced that it isn't due to the difference of nationality, but to that of our respective milieux. I have no doubt that there are people like them in Paris, too, in a certain set. Phelps drove in this morning by himself in Crosby's car and spent a couple of hours with Lady Makinson in her room. It makes me feel terribly bourgeois, but never for a moment can I get it out of my head that she's the mother of two children.

Nothing in Lady Makinson's attitude that day had given the slightest hint that she had been Ferdinand's mistress on the previous afternoon. She was exactly as usual and, though her leg was giving her some pain, fairly cheerful. At dinner the night before, Major Crosby had suggested she go to Stanleyville for treatment, pointing out that it was only a four-day journey in the car. She had turned him down, referring to her previous accidents, from all of which she had recovered.

"But suppose it leaves you with a limp?"

"Shall I limp, Ferdinand?"

"I don't think so."

"You see!"

The track was being cleared rapidly, and the plane had already moved three hundred meters. Ferdinand had told off Baligi for wearing a dirty dress. Camille was sulking again.

But this time was it on account of Baligi, or of the Englishwoman? Was he going to carry his mania to the point of falling in love with Lady Makinson?

Graux was very short with him throughout the day, so much so that on one occasion, when he had made a particularly unjustified remark, he felt called upon to apologize.

"Sorry! It's this damned rain that keeps holding off; don't you find it gets on your nerves, too?"

For after the rains had set in as usual, there had been a sudden break; hardly a drop had fallen for a fortnight.

I wonder if Emilienne's nerves will be able to stand the climate we sometimes have here. One has the impression that the air one breathes is charged with electricity. Even the elephants feel it and jib at everything one gives them to do. Today I changed my shirt four times. I cannot understand how Lady Makinson can be so unaffected by the heat. Even on the veranda I have to keep my double-decker hat on because of the glare, whereas she sits there for hours, bareheaded.

On this page there was a footnote:

Tell Emilienne to bring a good supply of quinine in cachets. The last batch I got is in tablets (I forgot to specify I wanted it in cachets), and it's nowhere near as effective.

Somehow he couldn't help adding:

Lady Makinson never takes quinine. To look at her you'd think her delicate, but actually she is tougher than most men.

Phelps left at five. Graux, who had been roaming his plantation for two hours under the sun, was streaming with sweat, his face blazing-red. On his return to the bungalow he found Lady Makinson sitting in the hall; Camille, assisted by Baligi, had carried her there.

Affecting not to see her, he went to the bookcase and took from it a book on economics, then poured himself a glass of water and drank it in little sips.

"Ferdinand!"

He made as if he had not heard.

"Listen, Ferdinand! If you don't behave more sensibly I warn you I shall have nothing more to do with you! I've been watching you for the last two hours. Go and change at once."

His shirt was sopping wet. He had tramped around aimlessly under a blazing sun, pretending to be studying the condition of his coffee bushes.

"Really, one would almost think you were about ten years old, from the way you act. No, don't come near me. Get out of those wet clothes at once!"

And he obeyed her. That may have been why he mentioned in his diary-letter that evening the fact that he had changed his shirt four times.

When he returned she was reading the book on political economy, a cigarette between her lips.

"Don't talk, please. . . . This book is quite interesting."

After some minutes' silence his nerves were steadier, and when she looked up from her book, she gave him an approving glance.

"Good. That's how I like to see you. Yesterday evening, when you took off your glasses, you looked so forlorn, like a poor lost child."

He did not remember having taken off his glasses, but it was quite true that when he did so his shortsighted eyes gave him a half-dazed appearance.

"Sit down. Now don't move."

Was she about to yield to a gentler mood, her mood of that memorable afternoon? No, it was not to be. And after dinner she went to bed immediately.

This evening, in the course of conversation, she gave me to understand that Phelps has been staying with them in Stamboul. Did she mean me to infer that her husband knows about their "affair"? Or does Makinson regard it merely as a flirtation?

This letter would be read in one of the big, somber rooms, dappled with glints of burnished copper, to which Graux Senior referred when saying to his son:

"Go up to your mother's place."

Indeed, it was so much her place, that quiet realm of silence and subdued light above the gunsmith's shop, that after dinner Ferdinand's father usually went down to his office, where he felt more at ease, to read the evening paper.

His younger son, named Evariste after his father, and like him in character and appearance, was to take over the business when the old man retired. Madame Graux, to distinguish him from his brother, always said "your son."

Whereas Ferdinand was his mother's son. He tried to picture her as she must have been at the age of thirty-two, Lady Makinson's age, and it set him wondering. . . .

In the last analysis, he wrote, morality is little more than a matter of class convention. Camille informed me the other day that girls in his village rarely marry until they have had a baby, and everyone takes that as a matter of course.

All the same, he added:

Spent two hours inspecting the plantation under a very hot sun. If the rain doesn't hold off too long, we should have a bumper crop this year.

Was she asleep? She had carried off to her room the book on economics and, to his surprise, seemed genuinely to find it interesting.

There were moments when he thrust angrily aside the memory of what had passed between them, as if it were something almost repulsive. Yes, he was ashamed of that insensate hour in the hot, stuffy bedroom, of those meaningless words they had babbled, of certain clumsy gestures—the grossness of it all.

And yet, when he recalled, for instance, the tone in which she had uttered his name, he felt a sudden rush of emotion and, clenching his fists, took a step toward her room. . . . But the hall, in which Camille was sleeping, intervened; and if he knocked, Camille would be sure to hear. . . .

Ferdinand found him still asleep there when he went out next morning, well before sunrise, for an inspection of the native huts.

About ten, when he returned, Camille was only just leaving the bungalow, and Lady Makinson had settled down in the hall. It struck him that Camille avoided meeting his gaze. As he was coming up the steps a voice hailed him:

"Good morning, Talatala!"

He stopped short. Lady Makinson was convulsed with laughter, but there was a hint of emotion, almost tenderness, in her eyes.

"Good morning, Talatala," she repeated.

A glance told him what had happened. There was an empty chair beside the one in which she was reclining. Obviously she had asked Camille to sit with her and they had been talking about him.

And Camille had confided to her the name the natives had for Ferdinand: Mundele-na-Talatala.

She was tickled by the idea of calling him by this name, little suspecting that Baligi did the same when they were together.

"Grumpy as ever? Now come and sit beside me, Talatala, and do try to look amiable for a change."

Talatala! It was absurd, but to hear her calling him by that name moved him so deeply that he had to look away. Evidently she noticed this, for she did not speak again for some moments, to give him time to recover his composure.

"Now let's have a talk, you and I. We have heaps of things to tell each other, don't we, and Phelps and Major Crosby will be here soon. Look at me, Monsieur Talatala. . . ."

Five

Tassin the notary was a small man with a quaintly lopsided appearance; that, anyhow, was one's first impression of him. Looking more closely, one saw that this was because one of his cheeks was bigger than the other; it bulged as if he always had a quid of tobacco lodged in it.

Indeed, many people meeting him for the first time believed he really did chew tobacco, for he had a speech defect that made him stammer and splutter like someone who is talking with his mouth full.

Like many undersized men, he had a habit of gesticulating, and, to make things worse, he suffered from a nervous tic that made him blink perpetually.

Beside him his daughter, Emilienne, looked like a giantess. Not that she was heavily built, but she was unusually tall; and she had very fine-grained skin, white as marble.

"No, Father," she interrupted in a decided tone, "it wasn't last year. It was two years ago. . . ."

He had lost his wife fifteen years earlier, and on her death his daughter had taken over the management of the household. A very competent young woman, she ruled him with a firm hand, as her mother had done before her. He took it in good part, for he had got used to being treated as a child—except by members of the Moulins Shooting Club, whose president he was, and by the bridge players of the little town, who regarded him as an authority on the game.

Dinner was nearly ended in the big dining room on the first floor above the gunsmith's shop. It was an evening in early June, and the windows stood open on the tranquil light of sunset, while the noises of the street provided a running accompaniment to the conversation.

Evariste Graux, Ferdinand's father, seated at the head of the table, wore an absent-minded look and paid all the less attention to what was being said as he knew the voluble little lawyer needed no encouragement to go on talking.

Evariste Graux, Jr., who was twenty-three, was waiting impatiently for the meal to end so that he could get away to a meeting of the Automobile Club of the *département*.

His sister, Marie-Thérèse, soon to be a mother, was looking pale, and her husband, a fair young man, almost as jumpy in his manner as Tassin, was putting in a word now and then to show his interest in what the lawyer was saying.

The maid, who had been with the family for twenty-five years, moved soundlessly around the room. On the other side of the street, level with the window, a huge red umbrella in painted tin projected from the wall: a shop sign that had been there since time immemorial.

Indeed, there was a curious timelessness about the scene, a sense that these people could remain exactly as they were now, keeping the same attitudes and expressions, forever, like a museum piece.

But just then Madame Graux made an almost imperceptible gesture, and the spell was broken; everybody rose. The men, instead of going to the drawing room, moved to the window and halted in front of it.

Madame Graux said to her daughter:

"You're looking tired. How about lying down for a while?"

Marie-Thérèse looked inquiringly at her husband, who observed:
"I'm not in favor of her getting too much rest in her present state."
Emilienne was standing in the background. She had had her eyes
fixed on her hostess for some minutes, and she knew that Madame
Graux was aware of this and understood.

"Will you come with me for a moment, Emilienne?"

No one showed any surprise. Emilienne followed Ferdinand's mother
into the linen room, where a sewing machine, with lengths of material
scattered around it, stood on a big deal table.

"Show me the letter, please."

Madame Graux put on her glasses and switched on the light, for the
linen room, which gave on an inner courtyard, was getting dark.

Emilienne said nothing, but the tense look on her face and the
unwonted stiffness of her posture conveyed her thoughts as plainly as
words. "You'll see, the situation's serious. We must put our heads
together, you and I."

Though not so tall as Emilienne, Madame Graux had all her natural
dignity; with her amply molded bust and close-fitting black dress, she
looked like the typical matron of old family portraits.

"Have you spoken about it to your father?" she asked.

"No, not yet."

Madame Graux fell to reading the letter, her lips moving like those of
a worshiper at Mass.

My dear Emilienne,

*This is my fourth attempt at writing a letter to you. It must go now,
such as it is, for the bus passes this morning. But really I hardly dare to
write to you in my present state. I might so easily say some foolish
thing, something I should regret bitterly all my life long.*

*I can only tell you that I am passing through a terrible emotional
crisis and ask you to bear with me till you get my next letter. Meanwhile, rest assured that I am doing my utmost to prevent anything's
being changed between us.*

*Go and see Mother; she will give you sound advice, I know. I am
feeling run down mentally and physically. And the rains are still
holding off!*

With love, Ferdinand

Madame Graux sighed and refrained from looking at Emilienne, who
murmured:

"Well?"

"I'd better show you the letter I've just got from him. The very first
line told me . . . something was amiss." She opened the linen cup-

board, in which she kept Ferdinand's journal-letters. "You'd better read this. There's nothing in it you shouldn't see. I'll be back in a few minutes. I must go and see to the coffee and liqueurs."

I imagine you saw in the papers that two English aviators, Lady Makinson and Captain Phelps, had disappeared with their plane. . . . Emilienne remained standing; she was not made for armchairs and easy attitudes.

For between myself on the one hand and Lady Makinson and her young airman on the other there's much the same social difference as that between the young Belgian couple and myself. . . . And farther on: *I am hoping they will leave tomorrow.* Only to be gainsaid in the next entry: *Lady Makinson will stay on till the new propeller she has ordered from England turns up.*

"Emilienne," said Madame Graux, who had just returned, "your father wants to know if you'll come back with him now; he wants to go to the club for a game of bridge."

"Ask him to wait a moment, please. I may have something to tell him."

She finished reading the last sheet:

There are moments when I wonder if I am not on the brink of a drastic change in my life. And the intense heat, the storm that goes on brooding and never breaks, plays havoc with one's nerves. Even Lady Makinson sometimes seems affected by it. In any case, it would be wiser for Emilienne to put off her departure for a few weeks.

"He asks if you'll come at once, for all the bridge tables will have been made up in half an hour."

Emilienne did not bother to answer; graver issues were at stake than missing a rubber of bridge. Still holding the sheets of airmail paper, she asked:

"What do you make of it?"

"What about you?"

Emilienne's eyes were dry, but her lips were paler than usual, and she never put any lipstick on them. Madame Graux had a sudden feeling of respect for this tall, stately girl, outwardly so self-possessed, who betrayed her emotion only by a slight movement of the throat, as if she were swallowing hard.

"I suppose I'd better go," she said at last. But she did not mean "go home" and enable her father to play bridge. It was Ferdinand she had in mind, and the advisability of setting out for Africa at once. Madame Graux evidently agreed with her, for she raised no objection, but stared at the floor, deep in thought. After a while she said:

"You must decide that for yourself, my dear."

"I know. . . . But can you explain it? It's so unlike Ferdinand to behave like that. Really, I'm almost frightened. Aren't you?"

But Madame Graux preferred not to answer.

"If I catch the plane in Brindisi, I can be there in a week."

Both of them, perhaps, felt the same anxiety, but it was Madame Graux who voiced it, rather hesitantly.

"Don't you think it . . . it might annoy him?"

Emilienne's only reply was a slight shrug of her shoulders that seemed to say, "I'll have to risk it. There's too much at stake for me to trouble about Ferdinand's *amour propre.*"

"Will you tell your father what you've decided?"

"Yes."

"How will you put it?"

Again her shoulders lifted slightly. Did it have any great importance how she broke it to him? Before leaving the linen room Emilienne kissed Madame Graux and asked, pointing to the sheets of paper:

"May I take them?"

"Certainly, my dear."

Slipping them into her bodice, she entered the drawing room. Marie-Thérèse and her husband were just getting ready to go. Tassin, who was standing at the window smoking a cigar and talking to Evariste Graux, beamed with delight when his daughter appeared.

"Ah, here you are at last! I thought you were never coming. With luck I'll be in time for a game. . . . But what's wrong, Emilienne?"

As she drew near the window the pale evening light brought out the wanness of her face, its tense immobility.

"There's nothing wrong with me. But I have something to tell you. I am leaving by train tomorrow evening for Brindisi."

"What's that you say? Leaving for Brindisi?"

Marie-Thérèse and her husband came back from the hallway to hear the rest of it.

"Yes, I must go to Ferdinand at once. He's not very well, and it's better I should be with him."

From the expression on the face of Madame Graux, the lawyer gathered that she approved of the plan.

"Is Ferdinand really ill?" asked Graux.

"Well, it's just as if he were," his wife replied vaguely. "Anyhow, Emilienne is doing the right thing. I'm convinced of that."

"But what about me?" wailed the little lawyer. One could see he was appalled at the thought of having to do without his daughter. "Really, it was most inconsiderate of you to spring this on me!" He looked as if he might burst into tears at any moment. "Yes, most inconsiderate," he repeated. "And when will you be coming back?"

"I have no idea."

Madame Graux took compassion on the little man. "Let me give you a glass of brandy," she suggested.

With the approach of night a hush had fallen on the town; the sound of footfalls in the street had ceased, the red umbrella on the opposite wall glowed a darker red, and the cobblestones in the street showed ashen-gray. A few minutes more and it would be time to close the window and turn on the lights.

And now, abruptly, all this evening peace had been shattered!

Marie-Thérèse and her husband lingered on, as if anxious to bear their part in the misfortune that had befallen the two families.

"Will you take the plane?"

"Yes, in Brindisi. I have a timetable at home."

Only Evariste Junior, who was now confabulating at the Automobile Club, knew nothing. His father betrayed his emotion only by making loud, wheezy sighs and pulling a long face. At last he put in a word:

"In any case, of course, you'd have been leaving in two months." He said it mainly to console his old friend the notary.

A moment later drops began to patter on the window sill. A brisk, warm summer shower had just set in, and all the windows in the street closed simultaneously.

"I want you to tell me something."

Lady Makinson made a faint movement of impatience. Here, too, night had fallen. The two long chairs were side by side on the veranda, where the lights had been switched off because of the insects.

Flooded with moonlight, the sky seemed infinitely remote, and the big stationary clouds with jagged edges looked like island continents set in a blue translucent ocean. The hillside facing the veranda was swathed in mist, and nothing could be seen but the tall, tapering form of the silk-cotton tree, leafless now. Periodically they heard the distant thudding of a tom-tom, and the blue darkness was full of furtive sounds: the padding of barefoot natives along the bush paths, the rustle of wild animals creeping through the scrub.

"What do you want to know?"

"I want to know just how much you've told Phelps."

She sighed. The question seemed to her so futile.

"He knows everything, doesn't he?"

"What do you mean by 'everything'?"

"That you're my mistress."

At that she nearly lost her temper, and there was more than impatience in her voice when she replied:

"But I'm not your mistress. And it's a horrible word to use. I'm free, and so are you."

But that he wouldn't admit, would never admit.

"No!" he cried impulsively. "That's not true!"

"Ferdinand, do, please, be sensible. I shouldn't have stayed so long, I know. . . ."

"I'm positive you've told Phelps . . . everything."

But she thought it best to keep silent. Lost in thought, they gazed up at the dark cloud masses rimmed with silvery light.

During the last ten days, at least, there had been nothing to prevent Lady Makinson's making a move and going to stay at the elephant farm with Phelps and the major. Almost every evening she had said she would leave next day, and several times had even done her packing—only to announce with a slight yawn at the last moment:

"No. I don't feel like moving today. Come for me with the car tomorrow, Jimmy, and I'll go back with you."

One of the things that puzzled Ferdinand most was that Phelps showed no jealousy whatever. He shook Ferdinand's hand as usual, with a conventional, slightly distant cordiality; and the major, too, behaved as if he knew nothing.

But surely that was incredible. There was no plausible reason why Lady Makinson should be staying on in the bungalow. The latest news from London was that the propeller would take at least a month to reach her; indeed, there were times when she spoke of leaving her plane where it was for the time being and returning to Stamboul by Imperial Airways.

"What have you told him?"

For not only did Phelps show no jealousy; to Ferdinand's surprise, his attitude now was much more friendly than at first. He had begun by almost ignoring Ferdinand's existence. Now he actually made advances and sometimes spoke of Lady Makinson as if there were a tacit understanding among the three of them. Thus, on one occasion, he said to Ferdinand:

"I really have a very great admiration for her husband. He is twenty years older than she, but he's one of the best—genial, broad-minded—and everybody likes him."

Ferdinand wondered what the young man was driving at with this laudation of the husband. Was he hinting that Sir Ronald knew of his wife's amours and tolerated them? Or was Phelps completely callous in such matters?

Another thing he confided to Ferdinand was that for two years he had been trying to cure Lady Makinson of the opium habit.

"If she asks you for opium—we had some in the plane, you know—don't get it for her. She's slowing down a bit, I'm glad to say, but a year ago I saw her smoke as many as thirty-five pipes in a day. Luckily she has a splendid constitution."

Another morning he remarked, with an air of seeming casualness:

"This is the first time I've known her to stay so long at one place. It's quite unlike her. You remember that when we turned up here our passports didn't have the proper visas. The reason's quite simple. The plane was delivered on a Wednesday. Well, Lady Mary wouldn't even wait till the Friday. She insisted on our taking off the very next day."

Ferdinand, too, had got into the habit of speaking of her, and addressing her, as "Lady Mary."

"Even when she was in her teens she was always doing unconventional things. Her father doted on her and let her have her way in everything. I hadn't met her then, but it's common knowledge among her set in England. She'd leave for the Rocky Mountains on a few hours' notice, the way other people go for a weekend in Brighton. When she was eighteen she used to stroll up Regent Street with a panther cub in tow."

All right, but why tell it to him, of all people? And why this uninvited frankness, behind which undoubtedly lurked a certain irony, and this complete lack of jealousy? In fact, the young man's attitude seemed often to convey to him, as clearly as words: "I'm leaving you a clear field. Make the most of it!"

On two occasions it had happened, and they were the crucial moments of the last few weeks—indeed, of Ferdinand's whole life.

Why on those particular days, rather than on others? The first occasion had been at breakfast, when they were seated around the checkered tablecloth. Camille, who was in one of his moods, had wolfed down his meal and left abruptly. In the morning light a spacious, comforting tranquillity brooded on the hillside, where the lush green foliage of the coffee bushes showed in sharp relief against the vividly red soil, dotted here and there with the dark forms of blacks. Absent-mindedly Lady Makinson had reached for her cigarette case, then drawn her hand back, murmuring:

"No!"

He looked at her wonderingly, then asked:

"What are you thinking about?"

"Nothing. . . . Don't talk, please."

He could see that she was deeply moved. And he could have sworn that she was yielding to the restful influence of her surroundings, perhaps to his personal influence as well, his sense of oneness with all that was most stable and serene in life and nature.

And then he had spoiled everything! For it was true, as she had often told him, he never knew when to hold his tongue.

"Do tell me what you're thinking about. Are you feeling sad? Mary! Look at me!"

And she had looked at him, but almost angrily. The spell was broken. She sighed:

"Oh, why *must* you always speak?"

"Because I love you."

He had struck the wrong note again! Her only comment was an impatient shrug, which rankled in his memory throughout the day.

The second occasion had been on the second day she was able to walk around a little. At night, when he was writing in his room, the door had opened. Lady Makinson stood in the doorway, leaning on her cane.

"I was wondering what you were up to, all by yourself."

He rose to his feet. From where she stood she gazed at the sheets of airmail paper on the table.

"You can read them," he said.

And that night she had kissed him in a different way, without a trace of sensuality, then frowned, as if trying to dispel a haunting thought.

"You queer old Talatala!" she said in a low tone. "No. Let me go to bed. Stay here."

In the vast and hospitable silence of the night they gazed at each other, each conscious of a quickening of the heart. Why, once again, had he blundered into speech?

"There are moments when I really think you love me. But no sooner have you left my arms than . . ."

"Ferdinand!"

"You see! It's as if you were ashamed, as if . . ."

She flared up.

"Won't you ever learn to hold your tongue? Don't you realize there are things a man who has any . . . any *savoir-vivre* doesn't speak about?"

"A man like Phelps, you mean?"

"Phelps, anyhow, knows when to keep his mouth shut."

"Yes, Phelps is a well-bred English gentleman, whereas I . . ."

"You always let your nerves get the better of you. . . . Oh, why must you spoil our last evening together? I'm leaving tomorrow."

"Yes?"

"And I want you to promise me to behave sensibly and take up your life as it was before I came. Yes, I assure you, that's the only thing to do. It's no use being romantic, my poor Talatala. I shall go back to Stamboul. I'll give tea parties at the embassy, play tennis, go yachting on the Bosporus—and now and then, perhaps, I'll send you a picture postcard."

There was an unwonted shrillness in her voice. He tried, without success, to make out the expression on her face.

"And Phelps will resume his post of gentleman in waiting," he said bitterly.

"You're either sillier than I thought, Ferdinand, or just spiteful. I'm handing over the plane to Phelps, who's quite determined to fly it to his country, New Zealand. It takes some pluck, you know; he has to cross the Indian Ocean, and after Madagascar there are only two small islands on the way."

"Why must you talk about *him!*"

"I thought it was you who started it."

"Are we going to have another quarrel?"

He clenched his fists, disgusted with himself, with the incapacity of human minds to rise above the petty and the mean. Here he was, airing his futile grievances, when all the time his one desire was to take her in his arms, to implore her to stay with him always, to link her life with his . . . !

"Mary!"

"Yes, Ferdinand? I'm here. But you go on talking all the time. I really think you enjoy tormenting yourself. You never seem to want to know anything about me, my life in Ankara, my children. . . ."

With an effort he kept silent, though words like those she had just spoken made him feel desperate; it was beyond him how she could say such things.

"When I met you for the first time," she went on, "you gave the impression of being a staid, levelheaded sort of man. Beside you Phelps cut the figure of a schoolboy. But when you took off those glasses you became just like him. No, not like him, like a nervous, temperamental youngster . . . I ought to have left the first day I was fit to be moved."

"Will you consent to answer just one question?"

"All right," she sighed, to have done with it.

"Tell me this: does Phelps know, or doesn't he . . . ?"

"Know what?"

"That . . . that I'm your lover."

"Oh, couldn't you have let that subject drop! Yes, Ferdinand, he knows."

"And he's not jealous?"

"Why should he be?"

"What? Do you mean to deny that he, too, is your lover?"

She stood up abruptly and tottered, as she'd forgotten to lean on her cane.

"Where are you going?"

"To bed."

"You haven't answered me yet."

But already she was walking through the doorway, her footsteps echoed by the tapping of her cane on the tiled floor.

Why, precisely at this moment, did he seem to hear a coarse voice shrilling in his ear:

"Do you hear, Georges?"

Yes, and how aptly someone might have said to him just now: "Do you see, Ferdinand?"

For the first time she locked her door—unreasonably enough, for he had never tried to enter her room without her permission.

With an effort, he, too, rose. As he stepped out into the hall he had an impression of something abnormal and switched on the light.

Camille was not there, and the blanket on his cot had not been drawn back.

Greatly surprised, Ferdinand went out to the veranda and started to walk around the bungalow, making as little noise as he could. On very hot nights Baligi sometimes brought her mat outside and slept in the open, near the kitchen door.

Tonight, as it so happened, it was on that side of the building that the moonlight fell. As Ferdinand was rounding the corner, something stirred on the ground before him, and a head and shoulders came into view.

It was Camille, who had been sleeping under the same blanket as the black girl and was obviously flustered at being caught in this position. Before he had time to rise to his feet, Ferdinand moved away. On entering his bedroom he, too, locked the door.

Next morning Lady Makinson did not appear till ten o'clock, but he heard her moving around in her room. At ten precisely a car hooted at the entrance of the compound, and some moments later Major Crosby and Phelps came up the steps.

"Good morning, Graux. Isn't Lady Makinson up yet?"

She had heard them coming, and her door opened.

"Come in for a moment, I have something to tell you," she said; then, turning to Ferdinand, "You don't mind, do you?"

The conversation in the bedroom lasted for a quarter of an hour. Twice Camille tried to buttonhole Ferdinand, and the second time got as far as:

"I owe you an explanation. . . ."

"That's all right, old boy. Don't bother."

As for Baligi, she had not put in an appearance yet. The rain still held off, though the sky was black with clouds and the earth scorching underfoot. There was hardly any water in the river, not enough to move the turbines.

At last the bedroom door opened.

"Any chance of a whisky?" asked the major the moment he was outside the door. Lady Makinson, who was close behind him, said:

"Can you come for a moment, Ferdinand?"

He had never seen her before in this costume, a white tailor-made outfit that made her look quite different. It would have been more appropriate on a Riviera beach or the promenade deck of a transatlantic liner than here in the heart of the Congo jungle. Also, Ferdinand noticed, she was holding a pair of white gloves. She said to him in an even tone, though her eyes were moving restlessly from point to point:

"I'm awfully sorry to leave you like this, Ferdinand, but it has to be done. Now you must promise me to be sensible. Your fiancée will be coming out quite soon. And in five or six days I'll be back at home with my children." They were alone, but he remained standing some distance from her, beside the door.

"I won't thank you," she continued, "for your hospitality; it might sound ironical. But I'm sure that someday we shall meet again, and I hope that when that happens we shall become great friends."

He said nothing. She still avoided meeting his eyes.

"Did you hear what I said, Ferdinand?"

Without thinking, she had begun putting on a glove. Then she picked up from the table, and replaced, a book on coffee growing that she had been reading and said with a smile:

"From now on, every time I drink coffee I shall think of your hillside and the waterfall, and that quaint silk-cotton tree, and the elephants. . . . *Au revoir*, Ferdinand."

She held out her hand with a frank, clean-cut gesture. Her aspect, too, in the white tailor-made costume, which brought out the slim lines of her figure, was clean-cut, almost statuesque.

"*Au revoir*, Talatala."

He bent forward to kiss her hand, but she withdrew it just in time and opened the door.

"Well, are you ready?"

Phelps and the major hastily finished up their drinks.

"We shall spend the night in Juba, I expect," the major said to Ferdinand. "That way we can see Lady Makinson off in the plane. We'll stop back here tomorrow. May we invite ourselves to lunch?"

She was crossing the veranda. Walking down the steps. Then she paused and seemed to be looking around for something. Finally she discovered Baligi peeping at her around the trunk of a banana tree, went up to her, and, opening her bag, produced a five-pound note.

The engine was running. The crocodile-skin bag had been placed on the seat beside the major, who insisted on another whisky before starting.

"Where's Ferdinand?"

He took a step forward on the veranda. Phelps shut the door of the car and waved his hand, and the major put it in gear.

He heard, or seemed to hear, her voice: "Talatala!"

Then he swung around abruptly; there had been a curious noise, like a sob, behind him. He saw Camille, the picture of misery.

"What are you doing there?"

"Nothing. I . . . ."

They could hear the drone of the car, out of sight now behind the elephant grass. It had passed the native village, and there was a sudden squeal of brakes as Crosby slowed down at a point where the road had caved in.

Graux sat down on the edge of the table and stared at Camille, frowning.

"If I'd known . . ." Camille paused uncomfortably.

"Known what?"

"I assure you I thought . . ."

"Don't be a damned fool!" Graux realized that Camille was still worrying over his lapse with Baligi. "How much gas is there in the car?"

"A hundred liters. Are you taking it out?"

"I don't know. . . . Now leave me alone, please. Wait! Get the car out of the shed in case I need it. Then go and see to the elephants."

When he had brought the car in front of the bungalow, Camille seemed unable to tear himself away. From the window of his bedroom Ferdinand shouted:

"Didn't you hear what I told you?"

"Are you going to Niangara?"

"That's it. I'm going to Niangara—perhaps. . . ."

The window closed, and, looking around, Camille saw Baligi crouching against the wall. She, too, was watching the car. In her hand was a five-pound note, but she seemed unaware of what she held and was rolling it into a ball, like a pocket handkerchief.

Six

Smith the hotelkeeper, who was as weather-wise as any peasant, had warned Major Crosby when the car was on its way through Bodi:

"Take my advice and start back at once. Unless I'm much mistaken we're in for some heavy rain, and likely as not the road to your place will be flooded once it starts."

Smith, a Belgian despite his name, had settled in these parts long before there were any airfields, or even roads. When one went home in those adventurous days one had to travel by jungle paths, on foot or in a machila—a hammock slung on a bamboo pole—to Stanleyville, then in a stern-wheeler down the Congo River, and the journey to Antwerp took altogether three months or more. The alternative route via the Sudan and Egypt was still longer—and hotter.

Crosby and Phelps had spent the night in Juba, so as to see Lady Makinson off next morning on the airliner. Then they had made the mistake of having a too copious lunch, started late, and reached the frontier after dark. By this time rain was coming down in torrents.

"You see I was right," Smith said, chuckling, when he met them at the hotel entrance. "I'll bet you anything you like the road's under water at Leopard's Leap. And only an idiot would drive by night in weather like this."

"Let's have a little whisky to start with," said Crosby.

Smith's hotel was very different from those of the Anglo-Egyptian Sudan. The first thing one noticed was a spacious park, all the more pleasing to the eye because the brick-red soil showed up the dark-green of the foliage to advantage. The main building, a bungalow set in a luxuriance of tropical flowers, contained only a big dining room, a lounge, and the kitchen. Dotted over the grounds were detached huts containing the bedrooms.

A homely, easygoing place run along typically Belgian lines, Smith's hotel was very different from the expertly managed, scrupulously clean hotels on the other side of the frontier, in British territory.

White-clad boys greeted arriving guests with amiable smiles, and Smith, too, treated them less like customers than like friends, joined in every conversation, and was always ready with helpful advice on every subject under the African sun.

"You'll have roast guinea fowl for dinner," he said to Major Crosby. "I bagged four this afternoon; they crossed the road just under my nose, the silly fools!"

Whether he was in his bungalow or on safari, under a blazing sun or in a tropical downpour, Major Crosby, with his pink cheeks and well-brushed snow-white hair, his well-groomed clothes and carefully knotted silk tie, always looked the picture of health and spruceness. He had a theory that a man who has any respect for his appearance polishes his boots himself; his always had a dazzling shine.

Was he listening to Smith? So it might seem, for he was looking at him. But one also had the impression that his thoughts were far away and he was wishing the Belgian would leave him to them.

"By the bye," said Smith, leaning across the table, "did our friend get there in time? He was in a hell of a hurry, and you could see his nerves were shot. He filled his tank without saying a word and started off at once for Juba. 'Taking the plane?' I shouted after him. I couldn't quite catch what he said, but it sounded like 'Don't know.'"

"He caught it," said Phelps, squirting some soda water into his whisky.

"Has he had bad news from home?"

Crosby deliberately looked away but showed no other sign of annoyance. And probably he would have had to put up with Smith's loquacity for some time longer had not the entrance door been flung open just at that moment, and all eyes turned toward it. Drawn up by the steps was a small car, its pinpoint headlights blinking in the wet darkness. It was a strange and marvelous contraption, more fit for a museum than for the roads of Africa, with a high roof that gave it something of the look of a hansom cab.

"Hello, Smith!"

"Hello, Macassis! Where have you blown in from?"

A boy promptly stepped forward, grinning from ear to ear, and after a brief parley jumped into the driver's seat and took the car to the garage.

Major Crosby uncrossed his legs and swung himself half around in his chair so as not to face the newcomer. And, not to seem to be listening to

what the two men said—they were speaking in the native language—he
turned to Phelps and remarked, as though summing up his meditations
on the day's events:

"Really, Ferdinand wasn't playin' the game."

Graux had charged across the landing strip and scrambled into the
plane less than a minute before it started; he had taken the precaution
of buying his ticket in advance at the Airways office. His face was pale
and drawn, but there was a look of defiance in his eyes, as if he were
telling the world at large:

"Well, I've come, you see—and nothing will prevent my leaving."

Lady Makinson, who was already seated in the cabin, pretended not
to see him. . . .

Phelps had been observing the newcomer with some interest. He
turned to Crosby and asked in a low tone:

"Who is it?"

Crosby put a finger to his lips, showing that he preferred not to
explain for the moment. Meanwhile Macassis and Smith were still
talking away. Each seemed delighted to see the other, and Smith had
taken a napkin from the nickel-plated globe, mounted on a standard, in
which the napkins were kept, and was rubbing down the other man's
wet back with it.

For Macassis had nothing on but a pair of shorts. His body was as lean
and sinewy as an Arab's and tanned a rich brown all over. His long
narrow head was crowned by a shock of steel-gray hair.

His real name was as English as the hotel proprietor's, and he was, in
fact, an Englishman, but everyone from the Uele to Kenya called him by
his native nickname, Macassis, meaning more or less "The Tough."

He had been living in these parts for forty years, and he had recognized Crosby at once. By profession Macassis was an engineer. It was he
who had discovered the Watsa gold mine, and he still had a large
interest in it.

"No," said Crosby as he helped himself to another drink, "it wasn't
playin' the game. Not the act of a gentleman, what?"

Macassis wasn't a gentleman, either, by the major's standards, which
was why the two men were not on speaking terms. He had a wife in
London, whom he kept well supplied with money, but his taste in
women ran to local color, and nothing would induce him to leave
Africa. In almost every village he had a girl or two, and he made no
secret of it, often taking them out for drives in his comical little car.

In Crosby's view he had committed the unforgivable sin: he had
"gone native."

Turning to Phelps and Crosby, Smith announced:

"Yes, gentlemen, I was quite right. The road's under water at the place I told you. Macassis has just come from there; he had water up to his axles and just barely got through."

Mascassis had settled into a wicker chair and was drinking water. The air in the room was hot and steamy, but traversed by occasional wafts of coolness. They could hear the purr of the engine that supplied the electric light. The native boys were squatting in the background, having nothing to do for the moment.

"You didn't answer me just now, Major. Shall I roast a guinea fowl for your dinner?"

"No," said Crosby promptly. "I'll have ham and eggs, and some beer." He was aware that the kitchen, in which Smith himself did the cooking, was far from being a model of cleanliness.

No one spoke for ten minutes, and what with the heat of the room and the steady drumming of the rain, everybody was becoming drowsy, when the sound of a motor—not that of the power plant—made the hotelkeeper prick up his ears. It was so unexpected that before going to the door he peered through the dingy net curtain. The rain was glittering down before two powerful headlights. He hurried to the door.

"Come in, madame," he said, standing aside for the young woman in a raincoat who came hurrying up the steps.

The raincoat was streaming with water. The rain had forced its way through the roof of the car. As she slipped off her coat she looked around her.

"Is it true we can't get any farther tonight?" she asked after a moment.

A mulatto in a red-and-green sweater had come in behind her and closed the door.

"I told her that with all this rain we'd have to spend the night here," he explained. "That all right, Smith?"

This man, too, was a familiar figure in these parts. He owned an old car in which he taxied passengers from the Juba landing strip to their destinations.

"Do you have far to go?" Smith asked the girl.

"To the coffee plantation owned by Monsieur Graux. Somewhere between two and three hundred kilometers, judging by the map."

"You can't get through. The road's under water."

"Oh!"

"What's more, Ferdinand has just left for Europe."

Everyone, Phelps especially, was casting furtive glances at the girl standing by the door. They could see her turn quite pale and look around for somewhere to sit down. It was Phelps who came to the rescue, carrying the chair in which he had been sitting.

She conjured up a smile of thanks, then asked in a tone as casual as she could make it:

"Are you sure? Did he tell you that?"

"He went through yesterday with his car," Smith replied, "on his way to Juba. These gentlemen know him—they've been staying at his place—and they saw him catch the Airways plane."

She looked toward Phelps, who nodded.

Emilienne was wearing a very plain gray dress, which had nothing tropical about it, yet looked quite in keeping with her present surroundings. The driver, who stayed close beside her, as if she were under his protection, said:

"In any case you'll have to stay here for the night. I've ordered a roast guinea fowl. I assure you it will be quite all right; Smith is an old friend of mine. Tomorrow—by the way, do you still intend to go to the plantation?"

"Yes, I think I'll go there all the same. Anyhow, I'll let you know definitely tomorrow morning."

Quite unexpectedly, Macassis, who had been hovering in the background, put in a word:

"You're his fiancée, aren't you?"

"Yes. How did you know about that?" She looked with surprise at this half-naked brown man who seemed to know so much.

"Oh, I stopped by at the plantation this morning and had a talk with Camille. . . . Do you know anything about that letter he was expecting from Brussels?"

"A little."

If only there were no more urgent problems than that letter from Brussels! She guessed its contents, and she knew Ferdinand had been awaiting it anxiously since his return to Africa. It would inform him whether he was to be granted a permanent title to the plantation, which he now occupied under a lease taken over from a Belgian six years previously. One of the main objects of his recent trip to Europe had been to get in touch with the Belgian Colonial Office about the matter, and they had promised to give him a reply within a few weeks.

"The letter came in," Macassis continued, "on the day he left, and the authorities in Niangara want to see him about it as soon as possible. Camille doesn't dare to take any steps on his own authority."

"But if the road's under water . . ." she began, with another glance toward Phelps. He had roused her interest, for she had an inkling he was Lady Makinson's pilot and companion.

"The road's under water," said Macassis, "but you'll be able to get through by tomorrow morning. . . . Hey there, Smith!"

Smith came from the kitchen, where the guinea fowl was browning in the oven.

"Can you send someone with a message to Maliro?"

Smith picked one of the boys, who rather sulkily began to take off his white coat.

"You drive him there," said Macassis to the mulatto. "It's the third village up the road. Maliro will put a couple hundred men on the job and they'll have run a temporary dam up by the morning. Tell him it's very urgent and he must keep his men at it all night."

He repeated this to the black till the man had the message down pat. When the car had driven away, Macassis, still standing beside the door, called across to Emilienne:

"How much did he make you pay?"

"The driver? Three thousand francs."

"Sheer robbery! A thousand would have been enough. Do you know how to drive? Yes? In that case, the best thing you can do is to buy his crate outright. You'll need it for going to Niangara. I can get it for you for six thousand francs. When you've finished with it you can sell it easily enough for five thousand."

Crosby was staring at his whisky, so absorbed in contemplation of it that one might have thought he didn't hear a word of all this.

"Thanks," said Emilienne. "It's very kind of you." But there was a shade of hesitation in her voice. Who could he be, this odd-looking man who had abruptly taken her under his wing and seemed intent on safeguarding her interests? Now and then she threw a glance at Phelps, as if asking his advice.

"Do you by any chance have a power of attorney?"

The question came as such a surprise that at first she hardly took it in. After a moment she replied:

"A power of attorney? Let's see. Yes, I have one. Unless I left it in France . . ."

Before coming out to Africa, Ferdinand had joined with a young man of about his own age in launching a fertilizer business. His partner had proved dishonest, and the concern went into liquidation. As the court proceedings were still dragging on when he was about to sail for Africa, he had given Emilienne a power of attorney, drawn up by Maître Tassin, to enable her to guard his interests.

"I'll have more to tell you later on," said Macassis, with a sidelong glance at Phelps and Crosby.

From that moment he took no more notice of her, whereas Phelps kept fidgeting in his chair, evidently desiring to start a conversation. But it was she who made the first move.

"Captain Phelps, I believe?" she said quite naturally. "Excuse me if I'm mistaken."

He rose, bowed, and bent over the hand she held out to him.

"Ferdinand often mentioned you in his letters. Has he really gone?"

"Just a moment, please. May I introduce Major Crosby, who runs an elephant farm not far from the plantation, and of course knows Monsieur Graux?"

"I know. . . ."

A little stiffly, it seemed, Major Crosby rose from his seat, bent over Emilienne's hand, and put his lips to it as the young man had done. Both men remained standing.

"Please sit down."

"Won't you have something to drink? You're quite wet still. . . ."

She hesitated for a moment, then said:

"Thanks. I might have a liqueur of some sort. I was airsick yesterday in the plane, and I got up at four this morning." Then, staring at the floor, she added quickly, "Has Lady Makinson left, too?"

"Yes, she took the plane yesterday. We saw her off."

A faint smile, which the two men failed to understand, came to her lips. She had remembered her "intuition" on the plane.

During the flight she hadn't spoken to any of the other passengers, and they had been rather puzzled by this tall, fair, placid young woman who kept so severely to herself and whose appearance was so little French or Belgian. Once or twice she had actually been addressed in German.

On the previous afternoon, soon after leaving Malakal, they had passed another plane, going in the opposite direction. Following the Airways custom, the two machines had approached to salute each other and for a moment were so near that one could see through the windows the faces of the homeward-bound passengers.

True, she had not caught sight of Ferdinand, but suddenly it had flashed across her mind that he might be on board the passing plane. The idea was so farfetched that she promptly rejected it. Nonetheless, it left an imprint on her mind, for that evening at the hotel it had been on the tip of her tongue to ask if Ferdinand Graux had been seen there earlier in the day.

The only thing, indeed, that prevented her asking was her distaste for giving way to superstitious fancies.

"Will Lady Makinson be coming back?" she asked in a low tone.

Phelps could not hide his amazement, and even Major Crosby looked up sharply.

"Oh, no. She's on her way to Stamboul, where her husband is."

"Yes?"

They were talking in undertones. Macassis couldn't overhear what they were saying. A boy had just placed a glass of Chartreuse on the table in front of her, and Emilienne was sipping it.

"Did Ferdinand tell you anything about his plans?" she asked bluntly.

Phelps looked uncomfortable, and Crosby came to his rescue.

"No, we only had a glimpse of him, you see, just as the plane was taking off."

Dinner was served, and separated them, Emilienne being given a table to herself.

Smith and Macassis dined together in a corner. They were the only ones who talked, employing, as they always did, the native dialect; Phelps smoked cigarettes between the courses, watching Emilienne from the corner of his eye.

The car returned while they were having dessert, which consisted of biscuits and mangoes, whose smell of turpentine made Emilienne almost sick, though the flavor pleased her. Macassis had a long palaver with the driver, who looked furious.

"Would you come for a moment, mademoiselle?"

He did not rise as she came up to him, introduce himself, or hold out his hand.

"Sit down, please. It's all fixed up. He'll sell his car to you for six thousand francs, and because he overcharged you two thousand for the trip here, you need only pay him four. Do you have the money?"

"Yes." She opened her purse.

"No, don't give him French notes. Smith will change them for Belgian ones. You'll gain over the exchange."

The strangest thing was that he took all this trouble in her behalf without the slightest show of amiability. Sulkily the mulatto pocketed the notes, saying:

"And now, how the devil am I going to get back?"

"I'm going to Juba tomorrow, and I'll give you a lift." He turned to Emilienne. "There's no filling station between here and the plantation, so you must take a hundred liters with you. You go straight ahead for two hundred kilometers, till you see a mailbox nailed to a tree and a turnoff to the right. You take that turnoff, and the bungalow's forty kilometers farther on."

"You were talking to me just now about the concession. . . ."

"That's no business of mine. But I'll tell you this much. I advise you to pay whatever sum the Belgian government demands to make the title permanent. And to waste no time about it, in case they change their minds. There may be a new ministry any day, and I suspect Graux has some pull with the present one."

"Have you seen him recently?"

"Graux? No, I haven't."

"Did you use to see him often?"

"Not once in a year. But I know him well."

After a brief hesitation she asked in a low tone:

"Do you know why he's left?"

At which he merely shrugged his shoulders and looked away. After all, why should he know? She could make nothing of this queer, half-naked man, so unlike anyone she had seen before or even dreamed of. All the same, she realized he meant her well, and felt a little comforted.

"You've been most kind. I can't tell you how grateful . . ."

He cut her short. "Don't mention it!"

"I shall do my best . . ." she began.

"That's enough!" he said abruptly and, rising, went to get an electric lantern to light the way to his bedroom.

His "That's enough!" might have merely indicated that he wished to close the conversation, but Emilienne guessed its meaning was: "If you do your best, that's enough."

"Good night, mademoiselle."

"Good night, monsieur."

She was standing. When she went back to her chair, she had only Captain Phelps to talk to; the mulatto driver was playing checkers with Smith.

At eight in the morning it was still raining, but the clouds were a little lighter. The two cars were drawn up outside the hotel, their engines turning over, Emilienne's in front. Smith was moving to and fro between the cars, seeing that the luggage was properly stowed, the tanks full—he himself worked the gas pump—and everything in order. When Phelps walked up to Emilienne the major smiled to himself.

"Our friend Crosby," said Phelps, "will travel at his usual breakneck speed. As we have to stop at the plantation in any case, to have a look at

the plane, I suggest you take me in your car. But perhaps I'm indiscreet. . . ."

"Not a bit," she said promptly. "Come with me, by all means."

Macassis was hovering in the background, looking rather offended.
He resented her willingness to be in both camps at once, but of course
she knew nothing of the feud between them.

Phelps climbed onto the seat beside her, and the car moved off
through the rain-sodden compound and turned onto the road, which
was bordered by deep gullies full of water. Gradually the green walls of
the bush, behind which were hidden the black cones of native huts,
closed in on either side.

They had gone little more than three kilometers when the big car
with the aluminum body whizzed past and was almost immediately
out of sight.

Ferdinand Graux had never taken to Phelps, whom he regarded as a
conceited, not to say uppish, young man. Emilienne, however, from the
start felt on an equal footing with him; indeed, on a slightly superior
footing. For she realized that at bottom Phelps was shy, and the free-
and-easy manner he affected a defensive reflex.

It was she who first broached the subject, her eyes fixed on the road
ahead, on which twice already they had all but run over coveys of
guinea fowl.

"Did he take the same plane as Lady Makinson?"

"Yes, and it was a near thing he didn't miss it. We had no idea he was
behind us. He must have telephoned from Bodi to reserve his seat.
Smith would know; I forgot to ask him."

There was a silence. Two blacks appeared, walking along the roadside, the man carrying a bow and arrows, the woman a roll of mats
balanced on her head. On catching sight of the car they dived into the
bush and were hidden behind the tall, rain-drenched grass. At last
Phelps ventured to ask:

"Did Ferdinand know you were coming?"

"No. The arrangement was that I was to come out after the rains, and
the missionary in Niangara was to marry us there."

He made no comment. After another long pause he said:

"Sure you're not getting tired? Suppose I drive for a bit?"

"No, thanks."

Driving the car was doing her good; it kept her mind concentrated on
the problems of the road, which was dotted with potholes. And, to add
to her difficulties, the roof leaked, and flurries of drops kept sweeping
across her eyes. Each of them had one arm wet; she her left arm, he his
right.

At one point they came to a gang of blacks working on the road, the men Macassis had had called up. In the course of the night they had run up a dam of sodden earth to divert the torrent rushing across the road. Now, to make the road surface negotiable, they were cutting swathes of elephant grass and strewing them across it.

In spite of this the wheels slipped a good deal, and it took some skillful driving on Emilienne's part to get through. The village headman, the only one of the blacks who wore a cap, gave them a military salute; the fact that his friend Macassis had routed him out in the middle of the night to attend to the road had convinced him that the travelers were persons of importance.

"Is it the same sort of country all the way?" Emilienne asked.

"Much the same. But it looks very different when the sun is out."

"What are the natives like in these parts?"

"You've seen for yourself. Quite harmless people, really, just like children. Ferdinand told me that the Logos are the gentlest of the lot, and the best looking."

The most naked, too. The women had nothing on but a tuft of dry grass hung sporran-fashion in front, and the men a square of cloth worn like an apron.

"Was Lady Makinson badly hurt in the crash?"

"At first we thought so. She was convinced her leg was broken, but actually she'd only put her knee out. . . . Cigarette?"

"Thanks, I don't smoke."

"You don't mind if I . . . ?"

"Not at all."

Nevertheless, each time the smoke from his cigarette drifted toward her he flicked it away.

"Who's that man who made me buy this car?"

"Another Englishman! Really, you've no luck. On your first day in the Congo everybody you meet is English. And the only Belgian, Smith, has an English name and most likely comes from English stock."

"What does he do?"

"Smith, you mean?"

"No, the other man. Macassis, isn't it?"

"Oh, nothing much. He just enjoys life, in his own way. He discovered a gold mine forty years ago. But what he really discovered was Africa—and the charm of black women. Major Crosby can't stand him. He says an Englishman who goes native like that is a disgrace to his country."

"Was the major a friend of Ferdinand's?"

"They saw each other now and again. But Graux is a man who likes keeping to himself, I imagine. If it hadn't been for a pure fluke, a plane that crashed in his plantation the other day . . ."

"Yes," she said pensively.

"Sorry!"

"Why?"

"I mean, I shouldn't have mentioned that," he said uncomfortably. Nothing could have amazed him more than the question she asked him now, casting a quick glance at his face.

"And you?"

He guessed at once what she meant, but it caught him unprepared. "Oh, it isn't the same thing at all, you know." He forced a smile to his lips.

"No?"

"Lady Makinson was just a very dear friend, a real pal. . . . You see what I mean?"

"I'm trying to."

To his surprise, this young Englishman, trained from his public-school days to regard talk about his private feelings as taboo, found himself doing what he could never have done with another man: unfolding, to a girl whom he had met for the first time the previous evening, things of a most delicate nature and intimately concerning himself.

"Graux didn't understand a bit. He thought I was jealous!" He hesitated, but her calmness and the look in her eyes emboldened him to continue. "Lady Makinson was like a . . . a cousin to me, if you see what I mean. We met in a boat going to Tahiti; the other passengers were a stuffy bunch, mostly high officials. So we spent most of our time on the boat deck, sun-bathing and—would you believe it?—reading poetry. Lady Makinson is an awfully well-read woman."

"Is she?" There was a touch of petulance in Emilienne's voice.

"Sir Ronald, her husband, hates traveling. He's a great authority on military matters. All he wants is to be left in peace. . . . You see what I mean?" he added naïvely.

"I see." She managed to say it without irony.

"Ferdinand got it all wrong. Toward the end I tried to explain things to him, but it wasn't any use."

A silence followed. They were driving through a village, the natives scampering into their huts as they caught sight of the car.

"I think that once he's over there he'll understand," said Phelps at last.

" 'Over there'?"

"In Stamboul, I mean. Sir Ronald has rooms at the embassy in Therapia, but he usually stays in his big modern apartment in Pera, the European quarter of Stamboul. Do you know it?"

"No."

"It's something like your Auteuil. Full of kids who talk every European language, nannies in uniform. Life's one long round of teas, bridge parties, dances, soirées, and the rest of it."

What exactly did the young man mean, she wondered, when he implied that "over there" Ferdinand's eyes would at last be opened? Did he think that his glimpses of the pomp and circumstance hedging a British diplomat's wife would have this effect? Or the sight of Lady Makinson herself, with her children, among her friends?

"Another sixty kilometers," Phelps said, "will bring us to the mailbox."

Sixty kilometers of silence. Emilienne was the first to catch sight of the box with a big "F. G." painted on it. So that was where his letters to her had been dropped every week. She made a sharp swerve, apologized, and, involuntarily pressing the accelerator, reached the bungalow without realizing the distance they had covered. The aluminum car was pulled up not far from the plane, which had been brought across the river and was now quite near the bungalow.

A tall young man wearing leather gaiters rushed forward and opened the door of the car.

"Mademoiselle Emilienne!" He could hardly get the words out.

"Hello, Camille!" she said quite calmly.

"When Major Crosby came, I could hardly . . ."

"Would you mind taking my suitcases to the bedroom? My heavy luggage is coming by boat and won't be here for a month."

She was taking eager draughts of this unfamiliar air of Africa, noting every detail, yet outwardly she had the look of a woman who has come home after a few weeks' absence.

"What will you have to drink, Captain Phelps?" she asked as they stepped onto the veranda. "Been here long, Major Crosby?"

The major was pleasantly surprised; she had addressed him in English, excellent English, too, to which a slight accent gave an added charm.

"No, not very long," he replied.

"Camille!"

"Yes, mademoiselle."

"I hope that Major Crosby and Captain Phelps will stay for lunch. You have everything that's needed, don't you?"

"Oh, yes. There's fish from the river, and I can open some cans."

She hadn't realized how tired she was till she stretched herself in a hammock chair. Suddenly she felt incapable of making the slightest movement, or even talking, until she had had a long spell of rest and, above all, solitude. Nevertheless she summoned up the energy to say to Phelps:

"Help yourself to whisky, won't you, Captain?"

Then she laid her hand, still wet with rain, on her forehead, which was burning, though her cheeks were pale.

Seven

The drone of the receding car could still be heard in the distance when Emilienne, coming back to the room where empty glasses and full ashtrays marked the places of the departed guests, gave way at last and let her face relax. And not her face only. Her shoulders sagged, and, raising her hands in an impulsive gesture, she ran them through her hair, ruffling for once its smoothness; a long lock straggled down her left cheek.

"Oh, Camille!" she sighed, gazing forlornly around, too tired, it seemed, even to move to a chair and settle into it.

"It gave me quite a turn, seeing you like that," Camille confessed. "You were the last person I expected here."

At last she sat down, poured a glass of water, and sipped it slowly.

"They've worn me out."

All the same, it was she who had asked Phelps and the major to stay. And she had not only given them lunch, but also deliberately prolonged the conversation after it, desultory and trivial as their talk had been—precisely because she was dreading the moment that was bound to come, and had come now.

"Take a chair, Camille. You know quite well you needn't stand on ceremony with me."

They were of exactly the same age and had known each other from their earliest days. In those times Camille called Emilienne by her Christian name, and she still called him by his.

"How did it happen?" she asked, then, without waiting for him to reply, caught herself up. "That's a silly question! Of course I know the answer as well as you do. . . . Do you think he'll come back?"

"I'm sure of it," said Camille stoutly.

"Why are you so sure?"

"Because he's bound to get cured sooner or later."

She smiled weakly.

"So you think he's ill?"

Now for the first time she was able to take a good look at the house and its surroundings. Her eyes strayed to a shotgun hanging on the wall, and she recognized it as one he had bought for her, for when she came to the tropics.

"Was this the room they spent most of their time in?"

"No, they were more often on the veranda. It wasn't raining then. The last fortnight was really terrible; I've rarely known it so sultry, and one was always waiting for a storm that wouldn't break."

The cumulative weariness of the last few days was taking effect, her gaze had lost its keenness, and she looked now as she felt, a thoroughly exhausted young woman. After some minutes' silence she asked:

"Do you know a man they call Macassis?"

"Yes, he's a friend of Ferdinand's."

"Oh! . . . We'll have to start talking shop soon."

"Can't that wait till tomorrow? You'd much better have a rest."

"No, I'd rather tackle it at once. It'll do me good. By the way, that black girl who waited on us at lunch—is it she?"

He nodded.

"Ask her to come. I didn't get a chance to look at her then."

Baligi remained standing, her eyes wide with curiosity, while Emilienne gazed at her thoughtfully.

"So you're Baligi?"

"Yes, madame."

"You're a pretty girl. . . . Now go!"

She dragged herself to Ferdinand's room to get an aspirin from her dressing case. Her head felt heavy as lead, and there was a throbbing in her temples. The rain was still pouring down. It would soon be time to light the lamps.

She sat down on the edge of the bed, then stretched herself on it with the intention of resting for a quarter of an hour to let the aspirin take effect.

An hour later Camille began to feel uneasy at the silence in the bungalow. Peeping into the room, he saw her lying fully dressed on the bed, sound asleep; he tiptoed away.

In Moulins it was always she who drove the car, for her father had never mastered the art of driving; the result was that when he had appointments in the country, Emilienne always had to accompany him.

She was capable of sitting for hours at the wheel, her gaze so rigid that she seemed to be thinking about nothing except the road ahead.

Several times Camille, who sat beside her, tried to start a conversation, but all he could get out of her was an occasional nod.

At about nine, when they had already been on the road a good hour, there came a sudden break in the clouds, and, though rain continued falling, the sun showed, ringed with silvery haze, across a veil of tumbling water. Then abruptly, as if a tap had been turned off, the rain stopped, and half an hour later the road was bone-dry, though torrents were racing by on either side.

They were now only some twenty kilometers from Niangara. Suddenly Emilienne gave a slight start and listened intently. She had just heard a curious thudding sound, the source of which was quite impossible to locate; there was no knowing if it were close at hand or far away. An army on the march, the rhythmic shouting of an excited crowd, a subterranean disturbance—all sorts of explanations crossed her mind.

Camille, who had his eyes fixed on her face, noticed her look of anxiety.

"Tom-toms," he said.

"Oh? I've heard them before, but they didn't sound the same."

While he, too, was wondering what it could mean, they came upon some blacks carrying a covered litter in which a dignified-looking African, a native chief presumably, sat in state.

"Silly of me!" he exclaimed. "I'd quite forgotten. There's a Big Palaver tomorrow in Niangara.

"What's that?"

"Twice a year the chiefs come in to district headquarters for a ceremonial gathering. They discuss affairs of state and sit in a tribunal to try important cases—murders, adulteries, cattle thefts, and so on."

She had ceased listening and hardly gave another glance at the long files of blacks they were passing, trudging doggedly ahead like pilgrims on their way to some celebrated shrine. Now and again they came upon a chief dressed in European clothes, surrounded by his wives and a bevy of black retainers.

"Tell me, Camille . . ."

"Yes?"

"Oh, nothing . . ." What was it she'd meant to ask him?

Because she had left Moulins before the date originally fixed, the tropical outfit she had ordered wasn't yet ready. So she had traveled in a gray silk dress whose neat, provincial appearance clashed with the sun helmet she had bought in Alexandria on the advice of one of the Imperial Airways staff.

"Is that the town?"

"Yes. Turn to the left when we enter the park."

She took it all quite calmly. Even such an unfamiliar sight as a group of stark-naked blacks whirling in a tribal dance around their chief won from her no more than a fleeting glance. At the entrance to Niangara they passed another batch of dancers, holding grotesque masks in front of their faces as they capered around.

For some distance the road was flanked by wooden shacks that proved to be shops, crammed with all sorts of merchandise: hardware, canned foods, sewing machines, phonographs. Greeks and Armenians lounged in the doorways, and some of them stepped out into the road to watch the European girl driving past.

Then came a red-and-green park, like Smith's but much larger, in the midst of which were three stylish buildings, something like Riviera villas.

"Drive to the central building," Camille counseled. "That's where the office is. The big house on the right is the Commissioner's. His assistant lives in the other one."

The park was crammed with natives, some squatting on the roadside, others moving to and fro, grinning and bawling greetings at one another, and the cheerful bustle reminded Emilienne of a French village fair.

The entrance door of the central building stood open. After parking her car outside, Emilienne went up the steps, followed by Camille. In a big room the walls of which were plastered with notices in French and Flemish, two men were at work, a white and a black, the former in white ducks, the latter in khaki.

"Good morning, Monsieur Bodet," said Camille. "This is Mademoiselle Tassin, Ferdinand's fiancée."

Inkwells, blotting pads, file folders, sheaves of official forms. The air was like a furnace, and Bodet, who wore a stiff collar and a black tie, looked thoroughly unhappy.

"Sit down," he said, without rising. The harshness of his voice and the oddly furtive glances he was casting at Emilienne astonished her so much that she turned to Camille to see if he shared her surprise.

"I suppose you want to see the Commissioner," Bodet continued. "As it so happens, he's not in the office just now."

The man seemed a bundle of nerves; in fact, the curious glitter of his eyes made Emilienne suspect he had been drinking—yet it was only ten in the morning.

"Do you have a passport?"

"Yes. I've brought it with me."

"And a permit to reside in the Congo?"

"I shall apply for one. At present I have only a transit visa."

"You'll have to fix that up with the Commissioner."

"Where is he?" Camille asked.

Bodet pointed with his pen across the road, toward a sort of shed on which was a signboard inscribed "Police Court (Natives)." It was surrounded by a crowd of blacks.

"When will he be leaving court?"

"When he's had enough of it he'll adjourn."

Bodet got up and opened the door of a cupboard. While he was hidden by the door, they clearly heard the sound of a bottle being uncorked. After a couple of minutes he slouched back to his seat and asked rather crossly:

"Do you intend to wait here?"

His eyes settled on Emilienne for the first time. There was a vague hostility in them, as if he knew in advance that he was going to dislike her.

She, too, was feeling the heat; her hands were moist with sweat.

"Ferdinand often spoke of your wife in his letters. I wonder if I could look her up?"

He bounded to his feet as if he had been stung and looked as though he were going off into a fit of rage. Then suddenly he grew calm and chuckled to himself.

"So you want to see Yette, do you? That *will* be a treat! . . . It's that house there, on the left."

It was exhausting, indeed nerve-racking, to watch him, and Emilienne breathed more freely once she was outside.

"What's the matter with him?" she asked Camille.

"I don't know. But I shouldn't be surprised if he's in for an attack of dengue fever." Camille, too, had been startled by Bodet's appearance and behavior.

"We'd better leave the car here. We shall get there quicker on foot."

They crossed a lawn that was being mowed by convicts in brown-and-yellow uniforms and stopped at the steps of the bungalow Bodet had pointed out. Camille shouted several times:

"Anyone home?"

All the doors stood open; they could see a large, untidy room, a table set for breakfast, a man's pajamas lying on a sofa.

"Anyone around?"

Emilienne had noticed a boy peeping at them from behind the bungalow. But she preferred to let Camille go about it in his own way and watched him enter the bungalow, knock at doors, and finally turn the handle of one.

A woman's voice shrilled furiously:

"What is it? What do you want?"

Camille retreated, while Emilienne walked forward. A moment later Yette appeared, in a dressing gown, her hair straggling down her cheeks, which were beaded with sweat.

"What is it?" she said once more. She cut as strange a figure as her husband.

"I'm Ferdinand Graux's fiancée. You remember him, don't you? You came out on the same plane."

"What do you want from me?" She flung herself onto the sofa and started sobbing. "Go away! Oh, *please*, go away!" she wailed. "No! Wait! If you knew how sick and tired I am of—of everything!" Suddenly she jerked her head up. "Where's Ferdinand? Is it true he's run away with that Englishwoman?"

It was confusing to watch her movements. She sprang up from the sofa, walked to a low chair, but no sooner had she sat down on it than she jumped up again and pointed to a settee.

"Sit down, won't you? . . . You can't understand, of course. But let me tell you something, something worth hearing, and you can repeat it to everybody when the time comes, if you feel like it. Because I—I have no money, I can't get away by plane, I've got to take what's coming to me."

It was as painful as bursting in on a dispute between a married couple, and really it amounted to that, though one party was absent, which produced an eerie effect, like the ramblings of a medium in a séance room.

"Have you seen Georges? Yes? What was your impression of him? Tell me frankly."

"Well," said Camille tactfully, "I thought he looked a bit under the weather. I should say he has a touch of fever."

She gave a harsh laugh.

"Oh, that's what you thought, was it? So did I, at first. And I tried to nurse him, but he's been getting worse every day. I can tell you what's wrong with him; it isn't fever—he's losing his mind. And so am I! Cheerful prospect, isn't it? In fact, the only thing I'm wondering about is which of us will kill the other first."

"Really, it can't be so bad as that." Emilienne was heartily regretting having entered the bungalow. "I'm quite sure you're exaggerating. . . ."

"Exaggerating, am I? It's all right for you talk like that. You don't have to live in this damned house. Just you try it for a week, only a week! . . . Do you know Costemans? No? And that hellcat of a wife of his? They're to blame for everything."

She went on talking volubly, without pausing to take a breath.

"I wanted to do the right thing, and the first day I was here I went to call on Madame Costemans. I wonder how you'd have liked it, having the door slammed in your face and being told Her Majesty would see you when it suited her. What right had she to treat me like mud? Her husband's District Commissioner and Georges is only his assistant, but they're in the same service, aren't they? Of course I know all about it now. The fellow who had my husband's job before him resigned the service, gave up his pension and everything, rather than go on working under Costemans. The truth is, Costemans will never get a promotion; he'll have to stick it out in Niangara for the rest of his days. I've heard all about it; he got into a nasty mess some years ago, and that's why he was sent to this Godforsaken hole. He's only thirty, and it was a blow for him, and for his wife. She's the daughter of a well-known lawyer in Brussels, and she's always wailing about her husband's bad luck. The result is, they loathe everybody who comes here, especially the younger men who may climb over their heads one day and become vice governors. In no big government office would anyone dream of treating the most junior clerk the way Costemans treats Georges. He flies out at him if he comes to work one minute late."

Through the windows they could see the other bungalow, the Commissioner's, a hundred meters away.

"I was born in the part of Paris between La République and the Bastille, and I'm not ashamed to admit it. I believe in calling a spade a spade, and I didn't mince my words, you can bet, when I went to see our leading lady. Since then my husband and Costemans haven't been on speaking terms; when they have official business to discuss, they do it in writing."

There was no stopping her. She drew a quick breath, then hurried on:

"You noticed that Georges smelled of liquor, of course? He's always drinking, and he's in terror of losing his job and not being able to get another one. He says that he'd never have a chance in Europe, what with his attacks of malaria. And according to him, it's all my fault! Did you ever hear such nonsense? The man's crazy! We're always fighting. This morning he jumped up in the middle of breakfast, and when I ran after him to call him back he shook his fist at me—on the doorstep!"

Emilienne began to make a move to leave.

"Please, please don't go," Yette wailed. "I know I'm boring you stiff. But except for Georges, you're the first person I've had to talk to for ten days. . . . Oh, how stupid of me! I haven't even offered you a drink. What would you like?"

She smelled of sweat and sodden crepe de Chine.

"Any news of Ferdinand? No? Georges was speaking about him yesterday, and he said in that nasty, sneering way of his, 'You see the sort of man he really is, your precious Ferdinand!' That's because I was always talking to Georges about him, saying what a nice, sensible fellow he was. But now—oh, I don't know." She sank into a chair at last and mopped her streaming cheeks with a towel.

She did not want to let Emilienne go until she had promised to come back for lunch, but "I'll do my best" was as far as Emilienne would go.

It was a relief to escape from the bungalow. They had just caught a glimpse of a crowd of natives pouring out of the courthouse and a European in white walking rapidly across to the office. Emilienne and Camille reached it just as he entered.

"Do you want to see me?" Costemans asked as he sat down at his desk and opened a file that was lying on it.

"I'm Ferdinand Graux's fiancée."

"Oh? Pleased to meet you," he said vaguely, with a slight, stiff inclination of his head, then waited.

"I believe you have received from Brussels a communication relating to his estate, and since he is away, I've come to see you about it."

Costemans was as lethargic as Bodet was excitable, and he, too, looked as if his health were bad. Young though he was, there were big, sallow rings under his eyes.

"I have a power of attorney," Emilienne added.

He reached forward to take the document, murmuring:

"Excuse me. . . . It was so terribly hot in that courtroom. And you can't imagine what the smell of forty or fifty bodies in a confined space is like until you've experienced it!"

Bodet was writing away busily in the background.

"Yes, this power is quite in order," the Commissioner said, after studying the document. "But I suggest we quit for lunch now. Yes, yes! My wife will be delighted to make your acquaintance."

This insistence came as a surprise; his cordiality seemed as labored as his courtesy.

"Good! We'll step across to my bungalow."

"But . . . !" She threw Bodet a glance, as if to say it wasn't her fault. . . .

The lamps had been lit, the door of the bungalow closed for the night, and Emilienne sat facing Camille across the red-checked tablecloth. As she took her napkin from the embroidered case, she felt an access of dizziness such as she had sometimes had as a little girl, in early spring, after a long day's outing in the country.

To steady herself she set her gaze roaming over the red brick walls and the plain, massive furniture made by local carpenters, and Baligi serving them with shyly downcast eyes.

But memories of the day kept ranging through her mind, unpleasant memories almost without exception.

What was it Madame Costemans had said as they were sitting down to lunch?

"I saw you going into her bungalow. . . . Really, you can't imagine how dreadful it is for us. Because she comes from Paris she thinks she ought to run the place. But she's a gutter-bred Parisienne, quite impossible. If you'll excuse my using such language, she's a common little slut. It makes it so awkward, having a woman like that trying to thrust herself upon one all the time."

The Commissioner's wife was wearing a bright-blue silk dress. The furniture was one of those ready-made suites turned out by the thousand by the big stores, with everything thrown in, down to mustard-yellow cushions each adorned with a black cat in velvet. Antimacassars, a piano, knickknacks everywhere, a lavish gilt dinner service . . .

"Bodet is a hopeless fool and drinks like a fish. My husband's got so tired of trying to keep him in his place that he's given up speaking to him. It'll end badly, I feel sure. Really, they ought to be more careful about the sort of men they send out to the Congo."

They had discussed the question of the plantation in the drawing room, so as to avoid going to the office. "There's no reason why the Bodets should know all about it," Madame Costemans had pointed out, then stayed to listen to the conversation between her husband and Emilienne.

The Colonial Office had advised Niangara that Graux could buy the estate outright for two hundred thousand Belgian francs, in which case he would enjoy all the privileges accorded to Belgian planters with regard to the development of his land and preferential tariffs.

"Really, all you have to do is to send a check to the treasurer of the Colonial Office. I'm merely a go-between in the transaction. Now I'll explain the procedure. . . ."

It turned out that taxes on the plantation were in arrears for about four thousand francs, and Emilienne promptly gave the Commissioner a check. That was the one bright spot of the day; as she signed the check she had the feeling that at last she was doing something of practical use.

"Do you have a car?"

"Yes."

"In that case I'll be going. We have to get back to the Big Palaver. If it would interest you to have a look . . ."

"Thanks—but I'm rather tired."

She wanted to say *au revoir* to Yette and walked toward her bungalow. Evidently she was seen approaching, for just as she put her foot on the first step the door shut with a bang! She was of half a mind to go up and knock nevertheless and explain why she hadn't been able to come to lunch. The thought of the young woman nursing her grievances in the empty bungalow, however futile and unreasonable these might be, weighed on Emilienne's mind; indeed, she felt quite remorseful, conscious that Yette must be thinking she had let her down.

"Really, I feel I must have dreamed it," she remarked as they were leaving Niangara. "It was all so fantastic."

"Speaking of fantastic things," Camille put in, "do you know what I was told just now? This afternoon two niggers are coming up for trial, an old man and his son-in-law. They killed the son-in-law's wife and made a meal of her between them."

The light had the same pearly luster as in the morning, and the sky the deep translucence of a mountain lake. Now and again a black woman loped past the car, treading so lightly that she seemed to walk on air, her long, sleek thighs and high-set breasts dappled with silvery glints.

"Tell me, Camille. What's your idea about Bodet? Do you think he really may do . . . something desperate?"

"All I know is that he was in a bad way already when he came out. And she—well, at first she took the Congo as lightheartedly as if she were at a picnic in the Paris suburbs. She giggled at everything she saw, and one had to keep reminding her to put her topee on."

And then, without thinking, Camille came out with a remark that was to linger in the minds of both:

"It's not everyone who's as levelheaded as Ferdinand."

Once again, half unconsciously, as they came in sight of the bungalow, Emilienne ran her eyes over it; and now she realized even more clearly than before how practical and solid it was, as if its very shape and structure—so unlike the bungalows at Niangara, for instance—

were a reflection of its owner's levelheadedness. It was new, it had no "style," and she had seen nothing of its kind in Europe; yet it had something of the dignity and spaciousness, the harmonious lines, of the old houses one sees on riverbanks in France, which give one the impression of having been there since time immemorial.

Outside, the warm darkness was murmurous with tiny sounds; there was a ceaseless chirring, not unlike that of cicadas—what insect could it be? she wondered—and while she listened she fell to picturing this house as it had been before her coming, during the last six years. With her mind's eye she saw Ferdinand seated each evening at his desk, covering sheets of airmail paper with those records of the day's events she knew so well; then, before turning in, settling down in a long chair to read a book on coffee growing or political economy.

Camille, too, seemed lost in thought and, when they had finished dinner, sat on unmoving, forgetting even to light the pipe he had just filled. Mosquitoes were humming around the electric lamp, and Baligi was clearing the table soundlessly, her bare feet seeming to glance across the floor, hardly touching it.

Then the sound of a sob broke the silence in the room. Emilienne had given way at last, and, resting her elbows on the table, she buried her face in her hands, her shoulders heaving. Baligi stopped abruptly and stood gazing at her, wide-eyed, until Camille motioned to her to go back to the kitchen.

Emilienne couldn't have explained what had come over her. That morning, for instance, or even two days before, on the airliner, she had failed, when trying to visualize Ferdinand, to conjure up more than a vague and fleeting image of him, less like a living presence than the phantom of a daydream.

She had no doubts about her love for him. If she had left her home and family on a moment's notice, it was because the thought of losing him had filled her with dismay; and she was prepared to do much more to keep him, if the need arose. And yet there had been something dreamlike about all that, too.

But now, suddenly, just as the meal ended, after a day of chaotic, nightmarish experiences, she felt his real presence in this room; she even saw him standing there beside the table, large as life! And for the first time, perhaps, she had an insight into the man he really was, that secret self of which till now she had had no more than an inkling.

Tears were rolling down her cheeks, but they came as a relief and were far less bitter than the savor that, all these last fateful days, had lingered on her palate. When she looked up, her face was red with weeping, and it reminded Camille of her face as a little girl when she had hurt herself.

"Did he ever speak of me?" she asked.

"Every day."

"What—what sort of thing did he say?"

"He'd say, 'When Emilienne comes, we'll have to send for a re-frigerator.' Or, "We might run up a shanty for you in the compound. That way Emilienne will feel more at ease in the bungalow.' "

She looked at him eagerly, still sniffing now and again.

"Anything else?"

"He's ordered a first-rate phonograph and a box of records, which should arrive next week. Not jazz; good classical and modern music. We've already installed a wall plug for the pickup."

"Where is it?"

"Just behind you, to the right of the fireplace. He was awfully worried about the bricks, you know. . . ."

"What bricks?"

"I mean the walls. It was his idea to leave the walls bare instead of having them distempered or papered. And he was afraid you'd find them rather depressing. He was always wondering if he shouldn't change them, though it would have gone against his grain, I know. He built this room practically with his own hands."

"But I like plain brick, too," she said with a wan smile.

"When he came back last time he told me you'd got your nursing certificate, and he intended to make a lot of improvements in the infirmary, since you'd probably be spending much of your time there."

"When he spoke of me—what exactly did he call me?"

Camille seemed surprised.

"Why, 'Emilienne,' of course."

"Did he never say 'my fiancée'?"

"No, I never heard him say that. But he often used to begin a remark with "When my wife comes out . . .' "

"Oh, Camille! . . . No, don't take any notice, please." She couldn't stop crying, but the tears were coming more slowly now. She took a handkerchief from her purse.

"Should I leave you for a while?" Camille suggested.

She shook her head. It did her good to sit here with Camille, exactly as Ferdinand used to sit here night after night, listening to the jungle sounds outside.

"What animal is making that queer howling noise?"

"A hyena. He did his best to get rid of them, but they keep coming back. You get used to their noise."

Still, she could not repress a slight shudder. She felt hot and cold all over. Camille, who had been listening, remarked:

"Do you hear? The rain's started again. We have two full months of it before us yet. Still, it might be worse. In some districts the rains last for six months of the year. At Matadi, for instance, Bodet's first station."

An unfortunate remark. The last thing she wanted was to have the tiresome little civil servant intruding in her thoughts, especially since he brought in his train Yette, Madame Costemans, and her baby—for the good lady had a baby.

Emilienne rose. She almost dreaded the solitude of her bedroom, which had been Ferdinand's. . . .

"Camille!"

"Yes?"

"Tell me"—she looked away—"did she ever sleep there . . . with him?"

"Never," he said emphatically. It was only a half lie. They had never spent a whole night there together.

"Don't wake me tomorrow morning, please. I need a good long rest."

And it was Camille who had tears in his eyes when he shook her hand and bade her good night. As he undressed he was muttering to himself, and Baligi had passed clean out of his mind.

Eight

Sometimes Phelps had to wait an hour or more before she appeared, but he did so without the least sign of impatience. On the contrary, he seemed to relish having the bungalow to himself and making himself at home in it.

He always arrived at the same hour, four exactly, in Crosby's car, which had already done its daily two-hundred-kilometer run, and his first glance around told him where Emilienne was that afternoon.

When it was raining, the infirmary door stood open, which meant that this was where work was going on, for she had decided to carry out at once the alterations planned by Ferdinand.

On fine afternoons he had glimpses of her—always with Camille, looking like the model "factor," in attendance—walking on the hillside among the coffee plants, or on the riverbank inspecting the turbines.

He never went down there to join her but stayed on the veranda smoking cigarettes and gazing vaguely at the view. Camille had revealed to him the existence of a small ice-making machine, run by hand, and he turned the handle with exemplary persistence till Emilienne came back to the bungalow, usually tired out.

Two tumblers stood ready on a table. He always sprang promptly to his feet, dived forward to kiss her hand, and announced with an air of vexation:

"It isn't here yet."

A remark that had come to have, for them, a double meaning. Officially, so to speak, Phelps drove to Niangara every morning to find out if the propeller had arrived in Juba, where Imperial Airways was to deliver it.

But on the second day Emilienne had said to him in a casual tone:

"By the way, if there's a telegram come in for me, you might bring it along."

And so, when ostensibly referring to the propeller, they had a second thought in mind.

The manufacturers had reported that they had no spare propeller suitable for Lady Makinson's plane in stock and were having one made, which meant considerable delay. To make things worse, there had been some muddle over the first cables exchanged.

And likewise no news of Ferdinand had come through. But they professed not to be surprised at this, and indeed went further, talking about him as if his absence were quite natural—as though, for instance, he were on a business trip.

It was Phelps who, with an innocent air, had invented the rules of this game of make-believe. Camille had taken the longest to get the hang of it and still was apt to break the rules by showing signs of discouragement.

"Tell me, Camille! Is there any special reason for not having curtains on the windows?"

Camille gave a start; his thoughts were far from window curtains.

"Any special reason? No, of course not. I believe there's material for them somewhere around. Somehow we never found time to attend to them."

She unearthed the material and was busy making the curtains when Phelps arrived from Niangara with the usual negative report.

He promptly sat down beside her and, just as he used to hand lit cigarettes to Lady Makinson, fell to handing her the scissors and thread-ing needles when she needed them.

He made no attempt to flirt with her. At any moment she could look into his eyes and see nothing there beyond frank camaraderie; and indeed they got along together excellently. He chattered away on all sorts of subjects, especially those that concerned him personally, with a naïveté that often took her by surprise. Thus very soon she knew all about his father and his uncle, the plutocratic owners of Phelps & Phelps, their eccentricities, their clashes with him and with their busi-ness rivals.

Phelps gave some more turns to the ice machine, then filled Emili-enne's glass. And when the curtains were sewed, it was he who climbed a ladder and put up the rods and brackets, not without hitting his fingers with the hammer several times.

Once he was in the bungalow he seemed reluctant to leave. On the first two days, when it was getting on toward six he rose from his chair and said lugubriously:

"Well, I suppose I should be getting back to Crosby's."

On the third evening, he stayed on while Baligi was setting the table, and Emilienne felt bound to suggest out of politeness:

"Won't you stay for dinner? Though I'm afraid there's nothing much to eat."

"That's all right. I never have much appetite in the evenings."

So he stayed for dinner, and thereafter it became an institution; a place was always set for him, and he never left before eight.

He did his best to make himself useful, brought small presents—English specialties, such as pickles, biscuits, chocolates, and the like—and Emilienne couldn't help smiling, since obviously all these things came from Major Crosby's storeroom.

She had sent to Brussels all the documents needed to complete the purchase of the plantation and written to her father asking him to remit two hundred thousand Belgian francs to the Colonial Office. She had some money of her own, left her by her mother; but in any case her father would never have dreamed of refusing this request.

The bungalow is very comfortable, she wrote to him, *and I think life will be quite pleasant.* And all she said about Ferdinand was: *He is away for the moment. When he returns . . .*

There was so much to be done that she had little time for brooding. She was up and about, always followed by the faithful Camille, from morning till night, under sun or rain, supervising work in progress, and often, when visiting the power plant, she took along one of Ferdinand's handbooks and with its aid studied the working of the machines.

Camille always glared at Phelps the moment he appeared at the bungalow. And Phelps retaliated by affecting not to see him, or treating him offhandedly.

One day Phelps persuaded Emilienne to come to lunch at Major Crosby's and take a look at the elephant-training farm of which she had heard so much. It disappointed her. There was no resemblance at all to Ferdinand's plantation or his pleasant, unpretentious bungalow.

One had the impression of entering military barracks, colonial barracks, it is true, but barracks nonetheless, what with the graveled courtyard ringed by low sheds each with a notice board over the doorway, barns for storing fodder, and, at the far end, a squat two-story building, Crosby's quarters.

To complete the military effect, all orders were conveyed by bugle calls, and a parade of the blacks took place morning and evening in the yard.

Emilienne did not see the elephants till they came back from the day's training, just before sunset, ridden by their mahouts, who let them splash and flounder for some minutes in the river to cool themselves and drink. After that they were led to their stalls, and there followed a methodical grooming down, along cavalry lines, under the severe eye of the major, whose hunting crop never left his hand.

Two or three times a year he organized an elephant hunt with a whole army of natives and some trained elephants. The captured wild elephants were gradually broken in, like horses, taught to kneel and rise at the mahout's order, then harnessed for traction work.

"Once they're thoroughly trained I can sell them for fifty thousand francs," the major told her. "The elephants that draw the trash wagons in Stanleyville all come from my farm. So do Ferdinand's elephants. And I hire out some of my stock to farmers for plowing, for ten thousand francs a year.

Nevertheless, Emilienne gathered, it was not a paying proposition, expenses being extremely heavy. And as Crosby had no private means, he had arranged to be subsidized by various British and Belgian groups.

Up to the hour of going to bed, despite innumerable whiskies, and though living by himself, Crosby kept up a standard of decorum in his habits and appearance that would have passed muster in his Singapore or London club.

Though it was pitch-dark when Emilienne left, Phelps did not insist on accompanying her back. All he did was to give her a loaded shotgun, which he placed beside her in the car.

"Perhaps there'll be some news tomorrow—of my propeller," he said as he bade her good night.

But there was no news of his propeller, or of Ferdinand. All the same, when, after bowing to kiss Emilienne's hand, he looked up, she guessed at once that there was something. But she preferred to match his discretion with her own and refrained from asking questions. She sank into an armchair, for, in spite of her show of energy, she was utterly worn out. In fact, she deliberately tired herself out day after day, so as to ensure a night of heavy, dreamless sleep.

"Do you know," he suddenly exclaimed with a friendly smile, "I'll feel quite lost when I won't have to come here every afternoon."

Just as he had felt "quite lost" when he'd had no more cigarettes to light for Lady Makinson. It seemed as if the young airman found it necessary for his peace of mind to live in tow of some young woman, even if this involved threading needles or hammering nails into a wall.

"Why do you say that?"

"Because the propeller's bound to be turning up one of these days."

Did he mean "the propeller" to be taken literally, or in a figurative sense? She had given a slight start when he spoke and couldn't help glancing at his pocket—which perhaps contained the telegram.

"Just think! I'll be two days and nights all by myself, with the stars above and a watery grave beneath!" When he smiled, as he did now, his white teeth showed to advantage, and Emilienne suspected he was conscious of this. It had struck her several times that there was a feminine streak in the young man, fearless though he was. "So I want to make the most of our little nook before I go." And his eyes roved the veranda, the brick walls, the big folding armchairs—all that went to make the "little nook."

Then at last he came out with it.

"There was a letter for me—from Stamboul."

He took it from his pocket. The envelope was addressed in a big sprawling handwriting; a woman's, Emilienne saw at once.

"You read English, I know. Yes, it's quite all right. There's nothing private in it."

While she was reading, he helped himself to a whisky and soda.

Dear Jimmy,

As you see, I've arrived sooner than expected, since it only took me four days to reach stamboul. I didn't feel like waiting for the boat at Port Said or Alex. and spending two days at sea. So I wired to Ronald to see if he could fix things up with the Admiralty, and I was flown across from Alex. to the Bosporus on a naval seaplane.

Ronald is very fit. The embassy has already moved to Therapia for the summer, and we shall rent a house there, so as to have the children with us.

If you had any anxieties about my journey, they were unnecessary. It went off without a hitch. In fact, I'm rather pleased with myself about it. I'll tell you the whole story when we meet at Aix-les-Bains in September—Ronald intends to do his cure there and I intend to go with him.

Any news of the propeller? I called up London but could get nothing definite.

All the best to Major Crosby and, needless to say, to yourself, dear Jimmy.

Yours, Mary

Emilienne felt too shy to question him, but she would have dearly liked to hear his views on two phrases, the only ones that mattered in the letter: "It went off without a hitch," and the next sentence.

But what had prompted Lady Makinson to ask to be taken across the Mediterranean in a naval plane instead of following the usual route? And why was she pleased with herself? To understand what lay behind those words she would have needed to know Lady Makinson—and she had never set eyes on her.

"I think we should feel pleased, too," said Phelps rather timidly, after some minutes' silence.

She swung around toward him, more eagerly than she might have wished.

"Do you really think so?"

"Yes, definitely. If Mary mentions those things, it can only mean . . ." He paused, obviously wondering how to put it in not too crude a way. "It can only mean that everything's quite all right now, if you see what I mean."

For everything to be "quite all right," the obvious condition was that the affair between Lady Makinson and Ferdinand had come to an end. Unless . . .

Unless—what? There was that unknown quantity, Lady Makinson's temperament, or, rather, her outlook on life. Probably she regarded it as "quite all right" when she traveled around the world with Jimmy, had him stay at her house, and watched him fraternizing with her husband—while all the time the relations between herself and the young man were hardly exclusively platonic.

Really, Emilienne would rather have had no news at all. Now that it had come, she would go on racking her brain to guess the meaning of those trivial sentences, open to so many interpretations.

"Oh, and I have something else to tell you," Phelps added, with a clumsy eagerness to change the subject. "Someone you know in Niangara came and had a talk with me. I wonder if you'd care to hear about it?"

She guessed it concerned the Bodets. She thought of them at times, and indeed that very morning, as it so happened, she had been wondering that there had been no new developments in that quarter.

"You know, I always park the car in front of the office when I call for telegrams. The Commissioner seems glad to see me; he speaks a little English and likes showing it off, I imagine. He has another white man with him, an assistant."

"Yes. Georges Bodet."

"Ah, you've met him? I gather the two of them don't hit it off. I've never heard Costemans say a word to the other fellow. This morning, as I was driving away, a Frenchwoman signaled to me to stop."

He seemed quite embarrassed. Evidently the whole business had got on his nerves; it outraged his sense of what was fitting.

"Have you met her, too? Quite a common little thing, isn't she? Well, no sooner had I stopped than she jumped into the car and said, 'I've got to speak to you.' "

For a moment Emilienne forgot all about Lady Makinson's letter and listened for what was coming.

"She jabbered away so fast that I missed a good deal. But I gathered that she was scared about something—terrified, in fact. All the time she talked she kept looking toward the office. She began by asking if Ferdinand had come back. When I said no, she clutched my arm.

" 'But don't you have any news of him? Can't you say when he'll be back?'

"When I said no again, she looked quite desperate. Then she made me drive on twenty meters; she said she was afraid of the two men in the office.

" 'Do you often see the young lady?' she asked. 'Listen! Tell her things are going from bad to worse. She'll know what I mean. They want to force me to go back to France. Georges has even spoken of divorcing me. Tell her I simply don't know what to do, but I won't let myself be driven away like that. If they insist, I'll do something desperate.' "

Phelps smiled, as if to excuse himself for repeating all this, then added:

"She got so worked up that I thought she was going to throw a fit or something. Really, it was most uncomfortable. Then one of the two

Europeans—the assistant fellow—suddenly came up. He didn't say a word. He just stood beside the car and stared at her. She jumped out at once and ran away to one of the bungalows. It was like a scene in a madhouse."

"I suppose I'd better go there tomorrow," said Emilienne, with a sigh.

"Do you really think it's as serious as she made out?"

"I shouldn't be surprised."

"And will you try to do something . . . ?"

"I don't know." She rose with a nervousness that was unusual with her and, after hesitating for some moments, said:

"Listen, Captain Phelps. Would you very much mind if I asked you to go now? I'd like to be alone this evening."

"I'm awfully sorry!" He sprang to his feet. "I'd no idea I was boring you."

"You weren't boring me at all, only . . . You understand, don't you?"

"I think so. Shall I stop by tomorrow as usual?"

"I'll be going to Niangara."

"Then perhaps we'll meet there?"

"Very likely. Good night . . . You're forgetting your letter."

Quite possibly he had left it on purpose, to give her an opportunity to read it again. But that was unnecessary; she knew by heart the two phrases that concerned her.

"Camille!" she called as soon as Phelps was gone.

He came from the kitchen, where he usually gave Baligi a hand in preparing the meal, and he saw at once that something serious had happened.

"I'm very worried." She was pacing up and down the room, twisting her handkerchief between her fingers. "An idea has just come to me—it had never entered my head before—and now it's the only thing about which I'm seriously alarmed. What's your opinion, Camille? Do you think Ferdinand's the sort of man who'd kill himself?"

The last words, spoken quite calmly and distinctly, shocked him beyond measure. A shiver ran down his spine, and furtively he touched wood.

"Why?" he asked with an effort. "Why on earth . . . ?"

"Let me tell you something I've just learned. Lady Makinson is in Stamboul, and Phelps has had a letter from her. She says the journey went off without a hitch and she's feeling rather pleased with herself. What do you make of it?"

He knitted his brows but said nothing.

"You see what I'm driving at?"

He nodded.

"During the last two or three days before he left, how did Ferdinand strike you? He was in a very—very emotional state, wasn't he? No, that was a stupid question. He must have been, to act like that."

"Yes."

She interrupted the thread of her remarks to say:

"I'm afraid the Bodets are on the brink of doing something silly." In the same breath she added: "Of course it's all pure guesswork. He hasn't written to anybody. If his mother had heard anything she'd have wired to me at once."

For by now a whole fortnight had elapsed without a word from Ferdinand to his family or Emilienne. Lady Makinson did not mention where she had seen the last of him, but presumably this was in Alexandria, for he would not have been allowed to travel by a naval plane.

But suppose he had followed her by sea? In that case, Lady Makinson might have written her letter before the boat arrived.

Emilienne regretted not having noted the date on the postmark. Still, even without it, by studying the airline timetable, checking dates and hours, might she not glean some information?

"Now leave me alone, please."

"May I say something first? I've been thinking it over, and I'm convinced that Ferdinand is quite incapable of—of doing what you said."

She looked him in the eyes and saw that he was not quite so certain of this as he professed to be.

"Let's get dinner over with quickly," she said finally. "Then I'll go to bed early, and tomorrow we'll see. . . ."

"He hates me like poison, don't you understand? I should have noticed that at the start, at Charleroi. What a fool I've been!"

Instead of going first to the office to ascertain if a telegram had come in, Emilienne had stopped her car outside the Bodets' bungalow, yielding to a secret craving to mortify herself and, perhaps, a vague idea that by acting thus she was propitiating fate.

Yette was wearing the same dressing gown as before, a hideous ready-made garment in blue crepe de Chine that flapped around her tiny body as she moved. Her bare feet were in loose slippers, and Emilienne noticed that they were dirty, as indeed everything was in the bungalow.

"Do sit down. Help yourself to a drink if you're feeling thirsty. Afraid I don't have the energy to play hostess. Last night I slept with a knife under my pillow. I'm pretty sure Georges had a revolver under his. That's what we've come to—after five months' married life!"

There was no need to encourage her to talk. Actually, Emilienne suspected that when there was no one in the house she kept talking to herself.

"I don't know how you and Ferdinand fixed it up between you, but I'm sure it was quite different from our engagement. I'd gone to Charleroi to spend the holidays with Grandma; my mother's Belgian, you know. That was where I met Georges—he was on six months' leave. His parents live two doors away from my grandmother's. His father's foreman at a coal mine. So he has no reason to put on airs, has he?"

Emilienne couldn't help throwing glances toward the office building, where she knew Phelps would be turning up at any moment, in Major Crosby's car.

"We went to the movies together several times. I was a good girl then, and Georges can't deny it. If he tried to, I'd only have to remind him of—of certain details. Not very savory details, either. You know what I mean, don't you? It was he who talked me into it, and one afternoon he got me to go with him to a hotel. . . .

"Didn't I have a perfect right to insist on his marrying me? First he agreed, then he started trying to back out. He kept on saying that the climate out here wasn't suitable for a white woman. When he took that line, I threatened to tell my parents everything.

"I had to go back to Paris, and I wrote to him three times a week to keep him in line. He was always trying to wriggle out of it, you know.

"And what do you think he's saying to me now? That I've spoiled his life! That his career is wrecked and he may as well put a bullet through his head and get it over with! Did you ever hear such rubbish? . . . Don't look at the bungalow, please; I know it's filthy. I don't feel up to cleaning it, or even giving orders to the boy. But I assure you I'm quite good at housekeeping, really. . . .

"Am I to blame if that Costemans bitch has her knife into me? Would you believe it, yesterday in the bazaar she stalked past me with her head up, pretending not to recognize me!

"I wasn't going to let her get away with it, you can just bet! I asked her to explain—in the presence of all those niggers. And imagine what she did. She called up a convict, one of the ones they use as policemen out here—crazy, isn't it?—and she told him to take me back to the bungalow.

"Last night Georges wouldn't say a word to me, but I saw him clearing his revolver and putting six cartridges in it.

"What am I to do? Can you suggest anything?"

Phelps had just driven up. When Emilienne began to make a move, Yette caught her by the arm.

"Do give me some advice! Your father's a lawyer, isn't he? What would you do in my place? Does Georges have any right to divorce me?"

"I'll think it over and let you know in a day or two." Emilienne was impatient to be gone. "And meanwhile, please try not to worry. . . ."

"Not to worry! That's easier said than done. They've got me in their power, damn them! It seems the Commissioner can have any woman turned out of the Congo on the pretext that she's damaging European prestige!"

Fortunately, just then Phelps, not finding her in the office, had begun to walk toward the bungalow. Emilienne went to meet him.

"Is that all you have to say to me?" wailed Yette, then added angrily, "I know what it is. You had lunch with that woman, and she's got you on her side!"

The sight of Phelps bending over Emilienne's hand to kiss it seemed to infuriate her still more, and she retreated into the bungalow, muttering to herself.

"So you came to see her?" Phelps said rather lamely.

"No telegram?"

"Yes—from London." He made haste to specify where it came from, so as not to rouse false hopes. "The propeller leaves on Saturday and should be here a week from then. I've wired Stanleyville for a mechanic to overhaul the engine. So you won't have to put up with me much longer."

She figured it out in her mind. He wouldn't be leaving for ten days, and surely some news of Ferdinand would have come through before then.

Camille's habit of dogging her steps when she was inspecting the plantation got on her nerves sometimes. With his studiously gentle manner he reminded her of a paid companion to an invalid.

The mechanic turned up three days later, and Phelps now had a good excuse for spending almost all his time at, or near, the bungalow. Between them the two men thoroughly overhauled the machine, and there was some leveling out of the ground to be done to ensure a good takeoff.

Phelps tried without success to disguise his exultation. Though the bungalow had agreeable associations and in some ways he was reluctant to leave, the prospect of taking to the air again had gone to the young man's head. Perhaps it was less the prospect of the actual flight that excited him than that of landing at the Wellington airfield and seeing the expression on the faces of those two old worthies, his father and his uncle. . . .

Next week another letter came from Lady Makinson, to say that she had settled down in Therapia in a big yali that had once belonged to a grand vizier, and she enclosed a snapshot showing the two children playing in what used to be the harem.

All this was something of a strain for Emilienne, but she put a good face on it and listened amiably to Phelps as he prattled now of Istanbul and the Bosporus, now of New Zealand and his family.

She got a letter from her father, who informed her that this year he was going to Vittel earlier than usual, so as to be able to take part in an August cruise to Spitsbergen, a trip he had been thinking about for several years. He "assumed" that all was going well at the plantation and the wedding would soon take place, and he specially warned his daughter to guard against malaria, citing the case of an uncle of his who had suffered horribly from it long after his return to Europe.

Madame Graux also had sent a letter:

I have said nothing about it at home or to your father. In the light of your first letter I can guess the reason for your silence. I sometimes wonder if you would not have done better to follow him. I make a point of reading all the news from abroad in the daily papers.

To see, presumably, if a Frenchman had committed suicide in Turkey . . .

The void was forming, or about to form, on all sides of Emilienne; not only did she hear the roar of the engine on the plane during two successive evenings, but Crosby, too, was making preparations for his annual trip to London.

One morning Macassis drove up to the bungalow and asked for a glass of water; as Emilienne was down at the infirmary, he merely left word with Camille that he was bound for Watsa and would call again when he returned.

Nothing in Niangara. Phelps went there now only on alternate days. He had not met Yette again, but her husband was always to be seen in the office, looking more haggard and distracted than ever.

Ferdinand had been away three weeks now, and Lady Makinson back with her family for over a fortnight. Might it not be that her talk of a pleasant journey and the rest of it meant purely and simply that . . . ?

Checking the thought abruptly, she called:

"Camille!"

"Yes, mademoiselle."

"When Captain Phelps has left . . ." She paused. Tensely Camille waited for her to continue. "I haven't quite decided yet, but I may be going on a short journey." At once, to reassure herself as much as him, she added, "I won't be away very long. I'll just go there and back without stopping anywhere."

For his last night Phelps slept at the bungalow, sharing Camille's room with Major Crosby, for he wanted to get an early start and, if possible, reach Dar es Salaam that afternoon.

He was bubbling over with a rather febrile gaiety, unable to talk of anything but the impending flight. At one moment, conscious of this, he apologized.

"Anyhow, I'll send you a wire." No sooner had he said it than he realized his blunder and tried to cover it up. "But I don't suppose it will interest you in the least; by then you'll have had another wire."

It went without a hitch. They breakfasted in silence, watching the flags set up at various points to show the direction of the wind. Though there was no rain, the ground was heavy, and the takeoff might be difficult.

The mechanic worked up to the last moment. Phelps was dressed in his ordinary clothes, and all he took with him was a Thermos bottle of strong tea, sandwiches, chocolate, and a few bananas.

As usual, he bent over Emilienne's hand, then at the last moment, after a brief hesitation, drew her to him shyly and kissed her cheeks.

"Good luck!" He said it in so low a voice that she had to guess the words.

The mechanic had spun the propeller, and across the din of the engine Crosby bawled, "Happy landing!," then, standing at attention, gave Phelps a military salute.

Strangely enough, as, after circling above the bungalow, the plane headed southeast, it was Camille, and Camille only, who furtively wiped his eyes.

"I'll take the mechanic with me," said Major Crosby to Emilienne. "If I can be of help in any way at all, don't hesitate to come and see me. I won't be leaving for three weeks."

And, suddenly, Emilienne was alone. . . .

Nine

It was another attempt to steal a march upon chance; instead of going to Niangara daily, as at first, she took to going every other day. Somehow she had got it into her head that the message would be handed her en route; in other words, that she would meet a runner with the telegram on the way.

For, though she could have given no reason for the notion, it was a telegram, and nothing else, that she expected. Chance had played a mean trick on her in this respect; her father had had the ill-inspired idea of wiring to her when the check was sent to Brussels, the result being that she did meet a runner on the road and, having no small change, gave him a hundred-franc tip.

But on opening the telegram all she read was:

DOCUMENTS MAILED TODAY. FATHER.

Two days later, on reaching Niangara, she found the offices closed. As far as she knew, there was no public holiday, and for a moment she felt her mind go blank—a curious sensation that had been coming over her rather frequently in these last weeks. She had not lost confidence, but her confidence was no longer of the active kind that meets destiny halfway. In fact, she was run down, mentally and physically, and inclined to clutch at any straw of hope.

"Let's see. Phelps got his propeller on a Wednesday. So next Wednesday's the day."

Then, looking back on her past life, she had to admit that Friday had always been her "lucky day." Sheer superstition! She tried to laugh herself out of it, but halfheartedly.

And now, turning toward the Commissioner's house, she saw a Belgian flag flying at half-mast over the veranda. Looking up, she saw another flag at half-mast above the office.

Her heart missed a beat. In vain she told herself that probably some member of the royal family had died in Belgium. Leaving her car on the roadside, she almost ran to the Costemans' bungalow.

For some time no one answered her knock. At last a boy appeared, a youngster who didn't speak a word of French. She tried to explain herself with gestures, but the boy was too stupid, or she too flustered, for him to understand. After some moments he went away, then came back, shaking his head. At last a plaintive voice came from the bedroom:

"Go around to the Bodets'." The words were half drowned by a baby's fretful cries.

A fortnight before, Emilienne wouldn't have lost her nerve so easily. Still, there was something really sinister in the atmosphere that morning. It was one of those sweltering, sunless days, with a sky the color of lead, that Camille called "Dead Sea days," and the flies were even more aggressive than usual.

There was no one on the Bodets' veranda, and this time she went up the steps without calling for the boy. On reaching the door she saw Costemans sitting in the living room talking to the white missionary, an old man who one morning when she was driving in had passed her on a motorcycle.

Costemans rose and came to the door. His face was drawn but calm, the rings around his eyes darker than ever.

"Do come in," he said. "I'm glad to see you, for we shall need your evidence."

The missionary, who had a long reddish-brown beard, merely bowed to her.

"Have you heard what's happened?" Costemans asked.

"I've heard nothing at all. I've just been to your bungalow and your wife told me to come here."

"Oh, you woke her up!" he exclaimed rather peevishly. "I'm sorry about that. She didn't sleep a wink last night."

Suddenly Emilienne opened her mouth, but something repressed the cry that rose to her lips. She had just caught sight of a table in the corner on which lay a body covered with a sheet.

"Who?" She brought the word out with an effort.

"Georges Bodet. Please sit down. Can I offer you something to drink? Unfortunately there's no other room to which I can take you. . . ."

"And Yette?"

"Father Julien says she may pull through. Needless to say, the doctor's out on his rounds, as usual."

Costemans seated himself at another table, on which were a pen and ink and some sheets of foolscap. Evidently he had been writing when Emilienne came.

"The tragic event took place yesterday morning. To be more exact, it was yesterday morning we heard of it. If I could have got in touch with you I would have done so, for your evidence will be very helpful. But I felt sure you'd be coming in today."

Father Julien was smoking a huge meerschaum, and Emilienne caught herself wondering if the brown streaks in his beard were due to nicotine. Contritely she switched her attention back to what the Belgian was saying.

"Bodet didn't come to the office at six. At half past I sent an orderly to his place to fetch him. . . . It will be simpler if I read the report I have drawn up:

" 'The body of the deceased, Georges Bodet, was lying on the floor at the foot of the bed. A 6.35-caliber revolver (made by the Heristal Small Arms Factory) lay within reach of his right hand. Henriette Bodet, his wife, lay on the bed, with a bullet wound in her left cheek, and appeared to be *in extremis*.

" 'The houseboy was away. Searches were made for him, since suspicion naturally fell on him. Yesterday evening he was discovered hiding in the bush; there seems no reason to disbelieve his statement that in his panic at what he had seen he took to flight.' "

Costemans ceased reading and looked up with a lugubrious expression.

"I wired to Stanleyville at once, for I should have preferred not to take the responsibility of holding the inquiry myself, though I have full magisterial powers. There were special circumstances in this case—you understand what I mean? Anyhow, to avoid possible misunderstandings I have asked Father Julien to be present throughout the inquiry and countersign the depositions."

Emilienne dared not look toward the table on which the body lay.

"Is Yette in her bedroom?" she asked.

"Yes. You can go to her later. The bullet went out at the back of her neck. She recovered consciousness last night."

"Hasn't she said anything?"

The Commissioner seemed not to hear the question.

"My wife tells me she thinks she heard three shots in the course of the night but, since she did not turn on the light, has no idea what time that was. She assumed that someone was firing at a wild animal; we often hear shots at night. But I've been unable to find the third bullet. Perhaps, after he shot his wife, Bodet's hand trembled and he failed to hit himself the first time, in which case the bullet may have gone out by the veranda. Anyhow, there were three shells, all right." He pointed to a small sealed package on the table in front of him. "I have reason to believe," he went on in the same toneless voice, "that the Bodets confided in you to some extent, and I will ask you to make a statement, which I shall take down in writing and require you to sign."

When Emilienne kept silent, he suggested:

"Perhaps it would make it easier if I asked you questions?"

Father Julien went on puffing at his pipe. Blacks walking by outside stopped talking when they passed the bungalow and shot timid glances through the doorway.

"I'll begin with the obvious question. Did you see any indications that the Bodets did not get along well together?"

She nodded, then thought better of it, tried to say something, but found no words. True, they didn't "get along," but there was much more to it than that; only—how to explain it?

"Did Henriette Bodet tell you that her husband had threatened to kill her?"

Certainly she did. Emilienne nodded again, to get it over with, though conscious that these questions travestied the facts.

"Do you know the cause of their estrangement? Please note that, since Bodet is dead, there's no question of criminal proceedings. This report is being drawn up by me for what I might call 'moral reasons.' "

"I'm afraid I can't help you there," she sighed. "All I know is that they didn't hit it off—and they'd reached the breaking point. Now may I go to Yette?"

Father Julien rose and tiptoed into the next room, after carefully depositing his pipe on a small table. Holding the door ajar, he beckoned to Emilienne.

All she saw on entering was two eyes, eyes whose color she had never observed before, pale-gray flecked with gold, and there was something so harrowing in their fixity that she had to turn away.

For Yette, whose face was entirely swathed in bandages, was gazing at her intently, struggling to convey, it seemed, a message that she could not utter. And as she gazed, her body moved a little in the bed. The missionary stood beside her, and Emilienne, finding no words to answer the entreaty in her eyes, gave way to tears and hid her face in her hands.

"Try to keep calm," the missionary whispered, touching her shoulder. "She mustn't be excited in any way."

She left the room without having said anything. Father Julien explained as the door closed behind them:

"She's been like that since yesterday, and she won't, or can't, speak. Perhaps the shock has deprived her of the power of speech. Anyhow, the doctor will be here tomorrow, and we shall know how things are."

Costemans had something else to say, and he spoke even more stiffly than before, weighing his words.

"I foresee that people will talk about the strained relations between Bodet and myself. As a matter of fact, had I not, out of mistaken kindness, postponed taking the disciplinary action his conduct called for, this tragedy might perhaps have been averted. . . . It has been a great shock to my wife and, coming so soon after her *accouchement*, may well have serious consequences for her. . . ."

There was no telegram, needless to say, and as she drove back along the too familiar road Emilienne felt more tired than ever. It was more than physical fatigue; a sense of utter desolation, all-pervading, like the gray light on earth and sky, had settled over her. She was not suffering, but her body and mind had gone limp, and had the car stopped for lack of gas she might well have stayed for hours on the roadside, gazing dully into space. Everything seemed so hopeless, all effort so futile.

She was driving slowly. Suddenly, with a rattle of scrap iron, Macassis drove past in his ramshackle car, going in the opposite direction. As he passed, the little man leaned out, waved his hand to her, and shouted some question that she failed to catch. The last word sounded like: ". . . pleased?"

She shrugged her shoulders. "Pleased"—about what? This was one of those moments that came to her occasionally, when the thought of the monotonous tranquillity of the bungalow filled her with despair and she wondered if she could bring herself to stay there much longer. Nevertheless the idea of going back to Moulins, to her father's house, seemed equally unbearable.

How strange, she mused, that so many people get through life without once coming up against its tragic side! Her father, for instance. He had remained a child at heart. Was he capable of any really intense, *adult* emotion? Then her thoughts drifted back to her mother, who had died when Emilienne was nine; then back again to her father, delighted as a schoolboy with a long-awaited treat in prospect—the cruise to Spitsbergen.

DOCUMENTS MAILED TODAY. FATHER.

Even when she told him she was leaving at once, he hadn't said a word. Then suddenly a picture rose before her of his quaint, lopsided face, and she seemed to hear his voice uttering one of those kindly, commonplace remarks that were always on his lips—and a rush of emotion came over her.

"Poor Father!" she said aloud and slowed down still more.

But all the time, with an unconscious eagerness, she was watching for the dead tree, the first landmark, after which came, a little farther on, the group of three huts and a banana grove, and, finally, a chimney top showing above the green sea of the bush.

As usual, she drove the car into the garage and locked the door. Then, in the failing light, she looked around for Camille and saw him still at work on the distant hillside, with a gang of natives and an elephant.

She was really worn out, aching in every limb. To keep herself from brooding she had been overtaxing her strength and now was feeling the effects.

Tossing her sun helmet onto a table, she sank into a long chair and settled down to muse for half an hour or so in the gathering shadows.

Suddenly her eyes fixed themselves on an object just in front of her, and she sat bolt upright.

The odd thing was that for some moments she had been looking at that hat without really seeing it, never realizing that it was Ferdinand's double terai. Her pupils dilated. She rose to her feet, half dreading that her eyes had deceived her, or that by some cruel trick of chance it was a spare hat that Baligi had left lying there after cleaning out a cupboard.

Just then there was a sound outside, the door opened, and she saw Ferdinand coming toward her, a Ferdinand that she had so far seen only in photographs—in shorts and a bush jacket.

"Hello, Emilienne!"

She realized that he was acutely nervous, though he gave no sign of it; but just then her senses were stretched to a preternatural lucidity. In a flash she had sensed everything: Ferdinand's panic; the reason why the hat had been placed there, not thoughtlessly but as an intimation; the effort it cost him to speak in that studiously calm voice, and to approach her as he now was doing, with deliberately measured steps.

"Good evening, Ferdinand." How she got the words out she hardly knew.

And then, strangely enough, they kissed each other almost in the usual way , quite naturally, for all the riot of emotions in their hearts.

Emilienne thought quickly, "Everything depends on this." By "this" she meant the present moment, the first words they said, the first time their eyes met—for both were still so nervous that they dared not face each other and kept gazing around the room.

It was no accident that Camille had worked late in the plantation, or that he was starting back now and would be at the bungalow within five minutes.

"Is Yette out of danger?" Ferdinand asked.

"What! You *know?* Have you been to Niangara?"

"No, the natives told me what had happened."

She had forgotten about the "bush telegraph," the promptitude with which messages were sent by tom-tom, sometimes faster than by the white man's Morse.

"I understand now!" she exclaimed.

"What?"

"Oh . . . nothing."

What she had understood was the remark Macassis had flung to her as he drove past: ". . . pleased?" He'd assumed she knew already of the great event, Ferdinand's homecoming, heralded by the tom-toms.

With a faint, vaguely apologetic smile, she let herself sink back into the chair.

"Tired?"

"That doesn't matter—now. Sure you're not. . . ?" After a moment's hesitation she came out with it, rather shyly: "Sure you're not annoyed with me?"

Why he should be annoyed with her she hardly knew. Perhaps for having come here unannounced. For everything . . .

He appeared not to notice the question. All he said was: "The plane had a breakdown, you know."

That was so. Something had gone wrong with the engine between Malakal and Juba, and they had been held up for twenty-four hours. But from the way he spoke it almost seemed that he meant the breakdown to explain his absence of more than three weeks.

Camille entered, as usual without knocking, and reported in his most businesslike tone:

"I've set forty men to clearing plot three. And I've just had Mali taken to the infirmary. He's developed a temperature, poor old fellow."

All three were, so to speak, walking a tightrope, acutely conscious that the least imprudence might mean disaster. The main thing was to go on talking and behaving as if this evening were like any other evening, to avoid showing any sign of nervousness.

Emilienne was convinced that Ferdinand had grown thinner. At the beginning of the meal—served by Baligi's mother, for Baligi herself was ill—it struck her that there was some other change in his appearance; but, until she saw his spectacles on the tablecloth beside his plate, she did not realize why he looked so different.

"Camille's shown me the copies of the agreement sent to Brussels. It's very satisfactory. And you've done wonders with the infirmary."

"Well, I was rather worried about one thing: whether to put in a third window or not." She tried to smile. "Then it struck me that the sun would shine straight in through it at three in the afternoon, the worst hour of the day."

"You're absolutely right. One's apt to think of things like that too late, and, out here, it's just those things that have the most importance."

It almost seemed as if there were a double meaning in the words "Out here, it's just those things that have the most importance."

"I thought of having a footbridge thrown across the river," Emilienne said, encouraged by his approval. "It would save the trouble of going around by the waterfall to cross, and the men would gain a quarter of an hour each time they went to the hill."

Only another hour or so had to be got through before bedtime. And tomorrow—well, somehow both had the impression that things would go more easily next day; time was on their side. When at one moment there was an embarrassed silence, Camille came to the rescue. Turning to Ferdinand, he said:

"Tomorrow's payday. Shall we look through the payroll now? There are some changes to be made. Orders have come in from Niangara to pay forty centimes a day instead of thirty."

"Yes, bring the payroll, please."

He put on his glasses and, with a smile to Emilienne, asked:

"Feeling sleepy, aren't you?"

"A little."

"Then I suggest you go to bed right away. Of course you'll keep the room you're in. I'll sleep in Camille's."

For all his rather self-assured manner he was feeling far from at ease; indeed, he hardly dared to kiss Emilienne's cheek as he said good night to her at her door.

"Sleep well."

But he knew she wouldn't sleep—anyhow, not for an hour or two. He knew that once she was in the room her eyes would fall on a little pile of sheets of airmail paper lying on the blotter on the writing desk, seeming to have been left there by oversight.

She realized at once that he had put them there deliberately, and that at this moment he was far more preoccupied with her reactions to them than with the payroll.

These diary entries were exactly like those that he sent to his mother by every mail, and which she showed to Emilienne. Or, rather, there was only one difference—a long gap after the first entry, dated May 25 and consisting of a single line:

There's nothing for it!

On resuming the diary eight days later, he indicated the gap with a wavy vertical line.

June 2. This morning I saw her children, accompanied by a nurse-maid, walking in a big public garden like one of our Paris squares. The small boy is the image of his mother—so much so, indeed, that I can hardly imagine him growing up to be a man!

Somehow I can't get used to the idea. . . . Only six days ago we were in Khartoum, and in Khartoum everything was settled—irrevocably. My last chance!

During the flight Lady Makinson had pretended not to know Ferdinand—which was easy enough, for she was always surrounded by the English passengers, who, impressed by her personality, lavished attentions on her. It was she who presided at meals at the various stops, she for whom takeoffs were delayed if she was slow to make a move.

Watching from his corner seat, Ferdinand had guessed why she talked so volubly, why her laugh was unnaturally shrill and she smoked even more persistently than usual.

Probably at that moment, if I'd chosen . . .

But at that moment his brain was fogged; he had no clear idea what he wanted. All he knew was that he was urged on by a blind impulse to do something—no matter what—but at all costs to break irrevocably with the past.

Did it ever occur to her, when she shot glances at me across the full length of the cabin, that there were times when I'd just about decided to kill her and, after her, myself?

Of that crucial moment in Khartoum he had set little down in the diary. Dinner was over. The other passengers were settling down to bridge. For some reason—perhaps to calm her nerves—Lady Makinson had walked out onto the terrace, from which tables and chairs had been removed, for a sandstorm was approaching.

At that moment I realized that a man in certain moods is capable of—anything! Such a loose term as "mad" doesn't answer; there's more to it than that. I'd made up my mind to . . . no, I can't remember. Perhaps to throw myself at her feet and weep my heart out—or something equally preposterous! Did she guess this? Was she touched by pity? She watched me coming toward her, and I saw her fist clench suddenly and go quite white, as if she were digging her nails into the palm of her hand. Then very softly, imploringly, she whispered:

"Please . . ."

Just that one word. And I knew what she meant. She was begging me not to say the word or make the gesture that might have changed everything.

Yes, at that moment, if I'd chosen . . .

But I let the moment pass. And half an hour later I saw her writing a telegram in the hotel office. I understood when we reached Alexandria, where a hydroplane was waiting for her.

I don't know why I took the boat. I suppose I had to!

Bending over the payroll, the two men kept silent, listening. The only light came from a small lamp on the table. They could hear the steady drumming of the rain on the roof; as usual at this season, a downpour had set in with nightfall. Looking across the table, Ferdinand could see Camille's eyes fixed on him anxiously.

"She can't have read it all yet," he murmured.

He felt sure of that, for he was timing mentally the progress of her reading.

June 5. I wonder what would happen if I did not have an instinctive repugnance for losing my mental balance—if I had the temperament of a man like Bodet, for instance? And I wonder, too, what it was that really prompted me to come here, to Stamboul?

At the time I thought that I was being driven by fate, urged on inescapably toward some tragic end, in the style of a Greek drama! Yes, I had sometimes the most melodramatic ideas—of a wholesale killing, for example!

Another fancy of mine was that I could go on trailing after her indefinitely, obliging her to repeat day after day that half-pathetic "Please . . . !

The next day's entry consisted of only two words, written in a steadier hand.

Romantic folly!

Two unrecorded days. Then:

June 9. Saw her this morning in her husband's car. She didn't notice me, I think. But—I have been convinced of it since that brief contact on the terrace in Khartoum—I know that she, too, was tempted . . . for a moment. After which he had written again, in a gust of anger with himself: *Romantic folly!*

To which he had added, as a sort of postscript:

Her son is a really beautiful child. Tomrorrow she is entertaining the diplomatic corps at tea. If good old Camille could see me now . . . ! And Tom Thumb! When he doesn't feel well, he tries to slink away to the jungle to hide. I'm a sick animal myself. Dirty and bedraggled. I've given up shaving. I can see the hotel staff are worried about me; do they fear I may do something desperate?

Even the saints and heroes of the past must, on occasion, have been sick animals, must have smelled bad and had thoughts for which they blushed when they got well again.

Yet there's something almost voluptuous about it. I do absolutely nothing. Yesterday I spent a full half hour among a group of street loafers staring at two cars that had collided; it was quite an effort to switch back my mind to her!

June 14. What happened at the plantation—I mean, of course, what passed between us two—is growing blurred, and I can look back on it dispassionately. A vast relief. I can even smile at a certain grotesque detail, the first time—due to her injured knee.

Still, I can't eradicate that "Please . . . !" I keep on trying to recall the exact tone in which she said it, the hot smell of the approaching sandstorm.

Damned fool that I am!

June 15. No, not damned fool. Damned mountebank. This morning I felt like shaving and deliberately refrained. After that I prowled around her house in the hope she might see me. Why? Yesterday she dined at the Polish embassy and the papers say she wore a tiara. . . . It's to be feared the animal is still a little sick.

June 16. Am beginning to believe that Sir Ronald is right, after all. Poor Mary, she can't do without her cigarettes and opium, her mad rushes to and fro around the globe. I actually shaved this morning. But I think I'll do a "cure" at Cairo before returning. Am still a trifle afraid of the loneliness of the bungalow, and a possible relapse.

Sad but true; the romantic attitude is a fool's game, a piece of silly make-believe. Or else one has no business to start plantations, build roads and bridges, and regard man as a rational being.

Cairo, June 19. The sick animal is on the mend. Tried to make love with a woman of the street, but it was a dismal failure. I felt more like weeping! I wonder if, when I meet Emilienne . . . ?

June 21. The animal is cured! Sound in wind and limb—and mind! Have booked my passage on Imperial Airways. "Life is earnest!"

"Camille! Did you hear something?"

"Yes, that was the mattress creaking. She's gone to bed."

"But the light's still on."

No sooner had he said it than the gleam of light under the door died out.

"Good night, Camille."

"Good night."

At eight in the morning he came back from the plantation for breakfast, and his face lit up when he saw Emilienne in a white dress, flowers on the table, and Camille laughing and chattering away in the best of spirits.

All the doors stood open, including those of Emilienne's bedroom and the kitchen, and the level morning light was flooding the red-tiled floor, seeping under the bookcases and cupboards.

"Had a good night?" he asked.

"Fairly good. I woke up twice, thinking about poor Yette."

He sat down and, unthinkingly, leaned his elbows on the table. From his place he could see the writing desk in the bedroom; the diary sheets were gone.

"Ferdinand!"

"Yes?"

"Don't you think we should go to Niangara and see if we can do anything for her? Yesterday I felt quite ashamed, leaving her like that, but somehow I didn't feel up to staying."

"We'll go there after breakfast. . . . By the way, I see we have two cars now."

They fell to discussing whether it would be wiser to sell one of the cars or to keep both. Several times Ferdinand's eyes strayed toward the place where the diary sheets had been.

"Oh, by the way," Emilienne said, reddening. "Just now, when I was straightening my room, I threw some sheets of paper into the fire, without thinking."

"Yes . . . I understand. . . ."

Abruptly he rose and, despite Camille's presence, took Emilienne in his arms, letting his head sink on her shoulder.

"Oh, Ferdinand! What's come over you?"

"Nothing . . . Please, don't speak. . . ."

His spectacles had slipped off, and somehow he didn't want her to see him without them—not at that moment. He drew a deep breath, then said:

"Yes, dear, we'll go to Niangara."

He said it so gravely that she couldn't help smiling. From his tone one might have thought he was making a profession of faith, or announcing a decision of capital importance.

"We'll go to Niangara."

And really she did wrong to smile, for that day "Niangara" meant, above all else, the bearded missionary with the meerschaum.

Tropic Moon

Translated by Stuart Gilbert

One

Try as he might, he could not account for it, this feeling of depression and foreboding that had taken possession of him. Nothing untoward had occurred; no danger that he knew of threatened him. He told himself he was a fool to give way to his nerves like this—here in the midst of a particularly festive evening at the hotel.

"Foreboding," perhaps, was too strong a word; it was little more than a vague unrest or a mild attack of the blues, and he fell to wondering when it had first come over him.

Certainly not when he was leaving Europe. On the contrary, Joseph Timar had set forth for Africa full of courage and enthusiasm.

Was it when he had come ashore in Libreville and made his first contact with the Gabon Province of French Equatorial Africa?

The steamer had anchored some distance out, and all that could be seen of the coast was a streak of dazzling white sand topped by a dark fringe of forest. There had been a heavy swell, and Timar had stood for some time on the bottom rung of the Jacob's ladder, with the sea immediately underfoot, waiting for a chance to jump into the surfboat. No sooner had it wriggled up alongside than a wave carried it away again.

At last a bare black arm flashed out, gripped him by the waist, and whisked him into the boat. A moment later they had shot away, he and the black boatman, and were bouncing over the whitecaps toward the shore. After a quarter of an hour—perhaps more; he could hear the steamer whistling to announce her departure—they had come alongside a jetty made of concrete blocks piled anyhow one upon the other.

Not a soul in sight. No one was there to meet him. Stranded with his luggage on the deserted quay, Timar had wondered what on earth he was to do.

But it was not then that his depression had begun. He had risen to the occasion and hailed a passing truck that took him and his belongings to Libreville's only hotel, the Central.

How thrilling it had been, this first taste of the tropics, the real thing, an outpost of France placed exactly on the line of the equator! The restaurant, whose walls were hung with African masks, was just as it should be, and as he cranked up a phonograph with a big old-fashioned horn, and the boy handed him his first shot of whisky, Timar felt like a seasoned "coaster"!

The main incident of that day had been more humorous than tragic. Just the sort of thing one would expect in French Equatorial. And anything that had a touch of local color enchanted Timar.

His uncle, a man of means and influence, had got him his job with the Sacova Trading Company. One of the managers at the head office in France had told him he would be stationed in the bush, some distance inland from Libreville. His duties would consist of felling timber and selling cheap goods to the natives.

No sooner had Timar landed than he made his way to a tumble-down warehouse bearing the name Sacova over the entrance. He hastened forward toward a bored, dyspeptic-looking European, who merely gazed blankly at Timar's outstretched hand.

Timar refused to be rebuffed and said amiably:

"You must be the agent. Delighted to meet you. I'm your new assistant."

"Assistant? I don't need assistance. What the hell do you think you're going to do here?"

But Timar didn't turn a hair. It was the agent who looked most nonplused, goggling his eyes behind glasses that made them appear enormous. After a while he actually became polite, adopted an almost confidential tone.

The same old story! he lamented. Those follows in the Paris office trying to run the show overseas and fouling things up as usual! This job they'd given Timar, for instance. Ten days' journey by boat up the river. Well, for one thing, the launch was stove in and couldn't be repaired in less than a month. Also, the trading station was at present in the hands of an old nut who'd sworn he'd let daylight into anyone sent there to relieve him.

"Make your own arrangements," he concluded. "I wash my hands of it!"

The interview had taken place four days ago, and during those first four days in Africa Timar had come to know Libreville better than La Rochelle, his birthplace. It consisted of a long red laterite road, the Strand, along the foreshore, fringed by coconut palms; an open-air native bazaar; a warehouse every hundred meters. Farther on, outside the native town, were a number of red brick houses in big shady compounds, occupied by European traders and officials.

He had inspected the launch with the damaged hull. No one was at work on it. No one had received orders to repair it. As a newcomer, almost an intruder, he hadn't ventured to take any steps himself.

He was twenty-four years old. His conventional good manners made everybody, even the boys waiting on him in the restaurant, smile.

Was there, then, no reason for his feeling so depressed? There was. Only too well he knew it, and if he had toyed with all sorts of spurious reasons, it had been to put off the moment of admitting to himself the true one.

The reason was here, everywhere around him, at the hotel. It was the hotel itself. It was . . .

Yet at first sight he had been delighted by the appearance of the Central, a yellow building set back in a compound full of exotic flowers and shrubs, some distance from the wharf, fifty meters from the palm grove.

The main room, which served as lounge and restaurant, was pleasant enough. The walls were color-washed in cheerful shades recalling the south of France. There was an air of solid comfort about the mahogany bar with its bright brass fittings and tall stools.

Here it was that the unmarried Europeans in Libreville took their meals. Each had his own table, a personal napkin ring.

The bedrooms above were seldom or never occupied. Bare, sparsely furnished rooms, distempered like the restaurant in pastel tones, with an old jug, a cracked basin, sometimes an empty trunk on the floor.

On both floors alike, tall Venetian blinds broke the glare, with the result that the whole place was dappled with clean-cut stripes of light and shade.

Timar's luggage was the kind a young middle-class Frenchman would normally possess, and it looked sadly out of keeping with its new surroundings. He himself felt no less lost, to start with. He wasn't used to washing in a basin little larger than a soup plate, and still less used, for other needs, to have to go outside and squat behind a bush.

Nor was he used to sharing his room with swarms of noxious insects: gaudily colored flies, nimble scorpions, shaggy spiders.

It was in his bedroom that he had had his first attack of what, for want of a better name, he had called "the blues"—dark imaginings that fastened on him with the pertinacity of a swarm of angry bees. After he had gone to bed and put out his candle, he still saw glimmering around him the white cage of his mosquito net. Beyond that flimsy barrier lay an outer darkness teeming with tiny life, of which he was acutely conscious, and from it came small, disconcerting sounds, shrill dronings, furtive rustlings. Now and again something would settle on the net—was it a scorpion or a spider, or only a mosquito?

Lying well in the middle of the bed, he tried to follow up the various sounds, trace each to its source, locate the sudden silences.

Abruptly he jerked himself up into a sitting position. To his surprise, sunlight was entering between the slats of the blinds. The door was open, and the proprietress of the hotel, placid and smiling, was gazing down at him.

He suddenly became aware that he had nothing on. White and wet with perspiration, his naked chest and shoulders emerged from the rumpled sheets. Why was he naked? He struggled to remember.

Yes, that was it. In the course of the night he had woken up feeling terribly hot, drenched in sweat. He had an idea that the bed was crawling with small, invisible insects. Some time about midnight, that had been. He had tried in vain to find his matches. Then he had flung off his pajamas, with the result that his rather scraggy chest and shoulders were in full view of the woman beside his bed.

With a calmness that amazed him she closed the door, then asked: "Had a good night?"

She picked up Timar's trousers, which were lying on the floor, shook the dust out, and hung them over a chair.

He didn't dare to move so long as she was there. He was unpleasantly conscious that the bed smelled of perspiration, there was dirty water in the basin, and the comb lying on the washstand had lost several of its teeth.

All the same, he didn't want her to go. Though obviously she was laughing at him, she did it in such a charming way!

"I came to ask what you have in the morning. Coffee? Tea? Chocolate? Your mother came to wake you in the mornings when you were at home, didn't she?"

She was wearing a black silk dress. She had drawn aside the mosquito net and was still laughing at him. Showing her teeth—almost as if she wanted to bite him! Because he was so different from the tough-skinned "coasters," because he looked clean and had the bloom of delicately nurtured youth.

In her attitude was nothing of the wanton, or of motherly affection. Or a hint, at most, of both. What he sensed above all in this attractive woman in her thirties was a latent sensuality that seemed to permeate the soft, yielding body from head to foot.

Embarrassed though he was, Timar caught himself wondering if she had anything on under the black silk dress.

And at that moment he felt a sudden rush of desire, whose urgency was actually intensified by things remotest from it: the curious light effect produced by the Venetian blinds, the stickiness of the bed, the hangover of an uneasy night, disturbed by childish panics and fumblings in the dark.

"Look! You've been stung!"

Sitting on the bed, she laid a finger on his chest just beneath the left nipple, touched a tiny pink spot, and looked into his eyes.

That was how it began. After that everything had gone in a rush, chaotically, with a sort of clumsy haste. And, he felt convinced, she'd been no less taken by surprise than he. Settling her hair before the mirror, she had said to him:

"Thomas will bring you your coffee."

Thomas was the boy. For Timar he was just a nigger; he was too raw to Africa to distinguish one black from another.

Coming downstairs an hour later, he found the proprietress seated behind the bar, crocheting a scarf in a banal shade of pink. Not a trace remained of the orgies of emotion they had shared a little while before. She looked quite composed, serenely calm. Smilingly as usual, she inquired:

"What time will you have lunch?"

He didn't even know her name! His nerves were quivering, his senses aching with remembered pleasure. Clearest of all was the impression of a voluptuously yielding body, the amazing softness of her skin.

A black girl came in with a basket of fish. The proprietress picked out the best, without a word, and dropped some coins into the basket.

Her husband came up the cellar stairs, his head and shoulders emerging first, then the whole of his massive but enfeebled body. A flabby giant of a man, slow-moving, with a sullen mouth and sallow rings under his eyes.

"Ah, there you are!" he growled.

And, like the fool he was, Timar started blushing when the man addressed him.

So it had gone on during the last three days. Only she hadn't come again to his bedroom to call him. As he lay in bed he could hear her moving around in the restaurant below, giving orders to Thomas, buying foodstuffs from the native hawkers who stopped in.

She wore the same black silk dress at all hours, and Timar now knew she had nothing on beneath it. This knowledge worked on his imagination, so much so that often he dared not look in her direction.

He had nothing to do outside the hotel and stayed indoors almost the whole day, taking occasional drinks, reading three-week-old newspapers, or practicing strokes on the billiard table.

Meanwhile she did her crochet work, served customers, and chatted with them for a moment as they leaned on the bar. Her husband busied himself with the beer and wine cellar and straightened up the tables, occasionally asking Timar to go and sit somewhere else. In fact, he seemed to regard the young man's constant presence in the hotel as somewhat of a nuisance.

There was something unnerving, almost exasperating, about this overdose of leisure and, despite the sunlight, the atmosphere of gloom—especially during the hottest hours, when merely to lift an arm made one start sweating.

At noon and again at dinnertime, the "regulars" trooped in for meals and a game of billiards. Timar hadn't struck up acquaintance with any of them so far. They eyed him with a certain interest, without cordiality as without dislike. And, for his part, he was too shy to try to make the first move.

Then the much-advertised "gala night" had come. The show was in full swing. Within an hour everyone would be half-seas over—including Timar, who was drinking champagne at a table by himself.

The entertainer was a dancer called Manuelo, a female impersonator. He must have come to the hotel while Timar was in bed. The first time Timar had seen him was at eleven that morning, when he'd found him pasting handbills on the pillars of the restaurant, announcing that Manuelo was the greatest Spanish ballerina.

An attractive, gracefully built little man, with a smile for everyone, he was already in the good books of the proprietress; they got along together not as a man does with a woman, but as women do between themselves.

After lunch the tables had been rearranged to leave enough space for Manuelo's dances. Festoons of colored paper had been strung around the room, the phonograph overhauled and oiled.

For hours on end Manuelo had rehearsed his dances in his bedroom, making the whole hotel vibrate with the drumming of his high-heeled shoes.

Was it because Timar resented this break in a routine to which he had grown accustomed that he felt so morose? He had actually gone out that morning, braved the midday sun, and felt his brain sizzling under the sun helmet. Black women had stared at him and grinned.

The regulars' dinner had been rushed through on account of the show. Then some residents of Libreville had drifted in, Europeans Timar hadn't seen before; the women were in evening dresses, and two Englishmen sported dinner jackets.

Champagne had made its appearance on all the tables. Night had fallen swiftly, and suddenly in the darkness outside hundreds of blacks had seemed to spring to life, peering in at doors and windows.

Manuelo started dancing. He looked so much like a woman that one began to wonder if he really were not one. The proprietress was at the bar. By now Timar knew her name: Adèle. Everybody called her by it. Most of the customers were free and easy in their talk with her. He, apparently, was the only one who addressed her formally as "madame." Wearing the usual black dress, naked beneath the silk, she had come to his table.

"Champagne? By the way, do you mind having Piper? I have only a few bottles of Mumm left, and those Englishmen don't care for any other brand."

That had pleased, even touched him. Then why, a few minutes later, had that look of profound depression settled on his face?

Manuelo had performed several dances. The proprietor—everyone called him "Eugène" and seemed on easy terms with him—had slouched off to a corner and seated himself beside the phonograph, looking glummer than ever. All the same, he had an eye on everything, kept the bus boys on their toes.

"Don't you see, you fool? That massa there is asking for another bottle."

Then, with an unexpected gentleness, he changed the needle on the phonograph.

Seated by himself, Timar was listening to the conversations going on around him, picking up a phrase here and there. Most of what he heard baffled him completely. At the next table, for instance, there was a tall, rather vulgar young fellow who had just broached his tenth whisky—and his companions addressed him deferentially as "Monsieur le Procureur." He looked more like a third-year student than a public prosecutor. A timber trader was explaining:

"Provided you leave no scars, there isn't the slightest risk. I'll tell you how to fix it. You put a wet towel on his back. Then you can lay on as hard as you like. The rattan doesn't leave any mark."

On the black man's back, presumably . . .

Had Timar gone through a whole bottle already? In any case, the boy was bringing him another. His glass was filled again. From where he sat he had a partial view of the kitchen, and just at that moment he saw the proprietress striking Thomas with her fist. The black didn't flinch; motionless, steady-eyed, he took the blows.

Sometimes the same record was played ten times over. A few couples were dancing. Most of the men had taken off their coats.

At the windows there was still the row of silent black men watching the whites enjoy themselves.

Beside the phonograph sat the proprietor, his face set and drawn, like a mask of tragedy.

What was happening? Nothing much, no doubt. What a fool he'd been to drink so much champagne! Suddenly all his rankling discontents, all his forebodings, came back, settled on him like a black cloud.

He wanted to say something, no matter what, to Adèle—simply to feel in contact with her. He watched her movements, trying to catch her eye. Somehow he couldn't manage it. Then a man at the next table called her. As she walked past he boldly caught a fold of her skirt and gave a little tug.

A pause. A glance. An unexpected remark:

"Why haven't you asked your boss's wife to dance with you?"

She pointed with her chin, and he saw a plump, matronly lady in pink seated beside the Sacova agent. Why had Adèle said that to him—and in such a curiously jumpy way? Was she jealous? That would be too much to hope for, and besides, he hadn't even glanced at any of the other women in the room.

The usual smile on her lips, she chatted with the people at the next table. But after that she didn't go back to the cash desk. She walked to the end of the restaurant where there was a door opening onto the compound. No one noticed her—except Timar, who, without being conscious of it, had filled himself another glass of champagne.

"What a damned fool I am! How could I hope to be the only one?"

He would have given worlds just then to hold her in his arms, to feel the soft warmth of her body pressed to his. He had never dreamed a woman's body could be so supple as hers had been at one particular moment.

How many minutes passed? Five? Or was it ten? Funereal as ever, the proprietor was winding the phonograph. Timar noticed that he had a bottle of mineral water beside him.

Adèle was still outside. Perhaps Eugène had noticed her absence, for he kept looking around the room.

Timar rose to his feet uncertainly and crossed the restaurant, surprised at feeling so lightheaded. He went out by the little door and, after crossing the compound, came to a gate beyond which lay open fields. Someone came running toward him, brushed against him. Adèle!

"At last!" he murmured tenderly.

"Get out of my way, you fool!"

It was pitch-dark. He could hear the sound of music in the distance. The black dress vanished into the night. For some minutes he stood still, sick of himself, of life, of everything. . . .

The clock struck three. Manuelo had finished his dances some time ago and passed the hat around. A man again, he was drinking peppermint cordial at one of the tables and prattling about his triumphs in Casablanca, Dakar, and the Belgian Congo.

Behind the counter Adèle was filling glasses, wrinkling her forehead with the concentration she brought to the task.

The Prosecutor was lounging against the bar, between the two Englishmen. He was drunk and in a quarrelsome mood.

Most of the people had left. At two tables, however, there were still some timber traders; determined to make a night of it, they had ordered sandwiches and beer.

One of them shouted:

"Stop that blasted phonograph, Eugène, and come have a drink with us."

The man rose to his feet. His lips were twisted in a wry grimace. He stared at the untidy restaurant, paper streamers trailing on the floor, empty glasses, wine-splashed tablecloths. There was a feverish glitter in his eyes. He began walking toward the door, then stopped suddenly, swaying a little as if a fit of dizziness had come over him. After a moment he moved on again, saying rather shakily:

"Back in a moment."

Adèle was busy sorting notes into piles, which she fastened with rubber bands.

Limp, dejected, bored with the whole situation, Timar was mechanically finishing off his bottle. He had no idea what the time was or how long the proprietor was absent from the room.

When he came back he looked huger and flabbier than ever, like a half-filled balloon. Halting in the doorway, he called his wife by name.

She gave him a quick glance, then went on counting the notes.

"Has the doctor gone?" he asked. "Send for him at once."

A sudden hush fell on the room. Then the man's voice came again:

"Where's Thomas got to? I can't find Thomas."

Timar cast a glance around the room, as did the others. Only the two extra boys engaged for the entertainment were to be seen.

"Not feeling well?" one of the timber traders ventured to inquire.

Eugène glared at him vindictively without replying.

"Shut the place up!" he ordered. "Right away! And get the doctor to come at once, if he's not too tight. Not that he can do me any good. I've got that damned blackwater again, and this time I'm done for."

Timar didn't understand, but evidently the others did, for they rose tumultuously.

"Eugène, old boy, hadn't you better . . . ?"

"Shut your trap! And close the damned place!"

He stamped down the hall. A door banged. There was the clatter of a chair kicked over somewhere upstairs.

Adèle looked up. She had gone very white. She was listening to a noise that was coming nearer, of footsteps and men's voices. A group of four or five blacks halted at the door.

Timar could not make out what they said—a few queer guttural sounds hawked up from their gullets.

Then he heard one of the timber traders, a one-eyed man, translating.

"They've just found Thomas's body, two hundred meters away. Shot dead with a revolver."

Upstairs Eugène was thumping the floor with a stick. After a while he lost patience, opened his bedroom door, and yelled down the stairs:

"Why don't you come, Adèle? Don't you know I'm dying, damn it!"

Two

When Timar awoke he was tangled up in his mosquito net, which had come loose in the night, and the room was flooded with sunlight. But here the sun shone every day; a cheerless, hostile sun.

Sitting on his bed, he listened to the noises in the hotel. Several times in the course of a broken sleep he had heard people moving around, whispering together, and the sound of water being poured from a jug.

The moment the doctor came, Adèle had packed Timar off to his room, in exactly the same manner as she had bundled the others out of the hotel.

"If I can help in any way . . ." he had kept on repeating with ridiculous insistence.

"Fine. I won't forget. Now off you go to bed!"

Had her husband died in the night, as he'd predicted? Anyhow, they were sweeping out the restaurant; the life of the hotel was going on. Opening his door a cautious crack, Timar listened. Adèle was speaking.

"What, no Gruyère left? No cheese in the warehouse, either? Open a can of green beans. Wait! For dessert, bananas and apricots—the ones on the righthand shelf. Got it, you dolt?"

She didn't raise her voice, and she wasn't in a bad temper. That was how she always spoke to blacks.

When, without waiting to shave, Timar hurried down some minutes later, he found her at the cash desk, filing checks. The restaurant was trim and tidy, as usual. So was Adèle. Not a crease in the black silk dress, her hair in perfect order.

"What's the time?" he asked. He couldn't believe his eyes.

"Just nine."

An incredible woman! Eugène's attack had come on at four in the morning. At that time the restaurant had been in a filthy state, everything topsy-turvy. Adèle hadn't had a wink of sleep. And now here she was, spick-and-span as ever; she had already drawn up the bill of fare for lunch, had even thought about the cheese and fruit.

All the same, he noted, she looked paler than usual. There were dark rings around her eyes, which changed their expression. Then Timar's eyes fell on the outlines of her breasts, bare under the black silk, and he looked away, blushing.

"Is your husband better?"

She looked surprised at first, then must have remembered he was a newcomer to Africa.

"He won't last out the morning."

"Where is he?"

She pointed upward. He dared not inquire if the dying man was by himself, but she guessed what was in his mind.

"He's delirious, doesn't recognize anyone. . . . By the bye, I have a note for you here."

She hunted for it on the counter: a small official form summoning Timar (Joseph) to present himself at his earliest convenience at the police station.

A black woman entered with a basket of eggs for sale. Adèle waved her away, then turned to Timar.

"You'd better go before it gets too hot."

"Why do you think they want me?"

"You'll find out."

She didn't seem worried in the least. And, like her, the restaurant looked exactly as usual.

"You take the turn to the right just after the jetty, before you come to the Shipping Office. Don't forget your topee."

Was it just imagination? He could have sworn he noticed something queer about the natives' demeanor that morning. True, there was the usual cheerful hubbub in the bazaar, the usual picturesque confusion of many-colored *pagnes*. But now and again he noticed someone in the crowd staring darkly at him, and sometimes two or three natives would fall silent and avert their eyes as he walked by.

Though he was dripping with perspiration, Timar quickened his pace. He took a wrong turn and found himself in front of Government House. Retracing his steps, he discovered at the far end of a road that was little more than a cart track a ramshackle building with a signboard in front: "Central Police Station."

The letters were daubed on in white paint and the *c* in "Central" was upside down. Some barefooted native constables were seated on the veranda steps. Behind them was a darkened room from which came the clacking of a typewriter.

"May I see the Superintendent?"

"Massa having chit?"

Timar fished up the summons from his pocket and waited on the veranda. After a while he was ushered into an office all the blinds of which were drawn.

"Sit down. Your name is Joseph Timar?"

As his sight got used to the semidarkness, Timar made out a red-faced man with prominent eyes, dark pouches underneath them.

"When did you arrive in Libreville? Sit down."

"By the last boat on Wednesday."

"Are you by any chance related to Councilor Timar?"

"He's my uncle."

The effect of the words was magical. The Superintendent rose, a flabby hand outstretched, and said in quite a different tone:

"Do sit down, Monsieur Timar. Is your uncle still living in Cognac? I was Inspector of Police there for five years."

Timar felt much relieved. Not only had the dingy, forbidding aspect of the room depressed him from the moment he had entered it, but he had also been irritated by the Superintendent's attitude. There were five hundred Europeans, all told, in Libreville: men who led hard, often perilous, lives in the cause of what in France was styled bombastically "colonial expansion." And no sooner had he landed than he was hauled up before a police official and treated like a suspect!

"A very fine man, your uncle. He can be a senator any day he chooses. But tell me, what on earth made you come here?"

It was now the Superintendent who looked baffled, and his surprise was so obviously heartfelt that Timar became slightly uneasy.

"I'm taking a job with the Sacova Trading Company."

"Is the agent leaving?"

"No, the idea was that I should take over the station up the river, but . . ."

The expression on the Superintendent's face was no longer one of surprise, but of frank consternation.

"Does your uncle know this?"

"It was he who got me the job. One of the directors is a friend of his."

Timar was still seated. The Superintendent had risen and was prowling around him, scanning him with interest. Sometimes he crossed a ray of light, and Timar noticed that his upper lip was gashed and his face more robust and virile than it had seemed at first.

"Well, it's a damned crazy idea! We'll talk about it later. Did you know the Renauds before you came here?"

"The Renauds?"

"The owners of the Central . . . By the way, is he dead yet?"

"I hear he won't last out the morning."

"Is that so? I wonder now . . . ?"

Suddenly Timar realized what was making him uneasy, affable though the Superintendent had become. It was the way the man was looking at him as he paced to and fro. Almost the same look as Adèle's: astonishment mingled with curiosity, and even a hint of compassion.

"You'll have a little whisky, won't you?"

Without waiting for an answer he shouted to one of the orderlies squatting on the veranda.

"Naturally you don't know any better than the others exactly what happened last night?"

Timar felt himself blushing. The police officer seemed to notice it, which made him blush still more. The black man handed a bottle to the Superintendent, who poured out two whiskies, puffing and blowing as if prostrated by the heat.

"I suppose you've heard that a black man was shot dead less than two hundred meters from the hotel? I've just been seeing the Governor. It's a nasty business, a very nasty business."

The typewriter was still clacking away in the next room. The door was ajar, and Timar noticed that the typist was a black woman.

"Here's luck. Of course you can't understand. But in the course of the next few days you'll get the hang of things, I have no doubt. I sent for you to question you, like the others. They'll all tell me the same story—that they don't know a damned thing! Have a cigarette. No? You must come and lunch with us one day; my wife will be delighted. She comes from the north of France, but she met your uncle while we were living in Cognac."

Timar was relaxing, even coming to appreciate the semidarkness, which at first had got on his nerves. The whisky was helping him to feel at ease. Also the Superintendent seemed to have had enough of inspecting him and was staring at the wall. He ventured to ask a question.

"These Renauds you were talking about just now—what sort of people are they?"

"Hasn't anybody told you? I'm surprised. Eugène Renaud was expelled from France fifteen years ago and forbidden to return. White-slave traffic was the charge, but I suspect there were other things against him as well. We have several fellows of that sort in Libreville."

"And his wife?"

"She *is* his wife. I've seen the marriage license. They were already married when he was doing his dirty job in Paris. Oh, they're a pretty pair! . . . Finish your drink."

Timar finished it, and two, possibly three, more in quick succession. The Superintendent, who drank even, was waxing loquacious. But for an urgent telephone call summoning him to the Public Prosecutor's office, the conversation might have lasted a good while longer.

When Timar went out, the sun was beating down so fiercely that after walking a hundred meters he became seriously alarmed. The back of his neck was scorching; he couldn't digest the whisky; and Renaud's sudden collapse, along with similar stories he had heard, kept running through his head.

But always his thoughts kept harking back to Adèle, who when he was only seven had already been helping Renaud to recruit young women for South America. She had come with him to French Equatorial Africa in the pioneering days, when there were only log cabins along the coast. After days and days of travel in native canoes they had hacked their way through the bush and set about felling timber and rafting it to the coast. The picture Timar conjured up was a medley of scraps of reality and illustrations to Jules Verne stories.

He was walking along the red laterite road that skirted the bay. The palm trees stood out half against the sky and half against the leaden grayness of the sea. No waves, only the faintest ripple, like a timid smile, ruffled the sandy beach. Almost naked men with gaily colored loincloths were gathered around some fishing canoes that had just come in. Barely a kilometer away, at the tip of the bay, the river began.

In the spacious times of Adèle and Eugène there had been no red roofs of warehouses and government offices rising among the verdure. He pictured her wearing boots and a bandolier; certainly not a silk dress next to her skin.

He turned off into every patch of shade he could find, but it was as bad in the shade as in the open. The air itself was broiling; even his clothes were hot as fire. In the old days there had been no brick walls, no ice for cooling drinks.

After eight years of it, Adèle and Eugène had defied the law and sailed for France with six hundred thousand francs in their pockets. They'd spent the money—"blown it" was the Superintendent's phrase—in a few months.

How had they spent it? What sort of life had they led? In what haunts would a youngster in his teens, as Timar was then, have stood a chance of meeting them?

Anyhow, they had returned to Africa, gone back to jungle life. The man had had two attacks of blackwater fever. Adèle had nursed him back to health.

Only three years ago had they bought the Central Hotel.

And this was the woman Timar had held in his arms one morning, in a draggled, sweat-stained bed!

He didn't dare take off his topee to mop his brow. It was noon; he was alone, absolutely alone, on the blazing road.

The Superintendent had told him other stories, without any show of indignation, merely grunting disapproval when, to his thinking, someone had really gone too far.

That planter, for instance, who, a month before, suspecting his cook of trying to poison him, had hung the man up by his feet over a tub of water. Now and again he paid out the rope and let the man's head down into the tub. Finally he'd forgotten, for a quarter of an hour, to haul the man up again. When he thought of doing it, the black was dead.

The case was being tried. The League of Nations was putting its oar in. And now another nigger had been murdered!

"This time they're in for it," the Superintendent had concluded.

"Who are?"

"The people who killed Thomas."

"What about the other cases?"

"Oh, one generally manages to fix things up."

What had Adèle been up to on the night of the show when she went outside? And why had she struck Thomas in the face a few hours before?

Timar hadn't mentioned what he had seen. He'd never breathe a word of it. But might not other people have noticed her returning from the compound?

There, he'd lost his way again! Once more he had to retrace his steps. At last he reached the hotel, where today, he observed, the tinkle of knives and forks was unaccompanied by the usual hum of conversation. Everybody looked at him as he came in. He also noticed as he went to his table that Adèle wasn't at her usual place.

A new boy, a youngster, brought his lunch. Someone plucked his sleeve, and, looking around, he saw one of the timber traders, a heavily built fellow with the face and manner of a butcher, beside his chair.

"It's all over."

"What do you mean?"

The man pointed to the ceiling.

"He died just now. By the way, what did he say to you?"

Timar stared blankly. The pace was too much for him—especially in this stifling heat. Though aware that it would sound silly to his hearer, he asked:

"Who do you mean?"

"The Superintendent, damn it! He took you first because he thought it would be easier to grill a new hand. Our turn'll come this afternoon or tomorrow."

No one stopped eating, but all eyes were fixed on Timar, who had no idea what to say. He felt completely at sea, what with thoughts of the dead man upstairs and memories of the fantastic tales the Superintendent had been telling him.

"Did you get the impression that he knows something?"

"That I couldn't say. Anyhow, I told him that I hadn't noticed anything."

"Good for you!"

He'd gone up in their opinion, that was clear. They were looking at him more amiably. But it meant that they knew he knew something. So they, too, knew. . . .

Timar blushed, ate a slice of cold sausage, and was surprised to hear himself ask:

"Did he suffer much?"

An inept question, as he realized at once; it had certainly been a horribly painful death.

"The trouble is its happening so soon after that business of the nigger who was drowned," remarked the one-eyed man.

So they had tumbled to that, too! Everyone had tumbled to it. In short, they were all making common cause, and if they watched Timar with a certain mistrust, it was because he was an outsider, and they weren't sure of him.

Footsteps sounded in the room above. A door opened and closed. Someone came down the stairs.

It was Adèle Renaud. There was dead silence in the restaurant as she walked through, went to the counter, and took the telephone off its hook.

Nothing had changed in her appearance; as usual, one could see her breasts outlined beneath the clinging silk, and, though he realized how absurd it was, Timar felt slightly shocked—as though mourning called for undergarments.

"Hello! Yes, 25, please. Isn't Oscar in? No? What a nuisance! The moment he's back, please tell him it's over and I want him to come here with his outfit right away. The doctor won't let us keep the corpse after noon tomorrow. No, thanks; I can manage all right."

After hanging up she remained for some moments in a brown study, her chin propped on her folded hands, her elbows on the counter. When she spoke, to reprimand a boy, she hardly turned her head:

"What are you up to? Why don't you clear that table beside the door?"

She opened a drawer, closed it, seemed on the point of going away, but thought better of it, and resumed the same position as before. Someone called from one of the tables:

"Is the funeral tomorrow?"

"Yes. The doctor says it wouldn't be wise to keep him here any longer."

"If there's anything we can do . . ."

"Thanks. Everything's fixed up. The coffin will be here any minute now."

Timar was conscious that her eyes were lingering on him, and he dared not look up. Then he heard her say:

"Did you see the Superintendent, Monsieur Timar? Was he very nasty?"

"No. As a matter of fact . . . Well, it seems he knows my uncle, who's a *conseiller général*, and so . . ."

He caught himself up; again he had grown aware that the others were observing him with that look of rather bantering curiosity—tinged now with a shade of respect—which he always found so disconcerting. And at the same moment he saw on Adèle's lips an understanding smile, which flickered out immediately.

"I'm moving you to another bedroom. Your room's the only one where I can put the body tonight."

She turned toward the shelf behind her, took a bottle of Calvados, filled a liqueur glass, and drank it up with a slight grimace. Then in a toneless voice she asked:

"What have they done with the dead nigger?"

"The body's at the hospital. There's to be a post-mortem this afternoon. It seems the bullet went right through the shoulder blades—and hasn't yet been found."

The last words were spoken with a certain emphasis. Then the timber trader shrugged his shoulders and, after gulping down a chunk of apricot that looked like a poached egg, added:

"There's a native policeman watching the place to keep anyone from coming to take away the bullet, if it's still there. If it's still there! Who's up for a game of billiards?"

He wiped his mouth with his napkin, then rose to his feet. Noticing that no one responded, he suddenly grew abashed and murmured:

"Well, perhaps we'd better not play billiards today. Give me a Calvados, Adèle."

He went up to the bar and rested his elbows on it, facing Adèle, while the others finished their meal. The blood had risen to Timar's cheeks. He ate mechanically, giving a little angry toss of his head each time a big fly that had selected him for its victim tried to settle on his brow.

The heat was stifling in the restaurant. Not a breath of wind out of doors. One couldn't even hear the sound of the long ripples falling on the beach nearby.

The only sounds came from the kitchen, through the open hatch—an occasional tinkle of dishes. The assistant manager of the bank, a tall young fellow whose manners somewhat resembled Timar's and who took his meals at the hotel, was the first to leave, after lighting a cigarette and putting on his topee.

Soon after him the others rose. Some moved across to the bar for a liqueur before going. By two at the latest nobody would be left in the restaurant except Timar and Adèle.

Timar wondered whether to stay on till then. After those unaccustomed whiskies in the morning he was feeling muzzy, and his head was aching. But he couldn't screw up enough energy to go upstairs and settle down in a new room, now that his own had been requisitioned for the corpse.

One of the group at the bar, liqueur glass in hand, inquired:

"Shall we see him before he's nailed up?"

"I doubt it. Everything will be done by five."

"Poor fellow!"

The speaker was a man of about the same age as the hotelkeeper. There were younger men who had already had two attacks. Several of those present, as Timar had learned from the Superintendent, had made one or two fortunes, only to squander them in France in less than a year. The one-eyed man with a gold tooth, for instance. On one of his visits to France, when he was in Bordeaux and there was a gala night at the opera, he had chartered all the taxis in the city just for the fun of watching the audience, men and women in evening dress, starting to walk home under a torrential downpour. Now, because of the trade depression, he lived precariously on the income from an ancient truck, making deliveries and doing road repairs.

A bell started ringing at one of the warehouses—half past one. Soon there were only four persons remaining in the restaurant, then only three. Still seated at his table, Timar was staring at the floor.

The last man finished up his drink and took his topee from the hatrack. Timar's heart was thudding. In agonized expectancy he was wondering what words would pass between himself and Adèle.

Footsteps receded on the tiled floor. With an effort he raised his head. He had come to a decision. Like the others, he would go to the bar and have a liqueur, even if it meant his being laid out for the rest of the day.

But just as he was rising to his feet, Adèle sighed like someone with a tiresome duty to perform. There was a click as she closed the till. Then, without a word, without a glance in his direction, she went out. He caught a glimpse of her through the kitchen hatch; she was giving orders to the cook in a low voice. Then she started up the staircase, and a moment later Timar heard her footsteps overhead.

Three

At dinner the atmosphere was much like that at lunch—except that everyone was now aware that the corpse was no longer on a bed but nailed up in a coffin resting on two chairs.

When the meal ended, some meaning glances were exchanged among the regulars. Evidently they were reminding one another of a program fixed up among them. The man with the butcher's face acted as spokesman.

"How about closing now, Adèle?"

"Yes, I'm just going to."

"And—well, I suppose there'll be the usual business tonight; sitting up beside the corpse, I mean, with candles and all that. If so you can count on us, of course."

The contrast was comical between the man's forbidding jowl and the expression on his face, like that of a schoolboy asking for an hour off.

"What's the point of sitting up with him? He won't run away."

The man's eyes twinkled; it was all he could do to suppress a laugh. Five minutes later all of them, Timar included, trooped out.

"How about a stroll before turning in?"

"Not a bad idea! . . . Goodnight, Adèle. See you tomorrow."

But these efforts to make their exodus seem casual somehow missed fire; it was more of a stampede.

There were six of them standing in the moonlight on the road. Someone was cranking up a light truck. Behind the fringe of coconut palms the sea was murmurous, lit with silvery gleams; it was just such a scene as Timar had pictured in faraway France when trying to evoke a tropical nightscape.

Glancing back at the hotel, he was strangely affected by the emptiness of the restaurant. The boy was clearing up. From the cash desk, Adèle was giving him an order.

Timar noticed that the assistant bank manager had come along. When the truck moved off, they were side by side. Someone heaved a sigh of relief.

"Glad it's over! I don't believe in scenes, but really Adèle goes too far the other way. It almost put me off my feed . . . !"

One of the men bent toward the driver.

"Hey, you! Stop at my place. I'll get a bottle of Pernod."

It was hard to make out faces; or, rather, the moonlight distorted them beyond recognition. Six dark forms lurched and bumped against one another as the truck jolted along the ruts.

"Where are we heading?" Timar asked the man beside him in a low tone.

"Oh, to a native hut, I imagine—to make a night of it."

Timar noticed that the young man seemed different from his usual self tonight. He was very tall and slim, with a finely chiseled profile and sedate manners. Now, however, there was a glint of excitement, a curious shiftiness, in his gaze.

While they were waiting for the bottle of absinthe, Timar exchanged some remarks with him. He learned that Bouilloux, the man who looked so much like a butcher, had been nothing of the sort, but a schoolmaster, in early life.

In the midst of a remark the banker had a sudden access of good manners. Leaning forward, he held out his hand.

"Let me introduce myself. My name's Gérard Maritain."

"And I'm Joseph Timar, of the Sacova."

When the truck started off again, it turned up a road unfamiliar to Timar, and the noise of the engine made further talk impossible. The ancient vehicle gave the impression it might fall to pieces at any moment, but this did not deter the driver from taking corners at top speed. At each swerve the passengers slumped in a mass toward the side of the car.

At first some lights could be seen beside the road; then all was darkness. Presently Timar saw in the distance the glow of a fire and a group of squat black cones around it which turned out to be native huts.

"Maria's place?" someone inquired.

"Yes. That's the idea."

From that moment Timar seemed plunged into a grotesque nightmare. It was his first night out in Libreville. In the moonlight everything looked unfamiliar, out of focus. He had no notion where he was or where he was being taken.

Shadowy forms loomed up beside the road, only to merge at once into the blackness of the jungle. The brakes squealed. Bouilloux was the first to alight. He went up to a hut that was in complete darkness and kicked the door.

"Hurry up, Maria! Get up!"

The others, too, alighted. Timar stayed beside Maritain, who was more of his own kind.

"Who's Maria?" he asked, "a tart?"

"No, just an ordinary colored woman. But they're only too glad, all of them, to have a visit from a white man. Libreville doesn't run to cafés, so there's nowhere else to go."

Though night had fallen the heat was still oppressive. No one stirred in any of the other huts. Maria's door opened; a naked black man loomed up on the threshold and, after a perfunctory salutation, slipped away into the darkness.

Later on Timar learned that this man who so obligingly made off when the white men visited Maria was her husband.

A match was struck, an oil lamp lit inside the hut.

"In you go!" shouted Bouilloux, shepherding the others through the doorway.

In the hut it was even hotter than outside, the air impregnated with the musty odor of blacks' sweat. Timar had already caught whiffs of it when blacks passed him in the street, but here it was a concentrated stench that rasped the throat.

After lighting the lamp the woman began to wrap a loincloth around her naked body. Bouilloux whisked it off and flung it into a corner.

"Go and fetch your sisters, both of them. Make sure you bring the little one."

With the possible exception of Maritain, who looked rather self-conscious, all the white men seemed perfectly at ease here. There were two decrepit deck chairs, a table, a shabby cot that still bore the imprint of two sweaty bodies.

Nevertheless, three of the men seated themselves on the squalid coverlet. Noticing that Maritain and Timar had remained standing, Bouilloux shouted:

"Sit down, boys. Make yourselves at home."

Never yet, even at high noon, had Timar felt so hot. And it seemed to him that there was something unwholesome about this fetid heat—like the smell of sickbeds or foul diseases. He couldn't bring himself to touch anything in the hut, including the walls, and lingered in the entrance, his eyes fixed on Maritain, who was nearer the others.

"Doesn't compare with Adèle, does she?" Bouilloux had noticed the expression on Timar's face. "Have a drink. It'll buck you up."

A glass was passed from hand to hand to Timar, one of three glasses that nobody had thought of washing. Bouilloux had another in his hand. The one-eyed man had a third.

"Here's to Adèle!"

Neat absinthe. Timar gulped it down; he lacked the courage to stand up against the five men watching him. But his nostrils wrinkled with disgust; no less than the raw alcohol, the filthy tumbler nauseated him.

"Very sporting of you, pretending you don't understand. But, seeing as we've all been there . . ."

There would certainly have been a scene had not the door opened just at that moment. Maria came in first, a humble smile on her lips. Behind her was a black girl, little more than a child, who was promptly grabbed by the man nearest the entrance.

It was difficult to make out what happened after that; the tiny hut was so jammed with people wedged against one another. The women hardly spoke at all. Only a stray word now and then, or a broken phrase. Most of the time they merely grinned, with flashes of big white teeth. Maria pulled a bottle of peppermint liqueur from beneath the mattress, and when all the Pernod was drunk, the men polished it off among them.

There was an awkward moment when the one-eyed man inquired:

"What are they saying in the village about Thomas's death?"

The smiles died from the black faces. All the amiability, even the meekness, had gone, and they stared sullenly at the floor. Bouilloux saved the situation with a jovial outburst:

"Damn it, what's all the fuss about? Who cares a hoot about what happened to that rotten nigger? Let's have another drink, boys. . . . Look here! What do you say to a little jaunt in the bush, to wind up the evening?"

Once again, as during dinner, understanding glances were exchanged, from which Timar inferred some hidden meaning behind the words, a prearranged plan.

"Just a moment. Listen, Maria. Here's a hundred francs for you if you can dig up a bottle of whisky somewhere."

Somehow she procured one in the village, which seemed asleep, where, though there was not a sound, not a whisper, not a glimmer of light, Timar had a feeling that people were listening in every hut, missing nothing of what was said.

They bundled into the truck again, shouting and laughing.

Just as they were starting, they caught sight of a black woman standing beside the trunk of a silk-cotton tree.

"Hop in!"

Whatever else was said was drowned by the roar of the starter, then of the gears and engine.

Timar preferred not to see what they were up to in the truck. Resolutely he fixed his eyes on the treetops scudding past, etched in moonlight. They were traveling along a sandy road, changing speed at every moment.

Somebody handed him the bottle of whisky; it was half full and tepid, and the neck was slimy. He could not bring himself to drink and kept his lips shut as he tilted up the bottle; he felt whisky trickling down his chin and chest.

"We've all been there. . . ."

The words were echoing in his brain; he was fretting with impatience to confront that swine Bouilloux and demand an explanation. It was a damned lie, of course! Bouilloux or the one-eyed man, for instance— Adèle's lover! Too ridiculous for words!

His mood kept alternating between anger and despondency. At one moment he had an idea of forcing them to stop the car and getting out. But without a notion where he was, he had no choice; he had to stay with them.

It seemed to him that they had covered a good twenty-five kilometers. The car stopped where the road ended, beside a clearing near a riverbank. The noise broke out again: loud voices, drunken laughter.

"The bottle!" someone shouted. "Don't forget the bottle!"

Timar remained standing by the truck; no one seemed to notice that he had stayed behind. In front of him dim forms were scampering in all directions through patches of vividly green moonlight and intense darkness, and he could hear whispers, stifled exclamations, sometimes shrill, excited giggles.

A tall, shadowy form drew near. It was Maritain, who discovered Timar when he was only a meter away and hailed him with some embarrassment.

"What? Were you here all the time? We've just been having a little fun, you know."

A bulkier form could be seen zigzagging heavily across the clearing. Suddenly it swerved toward them.

"Quick! Jump into the truck. We'll play 'em a good trick!"

It was Bouilloux. Another dim figure hurried forward. Then a group of three. Then a black girl.

"Hold on, baby! White men first."

They climbed into the truck. The three women waited for their turn. The engine was running.

"Off we go!"

The car plunged forward. The women started running after it, yelling, trying to scramble in.

"Hands off! Bye-bye, girls!"

They were naked, naked as creatures of the wild, sleek black bodies drenched with silvery moonbeams. They waved their arms distractedly, shrieking, imploring.

"Step on the gas, sonny, or they'll catch up with us."

The truck seemed to be rattling itself to bits. It bumped against a tree stump, toppled over, righted itself just in time.

The women were still in hot pursuit but gradually falling behind. The black-and-silver forms grew smaller, dwindled into darkness; their cries grew fainter.

"Good! We've done it."

Two or three chuckles of satisfaction; no more. Somebody said:

"By the way, who the devil was she, that fat old hag?"

Maritain, who was standing beside Timar, lowered his eyes.

Some bawdy jokes were exchanged; then gradually all relapsed into a gloomy silence.

"I've had a summons to come to the police station tomorrow."

"So have I."

"How about Adèle? Look here, let's all chip in for a wreath."

It was hot and cold at once. Timar was sweating profusely, and his shirt was stuck to his body. The furnace-hot air seemed to be burning up his lungs, yet at the same time the draft caused by the motion of the car made him shiver with cold.

He had given a start when Adèle's name was pronounced. The moon was setting behind the forest; he could not see the men around him. But he had already noted the place where Bouilloux was standing.

"You mentioned Adèle's name just now. I should like you to tell me . . ." His voice sounded so unnatural that he lost his nerve and couldn't go on.

"What the hell do you want me to tell you? Have a good time if you feel like it, like we did this evening. But cut out the Sunday-school stuff—we've got no use for it out here."

Timar kept silent. They dropped him at the wharf. He shook hands with one man only, Maritain, who murmured rather awkwardly:

"Good night, Monsieur Timar. See you tomorrow."

At last he was alone, alone in the warm, starlit darkness. The only light at the hotel shone in an upper window. The front door was bolted, and somehow he couldn't face the idea of making a noise by knocking, partly out of deference for the dead man within, and also because, after the nervous tension of the last few hours, he was in a state bordering on panic and shaking in every limb.

He crept around to the back of the building. The sound of his footsteps appalled him; his heart missed a beat when a cat scurried across his path. He had a feeling he must be coming down with an illness, because, though he was drenched in sweat, cold shivers were running through his body. At the least movement he felt drops of sweat oozing from every pore.

The back door, too, was closed. He came back to the front of the hotel, and as he stood wondering what to do, he heard a bolt being drawn.

Placid as ever, still in the black silk dress, Adèle was gazing down at him, a candle in her hand. She held the door open just enough to let him pass and closed it at once behind him. In the wavering candlelight the restaurant looked quite different. He tried to think of something to say. He was desperately miserable and furious with himself, with her, with everything. Never in his life had he experienced such a ferment of emotion.

"Hadn't you gone to bed?"

As he eyed her morosely a sudden change of mood came over him. Was it an aftereffect of the squalid scenes he had been forced to witness? Or was it not, rather, an angry protest of his secret self, an itch to take revenge on her? For in the rush of desire that set his senses tingling there was a streak of hatred.

"Your new room's on the left."

He followed her supinely as far as the foot of the staircase. He knew she would halt there, holding up the candle to light the stairs, letting him go in front.

And as she did so, he clasped her in a rough embrace—though even now he could not have said what he proposed to do. She did not struggle. A drop of wax from the candle she was holding fell on Timar's hand. All she did was to stiffen up, and such was her strength that, woman though she was, he was unable to draw her body toward his. And all she said was:

"You're drunk, my dear. Go to bed."

He gazed at her bemusedly. He saw her pale face flickering in the candlelight, her mobile lips on which even now there seemed to hover that familiar, half-mocking, half-affectionate smile.

With awkward haste he ran up the stairs, stumbled, started to enter the wrong room, while she repeated in the same gently indulgent tone:

"The door on the left."

A moment later he heard her coming up, opening another door, then closing it. The last sound he heard was two light taps, her slippers dropping one after the other onto the floor.

Four

It was in the graveyard that an immense homesickness descended on Timar, a sense of isolation like a great wave sweeping him off his feet, leaving him faint and gasping. At first he was inclined to attribute it to the strangeness of his surroundings: the feathery, golden-green palms, the surging crowd of blacks, their queer, singsong voices.

Then he realized it was something more: the full meaning of certain words had only just struck home. "There's no escape from Africa except by sea. Only one ship calls each month, and it takes three weeks to reach France."

It was eight in the morning. They had left the Central at seven, before the sun was high. But it wasn't only the sun that made one feel so hot; heat welled up from the ground, from walls, from every solid object. Even one's own body was a source of heat.

Timar had gone to bed at four and awakened feeling wretched, which led him to think he'd been more drunk than he'd realized the night before.

All the habitués of the Central were present, including Maritain. As at French-provincial funerals, the mourners clustered in groups around the cemetery gate. The only difference was that here everybody wore white suits and sun helmets. Adèle, too, who was walking behind the coffin in her usual black silk dress, had a topee on.

Draped in black cloth, the truck of the previous night's jaunt now served as hearse.

After going some way along the familiar red road, the truck-hearse turned up a steepish track bordered by native huts. Was one of them Maria's? Timar wondered.

Hot though it was, they moved at a brisk pace, for the truck engine stalled at a low speed. Adèle walked by herself, in front. She showed no signs of distress, and now and then moved to the side of the track or cast a casual glance around; to judge from her demeanor, she might have been on a morning's shopping expedition.

The cemetery was on a hilltop, with a view across the town and the bay. On the left, where a river issued from the jungle, a black-and-red cargo boat was loading timber, and each detail of the distant scene—was it due to the clearness of the air?—stood out in bright relief.

They could see rafts coming up alongside, towed by a tiny tug, and the chug-chug of its motor reached their ears. There was a jingle of chains being secured around the logs, the hum of windlasses.

Beyond the river mouth lay the open sea. And very far beyond—twenty days' voyage by the fastest liner—the shores of France.

Somehow Timar could not feel that he was in a real cemetery. True, there had been some attempt to conform to tradition. Two or three tombstones, a few wooden crosses. But everything else was lacking. No chapel, no wrought-iron gates, not even a surrounding wall. The nearest approach to one was a hedge of grotesquely twisted shrubs with big purple berries—which themselves reminded one how far away was Europe. And the soil was brick-red. A hundred meters away, half hidden in the scrub, were rows of rectangular hummocks, native graves. The centerpiece of the scene was an enormous baobab tree.

Some people who had not taken part in the funeral cortège, among others the Governor and District Commissioner, had come by car and were smoking cigarettes as they waited for the service to begin. They took off their hats to Adèle.

The burial service had to be rushed through, for there was not a patch of shade in the cemetery. It was accompanied by the clatter of winches

on the cargo boat and the thuds of falling timber. The pastor looked ill
at ease.

In his lifetime Renaud had been, if anything, of the Catholic persua-
sion. As it so happened, the local priest had just left on a pastoral tour
upcountry, so the Protestant minister had been asked to officiate in his
place.

Four blacks lowered the coffin into an indecorously shallow grave,
then scraped the earth back over it with hoes.

The thought that one day he might be laid to rest in this slapdash
fashion again brought unpleasantly home to Timar the distance he had
traveled since leaving La Rochelle. No, this wasn't a real cemetery. This
was not a real funeral. . . . This country was not his country.

He could hardly keep his eyes open, and he had a queer pain inside.
And the heat, which, creeping in under his topee, was searing the back
of his neck like lambent flames, made him apprehensive.

The moment the service ended there was a general stampede. Timar
would have preferred to walk back by himself, but he saw a tall form
edging its way over to him. It was Maritain, who murmured rather
apologetically:

"Hope you got home all right. By the way, have you been summoned,
too? I hear the Governor intends to be present when the witnesses are
examined by the police."

Timar had a glimpse of the bazaar and recognized the side street
leading to the police station. His shirt was stuck tight under his
armpits. His throat was parched.

As there was no waiting room, some chairs had been set out on the
veranda. But the sun beat in so fiercely that everyone had to keep his
topee on.

Black police orderlies squatted on the wooden steps. The door of the
office stood open; the Governor and Public Prosecutor were already
seated in it. The typewriter was clacking away as usual in the adjoining
room. Only when it halted for a moment could one hear what was being
said in the Superintendent's office.

The Governor had sent for Adèle first. The timber traders had exchanged glances when he did so, and grinned ironically when they
caught snatches of the remarks he was addressing to her in an almost
deferential tone:

". . . you must excuse us . . . your sad bereavement . . . got to be cleared
up without delay . . . a most regrettable affair."

It lasted barely five minutes. A chair scraped on the floor. Adèle came out looking quite composed, went down the steps, and started off toward the hotel.

From within, the Superintendent shouted:

"Next!"

Bouilloux made a face for the benefit of the others and went into the office. With the typewriter rattling away all the time, nothing could be heard of what he said. He came out shrugging his shoulders.

"Next!"

Timar, who was last in the row, was longing to ask an orderly for a glass of water but couldn't summon up the courage.

"What makes it so funny," Maritain whispered in his ear, "is that she used to be the Governor's mistress."

Timar gave no reply and merely moved one seat up when it was the banker's turn to enter the office. He heard the tail end of the interview:

"So you're positive no one went out of the restaurant between midnight and four in the morning? Right. Thank you."

The Superintendent came as far as the door with Maritain and, glancing down the veranda, caught sight of Timar.

"Oh, you're there, are you? Come in, please."

His bullet head was shining with perspiration. Timar followed him into the office, which, compared with the glare outside, seemed plunged in total darkness. After a moment he made out some shadowy forms, one of them seated, knees spread apart, beside a little table covered with glasses.

"This, sir, is the young man, Monsieur Timar, whom I was speaking of just now."

The Governor held out a moist hand.

"Glad to meet you. Sit down. You know, my wife also comes from Cognac; she used to know your uncle very well when she lived there." He turned to a man seated beside him. "Monsieur Timar comes from a very good family." Then, addressing Timar again: "Let me introduce you to Monsieur Pollet, our Public Prosecutor. . . . Can you find another glass, Superintendent?"

In the dim light filtering through the Venetians Timar saw the Superintendent pour out some whisky, then pick up a siphon.

"What gave you the idea of coming to these parts?" the Governor inquired. He was a burly, red-faced man in his sixties, with thick white hair and glowing cheeks that gave him a certain handsomeness. He had the hearty manner often found in elderly men who exercise authority and enjoy it—though not as much as they enjoy the pleasures of the table and strong drinks.

"And what possessed you to join the Sacova, of all companies? Why, they'd have been in the bankruptcy court by now if we hadn't gone easy on the fines imposed on them."

"I had no idea, sir. My uncle . . ."

"By the way, is he running for the Senate at the next election?"

"I believe so."

"Here's to your health, young man! Well, well, you must have a fine opinion of Libreville. Things had been going pretty smoothly for two years, but just lately we've had a whole crop of disagreeable incidents. There was another one last night, I'm told: a gang of drunken hooligans carried off some women and dumped them in the middle of the jungle. Which doesn't make my task any easier just now, when all the natives are up in arms about Thomas's death."

The Public Prosecutor was a much younger man. Timar had already seen him on the night of the show, having drinks with the two Englishmen.

"Any questions to ask him, Superintendent?"

"No, I can't think of anything. As a matter of fact, I sent for him yesterday; that's how we come to know each other. By the way, Monsieur Timar, if you're staying on at the hotel I advise you to be . . . circumspect. The inquiry has brought out certain facts. . . ."

He seemed doubtful whether to go on. The Governor, however, evidently judged Timar worthy of being taken into their confidence, and proceeded:

"It's quite clear Thomas was killed by that woman. We have a piece of almost conclusive evidence. The shell of the bullet that killed him has been found, and it's of the exact same caliber as the Renauds' revolver." He held out his cigarette case. "You don't smoke? A great pity it should be her of all people, but there's no getting away from it; this time we've got to make an example. You see what I mean? We're having all her movements watched. The first slip she makes . . ."

"What puzzles me," murmured the Public Prosecutor, who so far had said nothing, "is what on earth the boy had done to make her act like that. She's a pretty levelheaded woman as a rule and knows what she's about."

Timar would have much preferred to be questioned formally like the others, standing in front of the desk. It passed his understanding why he should always be stared at as if he were a man apart, different from everybody else, and accorded special treatment. These high officials, now, seemed to be accepting him as one of them, taking him into their confidence.

"I don't suppose you can tell us anything? Of course, those fellows in the timber companies all hang together. None of them will say a word; that was only to be expected. At any other time we could probably have managed to hush up the affair. Sure you didn't see anyone leave the restaurant that night?"

"No one."

"You must come to dinner at Government House some evening. My wife will be pleased to see you. Oh, and don't forget we have a club of sorts, just opposite the jetty. Only a one-horse show, of course; still, it's better than nothing. If you ever feel like a rubber of bridge . . ."

He rose to show the conversation was over, with the ease of one used to official interviews.

"*Au revoir*, then, Monsieur Timar. If I can help you in any way, don't hesitate to ask."

Timar made a clumsy, somewhat too ceremonious bow as he went out.

The sea was calm as a lake, and as he gazed at it there rose before his eyes a picture that had been haunting him all the morning—or, rather, not a picture but a map: the map of France. A tiny, compact fragment of the continent breasting the Atlantic. How familiar was that map with its towns, rivers, and *départements* whose boundaries he could have reproduced from memory! The Governor came from Le Havre, his wife from Cognac. One of the timber traders came from Limoges, another from Poitiers; Bouilloux's birthplace was in Le Morvan. Almost neighbors! From his home in La Rochelle he could have reached any of theirs in a few hours. And on a shallow belt of land won from the equatorial bush these men, a handful of Frenchmen, had cast their lot together. Boats came and went, liners and little tramps like the one he'd seen loading timber, precarious links between the jungle and the motherland. And—grim reminder!—on the hilltop overlooking Libreville was the cemetery—no, the imitation cemetery!

Walking past the Sacova warehouse, Timar had a glimpse of the agent at the counter, surrounded by a crowd of black women. They greeted each other with a limp wave of the hand.

And then it was not only a feeling of poignant homesickness that made his heart sink, but a sense of utter futility as well. Everything was futile: his presence here, his struggle to ward off the sunlight seeping in through every pore, the nauseous nightly doses of quinine. Wasted effort. It was as futile to live here as to die here—and be buried in a make-believe cemetery by half-naked blacks.

"What gave you the idea of coming to these parts?" the Governor had asked.

For that matter, what had given the Governor the idea of coming here? And what about all the others, not to mention that Sacova agent in an upcountry station who had threatened to shoot the first man who tried to take his place?

He pictured his friends, girls and young men of his age, basking on the sands beside the mouth of the harbor in faraway La Rochelle.

"Timar? He's got a job in Africa."

"Lucky devil! Wish I was in his shoes."

That's what they probably were saying on the tamarisk-fringed beach at this precise moment when he was dragging himself along, more dead than alive, across a scene of leaden-hued desolation.

He had spoken the truth when he said that Gaston Timar, the *conseiller général* and senator-to-be, was his uncle. What he had omitted to mention was that his father was a municipal employee; that he'd had to leave the university for lack of money, and for the same reason had often been prevented from joining parties of his friends at cafés or in the casino. . . .

The launch that was to take him upriver to his post was still lying high and dry among some native craft. No one was at work on it; no attempt had been made to repair it.

Suddenly, so precipitantly that he was startled by his own temerity, he came to a decision and put it into execution. He had noticed on the Strand a garage where not only cars but also boats were being repaired. Entering, he found a European trying to start up an old car by having some natives push it.

"Can you repair the launch that's on the beach over there?"

"Who's paying? The Sacova?" The man gave Timar a wink that indicated, "Nothing doing."

"*I* shall pay you."

"That's a different story. I suppose you know it'll cost you a thousand francs or so?"

Still egged on by a secret craving to play the man of action, Timar produced his wallet.

"Here's a thousand on account. But I'm in a hurry."

"She'll be ready inside of three days. . . . Have a drink?"

"No, thanks."

So the die was cast; in three days Timar would be setting forth to conquer his new domain—a conquest that, if accounts were true, would be far from simple!

Still the man of action, he flung open the door of the hotel with a brisk, emphatic gesture. The restaurant was empty, bathed in the half-light of all African interiors. The tables were set for lunch, but only Adèle was in the room, at her usual place behind the counter.

Before sitting down, Timar announced, without looking at her:

"I'm leaving in three days."

"Yes? For Europe?"

"No. Upcountry."

To Timar's chagrin, this statement, which had been so agreeable to make, merely brought the usual vague smile to Adèle's lips. He retired in dudgeon to a corner and pretended to bury himself in the newspapers, which he had already read twice. She took no notice of him, but went about her daily tasks, giving orders to the boys, putting bottles in their places, studying the ledger.

He felt outraged and determined to shake her out of her placidity. No sooner had he started speaking than he knew he was making a *faux pas*, but it was too late to retreat.

"Did you know they've found the cartridge case?"

"Really!"

"I mean the shell of the bullet that killed Thomas."

"I knew what you meant." She had her back turned to him and was arranging bottles on the shelf. "Why should that interest me especially?"

They were talking to each other across the empty restaurant, traversed by clean-cut bands of light and shadow. Once again a rush of desire for Adèle came over Timar, and this made him feel at once humiliated and still more annoyed.

"You'd better be careful!" He didn't want actually to frighten her. All the same, he'd have liked to make her show some sign of nervousness.

"Emile!" Her only answer was to call the boy, who ran up at once. "Put the carafes of wine on the tables."

From then on the boy kept moving around between them, his white coat flashing in the shafts of light as he went from table to table.

The timber traders entered in a bunch, then Maritain, then a lawyer's clerk and an English commercial traveler. The usual mealtime atmosphere prevailed, with the addition of some stifled laughs at reminiscences of the night's exploits.

Of all those present, it was Timar who had the most drawn face, the weariest eyes. . . .

After the evening meal he stayed on in his corner, pretending to read. Maritain had left early. The others had settled down with the lawyer's clerk to a game of cards, and at ten they had tramped out in a body. The boy had closed doors and shutters and switched off most of the lamps.

During all this time Timar had not spoken to Adèle or even glanced in her direction.

Now in the shuttered, dimly lit room she seemed nearer to him; they were drawn together by the secrecy and silence of the hour. He heard her lock the drawers of the cash desk and wondered: Did she guess his thoughts, was she looking at him? Had she looked at him now and again in the course of the evening?

He heard the boy say:

"All done, madame."

"Right. Go to bed."

As the power plant supplying the electric light might be stopping at any moment, she lit a candle. Timar rose and walked uncertainly toward the counter. Candle in hand, Adèle moved toward the stairs.

"Coming up?"

He followed her to the door. As she started up the stairs, her dress billowed out, and he caught a glimpse of her bare legs. She stopped on the landing.

"Which room do I go to?" he asked in a rather shaky voice.

"Why, the old one, of course."

The one he had been in first, to which she had come that unforgettable morning, and from which he had been evicted to make room for a corpse. She held out the candlestick; he realized that once he had taken it, it was the end. She would retire to her room, and he would have to go to his. He gazed uneasily at the candlestick, which she was moving to and fro at arm's length to indicate he was to take it.

"Adèle!"

What more could he say? Like a child who whimpers without any reason, he didn't know what he wanted. All he knew was that he was feeling low-spirited, discouraged by everything—though by nothing in particular.

Adèle's face was little more than a white blur in the shadows, but he seemed to see her smile as she walked toward his room and opened the door. She let him enter first, then closed the door behind them and placed the candlestick on the washstand.

"What's the trouble?" she asked.

In the pale candlelight the black silk dress had gleams of rusty red; the outlines of her body showed in soft relief.

"I want . . ." he began, then stopped and, as on the previous night, stretched his arms toward her till his hands were on her shoulders, but this time dared not try to draw her closer.

She did not repulse him, hardly shrank at all from his embrace.

"You see, my dear, what nonsense it was, talking of leaving in three days. Get into bed."

As she spoke she was pulling off her dress. She lifted the mosquito net, tucked in the sheets, patted the pillows. Timar, who had taken off his coat, was seized by a fit of shyness.

Quite calmly she slipped into the bed and lay there waiting for him to join her. Timar's shyness passed; it was as if they had always slept together.

"Blow out the candle, dear," she said.

Five

He awoke feeling much calmer. Before he opened his eyes he had a feeling that the place beside him was empty. He laid his hand on it and smiled, while listening to the noises in the room below. The boy was sweeping it out. Adèle, he supposed, was seated behind the counter. With an effort he sat up in bed, and when he saw the window his first idea was:

"It's going to rain."

Just like Europe. And, as in Europe, he caught himself grimacing at the thought that he'd need an umbrella when he went out. The clouds hung low; a dark, unbroken pall of gray. One had a feeling there was bound to be a deluge within the next few minutes, and yet the air was throbbing with the languid warmth of an unseen sun. No, it wouldn't rain. There was not the least chance of rain for another six months. This was Equatorial Africa. A resigned, if slightly bitter, smile hovered on his lips as he walked to the washstand.

He had had a restless night. Several times he had wakened and gazed through half-closed eyes at the dim form of the woman lying at his side, her head pillowed on her folded arm.

Had Adèle slept? Twice she had made Timar change his position because his breathing grew labored when he lay on his right side. The last time he had opened his eyes it was daylight, and Adèle was near the door, looking to see if she had dropped any hairpins on the mat.

Timar plunged his face into the basin and, after drying it, stared at his drawn features in the glass. Though he did his best to keep his mind off it, he was fretting over a tiresome little problem that had occurred to him in the course of the night. Adèle was certainly giving herself to him—in the accepted meaning of the phrase—but he had the impression that she was doing so in a half-hearted way: as if she were out to give him pleasure, yet did not really enjoy it herself. However, he knew too little about women to come to any conclusion.

He was practically sure she had not closed her eyes, but had spent a sleepless night beside him, staring up into the darkness. What inference was to be drawn from that?

Hopeless problems! He could gain nothing by brooding over them, and he decided to let things take their course, come what might.

As he walked downstairs, he realized that the cloudiness of the sky had made the heat still more oppressive, and he was perspiring freely by the time he reached the door of the restaurant. Adèle was at the counter, the tip of a pencil pressed to her lips. At a loss how to greet her, he held out his hand and said rather uncertainly:

"Good morning."

Her only answer was a flutter of her eyelashes. Then, after moistening her pencil, she went on with her accounts, only looking up to say:

"Boy! Bring Monsieur Timar's breakfast."

Twice he noticed her looking musingly toward him, but perhaps she did not know that she was doing so.

"Not too tired?" he asked.

"Tired? No, I'm quite all right, thanks."

She closed the till, tidied up the papers lying on the counter, then walked around it and seated herself at Timar's table. Before speaking she looked at him again; there was still a trace of indecision in her gaze.

"Are you on very good terms with your uncle?"

She could hardly have given a more unexpected opening to the conversation. So she, too, was interested in that precious uncle of his!

"Yes, on quite good terms. He's my godfather, and I went to say good-bye to him before I sailed."

"Is he left-wing or conservative?"

"He belongs to a group that calls itself the Popular Democrats or something like that."

"I suppose you know the Sacova's bankrupt, or will be one of these days?"

Timar took a sip of his coffee. What an amazing creature Adèle was! He could hardly believe that this woman who weighed her words and spoke in crisp, businesslike tones was the same woman with whom he had slept last night. And yet, on second thought, he asked himself: was she really so very different from the Adèle he had held in his arms?

It was the time when the restaurant was at its homeliest, the hour of small domestic activities, polishing and scrubbing. The noises of the bazaar drifted in, though it was four hundred meters away, and black women could be seen passing along the road, draped in flowing *pagnes* and carrying bottles or packages of food wrapped up in plantain leaves on their heads.

Looking at Adèle across the table, he was struck by her pallor. But probably she had always had that smooth ivory skin that seemed never to have been exposed to the open air. He wondered if in her youth her eyelids had already had that delicate tracery of tiny wrinkles.

Timar, as a small boy, had fallen deeply in love, and even now the thought of it brought a remembered thrill. The object of his devotion had been the village schoolmistress; in the place where he lived little boys and girls went to the same school. She, too, always wore black, and her expression had the same mixture of severity and affection, and above all the same repose—so foreign to Timar's own temperament.

Just now he was yearning to clasp Adèle's hand, gaze into her eyes, indulge in all sorts of silly, sentimental remarks, thinly veiled allusions to the previous night. But the look on her face, exactly that of his schoolmistress when correcting his exercises, overawed him and even made him blush; yet never had he felt he wanted her so much as now.

"As things are, if you go back to France you'll go with empty pockets."

On the face of it a crude, almost offensive remark. But somehow the way she said it made it sound actually affectionate. The crudity was redeemed by an undertone of tenderness that was her special gift, owing nothing to the choice of words or any gesture that accompanied them.

The boy was polishing the brass rail of the bar. Adèle's eyes were fixed on Timar's forehead, but she seemed to be looking right through it at something infinitely remote.

"On the other hand," she continued, "there's a way you can make a pot of money within three days."

Once again, if anybody else had said that, he'd have found it vulgar. She rose to her feet and started pacing up and down the restaurant, speaking in a still more businesslike tone. Clean-cut phrases, spaced out with equal pauses, set to the rhythm of high heels clacking on the tiles. Some would have said a vulgar voice, yet in Adèle's intonation there was something highly personal, if not unique; sometimes low and vibrant, sometimes jarring the ear with a tawdry stridence, it accorded marvelously with her smile.

What was she saying to him? It was all jumbled up in his mind with other impressions: the black women swinging down the road, the black sinewy limbs of the boy in cotton shorts, the thudding of a diesel engine being tuned up somewhere nearby. And there were other pictures, conjured up by what she said. When she mentioned timber felling, he at once saw Bouilloux's face lit up by the oil lamp in Maria's hut.

"One doesn't buy the land; the government gives three-year concessions."

Why, as he looked at her now, did he suddenly remember that glimpse he had had of her some hours before, hunting for hairpins on the floor while he pretended to be asleep?

She took a bottle from the shelf, placed two liqueur glasses on the table, and filled them with Calvados. Did she come from Normandy? he wondered. It was the third time he had seen her drink the Norman apple brandy.

"The early settlers got thirty-year concessions, sometimes even ninety-nine-year leases. Under the present regulations the properties are supposed to revert to the state on the settler's death. However. . ."

She never wore stockings or underclothes, and he had rarely seen legs as white as hers. He kept his eyes fixed on them because he was conscious of Adèle's gaze intent on him, as if she were trying to size him up.

A native came in and put some fish on the counter.

"Very good. I'll pay you next time."

She drank the brandy as if it were a medicine, with a slight grimace.

"There's a man called Truffaut who's spent twenty-eight years on the coast and gone completely native. Married a black woman and had ten or a dozen children by her. He wants to make a move, because nowadays, thanks to motor launches, his concession's only a day's run from Libreville."

Their eyes met. Timar could see she was aware that he was listening inattentively, but only the faintest shadow of impatience showed on her face. She went on with what she had to say, like that schoolmistress in his youth, who, even when the children were not attending, went indefatigably through the lesson to the last line.

In fact, it was the schoolroom atmosphere again, here in the restaurant, and Timar found his thoughts wandering just as they used to do in school, felt the same restlessness and the same resignation. He fell to picturing Truffaut, a patriarchal figure like a Bible illustration, surrounded by his coffee-colored tribe.

"With a hundred thousand francs . . ."

Another picture rose before him—of himself this time, handing one thousand of the three thousand francs that were all he had to the garage mechanic, who now presumably was busy repairing the company's launch.

"His eldest boy wants to go to Europe, to a university. . . ."

Adèle's hand closed on his, as if inviting him to give her a moment's, just a moment's, serious attention.

"I can supply the money. You can supply your uncle's influence. He belongs to the same party as the Colonial Minister. Your uncle can fix it up for us to have preferential treatment and . . ."

When he looked up again she was moistening the tip of her pencil as she had done at the bar. Then she started writing, pronouncing the words aloud, syllable by syllable:

SACOVA IN BAD WAY. RISK LOSING EMPLOYMENT. OPPORTUNITY HAS ARISEN FOR LAUNCHING ENTERPRISE WITH EXCELLENT PROSPECTS. ESSENTIAL YOU SEE COLONIAL MINISTER AND ARRANGE SPECIAL PERMIT FOR TRANSFER LONG-TERM LEASE REGISTERED UNDER NAME TRUFFAUT TO MY NAME. VERY URGENT, AS OTHERS MAY INTERVENE. HAVE FOUND COMPETENT MANAGER FOR WORKING CONCESSION. APPEAL YOUR USUAL KINDNESS TO TAKE NECESSARY STEPS. MY FUTURE ASSURED IF TRANSFER SANCTIONED. MUCH LOVE.

Timar smiled at the concluding phrase. Did Adèle really imagine that in his father's family the menfolk sent one another their love, or that he could address his eminent uncle in such gushing terms?

All the time she was writing he had been conscious of a growing feeling of superiority. It was his turn now to smile with rather pitying condescension, for her attitude, her trick of licking the pencil and laboriously spelling out the words aloud, implied at once a lack of education and the milieu from which she came.

"Is that more or less the way you'd have written it?" she asked.

"Well, yes. But I might change some words here and there."

"Change away!"

She returned to the counter and busied herself there for some minutes. When she came back Timar was rereading the amended telegram, still hardly taking it seriously. Indeed, he never knew at what precise moment he came to a decision, or, for that matter, if he really came to one at all. Anyhow, a little before noon the boy started off to the post office with a telegram, after Adèle had, quite naturally, given him the money for it from the till.

"Now I've got a bit of advice for you. Go and call on the Governor."

He hadn't been out yet that morning, and he jumped at this opportunity, though he had no intention of going to Government House. All the same, he changed his shirt, which was soaked through.

Bathed in bilious yellow light and sweltering in a peculiarly penetrating heat, unlooked-for on a sunless day like this, Libreville was still more depressing than usual. Timar noticed that even the black men's bodies were glistening with sweat.

Instinctively one was always expecting a clap of thunder. But none came. This nerve-racking atmosphere of a storm that never broke might easily wear on for days, or even weeks. And he didn't dare take off his topee to mop his brow.

As Timar walked past the Governor's residence, looking in another direction, the Superintendent, who was standing at the top of the steps, called to him.

"Going to pay a call?"

"How about you?"

"Oh, I'm just leaving. Go and have a whisky with the Governor. He'll be delighted. He's talked to me about you quite a lot."

Despite the languor in the air things moved fast, too fast for Timar's taste or comprehension. Before he knew what had happened, he found himself standing in a big reception room, much like that of any high official in La Rochelle or Nantes. If two or three leopard skins served to strike an exotic note, their effect was almost nullified by the furniture, obviously hailing from big Parisian stores.

"Ah, it's you, young man."

The Governor's wife was summoned, a middle-aged, middle-class lady of no charm, schooled to ply the teapot and dutifully listen to the men talking.

"So you come from La Rochelle. I wonder if you've met my brother-in-law; he's Keeper of Public Records for the *département*."

"Really? He's your brother-in-law?"

Whisky was brought. The Governor sat down, spreading his knees. He and his wife exchanged glances. Timar guessed why the Governor was so pleased to have visitors. He was a heavy drinker, but his wife kept a tight rein on him. When someone called she had to relax it; each time he filled his visitor's glass, he had a pretext for replenishing his own.

"To your health!" the Governor said. "Tell me, what are your plans? The Sacova's on its last legs. Of course this is strictly between ourselves. . . ."

The conversation lasted a quarter of an hour. No reference was made to the murdered black man or the inquiry. Once again Timar had become slightly fuddled before lunch, but he found this condition something of a relief; it gave a comfortable vagueness to his thoughts, blunting their rough edges.

In the restaurant he noticed people eying him with marked interest, which he assumed meant they knew he'd visited the Governor. He caught snatches of what was being said at the other tables:

"So I gave him a hundred francs and a kick on the backside. He went away pleased as Punch!"

Before long Timar learned that the speaker had been alluding to their jungle jaunt. Maria's husband had turned nasty, threatened to have a letter sent to the League of Nations. They had put together the hundred francs among them, twenty francs each. Timar had been left out; they hadn't dared ask him to contribute.

He slept till five, went downstairs feeling queasy, and steadied himself with a couple of whiskies.

"Did the Governor say anything?"

"Nothing of interest."

"I've sent a nigger to tell Truffaut we want to see him, to fix up the deal."

"But we don't know yet if . . ."

"That doesn't matter. If your uncle lets us down, we'll tell old Truffaut to go home, that's all."

Again she amazed him. Could this woman with the businesslike, almost masculine voice and manner be the Adèle with the soft, yielding body, so exquisitely feminine, who had slept beside him?

Shortly before dinner he went out for a stroll along the Strand and saw a man repairing the Sacova launch.

"You'll be able to leave in a couple of days," the man assured him.

A murky dusk had fallen; sea and sky were a poisonous green. The lamps were on in the restaurant when he got back. Then came dinner. After it games of billiards and a card party in which the lawyer's clerk, who had an enormous paunch, took part.

Maritain asked Timar:

"Do you play chess?"

"Yes, a little. But I don't feel up to it tonight."

"Are you ill?"

"I don't know."

The truth was he didn't know what to do with himself, couldn't settle down to anything. He kept on wondering what attitude to adopt toward Adèle when bedtime came. Would they go to the same room, as a matter of course, and sleep in the same bed? That would be like making a habit of it, and somehow Timar didn't relish the idea—especially when he remembered that Eugène had been sleeping his last sleep in that very bed only four days before.

Yet he fretted whenever Adèle left the room or one of the men addressed her by her Christian name.

Most of all he wanted to get an explanation from her—an explanation he did not dare, perhaps would never dare, to ask for—concerning Thomas's death. Was it really she who had killed the boy? Though practically sure it was, he could not bring himself to feel much indignation. All he really desired was to know how and why she'd done it, and also to solve the mystery of her calmness.

The restaurant, with its four electric globes, the click of billiard balls, and the chatter of the card players, was just like any French provincial café. Timar drank two liqueurs, then, taking advantage of a moment when Adèle was pouring out a drink, walked toward the stairs.

"Good night. I'm off to bed."

She looked up. He caught a glimpse of that disconcerting smile of hers, a smile of humorous affection. She was amused by him; she knew perfectly well what he was running away from and why he was doing so. And it did not disturb her in the least!

Contrary to his expectation, he slept soundly. When he awoke the sun was already high. Adèle, in her black dress, was standing at his bedside.

"Feeling better?"

"But how . . . ?"

How did she know he hadn't been feeling well? She sat down on the edge of the bed, as she had done the first time she came, when Eugène and Thomas were still alive. He stroked her dress, then drew her toward him and clasped her for a moment in his arms. Under the flimsy silk her skin was cold; she must have just taken a shower.

"I must go downstairs."

He, however, stayed in his room for two hours. He spent the time dawdling over his dressing, arranging on the shelf various small objects his mother and sister had put in his bags—such absurd and useless articles as a thimble, a set of spools of cotton of various colors.

"Out there you'll have to mend your own clothes."

There was even a box of buttons of all shapes and sizes. Evidently the two women had made the rounds of the haberdasheries in La Rochelle. He seemed to hear his mother saying:

"It's for my son who's leaving next week for the west coast of Africa. He won't have any woman there to look after him, poor boy!"

He went down, exchanged only a few words with Adèle as he had his breakfast, then told her he was going to see the Superintendent.

"A good idea," she said.

No sooner had he entered the office than the inevitable glass of whisky was served him.

"Anything new at your place? Aren't they wondering why the inquiry's hanging fire?"

"No, I haven't heard anything said about it."

"Thomas's father has come in from the bush. A native clerk, who put in two years at a lawyer's office, has got hold of him. He's urging him to press the case and ask for some fantastic sum as damages. By the way, has Adèle got a new protector yet?"

"I have no idea."

"Of course! A fellow like you could live here twenty years without even suspecting the sort of dirty work that goes on behind the scenes in Libreville."

Lunch. Two hours' unrefreshing sleep. An apéritif. Dinner. Once again Timar went up to bed before the restaurant closed. He could not sleep. He heard the murmur of conversation below, the click of billiard balls, the tinkle of small change in the till, then the boy closing doors and shutters. Finally Adèle's footsteps on the stairs. He hesitated, lacked the energy to rise, and spent two more hours sleeplessly, tossing around between the sticky sheets.

He was still asleep at ten in the morning when the door was flung open and Adèle burst in, waving a slip of paper.

"Your uncle's answer. Quick! See what he says."

Hardly knowing what he was doing, he opened the telegram. A cable, sent from Paris:

TRANSFER TRUFFAUT CONCESSION EASILY ARRANGED. ADVISE UTMOST CAUTION RE PARTNERSHIP AND SOURCE OF CAPITAL. PLEASE CONSULT NOTARY IN LIBREVILLE BEFORE SIGNING. BEST WISHES FOR YOUR SUCCESS. GASTON TIMAR.

Timar couldn't have said if he was pleased, vexed, or merely flustered, but he noticed a change in Adèle. Hitherto she had treated him with a certain condescension. Now there was admiration in her eyes. At last she was betraying frank emotion. Her gaze lingered affectionately on Timar; then all of a sudden she kissed him, on each cheek in turn.

"Yes, there's no denying it, you're *somebody*." Handing him his clothes, she went on eagerly: "Old Truffaut's here. He'll take a hundred thousand, with a case or two of whisky thrown in. Look! You've been bitten again!"

She laid a finger on Timar's chest, just above the right nipple, as she had done on that first morning.

"You have the skin of a girl. . . . I'll ring up the notary and make an appointment."

She went out. It was the first time she had shown signs of animation. Timar sat up in bed, staring dully in front of him. There was a clink of glasses below. Old Truffaut was being given drinks to make him easier to cope with.

". . . UTMOST CAUTION RE PARTNERSHIP . . ."

He cut himself shaving, looked in vain for the shaving block, and went downstairs with a smear of blood on his cheek. He had pictured the man he was to meet as a sort of human orangutan, hirsute and unkempt. To his surprise it was a dapper, white-haired little old fellow in well-ironed ducks who rose to greet him.

"I understand it's you who're . . ."

Was it that Timar's nerves were jangled? Was it the little stream of blood trickling down his cheek, or, more probably, the broiling heat, still more trying than usual that morning? He felt queer all over—a peculiar sensation he had experienced two or three times since coming to Libreville. He had noticed it especially when walking on the red laterite road at noon—a feeling that his topee was too thin and, if he didn't get into the shade at once, he would collapse on the spot. His vision grew blurred; everything he looked at seemed to shimmer as if he saw it through a cloud of steam.

The little old man stayed on his feet, leaning against the bar. Adèle watched the two men, a gleam of almost animal satisfaction in her eyes. Standing on a chair, the boy was winding up the wall clock.

Timar sat down, passed his hand across his forehead, rested his elbows on the table.

"A whisky, Adèle."

It struck him that this was the first time he had spoken to her thus in the restaurant: in the same tone and with the same assurance as the timber traders or the fat lawyer's clerk.

Six

"Happy?" she asked, resting her chin on her clasped hands and gazing into his eyes.

He drank off his glass of champagne before replying.

"Yes."

"By this time tomorrow we'll be there."

She spoke slowly, deliberately, keeping her eyes fixed on him. Timar had an uncomfortable feeling that he was being put to the test. Rather peevishly he said:

"Well, you can't say it's my fault we're not there already."

"Don't be unkind, Joe. I never said it was."

He was developing a morbid readiness to take offense and was run down physically as well as mentally. His eyes were unnaturally bright and restless, his features drawn.

"Well, children, how are you feeling?" asked the proprietor, who was dressed up for the occasion in a chef's uniform.

The new owner of the Central was none other than Bouilloux the municipal scavenger. The deal had been arranged in haste on one of the first evenings after it became known that Adèle and Timar had taken over a concession in the bush. The men had been playing cards, cracking jokes from table to table, while Adèle was busy with her accounts. Suddenly Bouilloux had looked at her over his hand of cards.

"Say, Adèle, who's going to run this place now?"

"Haven't had time to think about it yet."

"Are you asking much for it?"

"More than you could stump up, anyhow!"

They laughed. But some minutes later Bouilloux got up and went to the bar.

"We might talk it over, Adèle. I've never run a bar yet, but I wouldn't mind having a shot at it."

Next day everything was fixed up. Bouilloux paid fifty thousand francs in cash and signed IOUs for the remainder.

That had happened three weeks ago, but this was Bouilloux's first night in charge of the hotel. To celebrate it he was dispensing free champagne to all the regular patrons of the establishment. For the first time, too, since Renaud's death, the phonograph had been turned on, and some Europeans from the town had shown up in addition to the usual group.

Timar and Adèle had a small table to themselves; both were in a silent mood. Now and then Adèle would gaze intently at the young man facing her, and the slight frown that settled on her brow betrayed her concern.

Yet though he looked ill, he was only tired, desperately tired. Throughout this last amazing month events had moved too fast for him, and with such bewildering incoherence that he had never fully realized how much was at stake.

Hardly had he begun his stay in Libreville when he was rushed off to a lawyer's office by Adèle, who had drawn her chair up alongside his and started pointing her finger at clauses that needed changes or deletion. The concession was issued in Timar's name, but there was a deed of partnership between him and Madame Renaud, widow, who was bringing two hundred thousand francs into the joint venture: a hundred thousand for the concession and the balance for development expenses. The deeds were properly drawn up, and Timar, who had no objections to make, signed them one by one.

Since then there had been some minor incidents, but, above all, he had settled down into a daily routine that had become necessary to him. For instance, his morning walk along the red road beside the palm groves. He always made a short stop opposite the bazaar, and another farther on, at the place where the native fishing boats came in with their catch, and finally on the jetty opposite the Governor's residence.

The heat made the walk extremely disagreeable, but Timar went through with it as if it were a duty; nor did he fail to speculate on whom he'd drop in on for a whisky. Usually it was the Police Superintendent. As he sat down he would say:

"Don't mind me. Go on with your work."

"I've just finished. What's new? Have a drink?"

In the stuffy, darkened office they chatted amiably. And so it went until the story of the concession and Timar's partnership with Adèle got around the town. Then the Superintendent's manner had changed abruptly. He showed signs of discomfort and smoked his pipe with little fretful puffs, staring at the lines of light and shadow on the floor.

"You know the inquiry's not over yet, and we're still of the same opinion. I don't mind telling you the truth; to make out a cast-iron case we've got to find the revolver. Adèle's hidden it somewhere. But we'll lay hands on it one of these days." The Superintendent rose and started pacing up and down the room. "I'm afraid you may find you've made a mistake, a very great mistake. A young man like you, with a brilliant career before him . . ."

Timar had decided what attitude to take. With a rather superior, faintly derisive smile, he picked up his topee and rose to his feet.

"Let's drop that subject, if you don't mind."

He made a dignified exit, watching his step and assuming the jaunty air of someone who knows quite well what he's doing—till he was out of sight of the police station.

Of course the obvious thing to do, now that he had crossed into the enemy's camp, was to break off relations with the three persons who stood on the other side: the Governor, the Public Prosecutor, and the

Police Superintendent. But something egged him on to continue visiting them; whether a self-defensive instinct, a secret hope, or mere self-assertiveness, it was impossible to say.

At the Prosecutor's the procedure was simple enough. Timar was given three whiskies in quick succession; then his host slapped him on the back.

"You're making a mess of things, my friend. Of course it's none of my business. Still, take my advice and try to pull up before it is too late. Adèle's quite a girl to go to bed with, I grant you. But that's all. She's no damned good for anything else. See what I mean?"

Timar rose and walked out onto the veranda with his jauntiest air.

At the Governor's, however, he had a shock. As he waited in the vestibule, he heard the Governor's voice in the study where they had so often drunk together, saying to the boy who had announced his arrival:

"Tell the gentleman I'm very busy and don't know when I shall find time to see him." He did not even trouble to lower his voice.

Timar's ears were burning, but he showed no signs of his discomfiture. Indeed, even when there was no one to see, he rarely failed to wear a supercilious smile.

He walked back along the Strand to the hotel. The restaurant was in semidarkness, Adèle seated behind the bar, the timber men at their usual places. He went on behaving as if he were an ordinary guest at the hotel, took his meals with the others, and, in public, betrayed no intimacy with Adèle. Like Bouilloux or the one-eyed man he would shout:

"Adèle! A Pernod, please."

For they had taught him to drink absinthe. Other things, too, which had become a daily ritual. At noon, for instance, before they went to the table there was always a game of poker dice at the bar to decide who was to pay for the round of drinks. At night, no sooner was dinner over than everyone settled down to playing cards, and Timar played with them till the party broke up. Now and then someone, he or another, would shout:

"Adèle! Another round, the same again!"

He was even picking up "coaster" tricks of speech. Sometimes the others exchanged glances, as if to say, "He's making progress!"

But there were also moments when Timar was disgusted with himself for sitting on, hour after dreary hour, half fuddled with drink, dealing and drawing cards, in this pestilential atmosphere. At such moments he developed an extreme irritability, took offense over trifles, even at a casual glance in his direction.

It came to this: he had ceased to belong to the other camp, cut himself adrift from officialdom and respectability. But, on the other hand, he knew that even after twenty years of this sort of life he'd never feel at one with the men around him—that lawyer's clerk, for instance, who had a whole vocabulary of card-playing terms that Timar had never heard before.

The doors were closed. Candle in hand, Adèle went upstairs. The power plant stopped humming in the compound. Every night he had a moment's hesitation on the landing. Adèle turned and gazed into his eyes. Sometimes he merely said, "Good night." Then she, too, said, "Good night," handed him the candle, and entered her room, without kissing him, without even shaking his hand.

But there were other nights when he said, "Come!" It was no more than a flutter of his lips, but she understood. Quietly she turned into his room, placed the candlestick on the washstand, drew aside the mosquito net, tucked in the sheets, then lay down in the bed and waited.

"Feeling tired?"

"Not in the least."

He refused to admit it. Actually he could hardly stay on his feet— though all day he had not done a stroke of work, had not exerted himself in any way whatever. He supposed his lassitude was due to a sort of general debility; its symptoms were a feeling of blankness in his head, and accesses of dark, formless fear that sometimes set him trembling as if he were in instant peril.

The worse he was feeling, the more ardently he flung himself on Adèle, and as he strained her to his breast his brain seethed with unanswerable questions. Did she love him? What sort of love could she feel for him? Was she being unfaithful, and if not now, what of the future? Why had she killed Thomas?

But he never questioned her. He didn't dare. He was too much afraid of what the answers might be. For he could not do without her. When taking his solitary walks along the quay, he had merely to think of her white body, naked beneath the flimsy dress, to feel a rush of hatred for every man he saw.

What troubled him most was a curious feeling of being under observation. For some time past she had been looking at him a great deal, too much for his peace of mind. Even in the darkness of his room, when he held her in his arms, he was conscious of her gaze fixed on the pale blur that was all his face could seem to her. From her seat behind the bar she watched him during meals. She watched him rattling dice or playing cards. And for all its affection it was an appraising look, the look of someone trying to size another up.

What were her real feelings toward him? What would he not have given to know!

"You shouldn't drink Pernod. It's bad for you."

But he drank it nevertheless. Precisely because what she said was true, and he knew it.

Before the deal with Truffaut could be completed they had had to wait for certain official documents to come from Paris. These had arrived by the last boat, five days previously. Timar had refused to go to the jetty and had watched from his bedroom window the steamer from France dropping anchor in the bay; his eyes had followed the tender as it approached the quay.

"Since the hotel is sold, there's nothing to prevent our leaving tomorrow if you feel like it," Adèle had said. "It's only a day's run up to the concession."

But they had not left that day, or the next. Timar had made difficulties, invented pretexts, delayed their preparations.

Now he was raging inwardly because Adèle's eyes were fixed on him and he knew very well what she was thinking. She was thinking he was afraid to make the plunge into the unknown, was clinging desperately to the comfortable futilities of his present life.

There was an element of truth in it. These surroundings, which at first had seemed to him so appalling and which he had loathed with all his heart—he now was seeing them from a different angle. He had grown familiar with all their aspects, and much that had struck him as absurd or ugly now appealed to him in a curious way. That grotesque native mask, for instance, hanging in the middle of a wall. There was a subtle harmony between the tones of the mask and its background, vivid white on silvery-gray distemper.

Even the glossy mahogany bar was enough to give an illusion of security; it was exactly like the bar in thousands of French provincial cafés, and behind it was the same array of apéritifs and liqueurs.

He had come to like even his morning stroll, the sights and sounds of the bazaar, his daily halt to watch the fishermen hauling their boats up the beach.

In the restaurant there was a constant buzz of conversation around their table; now and again Adèle, without moving from her place, would answer a remark addressed to her. But all the time, her chin cupped between her hands, she kept on watching Timar as he incessantly smoked cigarettes, jerking the smoke out with little irritable puffs.

"Think you'll have some timber ready for that German tramp that's due in next month?" someone asked.

"Might have," Adèle replied, waving away the smoke that drifted between her and Timar's face.

On this opening night Bouilloux was in a waggish humor; on the tall cook's hat he was wearing he sported a red, white, and blue cockade that enhanced the comical effect.

"Permit me, noble lady, to serve you another glass of our delicious nectar. By the way, what will it cost me now? While I was a lowly customer I paid you eighty francs per bottle. But now I'm the boss. . . ."

Everyone laughed. Drinks were loosening Bouilloux's tongue.

"Will the noble lady sleep here tonight? With our young Adonis? Boy, conduct the Prince and Princess to the royal bedchamber."

Timar was the only one who did not laugh. And yet his discomfort was less mental than physical; he felt as if he were being forced to breathe polluted air. His forehead was clammy with sweat. He had already noticed that he sweated much more than the others, and felt ashamed of it, as of a bodily infirmity. Often when they were in bed Adèle would rub his chest down with a towel, exclaiming:

"How hot you are!"

Not that she herself did not feel the heat, but it was not with the same intensity, and what struck Timar most was that her skin always remained pleasant to the touch.

"You'll see; once we're up there you'll get used to the climate."

By "up there" she meant "in the jungle," but it wasn't jungle life that Timar was afraid of. Since coming to Libreville he had learned that wild animals do not attack men if they can help it, that fewer deaths are due to snake bite than to lightning, and that the fiercest-looking savages in the bush are usually quite harmless.

There were leopards, elephants, gorillas, gazelles, and crocodiles. Almost every day someone came back from a shooting expedition with a skin or two. The insects, even the tsetse flies he saw in the town, had ceased to trouble him much—apart from a brief, purely instinctive reaction of disgust.

No, he wasn't afraid. Only it meant leaving Libreville, the hotel, the bedroom stippled with light and shade, the red stone wharf, the palm-fringed bay, all in fact that he used to detest—including the rounds of poker dice for drinks, the card games laced with Calvados. But all these things had coalesced into a familiar, companionable setting in which he could move at his ease, trusting to his reflexes.

And that was a tremendous satisfaction, for he had become lazy, shamelessly inert. He had taken to shaving only twice a week; he sometimes remained seated in the same chair for hours on end, staring in front of him, his mind completely blank.

La Rochelle was dear to him, but he had left it cheerfully; watching his family waving handkerchiefs on the platform as the train pulled out, he had felt only the faintest pang of regret. But somehow Libreville had got a hold on him; it hurt to wrench himself away. Even when he saw the mail boat anchored off the coast he had had no real desire to leave—though during the next forty-eight hours he had felt exceptionally depressed.

He was disgusted with everything, himself included, and yet that feeling of disgust, like his own supineness, had become something he could not forgo. That was why his anger rose when he saw Adèle gazing at him broodingly. *She* understood—and what she didn't understand she guessed.

Then why did she love, or pretend to love, him?

He rose to his feet.

"I'm off to bed."

He cast his eyes over the other men, all of whom were half-seas over. Tonight, thank goodness, there was no need to wait till closing time. Adèle no longer ran the place. It was for Bouilloux to stop the power plant, have doors and shutters closed, and go upstairs last, candle in hand.

"Good night, gentlemen," he said.

Adèle had risen with him. And that was the first satisfactory thing of the evening; she had done it quite naturally, as a matter of course.

"*Au revoir*, everyone."

"Look here, Adèle, it's your last night. We won't see you again before you leave. How about a kiss all around?"

She walked from table to table, bending her cheek toward each man for a kiss. The one-eyed man, who was the most drunk of the company, started fondling her breast as he kissed her. Adèle pretended not to notice it.

"Coming?" She went to Timar's side.

They walked upstairs together, the voices from the restaurant echoing in their ears. They were occupying the room in which Timar had spent his first night in Africa.

"You haven't been looking at all well this evening. Anything wrong?"

"No. I'm all right, thanks."

The usual ritual. First she drew the mosquito net aside, then made sure there were no scorpions or small snakes in the bed and gave the pillows a shake. Finally she slipped out of her dress, with exactly the same movements as on previous nights.

"Don't forget, we've got to be up by five."

While taking off his tie before the mirror, Timar scanned his reflected self. The glass was tarnished and in the feeble light his face looked ghastly, almost sinister.

Suddenly he remembered Eugène, twice as robust as he, who had come downstairs on the night of the show to announce, in an almost normal voice, that he was dying of blackwater fever.

Looking around, he saw Adèle's naked form. She was sitting on the edge of the bed, taking off her shoes.

"Aren't you going to undress?" she asked.

At that moment he was thinking: Eugène's dead and *she* has survived him. He did not pursue the thought. He preferred to leave things vague. Still, he could not repress a slight shudder of superstitious fear. He was going with her into the bush; he would die like Eugène, and perhaps one day, in this same room, she would be saying to another man . . .

He checked himself abruptly, undressed, and started toward the bed.

"You've forgotten to put out the light."

He went back, blew out the candle.

"What time did you say?" he asked as the mattress creaked beneath his weight.

"Five."

"Have you set the alarm?"

He turned his back to her; his head found the familiar depression in the pillow; he felt the warmth of Adèle's body pressed to his. There was a long silence. To avoid being the first to break it he pretended to be asleep. But his eyes were open, his senses keenly alert. He knew she had not gone to sleep, but, lying on her back, was gazing at the white glimmer of the ceiling.

The silence went on and on, till he was on the verge of sleep. Then he heard a voice say:

"Good night, Joe dear."

He gave a slight start, but did not turn toward her. It seemed to him that the voice was not Adèle's ordinary voice; something had changed. Three or four minutes later he felt the bed shaking; he swung himself onto his back and sat up, peering into the darkness.

"Are you crying?"

The words were followed by a sob—as though his question had at last enabled her to give expression to her grief. Then she said in a stifled voice:

"Lie down, dear. Come. . . ."

She forced him to lie down again and took him in her arms, murmuring through her sobs:

"Oh, why are you like that? Why are you so unkind?"

Seven

Day was breaking when the launch cast off. Looking back, Adèle and Timar saw, outlined against the grayness, Bouilloux's truck, which had conveyed them and their luggage to the jetty. Bouilloux waved to them as the launch dipped into the trough of the first wave, rose, and was lost to sight again.

There was a short stretch of open sea. To enter the river mouth they had to meet the waves head on. A black was at the wheel. He wore a tattered cap, a black cotton bathing suit, and over it an old tweed coat, yet somehow he did not look ridiculous. With an inscrutable expression he was staring straight ahead, his hands—which were paler than the rest of his body—clenched on the wheel.

So long as Bouilloux and the truck were in sight Adèle remained standing; then she seated herself in the stern. She was in her usual costume, except that she was wearing riding boots to protect her legs from mosquitoes.

A dismal start. They had had to rise while it was still dark and had feverishly completed the last-minute packing. And now, to make things worse, the launch was pitching on a choppy sea, in the bleak light of dawn.

They did not speak, or look at each other, but behaved like strangers—in spite of what had passed between them in the night; perhaps, indeed, because of it. There had been a scene that had left a painful impression on Timar's mind, though he could recall none of the details. For he had lost not only his self-control but all grip of reality as well, all consciousness of what was happening.

"Why are you crying?" he had asked. "Do tell me why you're crying."

No sooner had he spoken than something seemed to break loose in his brain and he gave way to a mood of nervous irritation. And the prospect of having to listen to explanations, which would prevent his sleeping, added to his rancor. Then Adèle had said:

"Go to sleep, dear. It's over."

He had jumped out of bed, lit the candle, and poured out a flood of angry words. He accused Adèle of misunderstanding everything. What right had *she* to be miserable? Whereas he had every reason. He had worked himself up into a state bordering on hysteria, and it had been all Adèle could do to calm him down and coax him back to bed. The conclusion had been even more grotesque; he had apologized, pleaded to be forgiven.

"That's all right," she had said. "Don't worry any more, but try to get a little sleep before it's time to start."

He had gone to sleep aching in every limb, his head pillowed on her breast. And in the morning all seemed forgotten; there had been no demonstrations of affection between them—rather, a certain coolness. . . .

They were skirting the palm-fringed coast, half a mile offshore. When the last houses of Libreville were left behind and the launch swung around into the river, they were greeted by a burst of sunlight.

At last the night was ended, and ended with it all its absurd imaginings, phantoms of the darkness. After feasting his gaze on the green luxuriance of the riverbanks, Timar turned to Adèle with happy, laughing eyes.

"It's really quite pretty."

"It's even better farther on."

He lit a cigarette, and a wave of optimism swept over him. Adèle was smiling, too. She rose and moved to his side. They fell to watching the landscape gliding past, while the black at the wheel gazed steadily ahead.

Some canoes were anchored in midstream. They caught a glimpse of blacks, motionless as the craft from which they were fishing. There was a radiant peace, a tranquil ecstasy upon the river, that seemed to call for some majestic music, a swelling anthem, to drown the stridence of a sawmill on the bank and the thudding of the motor.

Slowly, leaving long trails of ripples in her wake, the launch forged upstream, throbbing with the beats of the propeller. They measured their progress by the big trees studding the banks. After the first bend the sea was out of sight, and there were no more sawmills. Only a riot of tangled foliage cataracting down to the water's edge, with queer, exotic trees standing up in its midst: mangroves whose roots spiked up from the mud, man-high; silvery-white silk-cotton trees with triangular trunks, leafless but for a tuft of foliage at the summit. Everywhere rushes and lianas; everywhere, too, a vast, brooding silence through which the steady chug-chug of the engine drove like a plowshare.

"Is it deep here?" Timar asked the steersman, with the naïve curiosity of a Sunday tripper on the Marne.

The man seemed unaware that the question was addressed to him, and it was Adèle who replied.

"About thirty meters, I would guess. But there are places where one scrapes along the riverbed."

"Any crocodiles?"

"One sees them occasionally."

Only one word conveyed his mood at that moment: "holiday." Yes, he was on a holiday. Even the sun seemed gayer than usual.

The first native village came into sight: four or five houses dotting the riverside among the trees, and half a dozen canoes moored in front of them. Some naked pickaninnies watched the launch go by. A woman who was bathing gave a squeal and let herself down, neck-high, into the water.

"Feeling hungry, Joe?"

"Not yet."

He was gazing at the landscape, missing nothing, with the sightseeing zeal of a tourist.

"Show me an *okume* tree."

After a moment she pointed to the bank.

"Oh, so that's an *okume*. Why does it fetch so high a price?"

"Because it's the only timber suitable for plywood. It's sliced up into plies by machinery; nothing's done by hand."

"And a mahogany tree."

"There aren't any around here. But you'll see some farther upriver, in an hour or two."

"How about ebony?"

"The same thing. All the valuable timber was felled long ago along the lower reaches."

"But we still have some ebony trees, don't we?"

The first time he'd said "we"!

"Yes, and mahogany, too. By the way, old Truffaut gave me a tip that may come in useful. The concession's full of orchids. He has passed on to me a book he had about them. Some of the rarer sorts fetch as much as fifty thousand francs in Europe, it seems. And he says he's come across some varieties like the pictures in his book."

Why was the world so beautiful that morning? Everything was going right. Even the landscape seemed to smile upon his prospects, and though the heat was as intense as usual, Timar was not affected by it.

They had been traveling for two hours. A moment came when the launch swung in toward the bank and grounded lightly on the sand.

Imperturbable as ever, the black stopped the engine and flung a mooring rope to a woman standing on the bank, whose only garment was a tuft of dry grass hung like a sporran below her navel. Never before had Timar seen such breasts—so amply yet so gracefully molded, and of such majestic opulence.

"What are we stopping for?" he asked.

This time the black deigned to answer.

"Engine plenty hot. Let 'im cool."

A village of a dozen huts, a few canoes. Timar and Adèle got out, leaving the boatman and the black woman chattering and laughing beside the launch.

In the center of a clearing was a miniature bazaar. Here also reigned a profound calm. Five women, wizened old hags with one exception, squatted beside mats on which their scanty stock in trade was exposed for sale.

Here human life and all that appertained to it seemed dwarfed out of recognition by the immensity of nature. At the foot of giant trees, in the heart of the vast, luxuriant jungle, all that lay on the mats was a tiny pittance: a few handfuls of cassava, some bananas, four or five small smoked fish. The old crones were stark naked, two of them smoking pipes. Another woman was suckling a two-year-old child who now and again turned to stare at the white folk with wondering eyes.

The women took no notice of the strangers and gave no greeting. Adèle, who walked in front, glanced at the little heaps of food and stooped to peer into the huts. She picked up a banana from one of the mats but did not offer to pay for it.

The natives showed no resentment, merely complete indifference. White folk were white folk and, being white, could do exactly as they chose.

Suddenly Adèle said:

"Wait for me a moment."

She walked toward the largest hut, which stood a little apart from the others, and entered it with a decided step. Timar remained behind, looking down at the bazaar mats.

Did she know somebody here? What could she be after in that hut?

He soon got tired of contemplating the old women and their wares, and walked back to the launch. The black man had gone ashore. Timar could see him, a dark form glimmering in a haze of broken lights where the sunbeams splintered on a tangle of lianas. He was standing with the naked black girl, very close to her, but they touched each other only with their fingertips. They were laughing, uttering slow, deep-throated sounds that seemed meaningless, mere grunts of satisfaction.

Not to appear to be watching them, he retraced his steps. Adèle had not come back yet. He thought of going to join her in the hut but didn't dare. At a loss what to do, he took a pack of cigarettes from his pocket. A small black hand was promptly stretched toward him, and he saw a pickaninny gazing up at him pleadingly.

Three meters away an old woman also put out a suppliant hand, and when he tossed a cigarette toward her there was a general scramble. All the women gathered around, giggling and squealing, trying to push one another away. As soon as a cigarette fell, they went down on their knees and fought for it in the dust. Just then Adèle came up. When she saw the women mobbing Timar she laughed.

"Let's go," she said.

On the way back to the launch she picked up another banana from one of the mats. Only when the engine had been started up did he think of asking:

"Where did you go?"

"Don't bother your head about that!"

"Know someone in that village?"

"I'd rather not talk about it."

The air was getting sultrier as the launch proceeded upstream. Timar felt a sudden twinge of annoyance.

"So you refuse to tell me why you went to that hut?" he muttered sulkily.

She smiled. A coaxing, affectionate smile.

"I promise you there's nothing for you to worry about."

Why did an incident that he thought he had forgotten come back to his mind just then? One of his earliest amours. He had been spending a few days in Paris just after leaving school and had let a woman take him to a bedroom in a squalid hotel on Rue Lepic. When they came downstairs again and were in the vestibule, the woman said to him, as Adèle had said just now:

"Wait for me a moment, please."

She had gone into the manager's office. He had heard a murmur of voices, and then she had come back to him, looking pleased.

"Off we go."

"Why did you go there?"

"Don't you bother about that. That's *my* affair."

Only several years later had he understood: she'd stopped in at the office to collect her cut of the room bill.

Why had he associated in his mind that juvenile experience with the incident at the village? Really they had nothing in common. And yet, when he noticed Adèle looking more cheerful than usual, the face of that other woman, whose name he had never known, rose again before his eyes.

"Who lives in that hut? A black?"

"Why, of course. There aren't any Europeans in these parts." When she saw him frowning, she added: "Don't look so put out, dear. I assure you there's nothing to worry about."

Under the torn, grease-stained cap the black's eyes were set upstream as he swung the wheel this side and that with small skillful jerks.

No doubt the mystery that Adèle was making over her visit to the native hut was not the only reason for Timar's sudden change of mood. The sun was straight overhead and the movement of the launch had ceased to give an illusion of coolness. And there was something exasperating about the unbroken sameness of the scenery on the banks.

He had breakfasted on a can of tepid *pâté* and a slice of stale bread. But he had already drunk two glasses of whisky and water.

It was the time he always needed a pick-me-up. Toward noon a sinking feeling invariably came over him, and not till he had had a drink or two did he feel relatively fit.

Adèle still seemed to be in high spirits, in almost too high spirits. Timar felt there was something forced in her gaiety. Usually she didn't take such pains to be entertaining. She was simpler, more placid, as a rule.

What could she have been up to in that hut? And why now this all too obvious eagerness to please and humor him?

Timar had stretched out in the well of the boat, and as he watched the treetops sailing past he felt the old rancor surging up again.

"Give me the bottle."

"Oh, Joe, please . . ."

"Well, what's the fuss about? Can't I have a drink if I feel thirsty?"

With a sigh she handed him the whisky bottle, murmuring so softly that he hardly caught the words:

"Be careful, dear."

"Careful of what? Of the black women I may choose to visit in their huts?"

That was unjust, and he knew it. For some time he had been catching himself talking to her in that vein, but the impulse was too strong to resist. At such moments he suffered an immense self-pity, saw himself as a victim with a legitimate grievance against the whole human race.

"*You*, anyhow, have no right to lecture me, considering you earned your living making people drunk!"

There was a gun beside him, ready for use if any game showed up;

but, except for a few birds, they saw no sign of animal life on the banks. There were, however, swarms of flies, which he had to keep brushing off his face. Each time one settled Timar gave a start, for he knew that tsetse flies abounded along the river.

Suddenly he jerked himself up peevishly and flung off his coat, under which he wore only a short-sleeved undershirt.

"Don't do that, Joe. You'll make yourself ill."

"That's my business."

He was no cooler without the coat; indeed, he felt hotter. But at least he didn't have that sticky feeling of sweat congealing on his chest and under his arms. It was now a different sensation, as if he were being toasted in front of a blazing fire, and he found it almost agreeable.

"Give me the bottle."

"Please don't drink any more. . . ."

"I told you to give me the bottle."

He was all the more insistent because he knew the black man, for all his air of stolidity, was listening to everything they said, sizing them up, him and Adèle. Defiantly he took a long draught from the bottle, then stretched out on the wooden seat running along the side of the boat, after rolling up his coat to serve as a pillow.

"Do listen to me, Joe. The sun's awfully dangerous and . . ."

But he refused to listen. All he wanted was to sleep. He felt so utterly exhausted that he would rather have died where he lay than move; even the effort of sitting up would have been too much for him.

His thoughts grew blurred, and he sank into an uneasy, vision-haunted doze. He had the strange feeling that his body had become part of the solid world and curious things were taking place within it. Was he a tree, or a mountain? Once or twice he opened his eyes and saw Adèle trying to protect his head from the glare.

Suddenly there was a hideous crash, a sort of cataclysm that jerked him off the seat on which he lay. He jumped up, his fists clenched, a red mist before his eyes.

"Can't you leave me in peace, damn it?"

The launch was listing heavily, water swirling past the gunwale at a dizzy speed. In a sort of half dream Timar saw the black man step over the side. It flashed into his mind that he'd been lured into a trap; they had him at their mercy. He flung himself at the black, crashed his fist against the man's face, and sent him spinning into the river.

"So, that's the idea, is it? Well, you won't get away with it like that!"

The river wasn't even a meter deep at that point. The launch had run aground in a rapid. As the black rose laboriously to his feet, Timar fumbled for the gun that he had had beside him in the morning.

"You murderous swine! I'll teach you to play your dirty tricks on me!"

But then his foot caught on something hard, a seat or, perhaps, the gun for which he was searching. He staggered. As he fell forward he had a fleeting glimpse of Adèle's face, stricken with panic and, above all, despair. His forehead bumped on some hard object.

"You swine!" he repeated, and then everything began to swirl around him, spiraling up and up, while from the zenith masses of solid darkness came toppling down.

Even after that, however, he had spells of partial lucidity. Once when he opened his eyes he found himself seated in the belly of the launch; the black man was propping him up while Adèle, raising his arms with difficulty, passed them through the sleeves of the cotton jacket.

Another time he saw Adèle's face bending above him. He was stretched on his back. Something damp and cool lay on his forehead; there was a hot, tingling sensation in his hands, along his spine and chest.

Then he felt himself being carried, not by two people, but by a whole crowd—ten, fifty, perhaps a thousand men—he'd no idea! An army of black men, their lean legs swinging to and fro, to and fro, level with his eyes.

They spoke a language he had never heard before, and Adèle spoke it, too.

Beyond the swinging legs were trees, myriads of trees, and then came a great darkness, pungent with the fumes of rotting leaf mold.

Eight

When he sat up in bed, it was not at Adèle, who was helping him to rise, that he looked first, but at the walls of the room. Pale-green walls. So it hadn't been a dream. And if one detail was true, all the rest must be true.

Timar frowned. His lips set in a hard line, and his eyes grew stern. He saw himself as a just but ruthless judge.

"How many days have I been here?" He watched Adèle's face, as if hoping to catch her out.

"Four days . . . But why on earth are you glaring at me like that?" she added with nervous laugh.

"Bring a mirror."

While she was getting it he stroked his unshaven chin. He had grown much thinner. His eyes had changed beyond recognition, and now, after making only a few movements, he felt quite exhausted.

"Where's Bouilloux?" He knew he was alarming her; he was conscious of the effect of his staring, fever-bright eyes—and he gloated over her dismay.

"Bouilloux? But this isn't Libreville. We're at home, at the concession."

"Answer my question, please."

He had plenty of other questions up his sleeve. Subtly misleading questions, the kind a lawyer uses to trip up a hostile witness. For, while he had been in bed with a temperature of 105°, he had seen and heard all sorts of things! And now he'd ascertained that the walls were really green, he knew where he stood!

It might have been the second day—anyhow, it was quite soon after their arrival—that Adèle, after tidying up the room, had made a wry face at the walls. Then he had heard her moving around on the ground floor, giving orders, and in the afternoon she had come back and distempered the walls and ceiling in green.

Evidently not realizing that his eyes were open and he was watching her, she had called someone in to help with the ceiling.

"Well, what about Bouilloux?" He was determined to get that question answered first; then he had another one to spring on her.

"He hasn't been here, Joe, I assure you."

He let it pass for the moment, though he was positive he had heard Bouilloux's voice downstairs, had even heard him say:

"Poor little Adèle, it's such a shame!"

And then one night hadn't he seen her holding the door ajar to let the man take a peek at him?

"What about the Greek?"

About him, anyhow, she couldn't lie. Timar had seen him not just once, but four or five times. A tall young man with sleek black hair and a bronzed face with a curious tic, he was continually blinking his right eye.

"Constantinesco?"

Obviously. After painting the walls she had made him hold the ladder while she did the ceiling. Timar had seen him quite clearly.

"What's he up to here?"

"He's our foreman. He used to work here before, and I've kept him on. Look here, Joe, do try to rest. You're dripping with perspiration."

But he felt a need to speak, to ask more questions, cut her to the quick, get his own back. There had been moments he shuddered to recall.

That night, for instance, when he had felt colder than he'd ever have dreamed it possible to feel. Though he was soaked in sweat from head to foot, his teeth were chattering, and he'd cried:

"For God's sake put some more blankets on! Light a fire!"

Adèle had answered gently:

"You've got four blankets already, dear."

"That's a lie. You want me to die of cold. Where's the doctor? Why haven't you sent for the doctor?"

Then had come a period of hideous nightmares. Timar saw Eugène in a bed beside him, eying him cynically and saying:

"You ain't used to it yet, sonny. But you'll get the hang of it in time. I'm an old hand, you see."

Get the hang of what? What the devil did he mean? Timar flew into a rage, shouted furiously for Adèle, who was sitting at the bedside. Oh, if only he could have killed her! But he had no weapon. She was laughing at him. So was Constantinesco, who tiptoed in and asked in a whisper:

"Still 105?"

Anyhow, he had decided to clear all that up right away. The fever had left him. There was nothing wrong now with his sight. Just to make sure, he blinked his eyes.

"I've had blackwater fever, haven't I?"

"Don't be so absurd, dear. Blackwater isn't a bit like that. All you had was a bad case of dengue. Almost everybody has one when he first comes out. It's not serious." Ah! So it wasn't even serious! "You must have been stung by an insect on the river, and being exposed to the sun all day made it come on with a rush. One runs a terrifying temperature, but nobody ever dies of it."

He was anxious to discover if she had changed in any way. He even leaned out of the bed to see if she was wearing her boots and saw that she was.

"Why are you dressed like that?"

"I have to go to the workshed now and then to see how they're coming along."

"What workshed?"

"Where the tools are being repaired."

"By whom?" He gave the words a threatening intonation.

"Constantinesco. He's a skilled mechanic."

"Who else?"

"We have two hundred native hands; they're busy putting up their huts just now."

" 'We'? Whom do you mean by 'we'?"

"Why, you and I, of course, dear."

"Ah, yes . . ."

He had thought she meant herself and the Greek. He was on the verge of collapse; the sweat that covered his body was cooling down. Adèle was gazing at him, clasping his hand tightly. There was no sadness in her look, only a hint of smiling reprimand, as when one sees a child behaving in a silly way.

"Now, Joe dear, do try to sleep a little. Tomorrow you'll be able to get up. Dengue comes on with a rush, but it goes away just as quickly. So we'll have a nice quiet talk together, you and I, tomorrow—about the concession. Everything's going well."

"Come and lie beside me."

For a fraction of a second she hesitated; knowing the bed smelled of illness, he felt secretly ashamed.

"Closer!"

He had half closed his eyes, and, seen through his eyelashes, her face was blurred. His hand slipped to the soft curve of her leg.

"Don't, Joe! You're not well enough yet. . . . Please!"

But he refused to listen. Somehow he had to assert his rights, to prove that she was his. Clammy, shivering, with loveless passion, he had his way. When he sank back exhausted, his whole body aching as if he had been beaten, she rose quickly, straightened her dress, and said without a trace of ill humor:

"Really, you're impossible, my dear! A regular spoiled child!"

He didn't hear her; all he heard now was the thudding of his heart, the pulses throbbing in his temples.

Next day, helped by Constantinesco and Adèle, he came downstairs and settled in the big living room. The Greek's slimness and jet-black hair gave him the look of a young man, but only at a distance; a closer view revealed a deeply lined face, ugly, irregular features. He was deferential, not to say obsequious. Whenever he spoke he was obviously courting Timar's approval.

The house was almost empty. Most of its previous contents, nearly all the furniture, had been thrown out and burned. All that was left was a large mound of charred debris in the compound. Only bare essentials had been kept—tables, chairs, a couple of bedsteads—and these had needed thorough disinfecting.

Timar was installed in a comfortable armchair. The room was surrounded on three sides by a veranda, and the walls, inside and outside, were in plain red brick, giving it a typically colonial aspect. On one side the ground fell away sharply toward the river, near which about a hundred and fifty blacks were putting up their huts. On the other three sides the house was ringed in by the jungle, less than fifty meters away.

"Where does Constantinesco sleep?" There was an undertone of suspicion in his voice.

"In a hut just like those native huts, behind the shed."

"Who does he have his meals with?"

"Oh, he has a native woman with him. They live together."

Conscious that Adèle was watching him, he looked away to hide the smile of satisfaction he could not repress.

"You see, Joe," she said, "it's just as I told you: we have a decent, well-built house to live in, the concession is the best in Gabon—I've gone around it, so I know—and I have no trouble in getting all the labor we can want. Now you must take it easy for a few days. Constantinesco will see the work is done properly."

"Right."

But all the same he felt depressed. He would need more than a few days' rest to make him capable of working like the others. He watched them walking around quite unconcernedly under the blazing sun, whereas the mere thought of facing even the milder glare on the veranda made him shudder.

How different he was from Adèle, who seemed so thoroughly in her element here, so brisk and at ease in her black silk dress, white sun helmet, doeskin boots! She chattered away with the blacks in their own language and handled them as if she'd spent her life among them. But he—where did he come in?

She had found some worm-eaten books among the things left behind by Truffaut; they included novels by de Maupassant and Loti, and a chemistry text.

He found the fiction almost unreadable, and yet in Europe he'd devoured it. Here, he wondered why any publisher had thought the pages worth the printer's ink.

When Adèle came back to the living room she found him engrossed in the book on chemistry.

Days went by, all alike as far as Timar was concerned. Each morning he came downstairs, by himself or leaning on Adèle's arm, and settled in the big living room, rising now and again to take a few languid steps.

By this time everybody else was at work; at six o'clock Constantinesco had rung the bell that summoned the men to their tasks. From time to time he came into the house, a hunting crop in his hand, and reported his progress to Adèle, who never offered him a chair and treated him in a strictly businesslike manner.

"I've kept twenty men here to finish off the huts," he would say, "and sent the rest of them to the jungle. The tables for the house will be ready by this evening. Oh, and I've sent the hunter out to shoot a buffalo; that will keep the men in meat for a day or two."

Timar was staggered by the amount of work that had been accomplished during his illness. As far as he remembered, every time he had opened his eyes he had seen Adèle at his bedside. Yet somehow all the while she had been superintending everything, keeping the natives at it. Marvelous woman! True, she looked paler, and the rings around her eyes were darker.

"We'll have to rig up a shelter for the launch, or one day when we need her we'll find the engine rusted through."

"I've thought of that. Two men are setting up the posts just now, to the left of the group of huts."

When he had gone, Adèle and Timar were left by themselves. But even then her hands were never idle.

"You'll see, Joe; you'll get used to it. This is one of the healthiest spots in the district. In three years we'll be back in France with a million francs in the bank."

That was precisely what dismayed Timar; he didn't have the slightest wish to return to France. What on earth could he do there? Where would he settle down? Would he go back to his family? Would he stay with Adèle?

Somehow he had struggled through the two novels left by Truffaut, and these had proved to him how utterly unfit for civilized life he had become. He simply couldn't picture himself going to La Rochelle, or sitting talking to his friends on the terrace of the Café de la Paix. And as for living with Adèle in Paris or anywhere in France—that was equally unimaginable.

No, he preferred not to think about it. Better to let things drift. Meanwhile he tried to adapt himself to his surroundings, to form habits, to get used to upcountry life. In a few days he'd be able to go out. He'd supervise that swarm of natives on the riverbank, go into the jungle and point out the trees to be felled.

But he was still too run down. After he had been walking for five minutes around the room, the floor of which, like the walls, was in red brick, his head began to swim and he staggered back to his chair.

"Sure Bouilloux didn't come here while I was ill?"

"Why on earth should Bouilloux want to come here?" She turned it aside with a laugh, as when he'd asked her why she entered that native hut, with the result that he was perpetually torn between confidence and mistrust—between love and hatred.

When she was not with him he grew restless, kept going to the veranda to see if he couldn't catch a glimpse of her. It was always a relief when he saw Constantinesco walking in a different direction from the path she had taken when leaving the house.

The third day was filled with adventure: though Adèle did her best to dissuade him, he went out of doors. He saw sixty black men harnessed to a huge log of *okume*, hauling it down on rollers to the river.

The first tree! *His* first tree! Though his legs were giving way beneath him, he prowled around the naked blacks, their acrid odor tickling his nostrils. Behind them Constantinesco, in rubber boots as usual, was shouting orders in a native dialect. The log moved forward, six inches at a time. Their bodies streaming with sweat, the men were panting.

"How much is that worth?" Timar asked Adèle, who had just appeared.

"About eight hundred francs a ton, but you have to deduct three hundred for the cost of transport. That log will bring us in about two thousand francs profit."

It surprised him that such an enormous mass of wood was not worth more.

"And if it were mahogany?"

There was no reply. She was listening. Then he, too, caught the hum of a motor in the distance.

"That's a launch."

The log had got stuck halfway down the bank; some men had stepped into the river and were tugging at the ropes. The sun was low. It would be quite dark in half an hour. Constantinesco, who had twenty years' experience of Gabon, had long since taken off his topee.

Just as the log, after being stoutly tethered like a captive monster, was allowed to take the water, a motor launch swung around the bend and grounded on the bank.

In it were two blacks and a European, who jumped on shore and shook Adèle's hand.

"Settled down already? Quick work!"

Once a month this motor launch came up the river, bringing food and mail to the European timber traders, calling at the stations along the riverbanks.

"You must be thirsty. Come to the house."

The young man had a glass of whisky, then produced from the satchel he had with him a letter addressed to Timar. It had a French stamp; the address was in his sister's writing. He read the first few lines before thrusting it into his pocket.

My dear Joe,

I am writing from Royan, where we are spending the day. The sun is shining, but not half so brightly, I'm sure, as in the wonderful country where you are now, you lucky fellow! The Germain boys are here, too, and I'm going surf-riding with them this afternoon. . . .

"Nothing for me?" asked Adèle.

"No . . . wait a minute. Do you know, old Bouilloux's engine conked out on the way down and he had to spend a night in a native village?"

Timar swung around and looked at Adèle, but she did not flinch or show the least concern.

"Really?" she murmured. But when she spoke again her sprightliness seemed forced. "What's the latest from the big city?"

"Nothing much."

They were sitting in the big red brick room, sparsely furnished with three long chairs and a table. On the riverbank the blacks who had dragged the log were mopping their brows and laughing. Constantinesco was walking toward the bell whose clang announced the start and the conclusion of the day's work.

"Except, of course, that business about Thomas," the young man added.

He seemed disinclined to continue. He gave the impression of being an amiable, rather gauche and shy young man. For three weeks every month he traveled up and down the river in his motor launch, in the company of the two natives, usually sleeping in a tent pitched in some jungle clearing. He had begun life as a commercial traveler in France and since coming to Libreville had opened up a busy trade with the villages of the interior, where he sold complete trousseaux, on the monthly-installment plan, to dusky beauties. Hail-fellow-well-met with all and sundry, but somewhat tactless, he carried on his business in the tropics exactly as he had done in the hamlets of Normandy and Brittany.

"They've found out who killed him. Another nigger, needless to say."

Adèle still betrayed no emotion of any kind. Her gaze shifted from Timar to the young trader.

"He was arrested two days after you left, or, rather, the headman of his village turned him over to the police. Since then there's been no end of palavers. The headman brought along some witnesses."

Timar was watching the young man's face and breathing heavily.

"Well, what's come of it?" he asked.

"Oh, the nigger's acting dumb, pretends he knows nothing about it. All the questions have to be put through an interpreter, and that holds things up no end. Still, one thing's proved, all right: the revolver was found buried in his hut. And there are witnesses who say that he and Thomas were after the same girl.

"By the way, what can I let you have? I've got some excellent canned lobster. If you're short of gas, I can spare twenty cans."

Timar had ceased to listen. He was gazing at Adèle, who replied:

"Right! I'll take the gas. And two bags of rice for our men. Do you have any cigarettes? I can sell them here at three francs a pack."

"I can give you some at a franc a pack in cases of a thousand."

Night was falling. The river was veiled in shadow. Constantinesco was starting the electric power plant; the lamps glowed red, then yellow.

"Tell me," Timar said. "That man they've arrested, what village does he come from?"

"Please, Joe . . ."

"Why shouldn't I ask him if I want to?"

"A little village downstream."

Timar got up and went out on the veranda. He could just make out the black mass of the log breasting the current like a ship at anchor. The blacks were kindling a fire in the middle of the ring of huts. The forest around the house was inky black but for the white, wraithlike trunk of a solitary silk-cotton tree tapering skyward.

All his senses were abnormally alert, and, though the words were whispered in the commercial traveler's ear, he distinctly heard what Adèle said:

"You blundering fool!"

Nine

"Stop, Joe, please!" she whispered. "He can hear everything."

The room was totally dark except for the glimmering rectangle of an open window, divided into two unequal parts by a thin, pale line, the trunk of the silk-cotton tree.

They were lying on their backs, and Timar knew that she was staring up at the ceiling. The traveler could still be heard moving around in the adjoining room, where they had given him a bed for the night.

"I insist on knowing the truth." Timar spoke harshly, without moving; he, too, was gazing up into the darkness. All he could feel of Adèle was her elbow, the smooth curve of a hip.

"Please wait till tomorrow. When we're by ourselves, I'll explain. . . ."

"No. You must tell me tonight."

"Tell you what?"

"You killed Thomas. . . ."

"Hush!"

She did not stir; there was not the faintest tremor in the body stretched out beside him.

"Well, will you speak? You killed him, didn't you?"

Holding his breath, he waited. Then there was a faint sound in his ear, a whispered "Yes."

He swung himself around, groped in the darkness, caught her roughly by the wrist.

"You killed him, and you're letting an innocent man take the punishment. You went to that hut to . . ."

"Joe dear, please! You're hurting me. . . . Oh!"

A cry of physical pain. He was crouching over her, belaboring her with his fists.

"Listen! I promise you that I'll explain everything, yes everything, tomorrow."

"And supposing I don't want explanations? Suppose I never want to see you again, to hear your voice, to . . . ?"

He choked, his arms went limp, he was sweating as never before. And suddenly he saw red, felt a wild desire to do something desperate—to crush her life out, to pound the wall with his bare fists. He started hammering on the wall. Adèle implored:

"Please, Joe! That man will hear. I'll tell you everything. But please stop doing that."

His knuckles were smarting. He turned, stared blankly toward Adèle. Was he looking for some other object on which to vent his rage?

Their bodies showed as two white streaks in the darkness. They had to strain their eyes to make out each other's faces. Adèle went up to Timar and sponged his chest with a handkerchief.

"Do go back to bed. You'll only bring the fever on again."

She was right; he felt it coming on. And the memory of the nightmare days he'd been through sobered him. He saw the dim shape of a chair beside him, drew it to him, and sat down.

"Speak away. I'm listening."

He did not want to be too near her, lest he should start using violence on her again. He had resolved to keep calm, but his calmness was precarious, at the mercy of any impulse.

"Do you really want me to tell you all about it, right away?" She felt bewildered, uncertain what to do with herself, whether to stand or to sit. Finally she sat down on the edge of the bed, about a meter from Timar.

"You didn't know Eugène. He was always jealous, especially near the end, when he knew he didn't have long to live." She spoke in a whisper, because of the man in the next room.

"As jealous as all that? And he used to shake hands with Bouilloux and the Governor and all the other men who've slept with you."

He could not see her, but he heard her catch her breath and swallow hard. For a while the silence was so intense that they could hear, through the window, the low, incessant murmur of the forest.

Adèle blew her nose. When she spoke again her voice was firmer.

"You can't understand. It wasn't the same thing. What I felt for you was . . ." She hesitated. Perhaps the word that hovered on her lips struck her as too romantic, too remote. "It wasn't the same thing," she repeated. "Anyhow, Thomas saw me coming from your room. He asked for a thousand francs. He'd been wanting the money for some time, to buy a wife. I refused. On the night of the show he tackled me again and . . ."

"You killed him," Timar muttered in a pensive tone.

"He threatened to tell Eugène."

"So really it was for my sake . . ." he began.

"No," she said quite frankly. "I shot him because I didn't want any bother. How could I guess Eugène was going to die that night?"

Timar had to struggle to maintain the unnatural calm he had imposed on his throbbing nerves. He stared hard at the window, the spectral tree trunk, listening to the palpitating silence of the jungle.

"Come to bed, Joe."

Unbelievable! Again he felt a mad impulse to cry out, batter the wall with his fists. She had confessed to murder, and now she was asking him to lie beside her—side by side with her warm, naked body!

It was so simple. She'd killed a man just to avoid bother. And now he,

Timar, was making trouble for her with his questions, keeping her from enjoying the peace she'd earned. When he referred to the Governor and the rest of them as her lovers, she didn't deny it. Only it wasn't the same thing! *He* couldn't understand—unlike her husband, who, for his part, saw the difference immediately.

There were moments when he felt on the point of flinging himself on her, thrashing her with what strength was left to him.

"And what about the poor devil they've arrested?"

"Would you rather I was sent to penal servitude?"

"Keep quiet. No, not another word! Leave me in peace."

"Joe!"

"Don't speak—please!"

He went to the window and leaned against the frame, letting the night breeze play on his sweating body. There were silvery gleams on the river, near the floating log. For five minutes or so he stayed thus; then he heard a voice behind him:

"Aren't you coming to bed?"

He stayed where he was without answering. But he wasn't thinking about Adèle all the time, still less about Thomas. All sorts of ideas kept coming to his mind. It struck him, for instance, that quite near him leopards were prowling, while at this very hour in the seaside towns of France, people were walking home from the casinos. Some of them, perhaps, had been to films about African life, with banana groves, a planter with a truculent mustache, love scenes to the accompaniment of exotic music.

His thoughts strayed back to the floating log. When the rainy season came it would be rafted down the stream along with all the other logs that had been felled. Hundreds of them would be hoisted on board a red-and-black tramp steamer moored at the river mouth. On their way down they would drift past the village with the hut that Adèle had visited.

How they had laughed, with dazzling flashes of square white teeth, the black boatman and that handsome girl with the big breasts, on the riverbank!

It came to this. All his life Eugène had tolerated his wife's having lovers, provided these were influential folk, people who might be useful to him. That, anyhow, was plain as daylight. And, after all, wasn't that, in a way, their métier, hers and his?

Timar looked around, got the impression that Adèle's eyes were open, and resumed his musings. He was feeling cold and sleepy. To keep himself in countenance he lit a cigarette.

What was to be done? The concession was registered in his name, and to obtain it he had employed his uncle's influence, dragged in his family.

Out there in the jungle there were elephants roaming, Constantinesco had informed him that afternoon.

Had Adèle slept with Constantinesco, too? . . . He heard her breathing more heavily, in a more even rhythm, and took the opportunity of slipping into bed.

Had he been mistaken? He sensed a slight change in her breathing now that he was beside her. Perhaps she had only pretended to sleep, or else he had awakened her and she was trying to control her breath.

Their limbs were not touching, they were invisible to each other, but each was intensely conscious of the other's nearness. The least tremor of their bodies was multiplied a thousandfold.

"She doesn't understand," he mused. "She's guided by her instincts and the life she has led. And yet she never seemed the sort of woman who cheapens herself with everybody. Somehow you'd never think it of her—all the men she's been with!" That was what had impressed him most, even more than the languor, the almost fluid softness of her body: that amazing sense of freshness, almost of purity, which emanated from her.

His thoughts swerved back to the forest. What did elephants do at night? Prowl around the jungle like the other, smaller, animals? Or did they sleep? . . . He could hear the sound of his own breathing, and it was like a sleeper's; perhaps he was dozing off at last. Adèle's hand crept toward him and settled on his chest, just above his heart.

He did not move or give any sign that he was not quite asleep. He knew no more till the jangle of the bell roused him abruptly, and sunbeams fretted his eyelids.

He opened his eyes. He heard the men padding across the sand toward the forest. He ran his hand over the place beside him. The sheets were stone-cold; Adèle had evidently been up for some time.

Before rising he spent a quarter of an hour gazing up at the ceiling and was amazed at his peace of mind, the tranquillity of a physically exhausted man or a convalescent who has burned up all his energy in a serious illness. His knuckles were still sore; the skin over the joints was cracked.

At last he rose, struggled into a shirt and trousers, brushed his hair. In the living room he found the commercial traveler reading an old newspaper while breakfasting by himself.

"Sleep well?"

Timar was looking out for Adèle, but he could see only Constantinesco, who was in the compound superintending half a dozen blacks at work.

"Has she gone out?"

He had nothing to say to Adèle, yet he missed her presence. Even if only to gaze at her indifferently, he wanted her around.

"She's left a note for you," said the young trader.

At that moment Timar was standing opposite a mirror hung on the wall, and he could see his face. Its impassiveness at once annoyed him and made him thrill with pride. And yet, within, his mind was in a ferment.

"A note, you said?"

"Here it is."

It struck Timar how like herself was Adèle's handwriting—clean-cut, vigorous, yet graceful.

Joe dear,

Don't be alarmed. I have to go to Libreville, but I shall be back in two or three days at the latest. Look after yourself carefully. Constantinesco will see to everything. And do please try not to worry.

Your Adèle

"So she took the morning train?" said Timar ironically.

"She must have started before daylight, in the launch. When I got up an hour ago, she was already gone."

Timar made no comment. He was pacing up and down the room, gazing straight in front of him, his hands linked behind his back.

"It's nothing serious, you know. As a matter of fact, I brought her the message. The magistrate wants to take her statement in connection with that murder case. That's all."

"Ah, you brought the message, did you?" Timar stared at the poor young man with withering contempt.

"There won't be any trouble. Now that the man has been sent up for trial, the case is as good as over. Only, as a formality, they have to take her evidence, since it was her revolver. . . ."

"Obviously."

"Hey! Where are you off to?"

Timar went straight to his room, shaved and dressed himself with a briskness he had not displayed for some time. When he came down he accosted the young trader, who was still at breakfast.

"Can you rent me your launch?"

"Sorry, no. I've only just started my tour."

"Two thousand francs?"

"Nothing doing, I'm afraid."

"Five thousand?"

"Not even if you offered me fifty thousand! It's the firm's boat, you know, and I'm carrying mail. So you see . . ."

Timar walked out without giving him another look. He heard an engine running in the shed where Constantinesco was at work and found him lying flat on the ground, tuning up the dynamo.

Without a word of greeting Timar asked him point-blank:

"Did you know what was going on?"

"Well, as a matter of fact . . ."

"Right. Now, listen! I want a canoe and boatmen at once. Have them ready within five minutes."

"But . . ."

"Did you hear what I said?"

"When she left she told me . . ."

"Am I the master here, or not?"

"I assure you, Monsieur Timar, that I'm only acting in your own interest. In your present state . . ."

"What about it?"

"Sorry, sir, to annoy you, but it's my duty to prevent your going . . ."

Never had Timar felt so calm. Yet never had he had so many reasons for losing his self-control. He felt quite capable at that moment of shooting the Greek in cold blood, or stepping into a canoe and making the journey by himself if boatmen were not forthcoming.

"Please, sir," the man implored. "Think it over! In a little while . . ."

"I want the boat *at once*."

The day was already warming up. Constantinesco put on his sun helmet and walked out of the shed toward the huts. The trader's launch was still alongside, and for a moment Timar thought of commandeering it. But why complicate matters?

The Greek was giving orders to some natives standing around him. They gazed at Timar, then at their dugouts, then downstream.

"Well?"

"They say it's late; they'll have to stop for the night somewhere on the way down."

"That's all right."

"They also tell me that it'll take them three days to come back, against the current."

The Greek was gazing at Timar with more compassion than surprise.

Probably he had run across similar cases, and his attitude toward Timar was that of a doctor watching the progressive stages of a disease.

"Very well, sir. I'll come with you."

"Certainly not. You must stay here and look after the concession. I want the work to go on as usual. Got it?"

Constantinesco had some more talk with the men, then came back to Timar, who was standing in the shadow of the house.

"May I give you some useful tips, Monsieur Timar? For one thing, don't let your boatmen touch a drop of alcohol, and you'll be wiser, if you don't mind my saying so, to keep off drinks yourself. In a motor launch you get a certain amount of coolness, because of the speed of the boat, but in a dugout the sun can be really deadly. Take the cot, in case you have to sleep out in the bush. There's another thing. . . ." He seemed much jumpier than the man he was addressing. "Look," he broke out, "you *must* let me go, too. I don't feel easy about you. Do you realize how badly your coming like this will complicate things? Madame Adèle, if she's left to herself, will get through it, but . . ."

"Ah, so she's been confiding in you?"

The Greek looked worried.

"No. I'm used to that sort of thing. I know the ropes, you see. But you're fresh from Europe, you don't see life here from the same angle. When you've spent ten years in Gabon . . ."

"I'll amuse myself shooting niggers, eh?"

"You'll be compelled to, one day or another."

"Have you killed many of them?"

"I came out to this country at a time when a white man in the jungle was greeted with a shower of arrows."

"And you returned the greeting with your revolver, I suppose?"

"One man I know had to throw a dynamite cartridge into a bunch of them to save his skin, and it was a near thing at that. . . . Have you had breakfast? No? Take my advice, have something to eat first; think it over. . . ."

"And give up my damn-fool idea?" Timar jeered. "Thanks all the same . . . Hello! You're still here, are you?"

The trader had just walked up to them. He asked Constantinesco: "Any message for up there?"

By "up there" he meant the higher reaches, where the jungle grew steadily denser. He turned to Timar.

"Incidentally, I'll be seeing that old nut you were sent out to relieve. You know whom I mean? The man who says he'll shoot on sight . . ."

Some minutes later the three Europeans came down together to the river's edge, beside the *okume* log. A black man started up the engine of the trader's launch; it shot out into midstream, then headed up the river.

Twelve men stood waiting beside a dugout in which they had stowed some palm oil, cassava, and a few bunches of bananas. The air was sweltering. Each puff of wind scorched like a fiery caress. Constantinesco looked Timar in the eyes, as if to say:

"There's still time."

Timar lit a cigarette, then held out the pack to the Greek.

"Thanks, I don't smoke."

"Too bad."

Futile remarks, to bridge an awkward moment. Timar's eyes strayed to the slope leading up to the house, to the newly built huts thatched with plantain leaves, then to a window on the upper floor, facing the silk-cotton tree: the window from which he had gazed upon the night-bound jungle.

"Let's go," he suddenly exclaimed.

The boatmen understood and settled down at their places in the dugout, with the exception of the head boatman, who waited to help the white man step on board. Constantinesco hesitated for a moment, then blurted out:

"Excuse me, Monsieur Timar, but . . . Look here, you're not going to give her trouble, are you? I mean, make things harder for her. She's such a splendid woman, I mean!"

Timar's eyes grew hard. He was on the point of answering, then changed his mind. What would be the use? With a sullen look he settled into his place in the dugout while twelve elaborately carved paddles flashed across the light into the river.

The house dwindled rapidly into the distance; soon no more could be seen than the red tiles of the roof, then nothing of the building, only the silk-cotton tree soaring in lonely eminence. The last time he had gazed at that silvery-white trunk had been when he was lying in the dark at Adèle's side, holding his breath, feigning sleep. He had kept silent. Yet perhaps a word would have sufficed, even a slight movement of his arm. . . .

And after a while, when her hand had stolen humbly to his breast, he had pretended not to notice it. Now he felt like weeping with rage, desire, despair, and, above all, yearning for her presence.

They were on the same river, no more than thirty kilometers distant from each other, she in the launch, he huddled on the bottom of the swaying dugout. The twelve paddles rose in a cataract of shining drops, hung for a moment poised in sunlight, and came down together with a great splash, while the boatmen broke into a plaintive, dirgelike melody, unvarying, timed to a massive rhythm that was to continue, without a break, until the day was out.

Ten

A small, gap-toothed black man rattled off a phrase of thirty words or so. When the paddles rose he stopped abruptly, and some moments of suspense ensued during which the dugout glided onward soundlessly, without the least vibration. Then, like the response of a litany, twelve voices answered, in deep-throated unison, while the paddles struck the water twice.

After that the little black man would start reciting again, in a high-pitched singsong voice.

The rhythm of the song tallied, beat for beat, with the two successive paddle strokes. There was always the same lull, followed by the same outburst of lusty voices. After this had happened some five hundred times, Timar started listening, frowningly intent, for the moment when the soloist was to recite, to see if he could make out some of the words. And soon he discovered that the man had gone on repeating exactly the same phrase, word for word—or almost so—for an hour on end.

He reeled off his patter without the slightest sign of interest in what he was saying, whereas the expressions of the others varied with each response; in turn they grinned, looked thrilled, or entertained, or even awed. And always, as the twelve paddles hung in midair before the downward stroke, the twelve voices broke out at precisely the same moment.

After a while Timar discovered that he was watching these black men with an interest that was almost cordial; taking stock of his mood, he was amazed at its serenity. He was angry with himself for feeling thus; it was like an act of disloyalty to someone, to himself, to this supreme crisis of his life.

All the same, he very soon returned to observing the black men as before, but with the difference that now he fixed his interest on each individually, one after another. There were stretches of smooth water and of rapids. Sometimes, though the boatmen strained their utmost,

the dugout swung out sideways across the current. Each thrust of the
paddles gave the boat a violent jar, and at first Timar found these
constant shocks highly disagreeable. Gradually he got used to them, as
he got used to the smell of the black bodies. Most of the men wore
loincloths, but three were stark naked.

The blacks stood facing the prow, and their eyes remained fixed on
the white man sitting there. Timar wondered what, if anything, they
thought about him personally, or if all white men were alike to them.

As for him, this was the first time he was observing blacks otherwise
than as decorative figures, tattooed so deeply that the intricate patterns
stood out in relief, some wearing big silver earrings or quaint objects
fixed in unlikely places—for instance, that boatman with a clay pipe
stuck like a flower in his fuzzy hair.

Today he was looking on them as human beings, individuals with
lives of their own, and just now this seemed quite simple, thanks,
perhaps, to the primeval forest, the dugout, this river that for untold
centuries had borne such primitive craft seaward. Yes, these naked
savages were far more understandable than the trouser-wearing blacks
of Libreville, or bus boys like Thomas.

The scene was picturesque to a degree, and Timar could imagine his
sister's and her girl friends' little shrieks of wonder, his male friends'
more sophisticated smiles, if they could have seen a snapshot of it. It
answered exactly to the homekeeping Frenchman's conception of a
settler's life in Equatorial Africa: the dugout; Timar seated in the bows,
clad in white ducks, sun-helmeted, and over him an awning of plantain leaves which, without being told, the boatmen had fixed up in the
prow, and which gave him, if not a majestic, an imposing air; and
finally, having the most local color of all, the twelve naked, or all but
naked, blacks standing in a line along the boat.

Actually the impression it produced on Timar was less of pictur-
esqueness than of something natural and restful which soothed his
nerves, took his mind off himself and his perplexities. Sounds, scents,
and pictures crowded in upon him, but all were blurred by the intense
heat and the glare, which constrained him to keep his eyes half closed.

He saw these blacks as simple, primitive folk with a certain natural
bonhomie and a childish sense of fun, who set up an ear-splitting din
whenever the dugout passed a village or even a solitary hut. At such
moments they drove the boat ahead at an amazing speed, whirling their
paddles aloft and emitting yells of triumph that evoked answering yells
from the riverbank.

At one point some young blacks plunged into the river and started trying to race the boat, which easily outpaced them. One of them shouted to Timar, "Cigarette, massa! Give cigarette!," making the gesture of flinging something into the water. Timar tossed a handful of cigarettes toward them and, looking back, saw the youngsters fighting for the sodden cigarettes in a cloud of golden spray, then scrambling up the bank with their trophies and capering away into the forest.

Above all there had come over him a great calm, though, for some reason he could not fathom, it was tinged with sadness. Yet some capacity for emotion remained, even if it lacked a specific object, and it pleased him to feel that he was on the point of understanding this mysterious continent that until now had brought out only his least healthy instincts.

On entering a stretch of sluggish water the boatmen brought the dugout alongside the bank and made it fast. Though wholly unprotected and incapable of making himself understood by his men, Timar did not have the faintest sense of apprehension. On the contrary, he had a feeling that they had taken him under their wing, were treating him like a child for whose safety they were responsible.

Standing waist-high in the river, they sluiced their heads and shoulders, took mouthfuls of the water, gargled, and spat it out. Timar felt that he, too, would relish the coolness of the water on his lips. But as he bent down, the gap-toothed black, noticing what he was up to, shook his head.

"No good for white man!"

Why wasn't it good for white men? Timar had no idea, but he felt sure the advice was sound. And when the black told him to eat, he obediently opened a can of corned beef. The blacks merely nibbled cassava or bananas.

Nothing could be seen in the darkness of the jungle, but on one occasion Timar noticed the boatmen listening intently. When he gave them a questioning glance, one of the men made a comical face, guffawed, and said:

"Macaque!"

The monkey kept out of sight, though its movements could be heard in the branches. The sun was still high. Two or three times Timar took a pull at the bottle of whisky, and gradually he relapsed into an agreeable, dreamy languor.

His eyes were still open and he fell to amusing himself by comparing the boatmen's faces with those of people he had known at home, tracing resemblances between them. From France his thoughts drifted back to Libreville: to the Governor, the Superintendent, Bouilloux, and

Adèle. And for a while the spell of peace was broken. Shutting his eyes, he felt the fever stirring in his blood.

Anger seethed up in him and he felt a need to egg himself on with drink to vent his rancor, had sudden impulses to shout, to inflict pain on someone—on himself as well. At one such moment he half opened his eyes and yelled at the blacks, who were singing the usual refrain:

"Shut up! Stop that blasted noise!"

At first the words took no effect. The gap-toothed man, however, who knew a few words of French, turned to the others and interpreted the order. No one protested. They stopped singing and gazed at the white man. No emotion was visible in the twelve pairs of eyes, yet somehow they made him feel uncomfortable, especially when he raised the whisky bottle to his lips. . . .

So those were the people whom any European shot down without the least compunction. Of course they were no better. Hadn't he been assured that every one of them was capable of poisoning a man without a qualm—in all innocence?

The word "innocence" brought a smile to his lips. That hit it very well. Here in Africa no idea of guilt attached to murder. Whites killed blacks, and blacks killed men of their own color and sometimes, but rarely, a European. Without malice. Innocently. Because one must.

Still, none of them had a murderer's face. Wait, though! What about that little gap-toothed fellow? He might well have killed someone. With tiny hairs, steeped in venom and mixed into the victim's food, that gradually bored through the intestines. Or else by scattering poisoned thorns in front of his victim's hut.

There was another halt. Timar was puzzled at first. Then two men came and arranged some plantain leaves behind him: they had stopped to protect his neck from the sun, which was nearing the horizon. Quite likely those two men were poisoners, too!

He took another drink, but the whisky did not have its usual effect. There was no rush of fury, no tension of his nerves. He lay down and, closing his eyes, gave himself up to melancholy brooding.

Only when night was falling did he come back to reality. Darkness spread across the sky like a patch of oil on a blue lake; there was no interval of twilight. They had come to a wide reach of the river where the current was slow. Beside the dugout, and under the trees lining the banks, the water was inky-black. Somewhere in the far distance a tom-tom thudded mournfully. As the white man had forbidden them to sing, the boatmen made do with a grunt at each stroke of the paddles.

It was useless for Timar to ask where they were. Even if they understood the question, he would not understand their answer. Where would he spend the night? What was he doing here? Adèle had promised to be back in two or three days. Why had he not waited for her at the concession, where at least there was another white man?

What would he do in Libreville? He had no idea. The truth was, he had resented being treated like a child, he was afraid of being looked upon as an accomplice, and above all, he was jealous. What had brought Bouilloux to the concession? And why had Adèle lied about it?

His unrest was returning. He gulped down some tepid liquor and felt so nauseated that for some moments he had to lean over the side of the dugout.

As night closed in, the boatmen ceased to keep stroke as accurately as before. They paddled feverishly, and sometimes two paddles clashed in midair. And instead of gazing at the white man they kept looking toward the forest, up to the moment when with one powerful thrust they drove the boat against the bank, amid the undergrowth.

Not till he had gone ashore did Timar recognize the spot. It was the village where he and Adèle had landed on their way upstream, where Adèle had entered a native hut and eaten two bananas.

A fire was burning in the middle of the clearing around which stood the huts, and shadowy forms squatted beside it. Timar dared not make a move until the little gap-toothed man, whom he had come to look on as his cicerone, had rejoined him.

When Timar's boatmen landed, the villagers seated around the fire merely looked over their shoulders at the newcomers, without moving. Three of the boatmen started toward the village, carrying Timar's camping gear. The little man beckoned to him to follow.

Few words, twenty at most, were exchanged between the villagers and the boatmen. The little man made a tour of inspection, opening doors and peeping inside the huts; none of the occupants thought of protesting. Finally he halted at a fair-sized hut and ordered out of it one of the old crones whom some days previously Timar had seen sitting beside their mats in the village market place.

The black man threw outside the mats strewn on the floor of the hut, then, pointing to the interior, said gravely:

"This plenty good place."

After seeing Timar's gear installed, he slipped away, leaving Timar alone in the hut. Only in the center could he stand without stooping. The air was thick with smoke; a fire had evidently been burning in the hut all day, and the ashes were still warm.

He spent ten minutes wrestling with the cot, whose mechanism baffled him, before he managed to set it up more or less securely. Then he went to the door and stood there smoking a cigarette. His boatmen, who had joined the villagers at the fire, were finishing their meal— shadowy forms crouching around the fire and plunging their hands into bowls of boiled cassava.

Someone was talking away as volubly as the chorus leader on the boat. Perhaps, indeed, it was he; the voice was just the same. After rattling off three or four sentences, all of which sounded alike, he would stop abruptly. A roar of laughter from his audience replaced the boatmen's chorus.

Was he talking about Timar? For a while Timar suspected it; then, after watching certain faces lit up by the firelight, he came to the conclusion the toothless man was talking gibberish. Timar could have sworn that he was uttering strings of disconnected words merely for the joy of saying them, and that the others were intoxicated by the jingle of the words and their own laughter. Like children who talk for talking's sake, without caring whether the words make sense.

In the air was the pleasant tang of burning wood and some highly aromatic spice unknown to Timar, and also the musty smell of the black bodies. And it was this last that most affected him.

He had no appetite and did not bother to open any of the canned provisions he had brought. Now and then, however, he took a sip of whisky, followed by a cigarette. Against the dark mass of the hut his white form must have been extremely noticeable, but no one cast a glance in his direction. Humiliated, almost aggrieved, by their indifference, he called out, "Cigarette?" and threw one toward the nearest black.

He had found twenty packs in the cot; presumably Constantinesco had stowed them there. The black man picked up the cigarette, rose to his feet, grinning, and exhibited it to the others. An old woman looked around and, after a moment's hesitation, held out both hands toward Timar.

He threw a whole packful, and there was a general scramble, a melee of capering shadows in the firelight. Some bolder spirits ran up to him, holding out their hands, laughing and squealing. There were women among them. Timar felt their bodies rubbing against him and, standing on tiptoe, stretched out his arms above their heads, dropping cigarettes at arm's length.

There were little girls as well, with tiny, budding breasts. The musty smell grew more pronounced as the crowd of women closed in on him. But Timar had eyes only for the handsome black girl he had seen on the trip upriver, talking to the driver of the launch. Though not so bold as the youngsters, she had come fairly near, and her eyes implored him to throw some cigarettes in her direction.

Timar launched three packs in succession. One was caught before it fell; a dozen pickaninnies scrambled for the others in the dust among the grownups' legs.

The black girl had big, firm breasts. Her hips, like a young man's, were narrower than her bust, but her belly was still plump, protuberant as a child's. They gazed at each other, she and he, across the surging throng. She was saying something in a pleading tone, and he could only smile in answer.

After tossing the last pack toward her Timar shouted:

"Finished! No more left."

But they went on holding out their hands until the gap-toothed black explained that the white man had no more to give them. Then the crowd dispersed as quickly as it had gathered, and a moment later all were squatting around the fire again. Thick lips pursed around the cigarettes, the blacks gazed proudly at the smoke curling up from their mouths. Often the same cigarette was passed from mouth to mouth among three people.

Timar remained standing in front of his hut. He was ready for bed, but the memory of the black girl would not leave his mind; what he felt was not mere lust but a vague yearning for affection. He found a low bench and sat down on it. He had forgotten to keep any cigarettes for himself. Women dragging small children after them were going into the huts, which very soon grew silent. No more wood was placed on the fire. The boatmen were the first to move off.

Where would they sleep? Timar neither knew nor cared. The girl seemed to have vanished, and he peered into the shadows, wondering when she had left the others and which hut she had entered. He was still quite calm, still mournful, but with a sadness of no thoughts, like an animal's. Only five or six dark forms lingered beside the fire, and no one spoke.

Suddenly a tremor passed through his body. There, quite near him in the shadows, was the black girl, leaning against the door of the next hut and looking toward him. Had she guessed? Had she taken a fancy to him, or was she merely submitting to his whim because he was a white man?

Bouilloux, he imagined, would merely have jerked his thumb toward the door of the hut, then followed her in. Timar was too shy; nor did he dare to move toward her. He was conscious of his inexpertness; in any case, he had not yet made up his mind whether he really wanted her.

However, he had risen to his feet. And now he saw her take a step toward him, hesitate, ready to retreat if he seemed not to want her. He remained standing at the door of the hut, leaving enough space for her to pass; with a slight movement of his hand he pointed to the interior.

She stepped hastily within, halted, her bosom heaving; none of the blacks by the fire had looked around. Timar thought of shutting the door but did not dare. And he was tongue-tied, knowing she would not understand a word of what he said.

She had ceased looking at him and was gazing at the floor of beaten earth, demure as a European girl visiting a man for the first time! With the difference that, but for a wisp of dry grass hung below her navel, she was naked.

He patted her shoulder. The first time he had touched black skin deliberately. It was smooth as satin, and he could feel the ripple of the muscles underneath.

He pretended to hunt for cigarettes, though he knew he had none left. He wanted to give her something and could see nothing but a Thermos bottle. Exploring his pockets, his fingers came in contact with his watch, a present from his uncle. It had a chain attached; he unhooked the chain and held it toward her.

"Present for you," he mumbled.

He felt terribly perplexed. Looking over his shoulder, he noticed that the blacks around the fire had gone. What was he to do? How to set about it? Did he really want her? He had no notion! His mouth was dry. The girl was standing motionless in the center of the hut, the gold chain resting in the palm of her hand.

He came near her again, fondled her shoulder as he had done before, then let his hand stray downward and cup her breast.

She neither encouraged nor discouraged him. She was staring at the gold chain.

"Come!"

He walked toward the cot. She followed submissively.

"Are you . . . ?" He wanted to ask her if she was a virgin, for in that case he'd have refrained. But he could not make her understand.

"Sit down."

He pressed on her shoulder to force her onto the edge of the bed. Extraordinarily embarrassed, he picked up the whisky bottle and tilted it to his lips, then stumbled to the latchless door of the hut and pushed it closed.

Eleven

Quite early in the morning's run something happened that put Timar in a bad humor. They were shooting some rapids, and the boatmen took a mischievous delight in paddling for all they were worth, their mouths agape as much with laughter as with the effort. The dugout hurtled along like a speedboat. At the foot of the rapids there was a bend in the river and a patch of backwater, which they proposed to take with a rush.

A branch trailed in the water just ahead, and its dense leafage made it look like an island in midstream. The dugout could have cleared it easily, but out of devilment the blacks headed toward it, plying their paddles more frantically than ever.

Twelve pairs of big round eyes beamed with childish glee as they gazed at the half-submerged branch, then at the backwater, then at the white man's face. Their idea was to crash through the leafage and give Timar and themselves a little thrill.

They negotiated the first meter or so of the branch without mishap, but then there came a violent shock, and the boat seemed to leap out of the water, listing heavily. It was so sudden that Timar had no time to figure out what had happened. There was no great danger. Before it could capsize the natives righted the dugout by making a concerted lunge with the full weight of their bodies to one side. But they had shipped a good deal of water, and Timar found himself sitting in a pool.

Abruptly he lost his temper and started hurling futile insults at the boatmen. The knowledge of what a sight he must look, splashed with muddy water from head to foot, added to his vexation.

Another source of annoyance was that he had no cigarettes. And rankling always at the back of his mind was the memory that he had slept with a black woman.

She had slipped away some time in the night; on waking he had found her gone. When he went to the dugout, followed by his boatmen, he had seen a group of women and children on the riverbank. Among them was the girl, but she had not dared to make herself conspicuous by showing signs of recognition, making any gesture.

When he caught sight of her he all but stopped, then thought better of it and went to his seat in the bows, while the men, paddle in hand, lined up at their places in the boat.

He saw the girl edging away from the others and looking hard at him.

The twelve paddles struck the water, and instantly, it seemed, the dugout was twenty meters out, in midstream. Only then did Timar see the girl raise her arm or, rather, move it hesitantly a few inches from her body in a timid gesture of farewell.

The hull had been slightly cracked by its impact on the snag, and one of the men had to keep bailing out, his two hands cupped together.

After watching him for some time Timar opened his last can of corned beef, threw the contents into the stream, and handed the empty can to the black.

The boatmen gaped at him, dumfounded. They knew that a can of corned beef cost a good twelve francs, about what one of them earned for a fortnight's work. The man who used the empty can as a scoop seemed fascinated by the white flash of the metal as he plunged it into the water, and the others cast envious glances at him.

But Timar had lost interest in the blacks. As he neared his goal, the old anxieties came crowding back into his mind. Presumably Adèle had reached Libreville fairly early in the previous afternoon, since the launch had been aided by the current. Where had she slept? With whom had she dined? What had she been doing all morning?

During the first few hours his adventure with the black girl still lingered in his mind. But as the sun crossed the zenith his thoughts were all of Adèle. Above all he was haunted by memories of that last night, the night they had spent side by side staring up at the ceiling, feigning sleep but keeping watch on each other in the darkness, every sense keyed to its highest pitch.

He would have liked to learn at what time they expected to reach Libreville, but couldn't make the gap-toothed man understand his question. The hours dragged on. Twice he had them stop the dugout and readjust the awning of leaves above his head. At one moment he asked roughly:

"Why the devil don't you sing?"

As the boatmen failed to understand, he himself started the refrain. Then they exchanged happy glances, as if a load had been lifted off their minds, and the little man launched into a recitative even more prolix than his previous efforts.

But now Timar didn't listen. After five minutes he ceased even to be aware the men were singing. . . . Why had Bouilloux come to the concession? Why had Adèle left without letting him know?

He dozed off occasionally but never slept for long. In fact, it was not sleep but a sort of coma brought on by the glare and heat. At last the sun dipped behind the forest, there was a brief dusk giving an illusion of coolness, and the milder light restored its colors to the landscape. A quarter of an hour later darkness had fallen, and Libreville was not yet in sight. Timar was furious, all the more so because it was impossible to make the boatmen understand his questions.

After they had been moving for an hour along the night-bound river, two specks of light appeared, one green, one red. Higher up, in the sky, another light, not a star, was twinkling. And a moment later Timar heard a clatter of footsteps on a deck and the sound of a phonograph.

The black bulk of a cargo steamer loomed up overhead. They had entered the estuary at the point where Timar had seen the other steamer loading timber. The record ran out, but they forgot to stop the phonograph; in the stillness the scratching of the needle could be heard distinctly.

A searchlight blazed out, and the vivid beam raked the surface of the river for some moments before settling on the dugout. It was directed from the captain's bridge. Leaning on the rail, three men watched the boat glide past. They evidently noticed that there was a European on board, for someone shouted:

"Hello! Who's there?"

Timar kept silent—why, he didn't know. He remained crouching in his corner, lost in gloomy meditation, then gave a start as the dugout came into rough water and started pitching.

Before him lay the open sea and on his right a string of lights, a wharf like any other, like a real wharf in Europe, and motor headlights flitting through the night.

The dugout grounded on the sandy beach where the fish bazaar was held each morning, among the native craft. Blacks in coats and trousers, others in Arab dress, were walking on the quay. For Timar it was like a homecoming after long absence in foreign parts.

The red road glowed darkly under the electric lamps; the green of the foliage was so vivid as to seem artificial. It reminded Timar of a stage setting, especially the palm grove, whose leafage, lit up from below, stood out in bright relief against the velvety black sky.

And there were noises: voices, footsteps, rumbling wheels; a passing car whose passengers did not even glance to see who was the lonely traveler coming up from the dark foreshore.

The three naked blacks hastily wound strips of muslin around their loins, while the others dragged the boat higher up the beach. Timar wondered what to do. Should he tell his men to go back to the concession, or keep them here? Was it up to him to provide them with food and lodging? Would they manage to fend for themselves in a town? He went to the gap-toothed man and tried to get some information.

"You can sleep here?" Putting his hand against his cheek, he bent his head to one side, closing his eyes.

The black man grinned, made a reassuring gesture.

"Me go see madame."

Of course! The decision rested with her, and Timar had no say in it. The boatman had put him in his place, and his place was that of a sleeping partner. "Madame's" satellite! He wasn't even a real "coaster," for he could not speak the native language, he hadn't taken a pot shot at the wild duck flying overhead during their journey down the river. Instead, he had lavished cigarettes. He hadn't knocked a single black man down. He hadn't pointed out the places to stop. In fact, he was an amateur, a greenhorn.

"Me go see madame."

Turning his back on the man, Timar stepped onto the lamplit road. His clothes were soiled and shabby as a result of the accident to the dugout. There was a two-day growth of beard on his chin. Just as he came under a street lamp he heard a car slow down. A face peered from the window, and he recognized the Police Superintendent, who did not stop the car, though he looked back twice as he drove on.

The hotel was less then three hundred meters away. In a dark corner of the quay a black woman in a blue *pagne* was giggling as she rubbed herself against a smartly dressed black man. She was plump, like most city-dwelling black women, and her fuzzy hair was built up into an elaborate coiffure. She had lost the respect for Europeans that comes naturally to almost all upcountry natives, and though she stared at Timar in silence while he walked by, he heard her going into shrieks of laughter when he was a few meters away.

Trivial details! Still, in his present mood, they affected him unpleasantly and added to his rankling sense of grievance.

At the hotel the phonograph was on full blast, playing a Hawaiian record that he had heard fifty times before, and billiard balls were clicking.

He halted for a moment on the threshold, frowning, in an unconscious effort to give himself an intimidating air. A wasted effort; nobody had noticed his arrival. The potbellied clerk and one of the timber traders, who were playing billiards, had their backs to him and partially masked him from four other men seated at a table near the phonograph. The four men had their heads bent together like people engaged in a secret and important conference. The clock pointed to eleven. There was nobody at the bar.

Stepping back to make a stroke, the clerk collided with the counter, and looked around.

"Hello! So you're here!" The tone was cordial enough, but the man was obviously flustered. He shouted to the others, "Look who's blown in!"

Everyone stared. They didn't seem particularly surprised, but there was no mistaking their vexation. Timar was the last person they wanted to see just now. Some glances were exchanged; then Bouilloux rose and walked toward him, exclaiming with false heartiness:

"Well, well! What a surprise! How the devil did you get here? By plane?"

"By boat."

Bouilloux gave a little whistle of admiration for the feat. Then he held out his hand, saying:

"How about a drink?"

Timar shook hands with him reluctantly, not daring to ignore the other's gesture. He could see that Bouilloux had had an inkling he might come, and that this was what he had dreaded most.

The billiard players went on with their game. Someone put another record on the phonograph.

"Had your dinner?" Bouilloux inquired.

"No . . . I mean, yes. I'm not hungry."

"Look, my boy, you haven't been taking your quinine regularly. One has only to look at your eyes. Damned foolish!"

Bouilloux's tone was genial enough, almost paternal, but his attitude was stiff. The one-eyed man, in the group at the table, was watching Timar glumly. Suddenly Maritain, who was with him, rose.

"It's late. I'm off to bed."

He shook hands quickly, giving the impression of someone who anticipates a scene and wants to get away before anything unpleasant happens. For the first time in his life Timar found himself the focus of interest in a dramatic situation. Obviously the part that fell to him was that of a potential troublemaker who needs humoring—which reminded him that he had a revolver in his pocket.

"Come and have a drink on the house."

Bouilloux shepherded him toward the bar, slipped behind it, and poured out two glasses of Calvados.

"Here's luck! Take a seat."

Timar climbed onto one of the high stools and drank the liqueur in one gulp, staring grimly at the man behind the bar. They weren't going to play fast and loose with him—he'd see to that! He had a feeling that the billiard players were going on with their game merely for appearances' sake, the men near the phonograph talking merely for talking's sake.

At that moment nothing mattered except himself and Bouilloux, or, rather, the clash of wills that was impending between them.

"The same again," said Timar, holding out his glass.

Bouilloux hesitated. He was afraid. Noting this, Timar deliberately accentuated his scowl, feigning a self-assurance he was far from feeling.

"Where's Adèle?"

Bottle in hand, the other man grinned at him and said with a chuckle, trying to gain time:

"Aha! Still as much in love as ever? What a time you two lovebirds must have up there all on your lonesome, with no damned spoilsports butting in! You don't know your luck."

Every word rang false.

"Where is she?"

"Where is she? How the devil should I know?"

"Is she at the hotel?"

"Why should she be at the hotel? To your health! Tell me, how long did the trip down take you in your boat?"

"Never mind . . . So Adèle hasn't been to the hotel?"

"I never said that. If you must know, she's been here, but she isn't here just now."

Timar had taken the bottle from his hand and poured himself a third drink. Suddenly he swung around to the billiard players and saw that they had stopped playing and were all ears. The clerk turned hastily to his companion.

"Your shot! That carom looks like a winner."

Never had Timar felt his nerves so violently on edge, and yet his brain so clear. He felt capable of anything, there was no extreme to which he couldn't go, without turning a hair. His gaze returned to Bouilloux, settled on him still more darkly.

He saw himself as a commanding, awe-inspiring figure—whereas in reality he looked merely like a sick man, in the throes of fever. His face was livid, he seemed on the brink of nervous collapse, and it was this that so perturbed the others. So much so that Bouilloux, picking up the two glasses, said quietly:

"Come with me, my boy. We'll have a little talk."

He led Timar to a corner where they could talk unheard by the others, placed bottle and glasses on the table, rested his elbows on it, and stretched his right hand toward Timar's.

The men at the other table rose and walked to the door.

"Good night, Louis. Good night, all."

Footsteps receded on the road outside. Only the billiard players stayed behind; there was something strained in their intentness on their game.

"Keep calm. It's not the moment to play the fool." The tone was gruff but kindly, bringing to Timar's mind the voices of certain priests he had known in his younger days. "Now let's have it out man to man. There's no point trying to beat around the bush, is there?"

While speaking, he watched Timar's face. He took a sip at his Calvados but moved the bottle away when he saw Timar reach toward it.

"Not yet."

The native masks hung at their old places on the color-washed walls. Nothing was changed. The only difference was that Adèle no longer presided at the bar; Adèle in her black silk dress, poring over her accounts or, her chin cupped in her hand, gazing dreamily into space.

"The case is coming up for trial tomorrow. You know what that means, don't you?"

He had brought his face near Timar's. A curious face. On a close-up view it had none of the coarseness Timar had got used to reading into it; once again it reminded him of a father confessor of his youth, who had the same gruff way of talking.

"Everything's fixed up. We've seen to it that Adèle won't be landed in trouble of any kind. And it took the devil of a lot of managing, let me tell you!"

"Where is she?"

"I tell you, I don't know. . . . Your name won't crop up at the trial. Oh, and by the way, there's no use letting it be known that you're in Libreville. Well, do you get it? Adèle's a dear little thing, and it would be too bad if she had to do a stretch."

A strange thing was taking place. Timar heard the words and understood them, but simultaneously he had the impression of seeing what lay behind them—as if they were a sort of latticework.

"A dear little thing." That was how they talked of her. And they'd slept with her, every man jack of them! Boon companions, a happy band of bedfellows—and now he'd come butting into the gang, an interloper. No wonder they loathed the sight of him. Like a child in a temper who refuses to listen to reason, he repeated:

"Where is she?"

Bouilloux nearly lost heart. He drank up his liqueur and stopped Timar from pouring out another one for himself.

"Listen! Out here white folk hang together. Whatever she did, she *had* to do it. Anyhow, it's done, and talking won't mend matters. I tell you everything's OK, and all you've got to do is sit tight and not worry. . . ."

"Look here! When she was your mistress . . ."

"No, my boy, you've got it all wrong!"

"But you told me . . ."

"That's a different thing. Do try to understand, damn it! It's a serious business, you know. I told you I'd slept with Adèle. Other fellows, too. But there's no connection . . ."

Timar gave a shrill laugh.

"I tell you that was quite a different thing. And that's why, as things stand, I'm damned if I'll allow . . ." He stopped abruptly. Timar had gone quite white, and Bouilloux noticed that his fists were clenched. "You have to take life as you find it," he went on hastily. "There are some things that can't be helped. Don't forget that in those days Adèle had Eugène with her. You still don't see what I'm driving at? Well, what proves it isn't the same thing is that Eugène never got jealous over . . . what she did. He knew better!"

Timar grinned, but he felt more like weeping with shame.

"With us coasters, and the bigwigs like the Governor and his crowd, it didn't amount to more than . . . than a sort of act of politeness, a business transaction, if you like. No more than that." His voice grew harsh, almost threatening. "I've known Adèle for ten years, and I honestly think you're the first she's felt like that for. And if I'd known how things were going to turn out, I'd have done everything in my power to stop her. So now you know!"

He fell silent. There was strong emotion in his voice when he spoke again.

"It's just as well Eugène passed out that night—or anything might have happened. You still don't understand? Damn it, have I got to explain *everything* I say to you? Now listen to me, young man: Adèle is in a nasty jam. It's a miracle she's managed to wriggle halfway out of it; only halfway, mind you, for the case won't be decided till tomorrow. So, as I said, there are some of us here who won't allow . . ."

Again he paused. Did he have an inkling he had gone too far? Or was it the look on Timar's face that alarmed him: its paleness mottled by glowing fever spots, the purplish lips and unnaturally bright eyes? And the thin fingers twitching on the polished table?

"Oh, well. Hard words don't get one anywhere. I'll only tell you this: Adèle knows what she's doing."

The billiard balls kept on clicking, the two men moving conscientiously around the table.

"So that's that. She's acting for the best. It'll all be over by tomorrow evening, and she'll go back with you to the bush. Here's good luck to you both! Whether she was right or not in leaving Libreville—well, that's her concern, and nobody else's."

"Where is she?"

"Where is she? I have no idea! And no one has any right to question her about it. You, least of all. See what I mean? You ask me where she is? Perhaps in bed with someone—trying to save her neck!"

Bouilloux swung around toward the boy who was standing motionless beside the bar.

"Close for the night. . . . And you," he added, turning to the billiard players, "clear out!"

It was he who was losing his temper now. Timar was at a loss what to say. But his hand moved toward the pocket that contained the revolver. There was the sound of closing shutters and the two men going away.

Bouilloux had risen to his feet and, almost as wrought up as Timar, was looking down on him, his huge bulk towering above the younger man's.

"If that's the only way she has of saving her skin, what damned right do you have to grouse about it, you . . . ?" He clenched his fists menacingly, while Timar's hand closed around the revolver.

Then suddenly the ferocity died from his face; he grew human, cordial, and tapped the young man on the shoulder.

"No, my boy, you've got nothing to worry about. It'll all work out. Just get a good night's sleep. By tomorrow evening she'll be out of the woods and you'll be able to take her home with you and make love to your heart's content."

Timar poured himself a final glass and drank it off. He still looked haggard, and there was a dangerous glint in his eyes, but when Bouilloux took his arm and led him to the door he offered no resistance. He heard Bouilloux's voice behind him as he walked upstairs.

"Yes, she's one in a thousand. We should all take our hats off to Adèle."

Almost everything that happened after that remained a blank in Timar's memory; he had no idea who handed him a candlestick, how he found his way to the bedroom in which, flinging himself fully dressed upon the bed, he tore down the mosquito net.

All he could remember was that he wept passionately, waked with a start just as the candle was guttering out, and hugged the pillow frantically to his breast, as if it were Adèle.

Twelve

Like the cemetery, the Courthouse had a makeshift air; all the traditions of a court of justice seemed to have been studiously avoided, and it was difficult to take it seriously. That, perhaps, was why Timar found his thoughts harking back to Eugène Renaud's funeral.

The big bare room might have been the interior of a warehouse. There was none of the dark oak paneling, the carved woodwork, or the impressive paraphernalia of a European courtroom. Whitewashed walls; four big windows opening on a veranda packed with blacks, the town dwellers wearing clothes, the jungle folk naked or almost naked, some standing, others squatting.

There was no seating accommodation for the public, no dock for the accused, no judge's bench. The portion of the room reserved for members of the court was merely roped off, and practically all the whites present were allowed within the official enclosure.

On the other side of the rope was a motley assemblage of blacks, Spaniards, and Portuguese, with a sprinkling of French people who, like Timar, had arrived late.

There was a table with a green tablecloth, at the center of which sat a man who was presumably the Presiding Judge. Were the men beside him assessors, Timar wondered, or did the decision rest solely with the Judge? And what were the Public Prosecutor and Police Superintendent up to, lounging in cane chairs as if the place belonged to them? And all those others, whom Timar had never seen before, and who had managed to secure seats for themselves near the Judge?

Behind the open windows the motionless forms of blacks stood out against the glare. All the Europeans were in white, and many had kept their topees on. Several were smoking; it was quite a family party!

Hemmed in by natives, Timar had difficulty at first in seeing Adèle.

He had not been able to get to sleep until the wee hours. Bouilloux, intentionally no doubt, had omitted to wake him, and it was striking ten when he opened his eyes. Hurrying downstairs, he found the hotel empty except for a single bus boy. Unwashed, unshaven, in his soiled and crumpled clothes, he had rushed off to the Courthouse, without even stopping for a cup of coffee. He had plunged through the crowd into the stuffy courtroom, then needed some minutes to get used to the atmosphere and take stock of his surroundings.

All the white men without exception seemed prostrated by the heat. In front of him, beside the rope that partitioned the room, a typical bush Negro, half naked and coarse-featured, was reciting some interminable story in a singsong voice. Now and then he made a timid gesture, displaying a surprisingly white palm; the rest of the time he stood stiffly at attention, his heels together.

Was anyone listening to what he said? The white men were talking among themselves. From time to time the Judge would glance at the windows and shout an order, and the crowd on the veranda moved back a few steps, only to surge forward again a moment later.

Timar had no idea who the native was, or what he was saying. But he could now see, not far from the Public Prosecutor, Adèle's black dress and a portion of her face. Evidently she had not observed his presence yet. She seemed to be signaling to someone.

The black gabbled on and on in a toneless, mournful voice. On the wall facing him hung a large clock of the kind found in all government offices, with a glossy white dial and a minute hand that moved in jerks. A servant pushed his way to the Judge's table and set on it a tray with glasses, a bottle, and a siphon. The men at the table helped themselves to drinks, paying even less attention to the witness than before.

Just then Adèle caught sight of Timar. She went very white and gazed at him with startled eyes; he returned her gaze with a cool, hostile stare.

He had not eaten anything since the previous afternoon. The stench of the serried mass of blacks was growing stronger all the time. He felt a sudden dizziness, which the strain of standing on tiptoe—the only way he could see anything—made worse.

Suddenly the Judge glanced at the clock, which stood at a quarter to eleven, and spoke for the first time.

"That's enough. You can stand down."

The black did not understand, but some instinct told him to stop speaking.

"Interpreter, translate his statement."

The remark was addressed to another black, who was wearing spectacles and European clothes: white trousers, a black coat, and a celluloid collar. He began speaking in a deep, guttural voice, like a distant growl of thunder:

"Your Honor, the man says he had never set eyes on Thomas, seeing as they come not from the same village, and he did not even know that such a man as Thomas existed."

This sentence took him a good three minutes to bring out. The Judge cried angrily:

"Speak up, man!"

"He says it is because of the goats he claimed from his brother-in-law because his wife ran off with a man from another village. She was one of the headman's daughters, and his head wife, and she went telling everyone . . ."

No one listened, including Timar. He didn't have the patience to try to follow the long rambling statement, some portions of which, moreover, failed to reach his ears. He was looking at Adèle. Whose bed had she shared last night?

Was she, as usual, wearing nothing under the black silk dress? Had some other man watched the whiteness of her body, the supple thighs and slightly drooping breasts emerging from their black sheath as she drew it over her shoulders? . . . The interpreter rumbled on:

"They would not give him back the she-goat, and so . . ."

Then four other blacks started speaking all at once in an upcountry dialect, sometimes questioning the man, sometimes wrangling among themselves. The accused, whose only garment was a rag tied around his waist, stared at them with consternation.

One had only to watch the proceedings for a while, without following them attentively, to find them utterly fantastic, like a grotesque dream or a piece of deliberate clowning. A whisky bottle stood on the "bench," the white men were passing around cigarettes, exchanging audible remarks.

Bouilloux was among them, with his boon companions and the lawyer's clerk. Standing beside a window, at the edge of the roped-in enclosure, they formed an intermediate group between the officials and the blacks. Bouilloux was the first to raise his voice:

"That's enough!"

Some of the other white men echoed him.

The Judge shook a little tinkly bell, more like a child's toy than an adjunct of a court.

"Now we have to hear Amami's wife. Where is she?"

From the doorway, where she had been standing, she was pushed forward through the crowd up to the rope. A black crone, with scraggy breasts, embossed tattoos on her chest and stomach, a shaven head.

She stayed where she had been placed, silent, unseeing. Subconsciously Timar's mind began to march again. He saw her, first in profile, then at another angle, and somehow she recalled the black girl who had slept with him two nights before. Not only her features, but also the line of hips and shoulders resembled the girl's. Perhaps she was the girl's mother. In that case the accused, the little man who had gabbled away for so long, might well be the father.

And suddenly he found himself contrasting the young, gracefully molded body he had possessed, a thing of vivid beauty, with the lamentable appearance of the old couple. But for a few rags they were naked; their skin was shriveled, lusterless.

They were standing a meter from each other. Timar intercepted a glance that passed between them, and realized that they had lost all track of where they were, what was expected of them, and, above all, why all these people seemed so angry with them. Especially the husband, who had a snub nose and small bloodshot eyes. In the panicked glances he cast around him there was a glint of madness.

No one was paying the least attention to them. Just then Timar noticed that Bouilloux was giving him a meaning glance, even making a slight movement of his head, half cajoling, half threatening, which clearly signified: "Watch your step, my boy."

The woman began to speak in a level tone, giving every syllable the same emphasis, mechanically knotting and unknotting her scanty loincloth as she spoke. To steady herself she kept her gaze fixed on a brown smudge, the remains of a squashed fly, just to the left of the wall clock.

Timar's eyes fell on one of his boatmen at a window; the man's face split in a wide grin. The heat was still increasing. One could almost see the steam rising from the bodies of the crowd. Fumes of pipe and cigarette smoke mingled with the stale odor of black men's and the more acrid tang of white men's sweat.

Sometimes one of the Europeans rose and walked quietly to the door, returning five minutes later. He had been to the hotel for "a quick one."

Timar was hot, hungry, and thirsty, but his nerves were keyed to their highest pitch, and he held out. Whenever he tried to catch Adèle's eye she looked away; just now she was listening to some long story that a white man Timar had not seen before was whispering in her ear. She was still pale; there were dark rings around her eyes.

Torn between conflicting emotions, he was at once enraged with her and full of pity. The thought, for instance, that she had spent the night in another man's arms made him want to kill her, and at the same time he longed to take her in his arms and weep over their common plight.

He heard the black woman talking endlessly; nobody tried to stem the flow of words. Perhaps they were glad of an excuse to defer the moment of making a decision. He gazed at the old creature's shaven head, the long rubbery breasts, the skinny, knock-kneed shanks.

Though sometimes she tripped over a word, she never paused for breath, and one could see her fierce desire to make herself understood and carry conviction. She used none of the artifices of the European, never waxed emotional or raised her voice. Instead of shedding tears or showing signs of weakness she made it a point of honor to face her hearers as still as a statue.

The voice would have sounded mechanical, inhuman, but for its intonation, which was that of an indifferent deacon plodding through the lessons. All the syllables sounded much alike and, unless one gave close attention, came to seem no more than incoherent noise, like the patter of raindrops on a window.

Her interminable monologue set Timar's nerves on edge; it had the same effect on him as certain lullabies still sung by nurses in French country villages, which sound less soothing than malevolent, like evil incantations. And all the time not a muscle of the black face stirred, and more and more clearly he glimpsed beyond it that other, younger face turning toward him as the dugout swerved from the riverbank, and the girl's shy, tentative gesture of farewell.

Other pictures rose to his mind, and he was amazed at their clarity of detail. The twelve pairs of eyes focused on him as the paddles flashed and fell, and through the golden air there rose the boatmen's song, monotonous and mournful, like this woman's voice. And the hangdog look on the men's faces when they had collided with the sunken snag and he lost his temper.

He had twinges of pain in his chest, due perhaps to hunger or to thirst. His knees were shaking with the strain of standing on tiptoe. Suddenly a wild idea came to him of shouting like the others: "Stop her! That's enough!"

But just as he was opening his mouth the Judge tinkled his absurd little bell. Failing to understand, the woman raised her voice a tone and went on doggedly with her monologue. The interpreter said something, and her voice went up another tone, and now there was despair in it. But she still made no gesture.

Timar was reminded of the *Parce, Domine* sung in churches in time of trouble, which is repeated thrice by the congregation, on three different notes, rising a tone each time.

Now her voice was high-pitched, and she was talking faster. She wanted to tell everything. Everything.

"Take her out!"

Some native policemen in blue uniforms led the woman out through the crowd. Did she know why she had been brought here, why so suddenly ordered out? She offered no resistance and went on with her monologue, unheeded, as they took her away.

Just then Timar caught Adèle's eye and saw a look of undisguised terror on her face. He had no idea that what scared her was his own appearance. All the exertions of the last few days, the heat, illness, exhaustion, had left their imprint, and he was looking ghastly. His eyes were bright with fever and shifting incessantly from the blacks to the whites, from the clock to the brown smudge on the wall.

Drenched in cold sweat, gasping for breath, he was able as little to fix his thoughts on anything as to control his eyes. And just now he felt a desperate need to *think*, to set order in the chaos of his mind.

"Tell us briefly what she said. Briefly, mind you! It was quite a speech! Well?"

"She says it isn't true."

The interpreter seemed full of himself, conscious of his importance. There were some murmurs at the windows. The Judge rang his bell imperiously.

"Keep quiet, or I shall clear the court."

Two other blacks stepped forward, unsummoned, to the place where previous witnesses had stood. The Judge, who had calmed down already, leaned forward, his elbows resting on the table, and asked:

"Do you speak French?"

"Yes, massa."

"What reason do you have to believe that Amami killed Thomas?"

"Yes, massa."

These two were evidently witnesses for the prosecution. And now Timar understood everything. He did more than understand; he visualized the whole sequence of events from the day he had left Libreville. While he was gazing at the black girl on the riverbank Adèle had gone to the headman's hut, offered him a handsome sum if he would pin Thomas's murder on one of the villagers, and handed the revolver over to him.

The rest was all plain sailing. The headman picked on a villager against whom he had a grudge, a man who had married his daughter and when she left him had dared to insist that the dowry be refunded. There had been a dispute about some goats and hoes. Five hoes, to be precise . . .

These two witnesses had been promised bribes, no doubt, and were doing their simple best to earn them.

"Yes, massa."

"That's not what I want! Tell me, when did you first hear that Amami killed Thomas?"

"Yes, massa."

Losing patience, the Judge rapped out:

"Interpreter, translate the question."

There followed a confabulation in the native language, which, since it showed no sign of ending, the Judge cut short. Imperturbable as ever, the interpreter announced:

"Your Honor, he says Amami has always been considered a bad sort."

Deadlock again. Though his wife had been sent away, Amami had stayed in the courtroom. He was staring dully at his accusers, sometimes trying to put in a word, only to be shut up promptly. He had lost what little grip he had ever had on what was happening.

Was the black girl Timar had slept with really this man's daughter? He blushed now at the thought that she had been a virgin, and that all the same he had possessed her, in a sort of blind rage, with a crazy idea that by so doing he was taking his revenge on the whole damned continent of Africa!

"Is that the revolver that was found in his hut?" The Judge pointed to the weapon lying on the table.

Timar was conscious of Adèle's gaze intent on him, and also that of the others: Bouilloux, the fat clerk, the one-eyed man.

Being unable to see his own face, he could not realize why, crucial as the moment was, Bouilloux suddenly started pushing his way toward him through the mass of natives. He did not even realize that the blacks near him were eying him with alarm. His breath came in wheezy gasps like those of a man in a high fever, and his hands were so tightly locked that the knuckles were cracking.

"Both of them swear that that is the revolver found in Amami's hut. All the witnesses give the same evidence. No European has visited the village since the crime took place."

The old black man was gazing at the interpreter with terrified, imploring eyes. He, too, had a faint likeness to the girl, though his skin was grayish-black and wizened like the old woman's.

The clerk and the man beside him watched Bouilloux forcing his way toward Timar. On the other side of the rope, the official side, the Prosecutor was bending toward Adèle. They were whispering together and casting furtive glances at Timar.

Suddenly a hand gripped Timar's arm. A voice said in his ear:

"Be careful!"

Why should he be careful? Careful of what, or whom? And then a queer sensation came over Timar; it lasted only a few seconds, but it left him sick with horror. He had identified himself with the miserable black, he *was* that half-naked old creature standing at bay with everybody's hand against him, beset and baited by the pack.

They were after him, too! Bouilloux had been sent to bring him to heel. The viselike grip was tightening on his arm.

Adèle and the Prosecutor were still watching him. Even the Judge looked around with an apprehensive air, as though he, too, had scented trouble. But he merely took another sip of whisky.

Did that poor devil of a black man have the same sensations, the same despair as Timar? Did he, too, feel surrounded by enemies, all these bodies, black and white alike, closing in on him, crushing out his life? Perhaps he did, for all at once he started speaking across the tumult in a high-pitched, whimpering voice, repeating the story to which nobody had troubled to listen.

Though Bouilloux's fingers were boring into his flesh, though Adèle was gazing anxiously at him and the Prosecutor observing him with a curious smile, Timar could restrain himself no longer. He drew himself up to his full height, swung himself up onto his toes, and, though every word rasped in his throat, raised his voice to a scream.

"It's a lie! It's a damned lie! He is innocent. It was . . ." Yes, he had to come out with it. Cost what it might, this nightmare must be ended. "It was *she* who killed that boy. And you know it as well as I do!"

Bouilloux twisted his arm, gave a sharp tug, and laid him sprawling among the black men's feet.

Thirteen

He guffawed and said aloud:

"Obviously! There's no such thing!"

Two passengers looked around. He returned their stare with a contemptuous shrug of his shoulders. More damned officials. Let them think what they liked! The steamer was getting under way. Timar was sitting in the smoking room aft of the first-class promenade deck.

Suddenly he jumped up. He had just realized that he was seeing for the last time in his life that yellow band of foreshore, those dark bastions of jungle, red roofs, and feathery palms.

His eyes were unnaturally bright, his features twitching, but it had become a habit with him to make faces, wring his hands, and mutter to himself, even when others were near.

"Now, I wonder who brought me to the train?"

He knew it was an absurd thing to say: that there was no station in Libreville, no one had come to see him off, no handkerchief had fluttered toward him from the quay. Yet "train" was definitely the right word, with its associations of good-byes, La Rochelle station, his mother and sister.

He had been very ill. So they had kept on telling him, and very likely it was true. As a result of being beaten up, of course. Never before had Timar been involved in any brawl, least of all in public. He was a well-brought-up young man, of a naturally peaceful temperament.

But when Bouilloux had started wrenching his arm in the midst of that surging crowd, he had seen red and lashed out blindly. He had felt that they were all against him. There had been a general melee of blacks and whites, and then the whole lot of them had been hustled out onto the road. Someone had kicked him in the face, drawing blood. His sun helmet had rolled away. The sun had blazed down on his head.

Sometimes he had seen street fights, but he had never taken part in one. Usually he gave them a wide berth. But in this one he had been the central figure. He had learned that blows hurt less than one might suppose, and no great courage is needed to put up a fight. Was everyone against him? Well, he'd show them that he, too, could use his fists! Which he did until, with no idea how he'd got there, he found himself in the semidarkness of the police station.

He had recognized at once those familiar stripes of light and shadow on floor and walls, the table on which drinks were served. He was seated, and the Superintendent was pacing to and fro, scrutinizing him in an odd way that puzzled Timar. Passing his hand over his forehead, he murmured uncomfortably:

"I'm awfully sorry. I can't quite remember what happened. They were all against me, you know." He conjured up a tactful smile.

The Superintendent, however, did not smile, but went on watching him with the same steady, hostile stare.

"Want something to drink?" he asked in the tone he would have used to a nigger or a dog. He gave Timar a glass of water only, then started pacing up and down the room again.

Timar rose from his chair.

"Stop!"

"What are we waiting for?" Everything still seemed rather blurred; he would not have been surprised to find it all a dream.

"Sit down," the Superintendent said.

It struck Timar that the man hadn't troubled to answer his question, and once more he had a vague impression of being trapped, the victim of a plot.

"Come in, doctor. How are you? I suppose you know what's happened?" The Superintendent cast a meaning glance toward Timar.

"What will you do about him?" the doctor asked under his breath.

"We shall have to put him under arrest. After such scandalous behavior . . ."

The doctor turned to Timar and remarked:

"So it's you who caused all the rumpus this morning?" His tone was as unfriendly as the police officer's.

While speaking, he had pushed up Timar's eyelids and peered into his pupils. After feeling his pulse for less than five seconds, he cast a glance over the young man from head to foot and muttered:

"Well, now."

He turned to the Superintendent.

"Come outside for a moment, won't you?"

They conversed in whispers on the veranda. The police officer returned, scratching his head, and shouted to a boy:

"Put me through to Government House."

He picked up the receiver.

"Hello? Yes, sir, it's as we supposed. Exactly. Shall I send him in a car? In any case, I'd have had to do so, since feelings are running high against him among the timber traders. Will you be there, sir?"

He picked up his helmet and said to Timar:

"Come along."

Timar followed, surprised at his own docility. He had lost all power of reacting; never would he have believed it possible to feel so tired, such a void in his head and body. He followed the Superintendent into the courtyard of the hospital, without even wondering why he was being taken there. The Governor's car had already arrived. In a spotlessly clean room, the first such room he had seen since coming to Africa, he found the Governor waiting and held out his hand. The Governor, ignoring it, said curtly:

"I wonder if you realize, young man, what you have done?"

No, to tell the truth, he didn't realize it—or only in the vaguest way. There had been a fight. He had listened to a black man and woman droning out some rigmarole in a stifling room, with Adèle in the background staring at him, trying to overawe him.

"Do you have any money?"

"I believe I have some left in the bank."

"In that case, let me give you a word of advice. There's a boat for France in two days. Take a passage on it."

Timar began to protest. With an attempt at dignity, he said:

"I'd like to tell you, sir, about this . . . business with Adèle. . . ."

"That can wait. Go to bed now."

The Governor and the Superintendent had left the hospital together. The manner of both had been distant, not to say contemptuous. Timar had gone to sleep. He had had an attack of high fever, acute pains in his head. He kept on saying to the male nurse:

"It's this damned little bone at the base of my skull that hurts. Why don't you do something about it?"

Somehow there did not seem to have been any intermediate stage between his going to the hospital and coming on board the *Foucault*. Still, he remembered that the Superintendent had come to visit him twice. Timar had asked if he could see Adèle.

"Better not."

"What does she say?"

"Nothing."

"And the doctor? He thinks I'm mad, doesn't he?"

That was what vexed him most. He realized he must look like a madman, yet he knew quite well he wasn't. Of course he made grimaces and, now and then, crazy gestures. Sometimes, too, he found his head buzzing with mad ideas.

"There's no such thing."

But he wasn't mad. That was obvious, for he felt quite calm, quite composed. He did his packing unaided. He even noticed that his white suits were missing and insisted on their being looked for, since he knew that everyone on board wore white as far as Tenerife.

On the quay at seven in the morning, when only his servants were with him, he had chuckled to himself as he gazed at the red road and the line of palm trees etched upon the brightness of the sky.

"There's no such place."

Obviously, in a sense, it existed—but he knew what he meant. Just as he knew that all this was only a passing phase. So there was no need to feel ashamed about it.

He had gone on board the tender. Suddenly he had buried his head in his hands, murmuring: "Adèle!" He gritted his teeth. Peering between his fingers, he could see the blacks grinning. The sea was smooth.

All that was ended, Africa out of sight.

The bar steward came up to him.

"Did you call me, sir?"

"An orangeade, please."

From the way the man looked at him Timar knew the steward, too, thought him mad. Probably the ship's officers had been told about him.

"There's no such place."

A train. What train? Ah yes, the La Rochelle train; his sister waving her handkerchief. Slumped in a wicker chair, he let his thoughts drift on. His tropical suits had not been found, so he was in black. But really he enjoyed being different from the other passengers. The boat was swarming with army officers. "Too many damned uniforms," Timar grumbled. And too many civil servants. And too many children rushing around the promenade deck.

What did it bring back to him? Why, of course—Adèle. She, too, always wore black. But she had no children, and nothing on under her dress. Whereas the black girl wore no dress. Naked and unashamed!

Yes, he could remember everything. Perfectly well. He wasn't the simpleton they thought him, not by a long shot. They'd wanted to convict the father of that black girl, but Timar had stood up for him. Then they had beaten him up. The whole crowd had turned on him.

Of course it was a plot. They were all in it. The Governor, the Prosecutor, Bouilloux, and his gang. For, of course, Adèle's bed was open to all of them!

White-clad passengers were pacing indefatigably up and down the deck, killing time.

"Murder? There's no such thing."

And suddenly the thoughts that had been racing through his brain slowed down, almost to a standstill. An all but lucid interval. He saw himself, a black figure with a sun helmet pushed well back, seated in the smoking room of a liner. Homeward bound.

Evidently he'd had some nasty knocks on the head. It had been a near thing he had not lost his reason. In fact, people thought him mad. But he'd get over it. So sure of this did he feel that he kept on postponing the moment of recovery, when he would have to think straight all the time. It was a knack one could acquire at will—thinking straight.

He closed his eyes and watched a pageant of mental pictures, all slightly out of focus, as in dreams, stream past. He listened to his thoughts. Dusk was falling. Four men, civil servants from their looks, were playing cards at a nearby table and drinking Pernod. As in Libreville, at Adèle's. He had learned the game they were playing. An easy game; he'd picked it up at once. The picture faded out into another. Another night, some weeks later. They were approaching the concession. In a launch. He'd had a sudden attack. Struggled, struck out with his fists. They had put him to bed. . . .

Adèle was lying, naked, at his side. They were spying on each other in the darkness, feigning sleep. Then he, Timar, had really fallen asleep, and she had taken advantage of it, to slip away. So next morning—no Adèle!

That black girl had been a virgin.

"There's no such thing."

He opened his eyes. A young lieutenant was passing, with his sun helmet on, though night had fallen. Another officer, a captain, called to him from the card table:

"Afraid of catching moonstroke?"

Timar swung around abruptly. Moonstroke! He'd heard someone use that expression before—when was it? When he was in bed—or was it during the fight? What's more, it had been said in just the same bantering tone. He glared at the officer aggressively, as if he expected an explanation or an apology.

The card players consulted one another, then rose to their feet.

"Time to change, isn't it?"

Timar's eyes followed them suspiciously as they walked off.

At dinner he had a table to himself. He felt absolutely calm, though occasionally he chuckled, when he saw people casting sympathetic glances in his direction. Now and then he would deliberately utter some words half aloud. There was a girl at one of the other tables who seemed to find this funny, and it amused him to see her holding her napkin before her face to hide her giggles.

What did it matter, anyhow? He knew so well this was a passing phase. Like the tide. There comes an hour, inevitably, when even the highest tide begins to turn. That was a law of nature.

The pictures forming before his eyes were steadily growing more clean-cut, less entangled one with another. Except at night. Twice he woke with a cry, sitting up in his bunk, drenched in sweat, quivering in every limb, and groping in the bed for Adèle. But that, of course, wasn't the same thing. Everything is different at night. And Adèle wasn't there—or, rather, she *was* there, but he could not reach her and bury his aching brow upon the softness of her breast.

To make things worse, the black girl was beside him in the bed. Inert, submissive . . . An awkward situation; he'd have to find a way out—perhaps go away, far away, with Adèle.

To stop all this damned gossip. To have done with Africa, the Gabon, timber concessions, and the rest of it. Let the blacks keep their damned *okume* log, and Constantinesco run the business!

Only Adèle counted. Adèle in the moist warmth of the bed, in the brindled twilight of the morning hours. When she'd gone downstairs, he would listen to the morning noises below, the boy cleaning out the restaurant while Adèle filled in her ledgers at the cash desk.

It was the ship's doctor who waked him, a silly young man who for some reason considered it necessary to make friendly conversation.

"I'm told we hail from the same parts, Monsieur Timar. Quite interesting, isn't it?"

"Where's your home?"

"La Pallice."

"That's not the same place."

Only three kilometers from La Rochelle—but three kilometers were three kilometers, weren't they? Not to mention that the fellow had a halfwit's face and ugly, bulging eyes. It seemed he wanted to know how Timar was feeling. Well, he was feeling calm.

"Had a good night?"

"Rotten."

"Sorry to hear that. I'll bring you some medicine to . . ."

"There's no such thing."

Damn them all! Why couldn't they leave him in peace? That was all he asked for, to be left alone! He didn't want people fussing over him. Least of all doctors. Didn't they know that he was cleverer than all the doctors in the world?

Cleverer than he himself had been in the past, for now he had developed a sixth—or was it a seventh?—sense. He perceived things that were too subtle for the ordinary run of people. He could even forecast the future; for instance, the visit that their family doctor would pay him in their villa at La Rochelle. He, too, would affect a hearty manner.

"Well, young man, what's the trouble? Tell me all about it."

His mother and sister would be fluttering around the bed. In the passage the doctor would whisper to them as he went away:

"Rest is all he needs. He'll get over it."

Why not? Then they'd coddle him. Then start talking to him again about his cousin Blanche, who lived in Cognac. One Sunday she'd turn up in a new pink dress.

Let them have their way. They wanted him to marry her; he'd do so. Just to have some peace. He'd accept the job that had been offered to him, at the oil refinery. In La Pallice, as it happened. In the part of the town where rows and rows of workmen's houses had been put up, a hundred meters from the sea. He, of course, would have a bigger house, with a garden, of the seaside-villa type. And a motorcycle. He'd settle down, make quite a good husband. Have a peaceful life. Never had he wanted that so much. Why, he might even consent to have children!

Those people who walked past him on the promenade deck or in the music room couldn't guess, of course, that he'd developed a sixth sense, but they looked back in a startled way, he noticed, and lowered their voices.

What did they matter, anyhow?

How wonderful, absolutely superb, was that moment when the twelve paddles rose together and, for the fraction of a second, the boatmen held their breath, their eyes fixed on the white man, then with a deep concerted grunt brought down the blades into the water, while straining muscles rippled in the light, and dusky bellies buckled! New beads of sweat shone on the sleek black bodies, cataracts of waterdrops were falling through the bright air, strings of rainbow-tinted pearls.

But it wouldn't be the slightest use talking about that. Nobody would understand. Certainly not the fellows at his office in La Pallice. Least of all Blanche, who was a really pretty girl.

"There's no such thing."

His eyes encountered the deck steward's. The man was smiling.

"Feeling better, Monsieur Timar?"

"Much better."

"Going ashore in Kotonu?"

"Ashore? There's no such thing."

The steward said with an understanding look:

"Anything to drink, sir? An orangeade?"

"An orangeade; why not? They've forbidden me whisky, you know. Anyhow—there's no such thing."

But he didn't really mean it. There were moments like that when, completely calm and lucid, he saw things in the bleak light of reality.

But that was just what he must avoid. For the present, anyhow. Or else . . . Why, he might even on a sudden impulse jump overboard! That, too, was something to be avoided.

With a faint hiss the bow cut through the gray-blue smoothness. The smoking-room veranda was in shadow. A sailor was giving a fresh coat of red paint to the interior of the wind scoops.

Timar resolved to make himself agreeable. With Blanche, with everyone in La Rochelle and La Pallice. He'd come to the wharf to see the liners bound for Africa, watch young men and civil servants going on board.

But he wouldn't say anything. Not a word. Only once in a while, at night, he'd have his moonstroke—an "attack," they would call it—and again would feel his senses swooning in the sultry air and, in a waking dream, see Adèle's pale form glimmering in the bed beside him—while his wife in her nightdress warmed up a potion on the stove.

People still stared at him uneasily as he walked by. He felt so calm, his brain was working now so smoothly, with such logical precision, that he couldn't resist the temptation of mystifying them a bit, playing to the gallery. With twinkling, fever-bright eyes he watched their faces as he said out loud:

"But there's no such place as Africa."

For a quarter of an hour more, as he paced the deck methodically, he kept on repeating in a calm, clear tone:

"There's no such place as Africa. No such place."

Aboard the *Aquitaine*

Translated by Paul Auster and Lydia Davis

One

The steward knocked three or four times on the cabin door with one knuckle, put his ear against the wood, and after a moment murmured: "It's four thirty."

Even though the fan was purring in Dr. Donadieu's cabin and the porthole was open, the doctor was drenched from head to foot, lying naked on top of the sheets.

He stood up lazily and, without bothering to look through the porthole, went into his bathroom, which was hardly larger than a closet, and prepared to take a shower.

He was calm and indifferent. His motions were automatic, the motions of a man who goes through the same rituals at the same times every day. The nap he had just taken was the most sacred of these rituals; after the nap came a shower with a rough sponge and then a series of minute operations that invariably took him until five o'clock to perform.

Today, for example, he looked at the thermometer, which read 115°. Other people—some of the ship's officers and some of the passengers—complained and protested and worked themselves into a sweat, even though they were used to the equator. But Donadieu felt a certain satisfaction as he watched the column of mercury rise.

While he was putting on his white lisle socks, the siren wailed somewhere over his head and the footsteps coming and going on the deck grew noisier and more hurried.

The *Aquitaine*, which had come from Bordeaux, was now at the farthest point in its voyage—the city of Matadi, by the sickly yellow waters of the mouth of the Congo.

The stay in Matadi was already over. It had lasted twenty hours, and Donadieu had not been curious enough to get off the ship. From the deck he had seen the wharf pilings and the docks, the shacks and sheds, a tangle of railroad tracks and railroad cars. It was a landscape crushed by the sultry sun. Crews of blacks panted as they worked, and an occasional European passed by, dressed in white, with a sun helmet on his head, a pencil stuck behind his ear, and papers in his hands.

Beyond this chaos there had to be a city with a railroad station, a half-built six-story hotel, houses scattered over the hillside.

As he dressed, Donadieu heard very little noise in his gangway and assumed that not many first-class passengers had come aboard.

The porthole did not face the city but the opposite side of the river, where there was nothing to see but a bare mountain with a few native huts at the bottom and some dugouts drawn up on the sand.

A whistle blasted several times. Donadieu dampened his hair with eau de Cologne, combed it carefully, and picked out a clean, dazzling-white and stiffly starched uniform from his closet.

The trip back was about to begin, with calls at all the same African ports. The most perceptible difference between the trip out and the trip back was that they had left Bordeaux with plenty of fresh provisions and would be returning with empty refrigerator rooms, forced to eat food that would become increasingly meager and monotonous.

The mooring ropes were cast off, the anchors were heaved, and the screw began to turn, while up on deck, as always, people waved wildly to their friends on land.

It was five minutes before five. For five minutes, Donadieu shifted various papers and small objects from place to place, then at last he took his sun helmet and went out. He knew that he was going to encounter stewards lugging suitcases through the gangways, that he would see cabins with their doors standing open and new passengers trying to find their way around, asking questions, or demanding to be moved to a different cabin. Three people were waiting in front of the purser's office. Donadieu passed them without stopping, glanced into the empty saloon, and walked in a leisurely way up the broad staircase. He thought he heard a weak cry, the cry of a small baby, but he paid no attention and emerged into full sunlight on the promenade deck.

The port of Matadi was still visible, as were the Europeans in white standing on the dock waiting for the ship to disappear from view. The *Aquitaine* was entering the river backwash at a spot known as the Cauldron, and no one had to look to be aware of this. In spite of its twenty-five thousand tons and its powerful engines, the ship vibrated in an abnormal way; the sensation was even more unpleasant than the heavy lurching during a storm.

Although farther downstream the Congo was nearly twenty kilometers across, here it suddenly narrowed between two brown mountains, seemed to flow backward, and eddied, while crosscurrents traced treacherous swirls on its surface.

Several dugouts rushed past; it was not clear what direction they were going in. One would have thought they were flying toward oblivion, and yet the naked blacks paddled them swiftly from one gulf to the next, taking advantage of the smallest eddy to stem the current.

On the portside there was no one on deck. Donadieu was still walking, rapidly and rather stiffly. As he passed the bar he stopped in surprise—which was unusual for him—and turned around to stare at someone he had not expected to see. He frowned and continued to walk around the deck.

The air was absolutely still, the bulkheads burning hot. And yet Donadieu had seen a doctor standing in front of the bar wearing the uniform of the colonial infantry, including a heavy country overcoat! There was something shocking about the thickness and the very look of the khaki cloth. As he passed a second time, Donadieu noticed that his colleague had black felt slippers on his feet and that instead of a sun helmet he was wearing a dark peaked cap with gold braid.

He was talking to the bartender. He was laughing. He seemed very animated.

The other passengers must have been busy moving into their cabins, and they only gradually appeared on deck.

Every now and then a sailor would run by and climb up to the bridge. Suddenly something unusual happened. The ship seemed to lift up into the air. The bump was hardly perceptible, but Donadieu had the strong sensation that for several seconds they had come to a stop.

Orders were shouted down the speaking tubes. A whistle blasted twice. The eddies behind the ship became more turbulent, and a moment later the ship resumed its normal course across the Cauldron.

Donadieu never went up to the bridge except to give his report. This was a principle of his: he liked everyone to stay in his place. The first mate came down looking worried and rushed off toward the engine room. Then a door opened. A passenger stuck out his head and spoke to the doctor:

"Seems we touched something."

Donadieu recognized him; the man had made the trip before. It was Lachaux, an old colonial who owned a whole province in the Congo. He had pouches under his eyes, yellow skin, a distrustful look.

"I don't know," said the doctor.

"Well, *I* know!"

And Lachaux, dragging his right leg, which was very swollen, climbed up to the bridge to talk to the captain.

The third-class deck was practically deserted. On the forecastle a dozen blacks who were going to leave the ship at one of the next ports had settled right on the bare sheet iron, and a buxom black woman wearing a dazzling blue head scarf was washing a completely naked little boy.

Donadieu was still walking. Four times a day he took the same unvarying walk with measured steps, but this time he was interrupted by the purser, little Edgar de Neuville.

"Did you see him?"

"Who?"

Neuville pointed with his chin at the bar terrace, where the man in the khaki overcoat was visible.

"That's Dr. Bassot. They're taking him back home. He's been waiting for a month, shut up in a cellar in Brazzaville. His wife has just been to see me."

A slight smile hovered on Neuville's lips. He always smiled when he talked about women.

"He's completely nuts. His wife is worried. She asked me if there was a padded cell on board and I showed her the cabin with padded walls. I'm sure she'll be calling on you."

The purser began to walk away and then turned back.

"By the way, did you feel the bump?"

"I think we touched bottom."

They went off in different directions. There were three new customers in the bar. Donadieu observed only one of them, a young man whom he noticed because of the worried look on his face. The doctor in khaki was still there; he seemed to be drifting from one table to another, watching the people curiously as he talked to himself and giggled.

He was a thin, blond young man, smoking one cigarette after another. When he saw his wife coming, he threw his cigarette overboard and looked anxious.

Donadieu went down to the infirmary, which had been set up on the second-class deck. Mathias, the orderly, was busy polishing some yellow shoes.

"Do you know what's happening to us?" he grumbled.

He was always grumbling. His forehead was always wrinkled and his mouth always tasted bitter, no doubt because even though he had been at sea for seven years he suffered from seasickness.

"What's happening to us?"

"Three hundred Annamites are being taken aboard tomorrow at Pointe-Noire."

Donadieu was used to hearing all the news from his orderly. Of course he should have been told first. But . . .

"There will be more people dying!" muttered Mathias.

"Do you have any serum left?"

This was not the first time they had shipped Chinese. Thousands had been taken to Pointe-Noire to work on the railroad, because the blacks could not tolerate the work. From time to time a number of Chinese on their way home were taken to Bordeaux, where they were put on a boat going to the Far East.

Donadieu lit a cigarette, out of habit paced back and forth for a moment in his consulting room, where Mathias's bunk was, and then went back to the first-class deck. It seemed to him that the boat was listing to starboard, but this did not surprise him, because the boat often listed, either to port or to starboard, depending on where the cargo was.

They had passed the Cauldron. They entered the estuary, and night fell at six o'clock, without any transition, as it always fell at the equator. In the dark, the heat became more unpleasantly humid.

Two white forms were leaning back against the railing—the chief engineer and little Neuville, who was talking softly. The doctor joined them.

"I'm sure Lachaux is going to try to make trouble," said Neuville.

"What's going on?" asked Donadieu.

"We really did hit hit bottom a little while ago, and a water-ballast tank was punctured. That's what's making us list. It's not important. The only thing we might have to do is limit the use of fresh water for washing. But Lachaux went up there demanding explanations. He claims that on every voyage there's some kind of problem; he's going to stir up all the other passengers."

In the dimness Donadieu looked at the chief engineer, who was smoking a short-stemmed pipe.

"Isn't one shaft already dented?" he asked.

"Just a little."

They had already felt the ship hit something as they were leaving Dakar on the way over.

"Why do the pumps run several hours a day?"

The engineer shrugged his shoulders, slightly embarrassed.

"The shaft did move a little. We sprang a small leak."

Neither of them was worried. Neuville looked toward the stern, where the madman and his wife were leaning with their elbows on the railing. This was ordinary, everyday life, the usual incidents.

"Have you found anyone for bridge?" the doctor asked the purser.

"Not yet. There are two young lieutenants and a captain on board; they like to dance."

All three happened to be sitting on the bar terrace with glasses of Pernod in front of them. Donadieu had not noticed them before. But didn't everyone look like everyone else on all these trips?

They were on furlough after spending three years in Equatorial Africa. The captain was wearing all his medals across the front of his white uniform jacket. He spoke with a Bordeaux accent. The two lieutenants, not yet twenty-five, were staring around looking for women.

There was time enough. Within three days, Donadieu would know everyone!

The steward walked by, banging the gong.

"Who does the captain have at his table?"

"Lachaux, of course."

"And you?"

"The officers and Madame Bassot."

"The wife of the crazy doctor?"

Neuville, a little uncomfortable, nodded.

"What about her husband?"

"He's eating in his cabin."

"So there's no one at my table?"

"No one so far. People will be getting on at Pointe-Noire, Port-Gentil, and especially Libreville."

It was always the same on every route, whether they were in the Gulf of Tonkin or Madagascar: the distinguished passengers sat at the captain's table, the purser had his choice of the pretty women, and for the first few days the doctor ate alone with the chief engineer. Then, when new people got on, particularly less interesting people, they were assigned to him!

The young man with the worried expression on his face went by, trying to find his way to the cabins.

"Who is he?" asked Donadieu.

"A minor employee in Brazza. A second-class passenger, but since his baby is sick, we arranged with the captain to let them travel in first."

"Does he have a wife?"

"She stays in the cabin with the baby, Cabin 7, the largest one. Their name is Huret, I think."

They finished their cigarettes in silence, waiting for the second sounding of the gong. The madman went by, holding on to his wife's arm, and she smiled at the purser as she walked past. The husband let himself be drawn along without enthusiasm. Just as they were about to enter the gangway, he hesitated, but his wife said something to him in a low voice, and he obeyed.

"Are we supposed to be taking on many people along the way?"

"By Dakar we should be full."

They left to wash before going in to dinner. When Donadieu entered the dining room, the captain was already there, sitting alone at his table. He was always the first to arrive. With his black beard, he looked more like a professor from the Latin Quarter than a seagoing man.

In another corner, Huret was also sitting alone, at a small table. He had been served some clear soup, which he was eating as he gazed absently straight ahead.

Lachaux arrived, panting and limping. He sat down next to the captain, spread out his napkin with an expansive gesture, began panting again, and called to the maître d'hôtel.

The atmosphere in the dining room was gloomy. The fans set up a continuous vibration in the air, and this was fatiguing. After the boat had left the river, a slight rolling had become perceptible.

"Rice and vegetables," ordered the chief engineer, who was sitting opposite the doctor.

He never ate anything else at dinner, and as he watched the regular meals being carried past, there was an expression of disgust on his face.

Now the three officers came in, hesitated over which table to choose, and finally followed the maître d'hôtel, talking more loudly than the other people in the dining room.

"Is the chef on board any good?" asked the captain with the medals on his chest.

"Excellent."

"We'll soon see if you're right! Give me the menu!"

Then came the purser, accompanied by Madame Bassot, who was wearing a black silk dress. It was not exactly an evening dress, nor was it an afternoon dress. She must have made it herself in Brazzaville, taking the design from a fashion magazine.

Donadieu ate in silence, and although he did not bother to observe the other people scattered throughout the room, which was ten times too big for them, he could still predict the pattern of the voyage.

Every three or four days they would take on new passengers at the various ports, but the original core, the small handful of people present at the moment, would continue to be the ship's solid foundation.

Already there was a noisy table of young people, the one where the officers and Madame Bassot were sitting.

There was the solemn captain's table with ill-tempered Lachaux, who would go on being insufferable all the way to Bordeaux.

There was Huret, who would no doubt remain alone, his wife shut up in the cabin with the dying baby.

There was the crazy man, watched by Mathias during mealtimes. . . .

The blacks on deck did not exist. But the next day the Chinese would come aboard; they would play dice every night, and in three or four days Donadieu would be called upon to treat some contagious disease. . . .

The only sounds were the purring of the fans, the clatter of forks, Lachaux's deep voice, and Madame Bassot's laughter. She was a plump brunette, one of those women who never seem to have anything on under their dresses and whose lips are always moist.

"The boat will have to go into dry dock once we reach Bordeaux," remarked the chief engineer in an indifferent tone of voice. "Have you taken your vacation this year?"

"Yes."

"I don't see how they're going to manage. Now two ships will be out of commission."

"I'm sure they'll assign me to the Saigon line. I like that better."

"I've only been on it once. At least it's not as hot."

"It's a change," Donadieu said simply. "Have you been smoking?"

"No. I haven't wanted to."

"Ah!"

They knew that he smoked, though in moderation, only two or three pipes a day. Maybe opium was the reason he was so phlegmatic. He did not get involved in anything, but remained calm and serene, with just a hint of stiffness in his manner, which they attributed to the Protestant origins of his family, an old family from Nîmes.

For example, the other officers wore uniform jackets with lapels, so that their shirt fronts and black silk ties showed. But he chose to wear high-collared jackets which made him look rather like a minister.

Poor Huret was badly dressed. He was uncomfortable speaking to the maître d'hôtel, who treated him in a slightly condescending way.

The captain and the lieutenants of the colonial infantry were eating everything, all five or six dishes on the menu, and halfway through the meal their voices grew more resonant because of the wine they were drinking.

Lachaux, sitting next to the captain, looked like a fat toad, and he chewed noisily, his napkin knotted around his neck. He was doing it on purpose. When he had first come to Africa he had been an unimportant worker from Ivry, without even an extra pair of socks to his name. Now he was one of the richest colonists in Equatorial Africa.

Even so, he lived in an old boat on different rivers and streams, and his only servants were blacks. For months on end he would tour his properties this way, sometimes on his boat and sometimes carried in a *tipoïe* by the blacks.

Countless stories were told about him. They claimed that at the start of his career he had killed dozens, perhaps hundreds, of blacks, and that even now he would not hesitate to do away with people who made mistakes.

His white employees were the most poorly paid in the province, and he was always involved in at least a dozen suits against them.

He was sixty-five years old, and Donadieu, who was looking at him and could guess what his physical problems were, wondered how he could bear up under that kind of life.

"The captain is annoyed!" said the chief engineer.

Good Lord, naturally! Captain Claude, who was meticulous, punctual, a stickler for the rules, hated nothing so much as guerrilla fighters like Lachaux. But even so he was obliged to invite him to sit at his table. The captain talked very little, ate very little, and did not look at anyone. The moment the meal was over he stood up, bowed solemnly, and returned to the bridge and his cabin.

Donadieu lingered in the dining room with the chief engineer. When he went up on deck, he saw that the ship was now out in the ocean. The water ran along the hull, making a silky noise. The sky was low and dense, not with clouds but with a uniform mist.

Music could be heard coming from the stern.

This was the hour when Donadieu would walk briskly around the deck ten times, through shadow and light, passing the bar every three minutes.

The first time he passed, someone had put a tango on the ship's phonograph, but no one was dancing. At a table on the terrace, the purser, the three officers, and Madame Bassot had just ordered champagne. Sitting in a corner by himself was a man the doctor could not see clearly.

The second time around, the champagne had been poured. He saw that the solitary form belonged to Huret, who was drinking the coffee his ticket entitled him to.

The third time around, the purser was dancing with Madame Bassot, while the lieutenants called out encouragements.

Beyond the boat lay darkness and silence. There was no one to be seen on the second-class deck but a couple leaning on the railing in shadow.

Donadieu was still walking. When he reached the bow he could see the third-class deck, the blacks lying here and there on the hatch cover, the black woman stretched out, too, holding her little boy in her arms.

He was not able to complete his ten rounds. During the ninth, while Madame Bassot was dancing with the captain of the territorial army, a steward came up to him.

"It's the woman in number 7! She's frightened because her baby doesn't seem to be breathing. I'm going to get her husband. . . ."

"Tell her I'll be coming down with him."

And Donadieu went up to Huret, leaned down, and murmured:

"Would you come with me? It seems the baby isn't very well."

The young lieutenants were roaring with laughter because their captain, who was twenty years older than they, was attempting to dance the *biguine*. As for the purser, he smiled as he watched Madame Bassot's rear end, which stuck out at every step of the dance.

Two

It was a long way to Cabin 7. Huret went first, hurrying forward and stopping at each bend of the gangway to look back at the doctor, as if asking whether he was going the right way.

He was still frowning and seemed unhappy. Or, rather, Donadieu had not yet succeeded in defining his complex expression, his nervous tension and extreme concentration, his need of something that was hidden from him. Huret was like a gun about to go off, and he seemed just as ready to explode in anger as he was to burst with tenderness.

His white twill suit was not badly cut, but the cloth was cheap. There was a kind of shamefaced mediocrity in his whole bearing. He must have been twenty-four or twenty-five and was tall and well built, but his sloping shoulders detracted from the impressiveness of his appearance.

He thrust open the door of a cabin and Donadieu heard a woman say: "Oh, it's you!"

Donadieu went in after him, but he knew everything just from having heard those few words and seen the woman from the back as she bent over a bunk.

"What's the matter with him?" asked Huret roughly.

He obviously bore a grudge against fate! He was already blaming it.

Donadieu closed the door behind him slowly and with ill humor breathed in the tepid air of the cabin, which was completely impregnated with the stale smell of the sick baby. The cabin was like all the other cabins, with enameled walls. To the right were two bunks, one on top of the other; to the left was only one, and the baby was lying on it.

Madame Huret had turned around. She was not crying, but it was obvious that she was holding back tears. Her voice was tired.

"I don't know what was wrong with him, doctor. . . . He wasn't breathing any more. . . ."

Her brown hair, pinned untidily at the back of her neck, formed a soft frame around her colorless face. It was hard for Donadieu to determine whether she was beautiful or ugly. She was tired, sick with fatigue. She had lost all sense of her appearance and had forgotten to button up her blouse, which hung open, revealing a breast that seemed somehow out of place.

With three people in the cabin, there was hardly room to move. The doctor leaned over the baby, who was having trouble breathing.

"How old is he?"

"Six months, doctor. But he was born a month early. I wanted to nurse him myself."

"Sit down," he said to the woman.

Huret was standing next to the porthole, looking at the child without really seeing him.

"I think no one ever knew exactly what was wrong with him. From the very beginning he wouldn't keep down the milk he drank. Later we fed him condensed milk, and for a few days he was better. Then he had attacks of colic. The doctor in Brazza told us that if we stayed in the colony any longer we would lose him."

Donadieu looked at her, and then looked at her husband.

"Is this your first term?" he asked him.

"I had already put in three years before I got married."

In other words, he had been barely twenty when he went to Equatorial Africa.

"Civil servant?"

"No. I was an accountant at the Société de l'Afrique Equatoriale."

"It was his own fault," said Madame Huret. "I always told him he should go into administration."

She bit her lips, close to tears, and her husband clenched his fists.

Donadieu understood the drama that was taking place. He asked one more question.

"Is your second term finished?"

"No."

Because of the child Huret had broken his contract, and because of that he must not have been paid.

There was nothing to be done! Donadieu was powerless before this baby, who had been worn out by the climate and yet still clung to life with all the strength in its fragile white body.

"At least you should feel encouraged by one thing," he said, getting up, "the fact that he has lived six months! In three weeks we will be out of the tropics."

The woman smiled skeptically. He observed her more closely.

"Meanwhile, you should take care of yourself."

The smell made him uncomfortable. Diapers that Madame Huret must have washed out in the basin had been hung from the upper bunk to dry. Donadieu noticed that Huret now looked to be in agony. He was breathing heavily, and his nostrils were gradually becoming pinched.

For an hour now the boat had been rocking in a heavy flat swell.

When the nausea overcame him, Huret did not have time to rush outside; he barely managed to open the door and bend over the basin.

"Excuse me for disturbing you, doctor. I know there is nothing we can do. The doctor there told me. But just the same . . ."

"You shouldn't stay in this cabin all day long."

Huret vomited and Donadieu went out, stood quite still in the gangway for a moment, and then slowly went up the stairs. A yellow moon had just risen, and it glazed the large undulations of the ocean. Echoes of Hawaiian music came to him from the stern, adding to the facile romanticism of the scene.

There was nothing missing—from the Chinese bartender to Madame Bassot dancing with the white-uniformed purser.

When the doctor had walked around the deck twice more, he went down to his cabin, got undressed, and put out the overhead light, leaving on only the oil lamp.

This was his hour. Slowly and patiently he prepared an opium pipe and smoked. After half an hour he felt no emotion when he thought of the baby, its mother, and Huret, who was seasick on top of everything else.

By the time the steward scratched at his door and announced that it was eight o'clock, they had begun bringing the Annamites on board (everyone called them the Chinese from then on, because it was easier). They came alongside in a whaling boat and climbed up the accommodation ladder like monkeys, most of them balancing their bundles on their heads. They were pushed toward the bow. As they moved forward, ship's officers studied pieces of paper and called out numbers.

Donadieu dressed at exactly the same pace as on any other day, sat down to his breakfast, and then went on deck just as the first-class passengers were boarding.

There were hardly any, only one family. But it was a very luxuriously turned-out family. Although he looked gentle and timid, the man was almost certainly an important person in the Congo-Ocean Railway. His wife was dressed as elegantly as though she were in a European city. Her little girl, six or seven years old and already a flirt, was being closely followed by a nanny.

As the purser went by, fussing over the new arrivals, he managed to glance meaningfully at the doctor. Was he already commenting on the new female passenger?

The ladder was drawn up. The whaling boats moved off toward the shore, which was as flat as that of a lagoon, while the three hundred Annamites settled calmly on the forecastle, showing no interest in their surroundings. Most of them were wearing shorts and plain khaki shirts; several had cork sun helmets on their heads, and others left their thick, black, crew-cut hair exposed to the sun. Some had taken their shirts off and were washing themselves at the faucet installed on the deck. The black passengers were huddled in a corner, either mistrustful or disdainful.

At the very end of the bridge, Donadieu came face to face with Huret, who was walking by himself.

"Are you feeling better?" he asked.

"Yes—because the swell has died down!" he answered aggressively, without looking the doctor in the eye.

"I told your wife she should get some fresh air."

"She took a long walk this morning."

"When?"

"At six o'clock."

Donadieu imagined her alone on the deserted deck as day was breaking.

"There is still some swell out in the ocean," Huret remarked.

On closer examination Donadieu saw that his face was rather childlike, and that in spite of his wrinkled forehead his expression was really very ingenuous. The fact was that he was only a kid struggling with his responsibilities as a man, a husband, the head of a family.

"Unfortunately there is no effective cure for seasickness," said Donadieu. "Tell your wife that I'll be down to see the baby soon."

The boat was moving again.The doctor went to the infirmary, gave the order to have the Chinese file in, and spent two monotonous hours with Mathias examining them one by one. They waited in a line in front of the door. Even as they stepped over the threshold they were already pulling off their clothes, sticking out their tongues, and holding out their left wrists. They had gone through the same formalities at least a hundred times since leaving their villages.

At a certain point Donadieu began to feel that something was amiss. He could not have said what it was. Perhaps the Chinese were slightly less impassive than usual.

"Have you noticed anything, Mathias?"

"No, doctor."

"Did you call the roll? Did they all answer?"

"They're all here."

But the doctor was still suspicious. Standing in the middle of the forecastle, he watched the Chinese who were swarming around him, going down to get tin mess plates and mugs from the hold reserved for them, and lining up again at the kitchen door.

Scarcely half an hour later a sailor solved the riddle: he found two Chinese lying behind the trunks and blankets in the hold.

Donadieu listened to their chests and took their temperatures, and then he understood. They were both seriously ill. Obviously they had not lined up to be examined at the infirmary; two of their companions must have passed through the line twice, taking their places.

Now they were afraid, not only of the doctor but also of the disease. Maybe they were even more afraid of being isolated—which was what immediately happened, since Donadieu had them put into two third-class cabins.

News travels fast on board a ship, though it is never clear who is spreading it. When the doctor went out onto the promenade deck, the first gong had just been sounded for lunch. The bar terrace was almost festive, because everyone was drinking apéritifs. Huret was there, sitting alone in a corner. The crazy man, in his khaki overcoat, was going from table to table, occasionally pointing at someone's face and murmuring apparently incoherent words.

Someone stood up. It was Lachaux.

"Would you have a drink with me, doctor?"

Donadieu could hardly refuse. He sat down. Lachaux looked at him with that peculiar expression of distrust which never completely left his face. At a nearby table Madame Bassot was surrounded by the lieutenants, but she managed to avoid seeming too gay or too intimate.

"What will you have to drink?"

"A little port."

Lachaux's insistent gaze was annoying. He waited until the drinks had been served and the bartender had gone away.

"Tell me, doctor, did you find the Annamites' health satisfactory?"

"Of course I did."

"You didn't notice anything abnormal? Of course maybe you haven't noticed that the boat is listing, too. . . ."

"That's because of the ballast tanks and . . ."

"Excuse me! You forget that yesterday we were leaning to starboard—today we're leaning to port. . . ."

It was true. And the fact was that the doctor had not paid any attention to it. Even now he was not very impressed.

"Do you know what that means?"

"They must have loaded the ship at Pointe-Noire. . . ."

"Absolutely not. They took on passengers, but no cargo. Well?"

"Then I don't know."

"Well, I'll tell you what's going on. After all, maybe they're hiding it from you, too. On this voyage alone, the *Aquitaine* has touched bottom twice, once leaving Dakar and then again crossing the Cauldron. The first time a transmission shaft was bent."

The purser had left the officers and the wife of the crazy man. He was sitting with the new passengers who had come aboard at Pointe-Noire. But he could guess what Lachaux was saying, and he was listening in.

"I've traveled on this line more than thirty times. I know the sound of the hold pumps. Last night they were running all night long."

"Do you think we're shipping water?"

"I'm sure we are. On the other hand, we're in danger of running out of fresh water. One ballast tank has been staved in. Go to your cabin and try to wash your hands!"

"I don't understand."

"I defy you to do it, because the water supply has been turned off, and from now on we're only going to have water four hours a day. I've just come from the bridge. I heard the captain give the orders."

Huret was listening, too, but from where he was sitting he could not catch everything that was said.

"Now let me ask you again—did you find that the Chinese, *all the Chinese*, were in satisfactory health?"

It was embarrassing. Lachaux was the kind of person who complained to the company after every voyage and refused to give tips because he claimed the service had not been good.

"All I found were two cases of dysentery."

"So you admit it!"

"You know as well as I do that it's going around."

"But I've lived in Africa long enough to know that sometimes dysentery is called by another name!"

In spite of himself the doctor shrugged slightly.

"I assure you . . ."

He was not lying. It was true that in the past Annamites coming aboard at Pointe-Noire had died during the voyage of a disease that resembled yellow fever. But this time he had honestly not found any symptoms.

"You're mistaken, Monsieur Lachaux."

"I hope so!"

The steward went by, sounding the second gong, and the passengers left the terrace one by one and went to their cabins to freshen up before lunch.

It had been a bad move to choose this moment to cut off the water. Bells rang, and cabin boys had to go from cabin to cabin explaining that there would be no fresh water until evening.

Now all of a sudden people looked worried and asked questions that were not yet anxious but were beginning to reveal some uneasiness.

The purser had permanently changed tables and was eating with the "new" people, the Dassonvilles, whose table was next to the captain's table.

This was the only table where there was some sense of elegance. Madame Dassonville had already had time to change her clothes. In spite of the heat, she was behaving just as she would have behaved in a restaurant at an elegant seaside resort.

Her husband, the chief engineer of the Congo-Ocean Railway, was only about thirty. He had obviously graduated from the Paris School of Technology with high marks. His surroundings did not interest him at all, and as he ate slowly, absorbed in his own thoughts, a flirtation sprang up between his wife and little Neuville.

Lachaux was grumbling. The captain said very little to him, looked elsewhere, and stroked his beard with his well-cared-for fingers.

Even Donadieu began questioning the chief engineer, who was sitting across from him.

"Are we really shipping water?"

"Very little."

"Very little?"

"Nothing to worry about. A few tons a day."

"Some of the passengers are getting alarmed."

"I know! The captain talked to me a while ago and asked me to do everything in my power to stop the ship from listing. The funny thing is that the list isn't important. People fix on that because they can feel it, but it doesn't make the ship any less safe."

"What are you going to do?"

"Nothing. There's nothing I can do. It's an unfortunate coincidence that the ballast tank happened to be punctured. When the pump is running, the passengers hear it and think we're leaking like a sieve. When it's not running, the list increases, and they get frightened and pester the sailors and stewards with questions."

The chief engineer was perfectly calm.

"This will be a bad crossing," he said. "Ever since we left Matadi, there has been a bad feeling on board."

They both knew what that meant. They were used to it. Some voyages went like magic from start to finish, the passengers lively and gay, the sea favorable, the engines effortlessly running at twenty knots an hour.

There were other voyages during which every possible problem came up, starting with the presence on board of a tough customer like Lachaux.

"Do you know what he told his cabin boy?"

"I can guess," sighed the doctor.

"He told him there were two cases of yellow fever on board. Is it true?"

The funny thing was that although the chief engineer had been calm enough while talking about the leak, now he had trouble hiding his fear.

This time the doctor was calm.

"I don't think so. I've isolated them just in case."

"Do they have blotches on their skin?"

"No."

Donadieu was willing to bet that before three days went by the purser would have his way with Madame Dassonville. He was all the more amused because the wife of the crazy man was looking dreamily at the younger of the lieutenants, perhaps in an attempt to make the purser jealous.

"Poor man!" he said, glancing meaningfully at Dassonville.

"Especially since he's getting off at Dakar and his wife is staying on," the chief engineer added.

They smiled. Every trip was the same!

The afternoon passed in the usual way. Everyone had coffee in the bar. Then people went to their cabins to take their siestas. Before closing the shutter over his porthole, Donadieu saw that Madame Huret had taken advantage of the empty deck to get some fresh air.

She seemed embarrassed to be in first class and looked timidly at the stewards who walked past her, as though they might ask to see her ticket and direct her back to second class.

She was wearing the same dark dress she had had on the day before, and her hair was loose on her neck. She did not even dare walk around. She would take a few steps, lean on the railing, walk a little more, very little, and stop, at a loss, leaning on the railing again and staring at the shining surface of the sea. Her sun helmet was faded and her bare legs were marbled with the beginnings of varicose veins.

Donadieu closed the shutter, and the cabin filled with a golden half-light. He wanted to brush his teeth, remembered that the water had been turned off, sighed as he undressed, and lay down naked on the bunk as he always did.

Someone scratched at his door, but even though the squeaking of his mattress indicated that he was awake, he did not hear the usual murmur—"It's four thirty. . . ."

A different voice, Mathias's voice, said:

"You must come look at the two Chinese right away."

At five o'clock, one of them died. The door of his cabin was carefully shut. As the doctor went to report to the captain he crossed the forecastle and looked at the other Annamites, most of them sitting on the deck and playing dice.

This did not stop them from observing him. On all sides dark eyes stared at him without eagerness, without indiscreet curiosity, even without bitterness. They had already seen so many companions die in Pointe-Noire!

Donadieu, somewhat ill at ease, walked among the groups of Chinese, stepped over blacks who were sleeping under the ladder, and made a detour to avoid Lachaux, who was slouched back in a deck chair.

On the upper deck he walked by the radio room. The door was open. A voice called out to him from inside, where the impenetrable darkness contrasted vividly with the bright light outside.

"Dead?"

Obviously everyone already knew!

The captain, who was getting dressed after his siesta, also asked:

"Did he have blotches on his skin?"

"No. It was amoebic dysentery."

But even the captain was suspicious and reluctant to believe him.

Three

The dead Chinese was buried at sea at six in the morning. To be more precise, the ceremony, which had been planned for six o'clock, was performed at five minutes to six, and this was done on purpose.

The Annamites had been told about the burial and allowed to send a delegation of four men. These four men arrived on the quarter-deck first, before the sun had risen. Around them sailors were noisily cleaning the boat, and lights were visible at the portholes of several of the cabins, where the officers who would be present at the ceremony were getting ready.

Donadieu came up slowly, in a bad mood, because he did not like having to deviate from his routine. Shortly afterward, the captain came down dressed in a wool uniform and shook the doctor's hand.

Two sailors carried out the crude coffin, the first rays of sun setting fire to the polished metallic sea and shining on the knotty wood.

Several times the doctor turned toward the bow, where soft noises could be heard. The Chinese must have been taking up positions everywhere they could expect to see anything, even though they had been forbidden to do so.

The captain looked at his watch. Donadieu understood: the only person they were waiting for now was the purser, and at last he appeared. But he was not alone—Madame Dassonville was with him.

The captain and the doctor glanced at each other. When the young woman came up to them they bowed coldly, and Neuville looked embarrassed.

There were still five minutes to go, but with an abrupt gesture the captain took off his cap, drew a small book bound in black from his pocket, and began the prayer for the dead.

The ceremony was performed in a perfunctory way. The presence of Madame Dassonville, who had begged the purser the night before during bridge to let her come, lent a false note to the occasion.

And soon Donadieu had reason to wish it would end even more

quickly, because another figure appeared, on the promenade deck, which overlooked the quarter-deck—a woman who had not known about the death of the Annamite until that moment.

It was Madame Huret, who was taking her walk as she did every morning and had stopped when she saw a coffin surrounded by men in uniform.

The coffin was put onto a slide and a sailor pushed it. It began sliding slowly down toward the sea, then gathered speed. There was a drop of several meters to the water. The four Annamites remained motionless, as if their minds were blank.

When the coffin hit the water, something happened that almost never happened, especially in a calm sea: it struck the surface in such a way that it burst apart. Madame Huret, up above, was the first to see it, and she cried out, putting her head in her hands.

The captain had enough presence of mind to signal to the officer on duty to increase the speed of the ship.

The four Annamites were leaning on the railing; Madame Dassonville bent over, pointing to something pale floating in the wake of the *Aquitaine*.

That was all. The captain saluted again, curtly. Standing behind the young woman, little Neuville explained in gestures that there was nothing he could do. Donadieu went down to see the Chinese man who was not yet dead. He lay without moving, his eyes on the ceiling, waiting for his turn to come.

The sun was up. Strands of warm mist hung above the sea. The only sound was the monotonous throbbing of the engine.

Donadieu had not yet decided if he would go back to bed. He moved to the promenade deck, walked halfway around it, and was surprised to hear women's voices. As he rounded the end he saw Madame Huret and Madame Dassonville talking.

He almost walked by without saying anything, but a look from Madame Huret stopped him, and he paused to ask:

"Did the baby have a good night?"

She tried to smile in thanks, but the spectacle she had just witnessed had shaken her so badly that her lips were still trembling convulsively.

Madame Dassonville felt called upon to explain:

"I understand what she's going through, doctor. To see 'that' when someone in your own family is ill! . . . Apparently another Chinaman is dying, too?"

"No, madame."

He was reserved, even rather distant.

Madame Dassonville pretended not to notice and maintained her composure. In spite of the hour, she was wearing a pretty pale-green silk dress which went well with her mahogany hair. As if she were in Paris or somewhere, her face was powdered and there was rouge on her cheeks and lipstick on her lips, and this emphasized the contrast between her and the pathetic figure of Madame Huret.

Donadieu compared the two of them and imagined Madame Huret well dressed, in good health, transformed by a happy smile.

"Doctor, do you think changing brands of milk will make any difference? The milk on the ship is different from the milk in Brazza. . . ."

"It's not important," he said.

He left them. Behind him the conversation between the two women continued, and he wondered what they could be saying to each other. It was certainly Madame Dassonville who had started it. She had noticed a woman on deck, and she had been curious to know who she was.

Donadieu shrugged. It did not concern him. He had an hour to spare before he had to be in his office to see second- and third-class passengers, and he decided to use the time to sit on his bunk and read. He was reading a book by Conrad that took place on board a freighter, but he had trouble keeping his mind on it. He was thinking that while his wife was on deck, young Huret was getting dressed in his cabin, which was too cramped and smelled of sour milk.

Anyway, Donadieu did not know why he was paying more attention to this kid than to the other passengers. Or, rather, he preferred not to admit it to himself.

He had a certain idiosyncrasy when he happened to be with someone he did not know, and it had nothing to do with his profession, since he had had it long before he decided to become a doctor.

Even when he used to return to school every October, he would look over his new classmates, pause over one face, and say:

"He's the one—something bad is going to happen to him."

For every year, out of all the students in a class, there is always one who will die or have an accident.

It was ridiculous. Donadieu did not have second sight. His choice, so to speak, was not necessarily the sickliest boy.

It was a very subtle thing. He would have had difficulty talking about it, especially since he did not quite believe in it himself. Yet he felt that some people were destined to suffer a catastrophe, just as others were born to live a long and peaceful life.

From the very first day he had been struck by Huret's face, though he did not know who he was or that he had a sick child.

Now he learned that the young man was already dogged by misfortune. He was married. He had responsibilities. His salary must have barely allowed him to make ends meet, and on top of it all his baby had become sick, forcing him to return to Europe.

"I bet they don't have a penny to their name! In fact I'm sure they have debts!"

Because they were the kind of people who would have debts, who would worry and worry without being able to extricate themselves.

The cabin boy scratched at the door and Donadieu shrugged, put back on his jacket, which he had taken off, and ran a brush over his hair. Was it any of his business? When he passed Cabin 7, the door was half open and he heard the sound of an argument.

"It can't be helped!" he sighed.

It was one of the hottest days yet, without the slightest breath of air. The sea and the sky were as pale, as iridescent, as the inside of a shell.

Donadieu managed to set the arm of a third-class passenger who had broken it falling in a gangway. At about ten o'clock, Lachaux called him into his cabin. He was sitting in the only chair, dressed in his pajamas, his feet bare and a glass of whisky within arm's reach.

"Close the door, doctor. Now, what about the Chinaman?"

"It's all over."

"Are you going to go on pretending it was dysentery?"

"My report is in the log. Did you ask me to come here to treat you?"

Lachaux grumbled and rolled his pajama bottoms up over his swollen leg. He had a habit of looking at people furtively, as though he suspected them of hiding something from him or planning some kind of mischief.

"You know what's wrong with you as well as I do," said Donadieu. "How many doctors have you consulted?"

This was another of Lachaux's obsessions. He consulted all doctors, proclaimed that he did not believe in medicine, and sneered:

"Now we'll see if you can do anything for me!"

There was nothing that could be done anyway. He had spent forty years in the bush and the equatorial forest without taking care of himself, literally collecting diseases to the point where he was rotting away.

"Are you in pain?"

"Not at all."

"In that case, there's no point in aggravating the disease by taking medication."

Donadieu wanted to leave. Lachaux held him back.

"In your opinion . . ." he began.

He turned away, uncomfortable, and swallowed some whisky.

"In my opinion?"

"Yes! I'm curious to know how much longer you think I'm going to live. That question bothers you, doesn't it? You can be honest with me!"

The funny thing was that Donadieu had no idea what to say. Although he did not even know if Huret was sick, he could have sworn that he would not live long. Faced with Lachaux's rotten flesh, he had no reaction.

"You're quite capable of living to a ripe old age," he muttered.

"Are you hoping for something?"

"I don't understand."

"*I* understand! But it doesn't matter. I would enjoy my whisky just as much if you told me I was going to die tomorrow."

Above them, two White Fathers who were traveling second class but had been allowed onto the promenade deck were dozing in deck chairs. A game of quoits had been started aft by Neuville, who was explaining the rules to the people who had not played the game before. The two lieutenants and the army captain were there, as well as Madame Bassot and Madame Dassonville. Donadieu was surprised to see Huret with a quoit in his hand. Huret seemed embarrassed and greeted the doctor awkwardly.

The doctor sat down in the shade. Because the reflections hurt his eyes he kept them half shut, so that what he saw through his eyelashes was blurred and seemed unreal.

The players moved into his field of vision one after another. Madame Dassonville was on the same team as Huret, who turned out to be quite skillful.

She was still wearing her green silk dress, and when she moved around in the sun her body was visible through the fabric, long and robust, more distinguished than Madame Bassot's but less voluptuous.

The officers clearly preferred the wife of the crazy doctor, with her unfailing good humor. She seemed greedy for pleasure, all kinds of pleasure, and without realizing he was doing it Donadieu looked at her wet armpits and could almost imagine how they smelled. After every turn, she burst out laughing, leaned on one of her companions, showed her teeth, and jiggled her chest.

"Bang! Bang!" said someone close to Donadieu.

It was the mad doctor, who was still wearing his heavy uniform overcoat. He was especially agitated but as usual was lost in his own world. He had noticed a spider on the bulkhead, and he was pretending to shoot at it.

"Bang! Bang!"

Suddenly he frowned. Something had nudged his memory. He lifted his head.

"Oh, yes. Coxyde . . . The trench . . ."

He was speaking quickly, and it was difficult to follow him.

"Trench . . . 'Artery-trench' . . ."

He was satisfied with the approximate word and, still standing very close to Donadieu, went on with his incoherent thought:

"Arterial tension . . . Fourteen . . . That's a lot, Admiral!"

His glance fell on Donadieu and he smiled at him in a friendly way, as if to include him in what he was doing.

"Admiral . . . admirable . . . honorable . . . mention . . . Menton . . . Nice–Menton–Monte Carlo . . . Carlovingians . . . Ha! Ha! . . ."

Donadieu smiled, too, because it was difficult not to, and also because the crazy doctor seemed pleased with his approval.

This went on for fifteen minutes with ups and downs—a jumbled succession of images, words, and puns would be followed by sudden silences, frowns, painful efforts during which Bassot would touch a certain place on his head. When the pain had passed, he would burst out laughing, as though he had been playing a good trick on the world.

His behavior was so extreme that for a moment Donadieu wondered if he wasn't acting, if he was really crazy. Whether that was the case or not, he still had some sense left. For example, he went up to the bartender, who had just served Donadieu. He was attracted by Donadieu's apéritif.

"Give me my red-currant syrup, Eugène!" he said in a sarcastic tone of voice. "Otherwise my wife will start shouting again."

He actually drank the red-currant syrup, while an ironic flame danced in his eyes.

An hour later Donadieu saw him absorbed in watching the little Dassonville girl, who was playing while her nanny watched.

Just before lunch, the purser said to the doctor:

"I don't know what the captain is going to decide."

"About what?"

"Bassot. A little while ago Madame Dassonville saw him hanging around her daughter. She went to the captain and asked him to keep the crazy man off the deck."

Donadieu shrugged his shoulders, but Neuville did not feel so detached about it.

"Obviously the madman does not belong on deck," he said.

He reddened as the doctor looked at him.

"It's not what you think. There's nothing between her and me. . . ."

"Not yet."

"But other children will be getting on at Port-Gentil and Libreville."

"What was Bassot before he became an army doctor?"

"He was a specialist in mental illness at Salpêtrière. He was beginning to behave strangely, and so they advised him to go to Africa. And instead of getting better . . ."

"Really!"

"Apparently he was drinking a bottle of Pernod before every meal. . . ."

They could hear Madame Bassot laughing and the sound of quoits clacking on the deck.

Lunch was more lively than it had been for days, because most of the passengers had got acquainted. And something rather significant happened: instead of eating alone, Jacques Huret sat down with the officers and Madame Bassot.

He was less gloomy. He forgot that his wife was spending all her time in their cabin by their baby's bedside, and that the baby might die at any moment. He joked with the others. The ship's captain, obsessed with good manners, found their table a little too noisy and grew slightly impatient.

"What about the ballast tanks?" Donadieu asked the chief engineer, whom he sat facing at every meal.

"They're holding up. I heard that this morning the Chinaman . . ."

They ate. For no good reason, Lachaux ordered champagne and looked defiantly at the doctor, who had not been able to help him. The Dassonvilles' little girl and her nanny ate at a separate table and spoke English together. As for Dassonville himself, he was preoccupied, because he was going to Dakar and then to Paris to present some rather delicate plans which he spent every day perfecting.

The sacred two hours of the siesta passed calmly, while the sailors took advantage of the time to polish the copper on deck.

The ship was supposed to arrive at Port-Gentil at about six o'clock in the evening and stay there two hours. When the dark line of the coast became visible, the three officers of the colonial infantry and Jacques Huret were playing *belote* on the bar terrace, while Madame Bassot leaned on the back of a chair and followed the game. On the table, ice melted in three apéritifs of different colors, and the smell of orange mingled with a more subtle fragrance of anise.

The *Aquitaine* sounded its first blast on the siren, and the city came into view at the back of the bay. It actually consisted of only a few light-colored houses with red roofs standing out against the dark-green

of the forest. Two freighters were loading billets of timber carried to
their sides by small tugboats. The air was full of the racket of capstans
and whistles blowing. For a moment the noise of the anchor being
lowered drowned out the other sounds, and a few minutes later a
motorboat came alongside.

The *belote* players did not stop their game. Some white men climbed
up the gangway ladder. People shook hands. In a few minutes the bar
was full and as lively as a café in Europe.

But most of the guests in the bar were not passengers. They were
people who lived in Port-Gentil and enjoyed having an apéritif on board
the ship once a month. They brought letters to be mailed and packages
to be taken to relatives and friends.

Night fell and lights went on along the coast, which seemed to move
closer. The purser was very busy, because he knew everyone, and
people were calling out to him from all the tables.

Two native dugouts had come alongside the stern. One was full of
colorful fish, and the other carried piles of plump green fruit—mangoes
and avocados. The cook in his white hat was arguing with the blacks,
who sat still without showing any impatience and occasionally spoke a
few words in their sharp voices.

Finally they reached an agreement. The fish and fruit were taken up
onto the deck, and coins were tossed to the natives.

Donadieu was watching the activity from a distance when the steward came up to him.

"The captain wants to see you in the saloon."

He was not alone there. He was sitting at a table with an army doctor
who was a general. The captain introduced the two men, and Donadieu
was invited to sit down.

"The general will be traveling with us as far as Libreville. I have told
him, doctor, about the request that was made to me this morning."

The army doctor was a good-looking man with a pepper-and-salt
mustache and very youthful eyes.

"I'm sure you agree with me," he said good-naturedly.

"About what?"

"About our unfortunate colleague. The captain has a serious responsibility. A passenger has complained. . . ."

"She has a child," the captain interjected.

"Madame Dassonville, I know!"

The captain hastened to add:

"I should also say that Madame Bassot herself would prefer to know
that her husband was in a safe place."

As if by chance the crazy man went by on deck, looking thoughtful and talking softly to himself.

"You don't want to lock him up in the padded cell, do you?"

"Well, if that becomes necessary . . . In any case, we could forbid him to go on deck at certain hours. . . ."

Cocktails were served. Donadieu drank only half of his and stood up.

"The captain will be the one to decide," he said. "Personally, I think Bassot is harmless."

A little later the crowd of strangers left the ship. The passengers gathered in the dining room, where there had been some changes.

The captain had seated the general at his table, and since the latter knew the Dassonvilles, he had invited them to the table, too; Lachaux was banished to the purser's table.

Two hundred tons of bananas had been loaded onto the deck. Because of this the ship was listing even more, so much that cups were sliding in their saucers.

"This is great!" the chief engineer said, smiling. "They've just told me there's a general on board. I'm supposed to do my best to right the boat!"

The second Chinese died during dinner, and Donadieu had to leave. He noticed as he went by that Jacques Huret, who. had had several apéritifs, had become quite animated and was talking in a loud voice.

The doctor plunged into the heat of the third-class area and found Mathias standing on the threshold of a cabin.

"It's all over!" he announced. "I found his money under the pillow."

There were two thousand three hundred francs. They had been earned during three years of laying down railway ties.

For Donadieu this meant a whole hour of filling out papers.

Four

The first contact between Jacques Huret and the doctor had taken place during the call at Port-Bouët a week after the ship left Matadi.

Life on board had changed again after Libreville. About forty passengers had come aboard, ten or twelve of them traveling first class. But the same thing happened that always happened: the original group of passengers hardly took any notice of them. With a few exceptions, the people who had just boarded seemed to them to be an anonymous crowd, as a crowd of new pupils is anonymous in the eyes of the older pupils.

The general had disembarked and had been replaced at the captain's table by a civil servant, a very thin little old man who had been in Africa for thirty years and yet had kept his ivory skin, his well-cared-for hands, his look of a finicky, sickly bureaucrat.

Lachaux returned to his place, and from then on the three men ate together at every meal.

Also on board were civil servants' wives, two little boys, and one little girl. The day after the ship left port someone had the idea of getting the children to dance the farandole hand in hand on deck, singing children's songs.

As early as eight o'clock in the morning, Donadieu would hear their rather shrill voices shouting:

"*Frère Jacques, Frère Jacques, dormez-vous, dormez-vous! . . .*"

Now he had to choose carefully when to take his walk, because there were almost always deck chairs across his path. Two of the new female passengers, one of whom was quite fat, sat knitting from morning to night, and ten times a day a ball of green yarn, acid-green yarn, would roll across the deck, unwinding as it went.

"Jeannot! Get my yarn! . . ."

Jeannot was one of the little boys.

What other changes were there? The lieutenants and the captain of the colonial infantry were not playing *belote* any more. They had stopped an hour after the ship left Libreville. What happened was that a timber man named Grenier who had just come on board was watching them play as he drank his apéritif. Donadieu noticed him because he was the only one on the ship not wearing a sun helmet. He did not look like a backwoodsman, either, but, rather, as though he belonged in the small bars in Montmartre or the Place des Ternes.

By the time the doctor had walked around the deck a second time, Grenier had struck up a conversation with the officers and Huret, who was one of the group.

The fourth time around, they had begun playing poker.

From then on it was settled, and in the evenings Madame Bassot had great difficulty finding someone to dance with her to the music of the phonograph.

In keeping with the rules, they played with chips, and the chips kept changing hands. But once the game was over everyone drew out his wallet.

The spirit of the group was no longer the same. No one would play quoits with the women. The smiles were more nervous. Donadieu may have been mistaken, but several times he had the impression that Huret was sending him a silent message.

They were in the waters of the Gulf of Guinea, where there was always a swell. Someone would occasionally leave the dining room very abruptly, and everyone knew what that meant. Later that person would be seen sitting on the bar terrace, where it was more comfortable.

Huret spent most of the day there. He was not actually sick, but his nostrils were pinched, and it was easy to see that the slightest imprudence would force him to hurry over to the railing.

When he met the doctor, he would greet him casually, like everyone else. But there was also a kind of shamefaced appeal in the way he looked at him.

Had he guessed Donadieu was interested in him?

"You shouldn't be playing cards," the doctor said to him wordlessly.

And he tried to walk past the tables when the players were cashing in their chips, to see if Huret had lost.

As for Madame Dassonville, she had almost disappeared from the crowd. People saw her without really seeing her. She no longer joined any of the groups. The purser had discovered that she played checkers, and for hours he would sit across from her in the back of the bar, where no one else ever sat, since the passengers preferred the terrace.

It was a dark room with black leather upholstered benches along the walls, heavy armchairs, and mahogany tables. The fan purred from morning to night, and only the silent white form of the bartender passed by now and then.

The couple was hardly ever disturbed. As people walked past on deck, they would glance briefly at the window and see nothing more than vague forms in the dim interior.

From time to time, Dassonville would sit down at a table with his files, his plans, and his blueprints and, a few steps away from his wife, would work steadily, with nothing else on his mind but his job.

Donadieu and the purser never talked about it. If they met, the doctor would simply ask:

"How's it going?"

And as though only one thing in the world was of any interest, little Neuville would answer with a wink.

The ship was still listing. The fresh water was turned off a certain number of hours a day. The original passengers had finally got used to it, but the newcomers would run after the chief engineer or the captain and ask:

"Is it true that the hull has been ripped open?"

They would try to calm the passengers' fears. The chief engineer went to great lengths to correct the listing as much as he could.

The morning they reached Port-Bouët, a little before they saw land, Donadieu met Madame Huret, who was getting some fresh air on deck, as she did every day. He went up to her and greeted her.

"How is the baby?" he asked in an encouraging voice.

When she looked up, he noticed a change in her. Her features had become not sharper but more indistinct. Her skin seemed to have softened and lost all its color. At the same time she was no longer in the least concerned with her own appearance and had hardly even bothered to comb her hair.

Perhaps she saw the look of surprise or pity in the doctor's eyes. Her eyelids swelled, her chin touched her chest, and she began sniffling.

"Come, come! The worst is over! As soon as we leave the gulf. . . ."

She was twisting a damp handkerchief between her fingers and sniffling, a tear running down her left cheek.

"Since the child has held out this long . . . Now you're the one who has to be looked after, and I think I will require you to be up on deck a certain number of hours every day. Are you eating well?"

She smiled ironically through her tears, and he was sorry he had asked. How could she have any appetite when her meals were brought to her in a cramped cabin lined with diapers hung up to dry?

"Is the motion of the sea bothering you at all?"

She shrugged almost imperceptibly, meaning she was resigned to it. Donadieu guessed that although she was not as sick as her husband, she felt a continuous nausea, a vague pain at the base of her skull, a bitter taste in the back of her mouth.

"I could lend you some books. . . ."

"You're very kind," she said without conviction.

She dried her cheeks and lifted her head, unashamed to show her red eyes and shining nose. She looked at him more firmly.

"Could you tell me what Jacques does all day?"

"Why do you ask me that?"

"No reason . . . Well, he seems different. He's nervous and irritable. One word and he flies into a rage."

"Have you had an argument?"

"It's not that. It's more complicated. When he comes down to the cabin it's as if it's a torture for him. If I ask him to do the slightest thing, he acts as if he's being victimized and gets seasick. Yesterday evening . . ."

She hesitated. They were alone on the promenade deck, and they could see the low line of the land and several bright spots that must have been houses. A dugout with a red sail passed close to the boat, and it was so frail, carrying only one bare-chested black man, that it was hard to believe it could have come out so far.

"Yesterday evening?" Donadieu repeated.

"Nothing . . . You'd better let me be alone. . . . I just wanted to know if Jacques had been drinking. . . . He lets himself be persuaded very easily. . . ."

"Does he usually drink?"

"It depends on his friends. When we're alone he doesn't. But if he's with friends and they're drinking . . ."

"Does he have trouble holding his liquor?"

"He's very cheerful for a while. Then he gets sad and disgusted with everything and cries over the slightest thing."

Donadieu thought about this and nodded. Of course he had not counted how many glasses Huret was drinking. Huret spent all day in the bar, but he did not drink any more than, say, the officers. Two apéritifs at noon. A liqueur after lunch. Two apéritifs in the evening . . .

"No, I don't think he's drinking too much," the doctor answered. "On land it would be too much, but on the ship there's nothing else to do. . . ."

Madame Huret sighed and cocked her ear, for she thought she had heard the sound of crying from the cabin directly below them. This was the hour when the other children began running along the deck shouting in their piercing voices:

"Miller, you're sleeping, your mill wheel's going too fast. . . ."

A few people were waiting for the doctor in front of the infirmary.

"In Europe things will be better."

"Do you think so?"

She did not have to say anything: he understood. Huret no longer had a job. He had heard talk about the Depression.

"What did he do before he went to Africa?"

"He worked at the Grands Moulins de Corbeil. We're both from Corbeil."

"I'll see you later," murmured Donadieu, walking away and sighing.

He did not understand at all! He knew Corbeil, because he used to go boating three kilometers up the river, at Morsang, just above the dam. And the memory he had was a summertime memory—the Seine, wide and flat, elongating the reflections of the peaceful landscape, the lines of barges, the narrow streets of Corbeil, the cigarette shop near the bridge, to his left the mills with their rumbling silos and the fine dust from the flour.

"Can't be helped! . . ."

He saw in consultation a woman from second class, crying because she was afraid she would give birth on board the ship. She had calculated when the baby was due to within several hours, and she begged the doctor to speak to the captain and have the boat increase its speed.

He could not do anything about this, either! On the forward deck, the Chinese had settled into a routine. All day long they were calm, cleaning themselves carefully, doing their washing, some of them helping to prepare the meals, since they had been allowed to eat their own kind of food.

But Mathias told how at night there were terrible fights in the hold, where they gambled wildly, even though they were being watched.

Out of prudence, their money had been taken away and deposited in the ship's safe. Altogether they had about three hundred thousand francs, but when the ship reached Bordeaux, the money would no longer be evenly divided up. Some of the Chinese would have nothing left, not even a pair of espadrilles, while others would have won as much as fifty thousand francs.

The anchor was lowered in the roads, rather far away from the beach, where the swell broke in a noisy surf. Almost nothing of the city could be seen: a few houses and a jetty on pilings, with small boats coming alongside.

Or, rather, they could not even come alongside, because of the surf. They had to perform a more complicated maneuver, and the same maneuver was being carried out on the ship.

Natives steadied small boats by the stern, opposite the cargo boom. The passengers who were getting off climbed into a rather ridiculous sort of basket that looked like the swings at a fairground.

The basket was raised with hoisting gear, moved through the air for a moment, and then deposited in a boat.

At the tip of the jetty the same operation was performed: a crane lifted the basket with the passengers in it and set them on terra firma.

This went on for hours. The heat was more intense than it had been anywhere else, and since the boat was riding at anchor, the swell was more perceptible; the passengers walked around white-faced, dull, and in agony.

In spite of this, the natives—especially the Arabs, who were wearing colorful robes and yellow slippers—swarmed up onto the deck like pirates, unwrapped their bundles, and made the ship like a fair as they covered the deck with ivory trinkets, African gods made of light-colored wood or ebony, little elephants, cigarette holders, snakeskin slippers, and badly tanned leopard skins that gave off a musky smell.

The Arabs were also sweating and smelled bad, and they clung to everyone, interminably lisping offers of services.

The hold had been opened, and loose rubber and bales of coffee and cotton were being loaded.

The passengers had looked forward to the visit as a period of calm, and now they waited impatiently for the ship to leave again. Departure was delayed because a high civil servant who was supposed to board the ship—and whose white villa was visible between the coconut trees that lined the shore—could not make up his mind to come. At the last momemt, for some reason or other, he had his secretary report that he would take the next mail boat.

It was just at this moment that Huret, who was walking by himself and zigzagging across the deck because of the list, came face to face with the doctor and looked at him as though he was reluctant to speak to him.

The two men were walking around the deck in opposite directions and could hardly avoid crossing paths again shortly afterward, and this time, too, Huret hesitated and went on walking.

The Arabs were still there, being jostled by the stewards, who were ordering them to pack up their merchandise and get off the ship. The first blast of the siren had sounded.

The third time they met, Huret finally stopped and made as if to remove his sun helmet.

"Excuse me, doctor . . ."

"Yes?"

Donadieu was only forty years old, and yet he inspired confidence, not so much as a doctor but more as though he were a priest; his mannerisms were a little like a priest's.

"I'm sorry to bother you. I would like to ask you . . ."

Huret was ill at ease. He blushed. He looked around at the Arabs, unable to keep his eyes still.

"Do you think the child will live?"

And Donadieu thought:

"You, my good man, are lying! You have not been stalking me all this time to talk about that."

"Why shouldn't he live?"

"I don't know. He seems so little, so weak. . . . He was born at a time when both of us were not feeling very well. . . . My wife was in a good deal of pain back there. . . ."

"Like all the women."

"I don't think so. It's hard to explain. . . ."

"I know what you mean, but it has nothing to do with what's bothering you."

"Do you think she will get her health back, too?"

"There's no reason for her to continue to be in pain. She is suffering through some hard times. When she gets to France and her life settles down . . ."

And Donadieu thought:

"Now that you've finished lying, come to the point."

Huret could not make up his mind to do it, but he could not leave the doctor, either. He seemed afraid that Donadieu would walk away, and added hastily:

"Maybe she has a little neurasthenia, too?"

"I didn't examine her with that in mind. Have you had any attacks of malaria?"

"I have. She hasn't."

"All you'll have to do will be to take some precautionary measures in France. Your doctor will undoubtedly cure you of it, because for some years now people have been able to recover."

"I know."

Still he did not say anything. What thought, what fear, was he hiding behind his stubborn forehead? For a moment Donadieu wondered if Huret was about to reveal that he had a certain more secret disease, but the doctor had not found any symptoms of it in the baby.

The Arabs left the ship. New passengers were wandering around the deck, taking possession of it.

"My wife didn't say anything to you this morning, did she?"

"Nothing special. She was tired. She was worried about how nervous you were."

Huret smiled briefly and hopelessly.

"Oh?"

"I know you get sick when you stay in the cabin, because it's so hot there. You can certainly tolerate the sea better on deck. . . ."

Huret understood. For a moment his eyes met the doctor's, and he might have been on the point of confiding in him.

"Sometimes all it takes is a kind word, a gesture," Donadieu went on, anxious not to lose his advantage. "Excuse me for saying this to you. When you go back down to the cabin, all you have to do is show a little . . ."

A little what? He could not think of the word. He had almost said "tenderness," but the word seemed to him ridiculous in a place like this. Just as his wife had done that morning, Huret bowed his head, and Donadieu was sure his eyes were moist.

But he was more nervous than she had been. He was actually consumed with nervousness; his fingers were hooked around one of the buttons on his jacket and he was about to pull it off.

"Thank you, doctor."

This time he went away, and the doctor simply continued to walk while the anchor was heaved and the boat moved out into the open sea, listing so much that the passengers had to hold on to the railing. As bad luck would have it, two glasses had slid off a table in the bar and shattered on the deck.

Lachaux was sitting there alone near a group of new passengers and the group of officers.

He was talking in a bitter, caustic voice, as if he were talking to himself yet making sure everyone could hear him. They all knew who he was. His forty years in Africa, his wealth, even his seat at the captain's table in the dining room, gave him a certain prestige.

"The governor was either cleverer than we were or better informed! He had reserved his two chairs, his luggage was at the end of the jetty, yet he didn't board the ship!"

Lachaux clearly enjoyed talking this way, especially as he watched the growing uneasiness of a young woman no one knew yet.

"I wonder if the company warned him. But for us, of course, the ship is good enough, with its hull torn open, the supply of fresh water strictly rationed, one screw bent. All you have to do is listen. Clearly one screw is not running true."

Everyone was tired. The visit had been demoralizing, what with the constant swell, the racket of winches moving continuously, the smell of blacks and Arabs who had invaded the boat, their shouts, their comings and goings, and on top of everything else the heat, which blew off the land in heavy gusts.

Men and women both had large wet semicircles under their arms. The ice in the glasses melted more quickly than usual, and after a few minutes the drinks were depressingly lukewarm.

Grenier, the timber man from Libreville who had started everyone playing poker, was one of the group on the terrace. He was not a civil servant or an employee of the company, so he could speak out.

"Do you think we're in danger?" he asked Lachaux.

"Well, if we run into a storm either here or in the Bay of Biscay, I don't know how we'll get out alive."

"In that case I'm going to get off at Dakar and take an Italian boat. There's one that leaves for Marseille every week."

The young woman squeezed her husband's arm and could not stop looking at the two men. Her wide eyes were naïve and frightened.

"I'll bet anything you like that the pumps will be running all night. They didn't dare have them running while anchored because it would have been too obvious, and they didn't want to frighten the passengers. I saw the same kind of thing ten years ago. . . ."

Everyone listened more closely.

"We drifted around at sea for a month before a German boat noticed us. There were no Chinese on board, but there were some blacks, and we weren't told that the blacks who were dying had yellow fever."

As he said this, Lachaux looked at Donadieu, who had just sat down and ordered a whisky.

"And I'll bet another thing! Before we get to Dakar at least two more Annamites will die, and we'll be told they had dysentery. . . ."

Huret, who had circles under his eyes, was leaning against a column on the terrace and listening. His eyes met the doctor's and he turned away.

After he finished dressing for dinner, Donadieu met up with the purser, who was on his way back from the captain's cabin.

"We have to amuse the passengers," he said. "Tomorrow we're going to start playing horse racing, with betting."

Something evidently struck him about the doctor's attitude or expression.

"Something wrong?" he asked.

"I don't know. . . . Maybe . . ."

It was only an impression, or not even that, a vague uneasiness with no identifiable source. Dinner was gloomy that evening. Certain passengers were uncomfortable because of the swell and left their tables, one after another. In the bar, the poker game was continually interrupted by hushed conferences.

Five

Donadieu sometimes blushed at his own thoughts. He found himself more and more preoccupied by Huret, and what he felt was not just curiosity. It was more complex than that.

His feelings reminded him of a problem he had puzzled over as a child. For an entire year at school, in fact, he had mulled over the mystery of fate.

His religion teacher had said that man is free to act. But he had immediately added:

"Ever since the beginning of the world God has known everything that would happen with the passage of time, including every act of the most humble animal."

Young Donadieu did not understand how man could be free if every phase of his life was known in advance.

He thought of this again in connection with Huret. It was almost the same problem. The moment he met him he "felt" that the young man was threatened by a catastrophe, that with almost mathematical precision it would swoop down on him at a certain moment.

And he watched Huret live his life; he kept watching him, and he started becoming impatient. The catastrophe did not take place, in spite of the oppressive atmosphere, which became more upsetting every day.

The proof that Donadieu was not wrong, that he was not letting himself get carried away by his imagination, was that most of the other people on board also acted as though some misfortune were about to occur.

Animals grow nervous several hours before a storm; all of nature becomes uneasy. Well, that same kind of uneasiness could be sensed in the most casual gestures, in attitudes that might have passed as normal.

For example, one morning, when Madame Huret was taking her walk on deck, Bassot appeared, dressed in his inevitable khaki overcoat. They met near the railing. The madman's eyes were dancing, and instead of uttering a long string of incoherent words, he said:

"Good morning, little sister."

She was afraid. She regained her composure, however, and he leaned on the railing next to her and talked to her. Donadieu could not hear what he said.

It did not mean anything. It was a completely banal incident, and yet what happened next increased the feeling of agitation in the air. Madame Bassot appeared on the promenade deck, rushed over to the couple, and grasped her husband by the arm, forcing him to leave with her. This was so unexpected, so abrupt, that Madame Huret was disconcerted and looked to the doctor for reassurance.

"What did I do to him?" she asked.

"Nothing. Don't worry. The passengers are nervous."

He was waiting for the situation to explode. Yet the morning was peaceful. The swell was not too annoying, and women in white dresses played quoits all along the deck. At about eleven o'clock, two sailors began preparing for the game of horse racing that would take place that afternoon, and it was amusing to watch what they were doing.

In one corner, near the bar, they had set up a cabin with a ticket window, and on it they wrote "Betting Office."

A race track was drawn on the deck in chalk and divided up into numbered squares.

The children were especially interested in the papier-mâché horses, which they would have liked to play with, but which were reserved for the grownups.

The only incident that took place was started by the madman. He was watching the children play when Madame Dassonville called to her nanny and said loudly:

"As long as that man is here, I don't want my daughter to remain on deck."

The other mothers, who had not been alarmed before, shuddered and gathered into a group. Bassot, having no idea that he was the center of attention, talked to himself as he wandered among the children.

Everyone knew what was happening when one of the women went toward the bridge. A few minutes later, in the bar, someone remarked:

"The crazy man said that if the children went on making so much noise he would throw them overboard."

Had he really said that? Donadieu was not able to find out for sure. But whatever the case, the captain came down and went over to Bassot, who seemed to sense that he was in danger, for he took several steps backward. The captain grasped his arm and led him away.

That was all.

"They've locked him in his cabin," someone said when they were having apéritifs.

Madame Bassot appeared. She was overexcited, and as she sat down at the officers' table, she said:

"I can't stand it any more! Unless someone makes some kind of arrangement, I refuse to take care of him any longer. Too bad if something happens!"

"Is he vicious?"

"With me, yes. Just now he blamed me for calling the captain, because he thinks everything is my fault."

Lachaux lay back in his wicker chair, which was being crushed by his weight. His face was greasy with sweat, and he seemed to be drinking in the general uneasiness with perverse joy.

But Huret was very calm. He avoided meeting the doctor's eyes and drank only one apéritif.

At four o'clock the races began. They were conducted as much as possible like real horse races, especially as far as the betting went.

First the animals were put up for auction. Since the proceeds were to go to the Orphans of the Sea, people turned to Lachaux, hoping that he would raise the prices, but all he did was pay one hundred francs for the first horse. The only one who added any excitement to the bidding was Grenier, the timber man.

Once the horses were in place, the Betting Office opened, and Donadieu saw Huret prudently bet ten francs.

The grownups surrounded the area marked off by chalk and pushed back the children, who were edging in, trying to watch.

The purser asked Madame Dassonville to throw the dice, and when she stepped forward it was clear that this had been arranged beforehand. After all, she was the most elegant woman there, as well as the most graceful.

Each throw of the dice corresponded to the advance of one horse, and soon the papier-mâché race horses were spread out along the track.

This was the first time the passengers had all gathered in one place this way. People who had never spoken a word to one another now struck up conversations. The captain had put in an appearance and stayed several minutes.

While the Betting Office was paying the winners of the first race, the doctor noticed Huret talking to Madame Dassonville. This was rather unexpected, especially since he was very cheerful, very much at ease. The purser was busy. Watching the couple, Donadieu saw them sit down at a table to have something to drink.

This was almost in defiance of Donadieu's predictions; Huret was a very different person from the feverish young man of the previous days. To judge by Madame Dassonville's bursts of laughter, he was evidently saying witty things to her.

And he seemed happy, his features relaxed out of his usual look of suffering.

Perhaps he guessed what was going through the doctor's mind. A shadow passed over Huret's face, but a moment later he was lively and youthful again.

He was not ugly. He was even a nice-looking boy, with something soft and childish about him, in the pout of his lips, his way of inclining his head. Madame Dassonville had discovered this, and Donadieu was sure she agreed with him.

"Now he's going to do something foolish," he said to himself. "To impress her he's going to play for high stakes, buy a horse in the second race, offer everyone champagne. . . ."

Because the timber man, whose stable had won, was buying champagne for the group surrounding the officers, and his example would be contagious. There was a relaxed feeling in the air. No one was thinking about the listing of the boat. Sails had been rigged up to provide some shade, and the temperature was bearable.

"The captain requests that you go see him at once."

Donadieu went up on the bridge and found the captain talking to Madame Bassot. Donadieu had not noticed that she was missing from the deck. She was drying her eyes, and her chest was rising and falling rapidly. The captain, sitting at his desk, looked worried.

"At this point there is nothing else we can do," he said without looking at the doctor. "Even madame herself wants us to do it. After one or two more stops there will be twenty children playing on deck, and I can't assume such a serious responsibility."

Donadieu had understood, but he did not say a word. . . .

"So make use of this opportunity, while the passengers have gathered on deck, to take Dr. Bassot to the cabin. . . ."

He did not dare say "padded cell."

And Madame Bassot continued to dry the tears from her full, rosy cheeks.

"Take three or four men with you, just to be sure."

"Will madame go with me?" Donadieu asked.

She shook her head vigorously, and the doctor left her and went down slowly, seeing from a distance that the horse racing was beginning again. The sun, already low on the horizon, was reddening, and on the forecastle the Chinese were contentedly lying in a heap.

Donadieu summoned Mathias and two sailors. The operation was a rather delicate one, since the cell with the padded walls was in the very bow of the ship, under the third deck, between the engines and the Annamites' hold. To reach it, they had to walk across the forecastle through the crowd of Chinese, descend a steep stairway, and then climb down an iron ladder.

The four men, standing in the first-class gangway, looked at one another and hesitated. Just in case he needed it, one of the sailors took off the rope he was wearing as a belt and kept it in his hand.

All along the gangway fans were humming. A chambermaid watched the scene from a distance, as did the maître d'hôtel, standing halfway down the stairs to the dining room.

Donadieu knocked at the cabin door, turned the key, opened the door part way, and saw Dr. Bassot. His face was pressed against the porthole, bathed in sunlight.

At that moment Donadieu was certain that Bassot was not quite as crazy as people thought. Not a word, not a gesture, from them was needed. Perhaps Bassot had been expecting this to happen for some time now.

When he saw the little group of men, he looked frightened and then outraged, and he plunged straight ahead without crying out, only groaning hoarsely.

He dived between the two sailors, each of whom seized one of his arms while Mathias stood by helplessly.

Donadieu mopped his forehead with a handkerchief. He watched Bassot fighting desperately and heard the sound of the khaki overcoat ripping.

In the corridor the door of Cabin 7 opened. Madame Huret, who had heard the noise, looked out.

"Hurry up," panted Donadieu, turning his head away.

The sailors twisted Bassot's arms and, after glancing at one another, lifted him suddenly and carried him off in that position, as he flung himself about, one leg slamming against the floor with anger. The chambermaid, surprised, ran away. From the deck they heard the sound of the bell for the betting.

They still had to cross the forecastle, where not one Chinese was moving. But three hundred pairs of cautious eyes followed the turbulent group as far as the stinking hatchway, which was next to the toilets. Below, hundreds of human beings lived on top of one another in such intense heat that just to lean over the stairway was unpleasant.

Donadieu was walking behind the others, listening to the banging on the sheet-iron bulkhead, which meant that Bassot was still fighting. But he could not see anything; they were walking single file. They had to let Mathias through to open the door of the padded cell.

"Should I put the strait jacket on him?"

Donadieu was incapable of saying anything and shook his head, looking away. He was familiar with the padded cell. It was a cabin one and a half meters wide and two meters long. The porthole, right at the water line, was so narrow that it could only be opened on the few days when the sea was absolutely calm. Because the engine rooms were so close and the walls were padded, the heat became intolerable.

Standing behind the others in the corridor, the doctor heard footsteps, a bang, the sound of the door closing, and then complete silence.

The two sailors looked at him as though waiting for another order or for congratulations, but Donadieu simply indicated that they could go. Mathias, his hair plastered to his temples, mopped himself off.

"He's going to die in there," he said. "Who's going to bring him his food?"

"You are."

Mathias hesitated. This was not the first time they had shut someone up in the padded cell, and in almost every case, when they had opened the door again, they had found themselves face to face with a raving lunatic.

"Come on. . . ."

Donadieu did not have the courage to go back to his cabin and write up his report. When he came out onto the third-class deck among the Annamites, he saw Madame Bassot standing with the captain at the end of the bridge. She had watched her husband's squirming body being dragged past below her.

"It's all over," he indicated, gesturing with his head.

And he reached the promenade deck in time for the end of the last race. The first person he saw in the crowd was Jacques Huret, whose face was glowing. He was waiting his turn in front of the ticket window, and everyone was going up to speak to him and looking at him with amusement, because he had just won a little less than two thousand francs.

It was an incredible piece of luck, considering that he had only bought one horse for one hundred fifty francs and bet thirty francs at the Betting Office.

His eyes were shining, his lips were moist. When he glanced at the doctor there was almost a look of defiance on his face. He seemed to be crying out to him:

"You always look at me in a pitying way, as if I were condemned forever! Well, fate has smiled on me. My hands are full of hundred-franc notes. I have spent the afternoon with the most beautiful and distinguished woman on board. . . ."

He was feverish, and in the confusion following the game he had trouble finding the people he wanted to gather together; he sat Madame Dassonville, the timber man, and the officers around a table.

"Champagne!" he cried to the bartender.

Donadieu saw a brief hesitation in his eyes. No doubt he had thought of going to tell his wife the good news. But in all fairness, how could he do that? When the timber man won the first race he had ordered champagne. Huret, who had won four times as much, had to do the same. And he could not leave Madame Dassonville there alone.

The shadow remained over his face for a few minutes. Then the champagne was served, and little by little the passengers settled down on the terrace in groups. Huret's group was the noisiest.

Donadieu was sitting by himself in his usual corner.

He was surprised that the purser, who had finished taking care of the Betting Office accounts, came up to him instead of Madame Dassonville.

"I hear he's been locked up."

Donadieu nodded.

"It's just as well. One accident, and the captain would lose his job. So would you. . . ."

Neuville, who was very bright, followed the doctor's glance, saw Madame Dassonville, and understood what the doctor was thinking.

"I'm cutting my losses . . ." he muttered, sipping his whisky.

"Already?"

"We were nearly caught twice, once by her husband and once by her little girl, only three hours ago. . . ."

"Oh!"

Donadieu smiled slightly, but the purser was taking it seriously.

"Her husband is getting off at Dakar. If she's this reckless with him on board, what will she be like afterward?"

Of course! Neuville was a smart boy. He carefully weighed his pleasures against any disagreeable consequences that might result from them.

Young Huret and Madame Dassonville, surrounded by the white uniforms of the officers, were sitting where Donadieu could see them without moving his head. There were three bottles of champagne on the table. Madame Dassonville was talking gaily to her companions, but every now and then she glanced furtively at the purser, whose back was turned to her.

"Do you think she'll leave you alone?"

"She already seems fully occupied. . . ."

And Donadieu thought about his old religion class again, and his childish doubts.

Huret was free to act! Huret was free, now, to look rapturously at Madame Dassonville. . . .

A short time before, as Donadieu had watched him, Huret had been calm and serious, his face relaxed, and Donadieu had doubted his own prediction.

"The designs of Providence are unknowable . . ." he recited to himself.

Another childhood memory. The first time he had read that phrase, hadn't he mistaken the meaning of the word "design" and imagined a rebus with tangled lines?

On the bar terrace morale was very high, so high that the captain, who rarely ventured here, came and sat at Lachaux's table to have an apéritif. Someone had mentioned the party that, as on every crossing, would take place immediately after the ship left Dakar. People were discussing possible costumes, and especially the question of whether the first and second classes could mix for once that evening, to make things livelier.

Dassonville was there, too—not with the excited group that surrounded his wife, but at the table of the old administrator, who was talking to him about the first work on the Congo-Ocean Railway and the work on the Matadi-Leopoldville line, which had taken place even earlier.

Madame Bassot was the last to appear. She had gone to her cabin to powder her nose and change her dress. There was a little too much powder on the right wing of her nose, and this made her look strange.

She hesitated when she saw that Madame Dassonville had taken her place, because, after all, she was the rightful guest at the officers' table. But one lieutenant very gallantly offered her his chair and called to the bartender to bring another glass.

The two women briefly exchanged looks. Huret triumphantly leaned toward Madame Dassonville to talk to her.

"Are we going to dance this evening?" he asked.

He had not yet danced on the ship, because he had not had a partner. He had always simply watched the others from the dark corner where he drank his coffee and liqueur.

"The records are always the same," Madame Bassot complained.

"I've heard that one of the engineers has some very good records, but somebody will have to go get them from him."

Huret said he would do it. He would have taken on all the sins of the world just to remain in that state of lighthearted optimism.

"Where is he?"

"As far below as you can go."

He got up. The champagne made him a little awkward, but after three or four steps he righted himself and plunged into the darkness of the stairway that led to the third class.

Madame Dassonville took the opportunity to keep looking at the purser, and when Donadieu told him, he turned around and smiled at her.

Then she stood up as though she were just going to stretch her legs.

"You're keeping to yourself today!" she said as she went by, mincing and showing her teeth in an aggressive smile.

"We were talking about something serious."

"And of course you won't be dancing this evening."

"That depends on how much work there is to do. We're going into port tomorrow. There are supposed to be ten more passengers in first class and nearly thirty in second. . . ."

She smiled rather spitefully to show that he was not fooling her.

When Huret came back, bursting out of the shadows the same way he had plunged into them, he was drunk with joy and carried a whole pile of records under his arm.

"Hip, hip, hurrah!" the officers shouted in unison.

Meanwhile Donadieu was reciting a phrase he had read somewhere: "Everyone has his moment in life. . . ."

He blushed. He was acting as though he was jealous of Huret, or, rather, as though he resented the fact that Huret was not confirming his predictions by heading straight into some kind of disaster.

Six

By the time they reached Dakar, the boat was almost full, but the newer passengers had not managed to form any relationships with the older passengers.

When the ship had stopped at Tabou no one had gone ashore, because the only way to leave the ship would have been by using the unpleasant basket system, and the swell had happened to be quite strong. But at Conakry all three army officers had gone off to take advantage of the few hours the ship would be in port. When they had come back, they had swaggered around like young peasants returning from the city. They had made remarks and winked at one another, as though no one else would understand.

The most important incident had taken place out at sea, two days before they reached Dakar. Night had fallen an hour earlier, and the passengers were having dinner in the dining room. At the beginning of the meal, people had noticed that the third officer had gone to look for the captain, but no one had paid any attention. Now, however, the screw suddenly stopped turning, the engines died, and the boat gradually slowed, drifting about in a disconcerting way.

People looked around at the other tables. Lachaux, whom the captain must have warned beforehand, ostentatiously continued eating. Dassonville, who was near a porthole on the starboard side, rose from his chair, glanced at the darkness outside, and gestured to his wife to go out on deck with him.

A moment later everyone except Lachaux and the civil servant, who was eating at his table, had left the dining room.

In the dark a short distance from the *Aquitaine* was a large steamer, festooned with such garlands of light that at first sight some passengers thought it was a city on the coast.

The two ships, which had come to a stop, rocked gently as a rowboat advanced between them through the water; voices rose from it.

"It's the *Poitou*," someone said.

It was another steamer belonging to the same company and traveling the same route, in the opposite direction. The *Aquitaine* let down its accommodation ladder, the boat came alongside, and a heavy-set man slowly climbed up the steps, followed by a sailor carrying his bags.

A few minutes later the two steamers continued on their way, and the passengers, disappointed, returned to dinner. As for the new arrival, he went into the dining room with the others. He was seated at a table with a family until a permanent place could be found for him.

Very tall, fat, and indolent, he had a mop of gray hair which made him look as though he belonged in the cabarets of Montmartre.

He did indeed live somewhere between Boulevard Rochechouart and Rue Lamarck, but he was not a song writer or a poet. He was a translator for a large newspaper, and there, in a room set apart from the rest of the staff, he spent ten hours a day annotating foreign newspapers and smoking a meerschaum pipe.

He had never before been outside of France. When he had turned fifty, a doctor had advised him to go to a different climate for several weeks, and so he had requested vacation time and bought a half-price ticket for Equatorial Africa.

As he had sensitive feet and hated moving around, he had not left the ship once and had not visited Tenerife or Dakar. One day, when he was checking the schedules, he saw that he had only just enough time to return to France before his vacation was over, and the *Poitou*, which was going on toward Pointe-Noire and Matadi, had handed him over to the *Aquitaine*.

It was he who reintroduced *belote* on board, so that everyone abandoned poker.

When the ship docked in the port of Dakar, the same thing happened as always. For several hours the passengers ceased to know one another. They all went on land, but each pretended to go his own way, to see what he wanted to see, do what he had to do.

Almost the only people left on board were Lachaux and the new passenger, whose name was Barbarin, and they remained on the bar terrace reading the fresh batch of newspapers that had just arrived.

This was how they happened to see four people come on board and go straight to the captain's cabin, where they remained for an hour, after which they examined the ship for a long time, especially the hold.

When the first passengers came back, exhausted from having walked through street after street in the city, they learned that this delegation, which was supposed to decide whether or not the ship was fit to continue on its route, had not yet finished work.

On deck there was the usual swarming mass of blacks, Arabs, and even Armenians selling the most incongruous assortment of objects. Barbarin did not see them. He had bought an enormous pile of newspapers, and through force of habit he was annotating them in blue and red pencil as he smoked pipe after pipe.

Jacques Huret was one of the first to return, because he had not found anything to do on land. Like a mirage, Dakar had disappointed everyone.

From the port you could see European-style blocks of houses, public buildings, taxis, and trolley cars. Once the passengers got off the boat they did find a few stores with real window displays, French goods, and two cafés similar to those in any small neighborhood in France.

But what was there left to do after drinking one or two apéritifs— which were much more expensive than the ones on board the ship? The streets were burning hot underfoot. Beggars caught at your sleeves, street merchants flung glass-bead necklaces around your neck or thrust colorful wallets into your hand.

As he passed Cabin 7, Donadieu thought he heard the murmurings of an argument, but several minutes later he found Huret pacing the deck. He had bought himself a silk jacket and a royal-blue tie and had put brilliantine on his hair.

The timber man, who had threatened to get off at Dakar and take an Italian ship, stopped mentioning his plan. The army officers returned to the ship.

There was a storm brewing. In fact, for several minutes some large drops of rain fell, but everyone's hopes were disappointed, and the coppery-red dusk was hotter than ever before.

This was the last port of call in Africa. From now on it would be a monotonous crossing on the high sea, with only one halt, in Tenerife, before they reached Bordeaux. The passengers bought presents for their relatives and friends, and all the presents were the same—little objects made out of ivory, crudely cut wooden statuettes, wallets or handbags of multicolored leather.

Donadieu did not have enough curiosity to want to watch the boat leave. From his cabin he could hear the din, the rapid leave-taking of the people who did not belong on the ship, the last instructions. He did not go to dinner, either, because that day Bassot had not yet been let out to get some fresh air.

The crazy man was still locked up in the padded cell, and Donadieu had been given permission to take him for a walk twice a day on the third-class deck, early in the morning and fairly late in the evening.

The first morning, Mathias had run up in a state of extreme agitation.

"Doctor! . . . Come quickly. . . . Our patient has had an attack. . . . He has broken everything. . . ."

It was not as bad as all that. It was even rather amusing. Bassot, locked up all alone in the padded cell, had not struggled, had not shouted, had not even banged on the walls the way ninety-nine out of a hundred would have.

Instead, with the tips of his fingernails, he had patiently pulled the stitches out of the cloth of his mattress and then the padding on the walls.

When the doctor went into the cabin, Bassot, still wearing his overcoat—which he refused to take off—was sitting in the midst of a mountain of feathers. A slight smile was floating on his pale lips.

"Where is Isabelle?" he asked.

"What Isabelle?"

"My wife! I bet she's having fun with the officers! She likes the officers, Isabelle does. . . ."

He forced himself to laugh though his face was twisted into an involuntary grimace. Then, almost immediately, he started speaking in incoherent strings of words, watching the doctor out of the corner of his eye. It looked as if he was doing it on purpose, as though he derived a malicious pleasure from fooling everyone.

"I tried to get the captain to give you a cabin, but I had no luck. . . ."

Bassot, who pretended not to listen, understood very well what was being said to him.

He refused to wash or shave. He even threw the pitcher of water at Mathias's legs when it was brought to him.

That evening, Donadieu tried again.

"If you're quiet and if you agree to clean yourself up, the captain will allow the two of us to take a walk on deck."

"That deck up there?" asked Bassot in an ironic tone.

"It doesn't matter which deck. You'll be out in the open. . . ."

It was upsetting to see how little the heat in the padded cell bothered Bassot. Donadieu could stand it only for a few minutes. The cell also smelled disgusting.

Yet Mathias cleaned it twice a day. Sitting on the bunk, which had a new mattress on it, the crazy man would silently watch him moving around, or else he would take the pencil he had asked for and draw on the door, which was the only surface not covered with padding.

Among the graffiti, next to the striking, very elongated faces he drew—some of them reminiscent of Memling's *Virgins*—it was rather surprising to see difficult algebraic equations and chemical formulas.

The walks went well. Mathias had been instructed to follow at a distance, ready to intervene if he had to, but it was not necessary. The Chinese lying on the deck moved aside to let the crazy man and the doctor go by, and watched them lazily.

The two men talked very little. Sometimes Donadieu's patience was rewarded with several coherent sentences.

"You'll see. In Bordeaux they're going to lock me up. My wife's brother is a doctor, too. He's the one who made me go to Africa. . . ."

That was all! Then he would start in on his improvisations:

"Africa . . . cash . . . don't have any . . . pennies . . . Pentagon . . . Pantagony . . ."

One time Donadieu gripped him violently by the arm and muttered: "Shut up!"

And Bassot looked at him in a frightened way, nearly smiled, and continued anyway:

". . . agony and . . ."

Can anyone ever know just how crazy a crazy man is?

Again that evening, as the lights of Dakar receded behind the ship and he was walking with his prisoner in the dark forecastle, Donadieu tried to understand.

Bassot was behaving well, saying nothing, breathing the night air deeply, and looking up at the sky, where a few stars shone through a gap in the clouds. Not far away from them, a deck passenger was operating a phonograph, playing records of Arab music.

The only light the two men had to see by was the diffused glow from the first-class deck, where the bartender was setting out glasses on the tables for the passengers who would be coming from the dining room.

Bassot was wearing his overcoat, but he had forgotten his cap, and his bleached hair was tousled. A three-day-old yellowish beard made him seem both thinner and more masculine at the same time. Under the khaki cloth he was wearing only rumpled pajamas, and his feet were bare in his worn-out slippers.

Sometimes Donadieu glanced at him quickly, but the crazy man was always aware of that glance. Most of the time he felt the need to spin around, smile, or speak incoherently.

He was not pretending; his case was more complex. It seemed as though he had been relieved to see the onset of his mental illness and had done all he could to accentuate it.

"Bang! Bang! The shell bursts. . . . My head bursts. . . . The bus stops short when a tire bursts. . . ."

Like a child he enjoyed making up meaningless rhymes, and his talk often resembled free verse or a song. The gunfire kept recurring.

"Bang! Bang!"

He looked around for his wife. He asked:

"Where is Isabelle?"

"She's eating dinner."

"With the officers!"

Donadieu had found out that in Brazzaville Isabelle had apparently slept with most of the officers, and that she had hardly bothered to hide this from her husband.

"Bang! Bang!"

Was this the explanation for the gunfire Bassot kept imitating?

He and Donadieu were the same age. The only difference was that Donadieu had gone to school in Montpellier and Bassot in Paris. Otherwise, they might have known each other from the time they were adolescents.

Bassot knew that the doctor was thinking about him and trying to understand. Didn't he sometimes want to say to him:

"All right. I'm sick. I'm crazy. Maybe there's a cure for it, but I don't want to be cured because . . ."

No. They walked along side by side like strangers, or even worse than strangers, since Donadieu could only regard Bassot as an animal under observation.

At one point the doctor looked up, sensing the presence of shadows on the first-class deck. A couple was leaning against the railing. The crazy man, who had also looked up, said as though to reassure the doctor:

"It's not her. . . ."

His wife was the only person who existed for him. The woman up there was whispering, her elbow touching Huret's elbow. She laughed softly every now and then. It was Madame Dassonville.

"Let's go back," said Donadieu, taking Bassot's arm.

He remembered something a friend had said to him one day on board another steamer, as they traveled down the Suez Canal after having crossed the Red Sea:

"People should call you God the Father!"

He had not laughed. He really was obsessed with the need to become concerned with other people—not in order to interfere with their lives or to make himself feel important, but because he simply could not remain indifferent to those who passed before him, who lived under his gaze, sliding along toward some joyful event or some disaster.

He had noticed Huret up there, and now he was anxious to get rid of Bassot, whom he locked up in his cell as usual after having patted him affectionately on the shoulder.

But he did not go up to the deck right away.

He stopped in front of the door of Cabin 7, listened for a moment, and then knocked.

"Come in!"

He had to admit that Madame Huret's voice, especially when she was in a bad mood, was vulgar and unattractive.

When he opened the door he saw the baby sleeping and, on the opposite bunk, Madame Huret lying in a black dress and bare feet, one arm under her head.

How long had she been lying there, staring gloomily at the ceiling?

"So it's you, doctor."

She got up hastily, looked for her slippers, and tossed back her hair, which was falling over her face.

"Have you seen my husband?"

"No. I've just come from third class. How's the baby?"

"The same as always!"

She said this in such a discouraged way that there was not even any affection, any anguish, left in her voice.

It was true that the case was discouraging. The baby was not really sick; at least he did not have any identifiable disease that could be treated. But he was not mending, as they say. He ate and yet did not derive any nourishment from his food. He was just as thin, just as limp, just as pale, as he had always been, and he was fussy the way all babies are fussy when they are uncomfortable, whimpering for an entire hour without stopping.

"In three days the climate will change."

"I know," she said condescendingly. "If you come across my husband . . ."

"Dinner probably isn't over yet."

All she had had to eat was a little cold meat and an orange, and the remains of her meal were still on the shelf at the head of the bunk. This was the way she wanted it. She had been asked if she wanted to take her meals with the children half an hour before the other passengers, while her husband watched the baby or Mathias stayed in the cabin.

"I don't feel like getting dressed up," she had said. "Not just so that people can stare at me as though I were a strange animal."

And Donadieu was reminded of Bassot, who was acting in somewhat the same way, refusing to shave or even to wash, deriving perverse pleasure from burying himself in the bad smell of his lair.

"If this goes on," she said calmly, "I'm going to ask you to give me some Veronal."

"What would you want it for?"

"To kill myself with."

Was this a pose, a romantic gesture? Was she trying to move him and arouse his pity?

"You forget that you have a child!"

She shrugged her shoulders, glancing at the baby's bunk. Could it really be called a child? Would it become something like a man one day?

"I'm worn out, doctor. My husband doesn't understand. Sometimes he's the one I want to kill. . . ."

Huret was standing up there leaning over the silky water, his shoulder against Madame Dassonville's bare shoulder, breathing in her perfume. Maybe their fingers had touched on the railing and furtively clasped.

What was Huret saying to her?

Dassonville had stayed in Dakar. Madame Dassonville was alone. Her cabin was the very last one at the end of the gangway, and her little girl slept with the nanny on the odd-numbered side.

"You've got to be patient. We're more than halfway there. In Bordeaux . . ."

"Do you think anything will change once we're in France? There's no reason for it to! It will always be just poverty and work. . . ."

At times like this she was particularly vulgar.

"It would be better if you gave me two tubes of Veronal, and then we would all be happy. . . ."

Her eyes were dry, her mouth turned down in scorn and disgust.

"What do you want me to say to your husband?" the doctor asked as he left.

"Nothing. You'd better not say anything. He should stay outdoors as much as he can. Besides, it's the only way to keep us from fighting."

Huret and Madame Dassonville had left the railing and sat down at a table on the terrace, and the two of them were having coffee alone together. They were as immodest in their behavior as happy lovers—smiling, hardly noticing anything around them, and inclining their heads toward each other in a way that transformed their most trivial remarks into important confidences.

The purser was sitting with Lachaux and Barbarin, who had ordered a glass of good brandy and was filling his pipe.

"Game of *belote*?" asked the timber man, who was sitting at the next table.

"A thousand points, if you like. I want to get to bed early."

"Are you in, Huret?"

And Huret answered, with an artificial air of embarrassment that delighted him:

"Not tonight."

Donadieu happened to catch Madame Dassonville looking at the purser as if to say:

"Did you hear that? Too bad for you! I hate you!"

The bartender brought the cards and a cloth, along with a little basket of chips. Lachaux grumbled and moved his wicker chair back. Some of the new passengers, who had not yet settled into any routines, walked around the deck and looked enviously at the regular customers of the bar.

The purser got up and went out for a moment, and several minutes later the phonograph began playing blues.

Most of the people who usually danced were busy doing other things. Two of the officers were playing *belote* with Barbarin and the timber man. The army captain was listening to Lachaux, who was telling him stories about ships being damaged on the high seas.

Just as the doctor turned toward Huret and Madame Dassonville, they stood up, not to take a walk but to dance.

The dance floor consisted of the whole rear part of the promenade deck, with the brightly lit bar terrace in the center. On either side there were corners in semidarkness. From below, the second-class passengers watched the couple moving around.

And over and over again Huret led his partner into the dimly lit corners, bent his head over her, and rested his cheek against hers. She did not push him away, but kept looking at the purser.

As for Huret, he seemed to be defying the whole world. He was no longer a worried little accountant demoralized by having been admitted as a special favor to first class, even though he held a second-class ticket. He was wearing his new jacket and his blue silk tie.

When the dance was over the couple stood still, laughing and waiting for the second record to come on.

It was already late, because dinner had not been served until the ship left Dakar. The captain was walking on deck with the chief engineer, and the two of them must have been talking about the inspection that afternoon.

"As long as we don't meet up with a storm," Lachaux said, "maybe the ship will hold out. But wait until we get into the Bay of Biscay! At this time of year we're almost sure to run into some heavy sea. . . ."

The couple danced only three dances. Then Madame Dassonville affectedly said good night to Huret, nodded to the other passengers, and went toward the cabins.

As for Huret, he stayed where he was for about fifteen minutes, sometimes glancing at his watch, sipping a glass of liqueur, and looking blissfully straight ahead.

At last he stood up, too, awkwardly acknowledged the doctor, who had to move his legs to let him by, and with an assumed air of nonchalance went inside.

The doctor did not have to follow him to know that Huret would not go to Cabin 7 but would stealthily continue on to the end of the corridor. He also knew that Madame Dassonville would be wearing a sumptuous dressing gown of embroidered silk—she had been wearing it once when she came to ask for some aspirin.

Donadieu got up and did his ten times around the deck, striding along by himself, and then went down to his cabin, slowly washed, and took the little pot of opium from his cupboard, along with the pipe, the oil lamp, and the needles.

He did not smoke any more than usual, because he was able to discipline himself. His thoughts did not become confused. They remained the same, dwelling on the same people, the only difference being that he felt more indifferent toward these people.

What did it matter to him that at this very moment Huret was lying in the arms of Madame Dassonville, whose body was so trim and graceful? What did it matter to him that Madame Huret, worn out and with the taste of nausea in her mouth, was gradually becoming indifferent to her baby, who was not managing to live? And that Bassot wrote equations on the door of his cell? And that Lachaux . . .

He lazily stretched out his arm, turned off the electric light, blew out the oil lamp, and closed his eyes. His last thought was that the wind was rising and the ship must be listing to starboard, since his back was pressed up against the wall.

Seven

Lachaux, the timber man, and a few others had already removed their sun helmets, and two or three women had worn coats on deck the evening before.

The *Aquitaine* had rounded Cape Vert and the water seemed more fluid, the sky lighter; the difference was almost imperceptible. Perhaps it was even an illusion, and yet everyone was cheerful.

That morning was also the day of the party, and right away it was obvious that this day would be different from the others.

There were now about fifteen children on board, and they were very excited because they had been promised that games would be played later on. Girls and older women lay in wait for the other passengers all along the deck.

"Would you like to buy some tickets for the raffle?" they would say.

Madame Bassot alone had sold two hundred of them, and she had been walking around the deck for so long, trying so hard, that there were patches of sweat on the back of her dress and large semicircles under her arms.

Madame Dassonville was supposed to sell tickets, too, but she did not appear on deck until about eleven o'clock in the morning, in a very smart dress, carelessly holding the tickets in her hand. She went up to Lachaux, who was arguing with Barbarin.

"How many tickets will you buy from me, Monsieur Lachaux?" she asked.

He looked her up and down. She was already tearing tickets out of her book and laying them on the table.

"I already have some," he muttered.

"That doesn't matter. Shall I give you twenty?"

"I told you I already have some!"

She did not understand that he was serious, and kept on insisting, whereupon he pushed away the tickets, which unfortunately flew onto the deck. Madame Dassonville bent down to pick them up, and Barbarin, embarrassed, helped her, murmuring:

"I have some, too. . . . But I'll take five from you anyway. . . ."

At that moment the bar terrace happened to be nearly deserted, so there was no one to wonder why Madame Dassonville hurried across the deck holding back her tears and slammed the door of her cabin violently after her.

The purser, with the help of some sailors and stewards, was preparing for the afternoon games—a tug of war, a potato-sack race, a quoits competition, and a pillow fight. They were looking for players to participate in a bridge tournament, and on a table in the middle of the dining room they were arranging the prizes they had collected to be raffled off.

There were bottles of perfume that the passengers had bought from the ship's hairdresser, fetish dolls, a few bottles of wine and champagne, chocolate, and objects made out of ivory that had been bought at the ports of call and which people were already sick of.

Donadieu had had a full morning, because two more Chinese had died and there had also been people at the second- and third-class office hours.

At eleven-thirty he was in his cabin with a female passenger. He was saying to her:

"You can get dressed now."

It often happened that his patients, especially his women patients, came to consult him in his cabin instead of going to the infirmary. And the doctor, who did not like to be disturbed, had found a way to get back at them.

This time it was a passenger he had not noticed before, a fat blond woman whom he could more easily visualize serving tea in a country tearoom than working in the colonies. She was determined to show that she was well bred. To excuse her intrusion she had reeled off phrase after phrase, to which Donadieu had not even listened.

"I'm sure you understand, doctor, that on a boat like this, where people notice every move you make and comment on it, it is rather hard to . . ."

He waited, looking at her in an abstracted way. She was wearing a pink dress, and under the cloth her ample bosom was shaking.

Finally the woman explained that she was afraid she had appendicitis and that in order to reassure herself . . .

"You know how it is, doctor. You imagine things. You can't sleep any more. . . ."

"Get undressed."

He said it seriously, looking away from her and pretending to busy himself with something else while she hesitated.

"Completely undressed?"

"My goodness, yes, of course, madame."

It amused him to make a woman who had been full of dignity and self-assurance until then take all her clothes off.

He heard the sound of cloth rustling.

"My girdle, too?"

"Absolutely."

And when he turned back, she really was naked; she stood there in the cabin, very white, not knowing what to do with her hands or where to look. Her arms and neck were sunburned.

"I don't know why I should be ashamed. . . ."

She was stout but her flesh was firm, covered with dimples. She occasionally leaned over to pull up her stockings, which were sliding down her legs.

Then Donadieu examined her and prodded her without much conviction.

"There's nothing at all the matter with you. What scared you was simply a stitch in your side. You probably went up the stairs too fast."

That was all. She got dressed again, and now she was no longer embarrassed. She talked. She was in no hurry. She fastened her stockings to her girdle and collected her underwear, which was strewn over the chair.

"Africa didn't do too much damage to me, did it? Of course I have always taken care of myself. . . ."

She was in her slip when someone knocked on the door, and only then did she become frightened, as though she were being caught in the act, and looked at Donadieu in a pleading way.

The doctor opened the door a crack and saw Jacques Huret waiting in the gangway.

"I'll see you in a few minutes," he said to him.

And the woman finished dressing, picked up a hairpin, and looked around to make sure she had not forgotten anything.

"How much do I owe you, doctor?"

"You don't owe me anything."

"But . . . I don't understand. . . ."

"Nothing! Nothing!"

Donadieu's eyes were laughing, but only his eyes, and he imagined his victim in bed, motionless and smug under his caresses. He was sure he was right: she was the very epitome of that kind of lover. . . .

He looked for Huret but did not see anyone in the gangway. He went back inside to wash his hands and was drying them when someone knocked on the door again.

"Come in!"

It was Huret, trying to seem confident but visibly embarrassed.

"Excuse me for disturbing you, doctor. . . ."

"Sit down."

Huret sat on the very edge of the chair and twisted the unbleached-linen cap he had been wearing since that morning in place of his sun helmet.

"Are you sick?"

Donadieu did not beat around the bush with him. In some way he felt Huret belonged to him. He had the feeling he had known him for an eternity.

"No . . . I mean . . . First I want to ask you a question. . . . Do you think my son will live?"

The doctor shrugged his shoulders cynically, because he knew that was not why Huret had come.

"I've already told you what I think," he muttered.

The fan hummed. A ray of sunlight twenty centimeters across passed through the porthole and fell in a quivering disk on the wall.

"I know! . . . It's my wife who is worried! . . . You don't have a very high opinion of me, do you?"

No! The doctor played with a letter opener while he waited for Huret to get down to business. All this was just words, nothing but words; the young man was talking to give himself courage. Donadieu was impatient and wondered what it was all about.

Huret managed to seem unself-conscious and talked in a natural tone of voice.

"You know that if the ship pitches at all I get sick. I can't stay in the cabin for more than an hour. You see? Even now I'm beginning to sweat. . . ."

It was true. His forehead was damp, and there were little beads of perspiration on his upper lip.

"On deck, in the open air, I feel better. . . . Even so, the trip has been agonizing for me. . . . My wife still doesn't understand. . . ."

Donadieu held out a pack of cigarettes, and Huret took one mechanically, then searched his pockets for a match.

"My wife also doesn't understand that I'm the one who has to bear all the burdens. The reason I'm talking to you about this is that . . ."

Now it's coming, thought Donadieu. "Is that" what? How are you going to get out of this one?

He did not get out of it at all, but groped for words without success. Then, bowing his head, he took the plunge:

"I came to ask you for some advice. . . ."

"If it has to do with medicine . . ."

"No, but you know me a little. . . . You know what kind of situation I'm in. . . ."

The doctor's face turned gloomy. He was suddenly sure that money was involved, and unconsciously he became defensive. He was not exactly miserly, but he disliked dealing with money or even talking about it.

"You're aware of the circumstances under which we left Brazzaville. The baby was hopelessly ill. The S.E.P.A, whose accounting offices I worked for, required that I stay another year. I was breaking my contract by leaving. . . ."

His face had reddened, and he was puffing awkwardly on his cigarette to keep up his self-assurance.

"They owe me more than thirty thousand francs, you know. Back there the local director told me to settle it with the Paris office."

He was hot. It was painful to watch him getting excited, and yet Donadieu did not miss the slightest wince in his expression.

At that point perhaps Huret regretted coming in, but it was too late to retreat.

"What I wanted to ask you was if you knew whether anyone on board could lend me a little money until we reach Bordeaux. . . . I'll pay it back the day after we arrive."

Donadieu knew that he was being cruel, but he could not help himself. His face had frozen, and his voice had become cool and crisp.

"Why do you need money, seeing that your passage has been paid for, including food?"

Didn't Huret feel that the game was already lost? He almost got up, raised himself slightly, then sat back again, deciding to push his luck as far as he could.

"There are minor expenses . . ." he said. "You know as well as I do. . . . Like everyone else I have an account at the bar. . . . As I said, it would be a loan. I'm not asking anybody for anything. Perhaps the company itself . . ."

"The company never advances money."

Now Huret was red and trembling like someone with a high fever. He was tearing his cigarette apart, and shreds of tobacco fell onto the linoleum.

"I'm sorry. . . ."

"Just a moment . . . The other day you won nearly two thousand francs at the horse racing. . . ."

"One thousand seven hundred fifty . . . I had to offer drinks all around. . . ."

"How much do you owe at the bar?"

"I'm not sure exactly. Maybe five hundred francs."

"And how much do you owe your partners?"

He pretended not to understand.

"What partners?"

"Yesterday you were playing poker again."

"Almost nothing!" Huret said quickly. "If someone would agree to lend me a thousand francs . . . or even . . . Here . . ."

Again he wanted it to be over. He had gone too far. He took a checkbook from his pocket.

"It wouldn't even be a loan. I'll write out a check in exchange. It can be cashed once we get to France."

He was on the point of tears, but something in Donadieu was forcing him to go to extremes, too.

"Do you have money in the bank?"

"Not at the moment . . . As soon as I reach Bordeaux I'm going to deposit some."

"You know very well that your company will not pay you what it owes you unless it is forced to by a court. The trial could go on for months."

"I'll have money anyway!" Huret exclaimed defiantly.

He was holding a dirty, crumpled checkbook he had brought with him from Europe two years before.

"I have family. . . . One of my aunts is very rich. . . . I even thought of sending her a telegram. . . ."

"Why didn't you?"

"Because I don't know if she's at home now. She lives in Corbeil, but she spends the summers by the sea or in Vichy. . . ."

"A telegram would be forwarded."

Wasn't he playing a cruel and futile game?

"My aunt would not understand. . . . I have to explain it to her. . . ."

"Does your wife know that you don't have any money?"

Suddenly Huret stood up.

"You're not going to tell her, I hope?"

Now he was an enemy. He looked at the doctor angrily, because he saw how Donadieu had driven him into a corner.

"As I said, I haven't asked anything of you. I was hoping you could give me some advice. I told you quite frankly what my situation was. . . ."

His lip distended. He stifled a sob and turned away.

"Sit down."

"What for?" Huret said, shrugging.

"Sit down! And tell me this: if you knew that you had no money, why in the world did you run up a bill at the bar and play poker and _belote_?"

It was all over. Huret bowed his head like a guilty man. His Adam's apple rose and fell, but his eyes were still dry.

"Does your aunt even really exist?"

The only answer Huret gave him was a look of hatred.

"All right. I believe she exists! But you're not sure she will give you what you need."

Huret, red in the face, did not move. He stared at the floor and crumpled his checkbook, which was all wet from the sweat on his hands.

"Nevertheless, I will lend you a thousand francs."

Huret raised his head with an incredulous look, while Donadieu opened the drawer where he kept his money.

At that point wasn't Huret tempted to refuse the money? He looked at the door and hesitated. Donadieu counted out ten hundred-franc notes.

"Make me out a check anyway."

And, uncapping a pen, he stood up to make room at the table for Huret, who obediently sat where he was told and turned halfway around.

"Who shall I make it out to?"

And with a wan smile, he added:

"I don't even know your name."

"Donadieu. As in 'given to God.' "

The pen squeaked. There was an ink blot near the signature. And Huret did not yet dare take the money.

"Thank you," he stammered. "Please forgive me. You can hardly understand. . . ."

"But of course I do."

"No! You can hardly understand. This morning I wanted to kill myself."

He was crying, moved by his own situation. The steward walked around the deck striking the gong to announce lunch.

"Thank you!"

He still wondered if he should put out his hand, and since Donadieu did not move, he backed toward the door, sniffed, dried his eyes, and rushed out.

He was late to arrive in the dining room. Because of the party, the din of voices was louder than on other days: people were debating whether they should put on their disguises for dinner or not. The ones who had costumes were in favor; the others were doubtful, wondering how they could make costumes out of what was to be found on the ship.

"Absolutely! I guarantee that you'll find whatever you need at the hairdresser's. . . ."

Almost no one took a siesta, and Donadieu had trouble sleeping because people kept walking back and forth on the deck over his head.

Barbarin had agreed to be chairman of the committee and behaved as though he had been doing this kind of thing all his life. It was clear just from looking at him that he was the most important person around. He was wearing beige twill pants, a white shirt with the sleeves rolled up over his hairy arms, and a blue arm band which he pretended to ridicule. He had also asked for a whistle, and at four-thirty he gave the signal for the games to begin.

For half an hour the only noise was the sound of children shouting, because it was they who began the games, playing tug of war, running with an egg balanced in a spoon held between their teeth, and waging a pillow fight.

The captain was obliged to attend. He stood out from the motley crowd and was aware of it, trying to smile as he distractedly stroked his beard.

"Aren't you playing?" he asked Madame Dassonville, whom he found standing in a deserted spot on the deck.

"Thank you, but I'm not in the mood."

He felt called upon to urge her, and did it awkwardly, so that the young woman looked at him impatiently. Madame Dassonville's bad humor was so obvious that Barbarin went up to her, too.

"Excuse me for following you around. Lachaux really is a brute. He deserves to be taught a lesson. But you shouldn't punish all of us! The party won't be complete if the most attractive passenger doesn't join in. . . ."

She smiled but stuck to her guns, and continued to stand there leaning on the railing and gazing at the sea.

Donadieu looked for Huret and found him in a group that was preparing to play a tournament of *belote* for the benefit of the sailors' fund. Huret was a little nervous, but he showed no trace of the morning's emotions.

What *was* upsetting him was Madame Dassonville's standing apart from the others. He watched her from a distance. Someone asked him to be the fourth, and he did not know what to say.

"In a little while . . ."

"It's time to begin the preliminary rounds."

"You'll be able to find someone else. . . ."

The officers were very jovial. Instead of taking a siesta, they had drunk a few glasses of liqueur, and by now they had already gone on to champagne. Since Madame Dassonville was not present, Madame Bassot had become the queen of the party and she brought to the role just as much enthusiasm as she had brought to selling raffle tickets.

After the children had finished, the adults began playing the traditional games. The sack race was first. Taking advantage of the fact that everyone's attention was distracted by the comical start of the race, Huret went up to Madame Dassonville.

From then on they stayed together, not sharing in the general animation. After spending a long time whispering and looking at the sea, they walked up and down as if nothing unusual had happened.

Madame Dassonville had a defiant look on her face. As for Huret, he tried to seem cheerful, but it was evident that he felt uneasy in his role. Wasn't Madame Dassonville deliberately walking back and forth in front of the terrace, which was the center of attention?

People were turning around to look at them. The new passengers, the ones who had boarded at Dakar, did not understand why they were keeping to themselves. One woman even thought they were newlyweds.

Barbarin rushed around busily, full of a Montmartre type of good humor.

"All right, madame," he said to a forty-five-year-old woman. "We still need one more contestant for the egg-and-spoon race. What are you afraid of?"

They laughed. He forced a spoon and an egg into her hand. The woman, blushing, looked around as though to excuse herself for appearing ridiculous.

"Listen for the whistle! . . . First prize is an electric razor! . . ."

Madame Dassonville and Huret were walking around and around the deck, as regularly as Donadieu did every morning.

The first few times he passed, Huret managed to avoid meeting the doctor's eyes, but he knew where the doctor was standing and chose to walk where he would not come face to face with him.

A little later this was no longer possible. His way blocked by contestants in the pillow fight, Huret found himself directly in front of Donadieu.

At that point he smiled, a shy, humble, and also unhappy smile that seemed to be saying:

"You can see that it's not my fault!"

Shortly afterward the couple disappeared, and the captain came up to the doctor.

"It would be better if you didn't take your madman out for his walk tonight. The third-class passengers have been doing a lot of drinking and are too rowdy. There could be an incident. . . ."

They could not stop one of the Chinese from dying, but no one except Mathias knew about it, and by eight o'clock the passengers were excitedly trying on costumes in their narrow cabins, while in the depths of the ship the chief engineer was being summoned.

Eight

By midnight the party seemed to be over. The phonograph was still playing on the first-class deck, but no one was dancing. In the second-class saloon on the quarter-deck, though, couples were still whirling around.

They might have had a particular reason for continuing to dance. There had been an incident. Immediately after dinner a young woman dressed as "the Republic of France" or, rather, as Lady Angot, had invaded the first-class terrace, with the excuse that she wanted to dance a farandole. With her were four or five young men dressed up more or less as pirates. Everyone had laughed. No one had bothered them.

Dinner had not been very cheerful. Only a few people had put on costumes, and others had simply worn evening dress—for the first time five or six tuxedos had been visible.

Madame Bassot had borrowed a sailor's outfit that was so tight she nearly suffocated, but in spite of this she and the officers tried to inject some liveliness into the atmosphere.

Madame Dassonville came to the table wearing her everyday clothes, as though she had not noticed anything was different, and Huret was also wearing his ordinary clothes.

At the captain's table, which was as dignified as always, Lachaux was wearing his linen suit, but Barbarin had drawn a large mustache and sideburns on his face with burnt cork; the rest of his disguise consisted of a red silk scarf and a worker's cap found in the trunk of party favors.

The "Marianne" in her liberty cap and tricolor petticoat was a pretty redhead who had drunk a good deal and was in high spirits.

Heavy, fat Barbarin danced for the first time. People ordered champagne. Another farandole was organized, covering the entire deck, while Huret and Madame Dassonville stayed in a corner of the bar not far from Lachaux, who was scowling.

Half an hour later, everything was spoiled. Lady Angot was still drinking, and she became more and more excited, kissing passengers on the mouth; and soon she was lifting her legs as high as she could, revealing her naked thighs, as she danced a quadrille step by herself that brought back the old Moulin Rouge.

The officers laughed. Barbarin became hot under the collar. But the ship's personnel reacted differently, and the purser said quietly to one of the young men in the group:

"I think you should try to take her away now. . . ."

The young man had been drinking, too. He called to the others and loudly told them that since the first-class passengers had now been sufficiently entertained by them, they were supposed to return to second class.

In a sense this was true and in another sense it was not. "Marianne" noticed that something was going on, asked what was happening, and before anyone could stop her unleashed a flood of insults, at the purser and the passengers, worthy of the lady whose tricolor petticoat she was wearing.

This had taken place at a little past eleven o'clock. Now it was midnight and everything was calm again, though the calm was rather heavy and stiff, since the party had been a failure. The phonograph was on, but no one was dancing. No more than a dozen passengers were sitting at the bar finishing up their champagne or whisky, and even Barbarin had washed his face and taken off his scarf.

He was sitting at a table with Lachaux and the timber man. The air was cooler than on the previous evenings, and Donadieu saw that his patient from that morning, wearing a very low-cut dress, was shivering. She was accompanied by her husband, a little man with a blond goatee.

It seemed the evening was over. Lachaux got up first, shook hands with Barbarin and Grenier, and walked away, dragging his leg.

Barbarin and the timber man emptied their glasses and followed him less than half a minute later, but stopped to talk by the railing.

Donadieu did not pay much attention to these details, and later he had some difficulty reconstructing their exact order, which turned out to be rather important.

For some time now Huret had been growing impatient, afraid that if he went down too late his wife would make a scene. But Madame Dassonville was lingering, and when he leaned toward her it was to beg her to go.

He finally got up and left her there. They parted quite coldly. Donadieu imagined that she was saying to him:

"All right! Go to your wife!"

Huret walked away reluctantly, his shoulders drooping, and passed close by Barbarin and the timber man, who were still talking. The purser had turned off the phonograph, and the bartender, irritated by the fact that the officers were playing an endless game of *belote*, began clearing the tables and even piling up the terrace chairs.

It was at this point that a cabin boy went up to him and murmured something. The bartender looked around, glanced at the tables, and meticulously searched the table where Lachaux had been sitting.

The steward walked away in the direction of the cabins, and before three minutes had passed Lachaux appeared, too, without his collar and wearing sandals on his bare feet.

It was clear from his behavior that he was about to make a scene. He looked cynically around at the people who were still there and scowled with his thick gray eyebrows.

"Bartender! Go get the purser for me."

"I think the purser is in bed."

"Well, then, tell him to get up!"

Everyone was listening. Barbarin, who had seen Lachaux from a distance, came back toward the terrace, while the timber man went inside.

And Lachaux said nothing, his broad, heavy body planted in the middle of the bar. The officers went on playing their game but did not take their eyes off him.

He had rarely been in such a bad mood as he was that evening, perhaps because two of the young men who had come up from second class were employees of his, unimportant young men like Huret, and he had pretended not to recognize them.

As they were being sent away, he had overheard someone in a group near him say:

"Some people here are traveling first class with second-class tickets!"

"Who?" Lachaux had asked the timber man.

Grenier had tipped his head toward Huret.

"I think it's him. He has a sick wife or baby, I'm not sure which."

Then Lachaux had muttered a threat to the company, saying that he would demand to be reimbursed the difference between the price of a first-class ticket and that of a second-class ticket.

This incident, far less noisy than the first, had gone unnoticed. Now the purser hurried up; he came more quickly than he normally would have, because he had been found in the shadows at the extreme end of the second-class deck, with "Marianne," insisting that he had had nothing to do with what happened.

"Purser, I demand an immediate investigation: there is a thief on board."

He had purposely spoken very loudly, and the ten or so people on the terrace heard him and turned their heads at the same time.

In cases like this, little Neuville was usually quite diplomatic. He answered hastily:

"If you will please come to my office with me, I will make a note of your complaint and . . ."

"Tsk, tsk, tsk . . . No need for offices or notes," Lachaux replied, laying his fat, soft paw on Neuville's shoulder. "The robbery took place right here, not ten minutes ago. I know why you want to take me away. The company doesn't like scenes, and next you'll be offering compensation. . . ."

The purser and Donadieu looked at each other. Neuville seemed to be asking for advice. The doctor had become very sober.

"Come here. . . . Just ten minutes ago I was sitting at this table with two people—Monsieur Barbarin, who is over there, and the timber man who got on at Libreville. . . ."

"Monsieur Grenier?"

"I don't care what his name is. At one point I took my wallet out of my pocket to show him a document, an article from a small newspaper attacking me and calling me a murderer."

It delighted him to shout this as loudly as possible.

"When I got up to go to my cabin five minutes ago, I left the wallet on the table. I'm sure of it! I'm not a child. When I got to my cabin I saw that it wasn't in my pocket, and I immediately sent the steward to look for it. The wallet was gone!"

The purser thoughtlessly asked:

"Was there much money in it?"

"That's none of your business! It doesn't matter whether I was robbed of a hundred francs or a thousand francs. That concerns only me. I want my wallet back. I want to catch the thief and teach him a thing or two."

This time the game of *belote* had stopped, even though the cards had been dealt out. The players looked at Lachaux's table, which was nearby, and they were clearly upset.

Everyone was upset, as a matter of fact, because everyone was open to suspicion, even Barbarin, who was now going up to Lachaux.

The woman who had had to undress in front of Donadieu that morning was still there with her husband, whose small worried head sat high up on his thin neck.

"I'll have to refer this to the captain," the purser stammered to gain time.

"Call him, if you like. In any case, I demand an immediate investigation, because the wallet can't be far away."

Neuville would have liked to take Lachaux aside, calm him down, and promise him anything to avoid a scandal. He knew there could not be much money in the wallet, since Lachaux had turned everything he had—about fifty-five thousand francs—over to him to be put in the safe. He could not have kept more than a few hundred francs for his daily expenses.

"Steward! Please tell the captain that Monsieur Lachaux insists on speaking with him on the bar terrace."

Lachaux walked back and forth, his hands behind his back, without paying any attention to Neuville, who in the meantime went and sat down by Donadieu.

"Were you here?"

"I haven't moved."

"Well?"

"I don't know."

"He's quite capable of demanding that we search the passengers and their cabins."

Barbarin, holding forth to the group of officers, was proposing the same thing:

"Let them search all of us! I for one will agree to empty my pockets immediately. I left after Lachaux. I went to the railing, and I came back almost at the same time he did. . . ."

"Of course! Search us!" the captain of the colonial infantry said, agreeing with him.

No one dared go to bed, for fear that it would look suspicious. The people in second class were still dancing; shadows moved back and forth behind the illumined curtains of the saloon.

When the captain appeared he was wearing the uniform overcoat he had worn at dinner, and even before he reached them he was obviously trying to figure out what was going on. The purser wanted to go meet him, but Lachaux stopped him.

"Wait a minute! I want to explain it to him myself. . . ."

He told his story to the captain with the same lack of civility with which he had told it to the others.

"There's a thief on board and he must be found," he concluded. "After God, you're the one in charge here. It's up to you to do what has to be done until I can lodge a complaint in Bordeaux. . . ."

Actually he found the incident rather soothing. Suddenly a valve had been opened, and he could pour out his bile. From now on these people were no longer passengers, colonials, settlers, civil servants, officers, employees of foreign trading posts: for him they were only suspects!

Barbarin, who ate at the captain's table, ventured to speak:

"These gentlemen and I have agreed that we should be searched immediately. Since the disappearance of the wallet we have not left the deck, and consequently we could not have got rid of anything."

The captain did not turn a hair. He remained quite dignified, but his self-assurance was only superficial.

"I can't stop you from proving that you're innocent," he said finally, after looking at the purser and Donadieu as though he would have liked their support.

The situation was both grotesque and dramatic. Barbarin emptied all his pockets one by one and set out on the table a bunch of keys, a pipe, a tobacco pouch, a tin of lozenges, a handkerchief, and the red scarf he had been wearing earlier. Then he turned his pockets inside out, and shreds of tobacco showered down onto the deck.

Then it was the officers' turn to stand up, and they took the affair very seriously. One of them, who had been drinking, even talked about requesting a signed inventory of what he was showing them.

"Me, too!" said a woman's voice.

It was Madame Dassonville, whom no one had noticed because her table was partly in shadow and she had not moved.

"Me, too!" the little man with the white goatee cried quickly, while his wife held out her empty hands.

"Who else was here?" the purser asked impatiently.

Donadieu chose to let the others answer. Barbarin looked at Madame Dassonville, who murmured:

"Monsieur Huret was with me. . . ."

"Where is he?"

"He went to bed."

"After Monsieur Lachaux left?"

"I think so. . . . I'm not sure. . . ."

"Grenier was here, too," Barbarin said. "We chatted for a few minutes, and then he went down to his cabin."

The captain turned to Lachaux.

"Are you going to demand that those gentlemen come here?"

"Absolutely not! They will have to be questioned in their cabins, and their cabins will have to be searched. . . ."

The purser and the captain stepped aside, spoke together softly, and gestured for Donadieu to join them.

"What do you think?"

All three were grim, because this was not the first time they had witnessed a robbery on board.

At the moment only ten passengers were affected, and these were assuming an attitude of detachment, though they felt burdened by the whole situation.

In the morning, a hundred passengers would know about it, would go up to one another with conspiratorial looks, would watch one another furtively. And there were still ten days to go before they reached Bordeaux!

"That only means searching two cabins," the purser said.

"Monsieur Lachaux!" the captain called. "Would you describe your wallet for us?"

"It's an old black wallet, worn at the edges, with several pockets."

"How much money did it have in it?"

This time he answered:

"Seven or eight hundred-franc notes. You know my money is in the safe. But it isn't the money that matters. It's the papers. . . ."

"Are they important?"

"To me, yes, and I'm the only one who can judge."

"If you will stay here for a few minutes, we'll search the two cabins. . . ."

Lachaux grunted his assent, but it was clear that he would have liked to be present at the search.

"Go ahead, purser," said the captain. "Take two witnesses with you. Monsieur Barbarin, will you go? And you, Captain?"

The two men nodded and followed the purser.

This was the most unpleasant fifteen minutes.

Lachaux remained alone in his corner, scowling in a menacing way, perhaps aware that people were looking at him rather hostilely.

The captain and Donadieu stood apart from the others, while Madame Dassonville lit a cigarette which glowed in her patch of shadow.

No one spoke of going to bed. They were waiting. Sometimes they heard bursts of music from second class, where the party was still on. Three or four passengers were completely drunk.

"Do you suspect anyone?" the captain asked quietly.

"No. No one."

An incident like this had to take place before the captain was willing to be at all familiar with his crew, because on board the ship he usually kept to himself, engaging only in strictly official relations and coming down from the bridge only to preside over the meals, the most painful aspect of his duties.

The sky was full of clouds that looked European, lighter and more lively than African clouds. That afternoon the ship had come upon whole schools of flying fish, but because of the party no one had paid any attention to them.

There would be one more stop, at Tenerife; the deck would be invaded one last time by Arab and other merchants, and then, almost without any transition, they would come to Portugal, and finally France and the turbulent waters of the Bay of Biscay.

The time seemed to pass slowly. People wondered what the purser and the two witnesses could be doing. At last the timber man appeared, wearing a faded bathrobe over his pajamas.

He was shuffling along in old worn-out slippers, and there was something intimate about his whole appearance that contrasted strangely with the long-necked passenger's dinner jacket and his wife's evening dress.

"What's happening?" he asked, going up to the officers' table and glancing at the captain. "What kind of people do they think the passengers on this boat are?"

His accent had never before sounded so common.

"Does anyone have a cigarette?"

A lieutenant held out his pack.

"I was already asleep when they came and woke me up, and the purser searched my cabin as though I were a criminal."

He spotted Lachaux, whom he had not seen at first.

"Tell me, are you the cause of all this? You could have waited until tomorrow morning!"

He did not leave. He stood there like someone who had already undergone a medical examination and was waiting for his friends to come out. He was calm. They had not found anything in his cabin.

"Did your wallet have a lot of money in it?"

Lachaux did not want to answer him. An uneasy silence fell after the timber man had spoken, because now the possible suspects had been narrowed down to one: Huret.

Everyone was secretly watching Madame Dassonville. Even Lachaux was looking at her, grimly, with a certain satisfaction. After she had offered him the raffle tickets that morning and he had thrust them away, Barbarin had said to him:

"You're going too far! You forget that she's a woman. . . ."

"A whore!" he had answered.

"You have no right to talk that way."

That had been the end of it, but Lachaux had not been swayed by the incident, and now he waited impatiently for the purser.

The captain had stopped talking, and Donadieu, leaning back against the railing next to him, was also silent.

At that moment all other life seemed suspended, as the boat slipped through the night with a wet sound, its muffled engines purring in its bowels.

But suddenly everyone heard the noise of hurrying footsteps, and then Huret's thin form appeared; he was wearing nothing but striped pajamas, open across his chest.

Huret had no need to look for Lachaux. Instinctively he headed straight for him.

He was panting, his hair was tousled, his eyes were shining.

"Were you the one who accused me of being a thief? Well? Was it you who demanded that they search my cabin?"

Lachaux was in an inferior position because he was sitting down, and he started to get up.

"You scoundrel—you starve people, you kill people, and yet you dare to bring suspicion down on others?"

Donadieu started toward him. An officer got up. They heard the footsteps of Barbarin and the army captain, who had been witnesses at the search, but the purser had not yet returned.

"You know very well that the thief is not the person you think it is! If there is one person here who has spent his whole life stealing . . ."

He had lost all self-control. He was trembling. His movements were jerky, and, having nothing more to say, he shouted, or, rather, howled:

"Scoundrel! Scoundrel! Scoundrel!"

At the same time he grabbed Lachaux's head, his throat, anything he could get hold of, and Lachaux, swinging around in his chair to get free, tipped it over and rolled onto the floor.

Huret tried to go down on top of him and grab him or hit him again, but Donadieu had grasped him by the shoulders.

"Calm down! Calm down!"

They could hear the young man panting; Lachaux, in his light suit, lay on the deck waiting; not until they took Huret back to a safe distance would he get up.

"Gentlemen . . ." the captain began.

But he could not think of anything to say, especially since other passengers, who had been woken up by the searches, were appearing on deck.

"Gentlemen . . . I . . . I beg you . . ."

Huret's thin chest was rising and falling rapidly, and when Donadieu looked questioningly at Barbarin, the latter shook his head.

They had not found anything in the cabin.

Nine

The next morning Donadieu learned some of the details from the purser. There was a surprise in store for the passengers when they woke up: rain was pouring down. And they were just as excited to see fresh rain as children rolling around in their first snow. It was a novel sight—the deck wet, the curtain of transparent drops falling from the upper bridge; over the continuous splattering of the rain, they could hear water pouring down the gutters.

In the forecastle the Chinese were smiling, though they had no shelter, and a few of them used an old bag or even a pot as an umbrella.

Some people took out dark woolen clothes for the first time, and it was strange to come across people dressed in blue and black.

The sea was gray, fringed with white. The ship rolled a little and stirred up a lot of foam because of the swell.

Donadieu had just finished his walk around the deck. On the bar terrace he had noticed Lachaux, Grenier, and Barbarin smoking in silence. Up ahead Madame Bassot was talking to one of the lieutenants. Madame Dassonville must not have left her cabin yet, and Huret was not there, either.

The doctor met Neuville as he was coming down from seeing the captain. There was no need to ask him anything.

"A dirty business," the purser muttered. "The captain has already talked to each of them."

"Huret and Lachaux?"

"Lachaux is yellow with rage. Huret has his hackles up like a fighting cock. And I'm the one who'll get it in the end for having put the Hurets in first class."

Donadieu and the purser strolled along together while a few of the passengers watched them. Neuville told about the searches the night before.

"We didn't have any trouble in the timber man's cabin. He had just gone to bed and turned off the light. He was very startled, but he went through the formalities with good grace. But in Huret's cabin . . ."

The purser's job had been as difficult as could be. When he knocked at the door of Cabin 7, he thought he heard something like a sob, but he wasn't paying attention. He had to knock several times before the door was opened. And Huret frowned and looked angry when he saw him.

"Excuse me for disturbing you, but there has been a robbery on board and it is my duty to . . ."

While Neuville had delivered his speech, Huret's face hardened.

"Why are you searching my cabin?"

"Yours isn't the only one. We've already searched . . ."

In a rage, Huret kicked the door wide open and they saw his wife sitting on a bunk, drying her tears. Neuville and the others had intruded on a domestic quarrel. The baby, lying on the opposite bunk, looked as though it was suffering. Its eyes were open.

"Excuse us, madame."

"I heard. . . ."

She had nothing on but a flowered dressing gown, and she got up and stood in a corner. Her husband stayed where he was for a moment, not interfering with the searchers, and then suddenly rushed outside and ran to the bar, where he attacked Lachaux.

"His wife didn't say anything?" asked Donadieu.

"She cried out. She tried to stop him, but he chose not to listen, and then she stayed put until we left. She shut the door behind us."

As for the scene on deck, it had lasted only a few minutes. The captain had gone up to Huret and then to Lachaux:

"Gentlemen, please return to your cabins. Tomorrow morning I will be entirely at your disposal to take whatever action is necessary."

Some of the passengers, the officers in particular, had continued to talk about the incident for a few minutes, but finally everyone had gone to bed.

This morning the rain came just in time to distract the passengers. Yet even so, everyone asked for the latest news of the incident. As they walked past the terrace, people glanced at Lachaux, whose enormous bulk was slumped down in the wicker chair. He endured their curiosity cynically.

It even seemed as though he was trying to be just as crude, as ugly, and as cross as possible. He was wearing a shirt without a collar, open on his chest, and although it was ten in the morning, he had nothing on his feet but a pair of old slippers.

This was the way he was dressed when the captain called for him.

"I suppose you want Monsieur Huret to apologize," the captain said. "I'm going to speak to him. I'll make him come to his senses."

"First of all I want my wallet back."

"The investigation will continue, and I won't stop you from making a formal complaint once we reach Bordeaux."

"There will also be nothing to stop me from notifying the company that I was struck and insulted by a passenger traveling first class when he shouldn't have been."

Nothing else had happened. Lachaux knew that everyone was afraid of him. He was also aware that action would be taken against the officers of the ship for having done Huret a favor.

A little later, when he was sitting on the terrace, he saw the young man go up to the captain's bridge, too.

The purser witnessed the interview. The contrast between Huret and Lachaux, who had just been there, was so striking that even the captain was upset.

Lachaux was massive, as hard as rock. Young Huret had attacked him with all the futile rage of his youth, and it had been in vain.

It seemed as though Lachaux must have manipulated hundreds, even thousands, of little fellows like him.

"First and foremost, Monsieur Huret, I assume you intend to apologize to your opponent of last night."

"No!"

He was thin and pale, as taut as a violin string, about to become aggressive again.

"It is my duty to intervene and make sure you put an end to this intolerable situation. You attacked Monsieur Lachaux. . . ."

"I said he was a scoundrel, and everyone knows it's true; you know it yourself!"

"I beg you to watch what you're saying."

"He accused me of being a thief!"

"Excuse me. A wallet was stolen from him and he asked that a search be made of the cabins of all the passengers who were sitting near his table when the wallet disappeared."

But it was useless to try to make Huret see reason. He became more and more stubborn, because he felt he was both right and wrong at the same time.

"I will not allow myself to be accused of theft by a scoundrel."

"I am only asking that out of consideration for all the passengers you simply say very briefly that you're sorry—so that the trip can continue peacefully."

"I'm not sorry for anything."

The captain had not wanted to use blackmail, but he was forced to bring up a certain subject.

"There is one matter, Monsieur Huret, which I hope you will excuse me for mentioning. Because your child was sick, the purser felt it his duty to . . ."

"I understand."

"Please let me finish. . . ."

"Don't bother. Aren't you trying to point out that I'm traveling first class when I'm not supposed to be—through charity?"

"There is no question of charity. It was Monsieur Lachaux who . . ."

"Don't worry. I'll move down to second class immediately and . . ."

It was impossible to calm him down. He was not red in the face, but pale and on edge. His voice was dull.

"You will not change cabins—anyway, all the second-class cabins are full. I will simply ask you not to take your meals in the first-class dining room and not to walk around in first-class areas."

Huret smiled a scornful, unhappy smile.

"Is that all?"

"I'm sorry this conversation had to end this way, but it's your fault for persisting in an attitude that cannot be permitted. Let me appeal to your good sense one last time. . . ."

"I will not apologize."

Nothing else had come of it. Huret had gone away, completely rigid, and no one had seen him since.

"Do you think he'll eat in the second-class dining room?" Donadieu asked the purser.

"He'll have to."

The two men went their separate ways. The doctor was tempted to knock on the door of Cabin 7, but what would he say? He doubted that he would be very welcome.

The rain had cooled off the decks, but it had made the heat in the cabins even more unpleasant, because the humidity was higher. Donadieu walked around among the passengers for half an hour. Lachaux continued to subject himself to their curiosity, sitting with Barbarin and Grenier, who looked as though they were testifying to his honor.

Madame Dassonville appeared, dressed in a suit no one had seen before. It reminded everyone that the ship was approaching Europe. As she wandered around the deck she was so pointedly casual that it was clear she was looking for Huret and becoming worried.

She had not had anything to do with anyone but him and the purser, and she did not dare ask what had happened after the incident the night before. She overheard snatches of conversation and tried to piece them together. Finally she sat down on the terrace at the same table she had occupied the night before, behind Lachaux, and lit a cigarette.

For a moment Donadieu thought of sitting down next to her and telling her the news, but that would be acting like God the Father again, and he decided not to.

He was uneasy. Something about the sequence of events irritated him, like the squeaking of a badly oiled gear. He would have liked to shove fate back on the right track.

He had foreseen catastrophes. He had felt that Huret was slipping down an incline he would probably never climb up again. But this was not how he had envisaged the fall!

It was too absurd, too paltry!

Had he really been stupid enough to steal a wallet, particularly Lachaux's wallet?

With his head bowed, Donadieu went back to his cabin to wash before lunch. At his door he came face to face with Huret, who was waiting for him.

"Did you want to speak to me?"

"I would like to return something to you."

The doctor opened the door and gestured to the young man to come in and sit down, but Huret refused the chair and took the ten hundred-franc notes Donadieu had given him the day before out of his pocket.

"After what has happened, I would rather not owe anybody anything. So please give me back my check. Here are the thousand francs."

Huret looked as though he were trying to defy all of humanity by himself. His very solitude and his weakness were intoxicating him. He had been caught by the fever of martyrdom, and for a few moments Donadieu forgot what was happening and observed Huret as he would have observed any strange phenomenon.

"Why do you want to return this money to me, since you have given me a check?"

"You know very well why."

"No, I don't," the doctor said sincerely.

"Yes, you do. When I came to see you yesterday, you forced me to admit that I had no money in the bank."

"But your company owes you . . ."

"You also pointed out to me that my company would not pay me without a long trial. . . ."

"Your aunt . . ."

He snickered.

"My aunt will probably tell me to go to hell, and you guessed that, too! You gave me that thousand francs without expecting to see it again, maybe because you felt sorry for me, maybe as a challenge. . . ."

He was not entirely wrong, and today Donadieu was the one who was disconcerted.

"You can repay the thousand francs whenever you can afford to," he said, not knowing what to do.

"I certainly intended to pay you back, but it might have been some time before I could."

"I'm in no hurry."

"Now it's too late. I don't want anything from anybody."

He was really only a child! Sometimes it seemed as though his fever would leave him and he would burst into tears like an abandoned kid.

"You told me you had no money to pay what you owed at the bar."

"I simply won't pay it."

"The company will make trouble."

"I don't care. I know what you're thinking. You're saying to yourself that the reason I'm giving you your money back is that now I have the money that was in the wallet."

That had actually occurred to Donadieu, and he blushed, even though he had immediately rejected the idea. No, he didn't think Huret had stolen anything! That would have been much too stupid.

"You're being unfair," he sighed.

"I'm sorry. Perhaps I have reason to be. Give me back my check, and that will be that."

Donadieu was reluctant to give the check back, because he had the feeling there would be something final about it, that it would almost amount to a condemnation of Huret. This was only an impression. It was not based on anything. Yet he clung to one last hope.

"Sit down for a moment."

"I assure you I have nothing to say to you."

"And what if I have something to say to you? I'm older than you are. . . ."

Donadieu's voice was full of emotion, and when he realized it he blushed again and did not know where to look. Nevertheless, he went on:

"I know your wife, and I know that she has suffered through some very difficult days. At this point there's hope that your child will be saved. Are you thinking of that, Huret?"

"Of what?"

"You know very well, you can feel it! This evening we'll be in Tenerife. In a few days you'll be standing on French soil again and . . ."

"And? . . ." the young man asked ironically.

"Listen, you're just a kid—I was going to say, a stupid kid. You're forgetting that you're not alone in the world. . . ."

It was only as he spoke that Donadieu realized what he was doing. He was actually talking as though Huret had said he intended to kill himself. Yet he had not said anything of the kind.

The doctor stopped talking and looked at the check he was holding, with its even signature and its ink blot.

"Give it to me or tear it up. It really doesn't matter. . . ."

Huret was about to leave. His hand was on the doorknob.

"Listen to me! It's not too late to fix everything. Apologizing to Lachaux would only be an unimportant formality, a difficult moment to get through. Everyone on board would understand. . . ."

"Is that all?"

"If you're not brave enough to do that, I will no longer have any . . . any respect for you. . . ."

Donadieu had stumbled over the word; perhaps he had almost said "friendship," or even "affection."

It had come about strangely; he himself could not have said how it had happened. More and more, he had the feeling that this moment would determine everything, and he persisted in trying to save Huret, as if it were in his power to do so.

"You respect me?" said the young man derisively, with a cynical attitude.

What could he say now? How could he answer?

"Take back your thousand francs, Huret."

"*Your* thousand francs."

"All right, mine. Take it back. We'll see each other again some day in France. . . ."

"No."

He turned the doorknob. Donadieu was sure that he, too, was reluctant to break off this conversation and trust to his luck. Something was holding him back—no doubt pride—and this was the most maddening thought of all: that a man could foolishly destroy himself out of pride.

Of course it was true that Donadieu was being just as foolish, allowing his sense of discretion to stop him from insisting further.

"Thank you for what you've done . . ."

The door was open. They could see the gangway and people walking toward the dining room. Already Huret was leaving, and Donadieu stood there with a bitter taste in his mouth as though he were seasick, too.

He was not disgusted by the sight of a man, a woman, or a child dying. He predicted coldly that before they arrived in Bordeaux at least seven Chinese would have died in all, and that about ten more would never reach the Far East. Perhaps because he was used to it, illness seemed to him to be a normal part of life.

Huret's baby might have died the moment he shrugged his shoulders. Huret himself might have suffered from an attack of blackwater fever, for example. . . .

No! What enraged him was the lack of proportion between cause and effect.

What had actually happened? A minor accountant from Brazzaville had a sick child, and after some weeks of hesitation he decided to return to Europe.

If this accountant had had, say, ten thousand francs waiting for him, things would have worked out. The proof of this was that the child had not died and could almost be considered saved now that the temperature had dropped.

But no. He had no money. He had been put in a first-class cabin like a poor relative. He was seasick. . . .

Mechanically, Donadieu washed his hands, ran a comb through his hair, and carefully cleaned his fingernails.

There was no real drama. Nothing but a series of absurd incidents. A succession of chance events! . . .

Like the purser's being scared off by Madame Dassonville's lust and indiscretion.

Like Madame Dassonville's choosing to pursue Huret the day of the horse racing, just to anger Neuville.

Like . . .

Everything! Even the incident involving the raffle tickets!

When these minuscule facts were re-examined objectively, they became all tangled up like a swarming pile of crabs.

The result . . .

But Donadieu shrugged. No one knew what the result would be, and he walked at his usual pace toward the dining room, because nothing could ever make him move any more slowly or quickly than he always did.

The captain, who had not dared to move Lachaux to a different table and yet undoubtedly did not want to appear to be on his side by eating with him, had sent word that he could not be present.

Madame Dassonville, sitting alone, tried to put a good face on things and exaggerated the casualness of her gestures.

Had anyone told her that Huret had been exiled to second class? And if someone had, didn't she feel humiliated?

Donadieu shook hands with the chief engineer, who was still sitting across from him.

"Nothing new?"

"Unless we run into a storm, we'll manage. The real test will come when we try to cross the bay. By the way . . ."

"What?"

"Apparently Lachaux is still up to his old tricks. Fifteen minutes ago in the bar he said loudly that if he saw the madman on deck again, no matter what time of day it was, he would complain to the company. He also demanded that running water be supplied to his cabin all day. . . ."

"What about the captain?"

"He's annoyed. He's going to want to speak to you about the madman. Since it's cooler now . . ."

Donadieu sighed and looked at Lachaux, who was eating a chicken wing with his fingers, being deliberately crude.

"As for the water, I don't see how they can give him water without giving it to all the passengers, since the same pipe runs to all the cabins."

"Are they going to give it to him?"

"As long as they can."

Huret, of course, was not there. Donadieu was very surprised to see the woman he had asked to undress in his cabin looking at him warmly. Her little husband was eating voraciously, as though trying to make up for the privations of life in the colonies.

"You've 'scored'!" said the chief engineer, noticing the woman.

"Thank you."

At any other time he might have been flattered. She was attractive, in spite of the contrast between her extremely white body and her sunburned arms. Naked, she looked as though she was wearing gloves up to her armpits.

"A rotten trip," muttered the chief engineer, without knowing exactly why.

When you're used to taking on passengers this way for a three-week-long voyage, you feel these things. It's a matter of intuition. On the very first day, you can tell whether the crossing will be good or full of sinister feelings.

"And how about your Chinese?"

"Another three or four will probably die," answered Donadieu, helping himself to some applesauce.

The purser, coming in late, leaned over the doctor and murmured:

"He's in his cabin. . . . I've just come from second class, and he hasn't set foot in the dining room. . . ."

Ten

Before he opened his eyes, even before he was completely awake, Donadieu knew that this would be a difficult day. He felt slightly sick. There was a persistent pain in his head which became more intense with the least motion. He remembered that the night before he had smoked three or four more pipes than usual. And when that happened, he was as upset as though he had been caught doing something shameful.

The sight of the little oil lamp was unpleasant to him. He put it away in his cupboard and prepared a dose of medicine for himself. Looking just as calm and serene as on any other day, he began to wash, sometimes pausing to listen to the noises of the boat.

Why should a night like that have left him feeling so bitter? He had smoked his pipes, as he did every night. And as always, he had been tempted to go on smoking. His hand had reached out toward the pot of opium, toward the needle.

He had given in. He was ashamed of it, but still he tried to recover some trace of the atmosphere of the night before.

It had not been very extraordinary, anyway. He had not had wild dreams; he had not felt anything unusual.

The boat was asleep. As they approached Tenerife there was not a breath of wind, and the sea was smooth, rising and falling slowly in the swell that came from far out in the Atlantic.

The porthole was open and fresh air blew in. He drank it as though it were water. Beyond, he could see a piece of sky colored silver by the moon.

He turned off the electric light. Only the little reddish flame in the night light danced, and the gusts of air from outside drove the stale smell of opium into every corner of the room.

But none of this mattered. What mattered was something else. Donadieu, stretched out on the bunk, stared at the light-blue disk of the porthole without seeing it.

Was he breathing? Was his pulse beating? It didn't matter! He was living a life other than his own. He was living ten lives, a hundred lives, or, rather, one multiple life, the life of the entire boat.

He was familiar with the scenery. He did not have to go up on deck to know that you could already see the high foothills of the islands, dotted with a few lights. Maybe the ship was even passing silent fishing boats, which immediately vanished from sight.

The captain was on the bridge, dressed in his wool uniform, watching the ship's course and looking out for the pilot boat.

Already the night had ceased to have an African feel. It was almost Mediterranean. The passengers had lingered on the bar terrace until one in the morning. Half an hour later Donadieu heard whispering and suppressed laughter, and he was aware that Madame Bassot was with one of the lieutenants, looking for a dark corner.

Even better, he could predict that the couple would end up on the embarkation deck, because all the crossings were the same, and the same people did the same things in the same places.

He was not envious. He enjoyed imagining Isabelle's white thighs emerging little by little from the silky material of her dress.

Madame Dassonville was asleep and had certainly gone to sleep in a bad mood. Hadn't she been affected by what had happened the day before? She had not even seen Huret after that, because he had not left his cabin all afternoon or evening. Now she knew that he was a second-class passenger who had been admitted to first class as a favor.

She was annoyed, and underneath she really blamed the purser. As for him, he remained quite offhand, with a malicious spark in the pupil of his roguish eye.

The screw was turning smoothly. The ship was hardly listing at all. Donadieu loved the large rocking motion of the swell, but Huret, in his stuffy cabin, must have suffered, must still be suffering.

During the afternoon the doctor had stopped before the door to number 7 several times, with the vague hope that it would open by chance. He had leaned over to listen. He had heard murmurs.

What had the couple been saying to each other hour after hour? Did Madame Huret know that her husband was the lover of one of the passengers? Didn't she guess the various reasons for his excitement? Had she been scolding him?

What reasons did he give her for the fact that he refused to leave the cabin? He had not had any food brought to him. At one o'clock and at seven o'clock his wife's meals had been brought, and Donadieu had thought that at last the door would open. It opened only a crack. Madame Huret, in a dressing gown, took the tray. She was barely visible.

Had they shared the food? Had Huret been completely obstinate and in a fit of rage stayed on his bed staring at one spot on the wall?

Donadieu could imagine them, Huret on the upper bunk, unable to sleep, his stomach upset, his teeth clenched, and Madame Huret below, half naked, the cover thrown back, her hair spread over the pillow.

Wouldn't she wake up from time to time to see if her baby was breathing? Wouldn't she ask softly, lifting her head:

"Are you asleep, Jacques?"

And Donadieu could have sworn that he would pretend to be asleep, chafing at his bonds in his solitude.

Now, when he thought about it, the doctor felt a weight on his chest, but the night before, after he had been smoking, it was not the same. Because this morning he was once again part of the universe and subject to its moods, while a few hours earlier he had been above everything, serene, hardly curious about the reactions of those little creatures revolving around the earth in the iron hull of the ship.

And it was only through force of habit that he called it a ship! It was a piece of matter with life inside it. And it floated, it moved ahead toward the rocks with a regular throbbing sound. Because, after all, the Canary Islands were also just rocks with life on them.

The important thing was that the air was cool, that Donadieu was so comfortable, naked on top of the rough sheet, that he did not feel as though he even had a body.

He knew everything! He was incredibly intelligent! For example, he heard the click of the telegraph and knew that the captain was signaling for the ship to be slowed down because he thought he could see the lights of the pilot boat. He himself could see those lights with his eyes closed, he could see them bobbing between the sea and the sky, in the blue-green water of a moonlit night.

Barbarin was snoring. He slept on his back, no doubt, and from time to time he moved, groaning.

As for Lachaux, Donadieu could see him, too, squashed on his mattress like an enormous sick animal, tossing and turning, panting, throwing back the covers without finding any relief. His sweat smelled bad. He called for a bottly of Vichy water and drank little sips of it all night long, every time he woke up.

In a moment Madame Bassot would kiss the young lieutenant one last time and leave him, satiated, stepping softly and furtively into the gangway and avoiding the service steward.

Wasn't it all perfect? A Chinese man was dying quietly, his eyes on the sky, alone in the infirmary, while Mathias slept the sleep of the just in the next cabin, where small bottles of medicine stood in rows.

The other Chinese were lying in a heap. They did not want hammocks. Half of them were asleep on the deck, as peaceful as docile cows.

The civil servant with marble-colored skin who ate at the captain's table would not be returning to Africa. From now on he would go fishing, and he would paint his own punt in colors as limpid as those of his village on the bank of the Loire or the Dordogne.

Huret would not be able to sleep, but what difference did that make? There have to be all kinds of people, and all kinds of destinies, too. Huret had been born to be eaten, just as Lachaux had been born to eat other people, and that was that!

Mountains were looming up on the horizon. The officers of the watch and the sailors prepared for loading, and hatchways banged as they were flung open. Always the same cargo: bananas.

The next day, all the passengers would pay ten francs for boxes of so-called Havana cigars and then throw them overboard two days later.

It was always the same! The madman was asleep in his padded cell. An ambulance would be there to meet him when they docked in Bordeaux, and he would be taken before hospital matrons, naked, pale, and nervous.

Meanwhile Lachaux would go to Vichy for the remainder of the season, and the third-class customers—no matter where you go there is always a third class!—would point to him and murmur:

"That's Lachaux. He owns more land in Africa than two *départements* in France. . . ."

And the rest? As for the timber man, he would rejoin his pals on Avenue de Wagram or Place Pigalle. Barbarin would begin his story:

"One day on the boat, while we were playing *belote* . . ."

What did Huret think he was accomplishing by hiding himself away? Nothing! He was ruined! That was Donadieu's opinion, and it did not bother him in the slightest.

Toward the end things became more confused. The telegraph was still clicking. The screw stopped churning the water, and there was a gentle bump on the starboard as the pilot's launch came alongside. A man climbed on board.

He would be offered something to drink up there—that was the tradition—but the captain would only pour himself a finger of alcohol to be polite and would go to bed as soon as the boat had been moored.

Donadieu heard the noise of a chain being unwound and then the capstans of the cargo booms were started up. . . .

. . . There was a gap in his consciousness, and he found himself brushing his teeth in front of the mirror in his bathroom. His mouth tasted bitter, and he had an evasive look on his face.

Mathias knocked, as he did every morning, to give his report, and stood leaning against the door.

"Anything new?"

"The Chinaman died."

"Nothing else?"

"The madman has a boil on his neck. He wanted me to give him my penknife to lance it with."

"Anyone in the infirmary?"

"You know very well they're all going ashore."

Of course. And for one hundred francs apiece the company would even take about twenty of them on an excursion by bus. The purser was the one who arranged it, but he sent his second in command along to look after the passengers.

"I'm coming, Mathias."

It was a clear day, the kind of day they had not had for nearly three weeks. There would be no more thick, syrupy skies. The air was still warm, actually very warm, but the heat was honest and healthy. It did not make you pant the way the heat along the coast of Africa did.

Through the porthole Donadieu saw real human beings, people who were not blacks or colonials, people who lived there because they were born there and were spending their lives there.

He could see boats painted all different colors, fishing boats and schooners that had come from La Rochelle or Concarneau. There were real trees, streets, shops, and a large café with a terrace facing the public garden.

This was Tenerife—in other words, this was almost Europe, a mass of colors and sounds reminiscent of Spain or Italy.

The passengers were already standing around, calling to one another.

"Don't forget the camera! . . ."

Of course, the camera!

Natives were waiting for the visitors in boats, and they slipped cushions under their buttocks.

They argued:

"He's asking five francs to take us to the dock. . . ."

"Francs or pesetas?"

"How much is the peseta worth?"

"Moneychanger, gentlemen! . . . Moneychanger! Better rate here than in the banks . . ."

There were ten of them on board; satchels heavy with coins hung across their chests.

Donadieu came out of his cabin and caught sight of the purser, who was overseeing the debarkation.

"How's it going?"

"Fine. You?"

"Has he come out?"

"Who?"

Donadieu nearly blushed, because he was the only one so worried about Huret.

"I haven't seen him. . . ."

"And his wife?"

"She hasn't come on deck."

So the two of them, as well as their baby, were still shut up in their dank cabin. Huret would not have shaved or washed his face. He was undoubtedly still wearing his pajamas, and he must be looking out the porthole and watching the passengers get off.

And they were all getting off! If the couple stayed on board they would be the only ones who did. And they would stay, because they had no money.

"Did they eat this morning?" Donadieu asked, stopping a steward.

"I carried them their breakfast as usual. The lady took it. I asked when I could do their cabin, and she said I shouldn't bother."

By ten o'clock the deck was deserted. Madame Dassonville had been the last to leave, wearing a white muslin dress that made her look like a butterfly, and holding her little girl by the hand. They were followed by the nanny in pale-blue with a white cap on.

"Are you having lunch ashore?" Neuville asked Donadieu.

"No."

In spite of the medicine he had taken, he had a headache and had not even drunk his coffee. He was suffering from an agonizing sensation he could hardly define. He felt like a man who notices that a fire has just broken out and who goes around giving the alarm. But no one listens to him! People stay where they are, though they are in grave danger, continuing to live their lives as though nothing were happening! . . .

He was obsessed with that narrow cabin where three people were shut up together. Involuntarily he kept returning to it, walking by the door to number 7 and vainly trying to hear something.

What could they be doing in there? What could they be saying to each other? Madame Huret was not the kind of woman who would keep quiet. Her love for her husband was not a blind love. Did she even love him any more?

She blamed him for taking her to Africa. She blamed him for making her pregnant. She blamed him for not earning any money, for being seasick, for not making life easy for her. . . .

The fact that Huret had stayed away from the cabin during so much of the crossing had made her bitter, but now that he never left the cabin, his presence must be an even greater torture for her.

Because Huret was incapable of pretense. Even in port the boat rocked, and Donadieu knew that this swell was the most difficult to endure. He was sick! He was hot! He no longer believed in anything, not even in himself!

Yes, what could they be saying to each other? What cruel words would they have been driven to say?

And wouldn't they end up knocking their heads against the wall?

That was the least serious of all the possibilities. Worse things could happen. Worse things would certainly happen.

If his wife blamed him, didn't Huret blame his wife just as much? Wasn't she the one who had brought a sick child into the world? She was the one who had not been able to endure the climate of Africa, who had also made him spend so much money, and who in the end had forced him to break his contract and leave without any money.

She was not even beautiful. If she had been beautiful to start with, her beauty would have faded immediately, and she would not even have stayed attractive.

Alone, Huret could live, he could play *belote* and poker, win at horse racing, and captivate a woman as elegant and distinguished as Madame Dassonville.

What did she think of him? What would she say to him if they met?

He did not even have the right to meet up with her, since he had been forbidden access to first class. In his cabin he must have seemed like someone on the quarter-deck with the plague! She would be able to see him from the top of the bridge. The second-class passengers, people like "Marianne" from the masked ball, would smile when he came into their dining room. . . .

And what about the scene that would take place in Bordeaux? Because in the end he would have to settle his account at the bar. All the passengers would go ashore, and he would have to wait for a company agent to come. He would have to tell him he didn't have a penny to his name.

It didn't matter, not at all, not in the least! The night before, after smoking, Donadieu had smiled when he thought of it, but now it made him sick with nervousness.

"All it would take would be one word," he said to himself, "one foolish remark from Madame Huret at the wrong moment, for example. . . ."

Hadn't she already talked about dying?

He could see the animated city, the cars, the people in white pants. All the passengers would come back with new shoes, because Tenerife was the city for cheap shoes. They would run across one another in the same restaurants.

By three o'clock a group had settled on the terrace of the Café Glacier, near the orchestra; you could almost hear the music as you watched the bows slide over the strings. Lachaux, Barbarin, and Grenier were preparing real Pernod the way they had before the war, balancing sugar in the slotted spoons.

"Did they eat?" Donadieu asked the steward.

"I took them a plate of cold meat which they returned almost untouched. . . ."

Damn! Didn't the doctor have the right to knock on the door, to say, for example:

"Listen, children, this isn't the moment to act like a couple of idiots. What's bothering you is not important. In life everything works itself out, believe me, and it is always wrong to make extreme decisions. . . ."

The boat was almost empty. The sellers of lace, souvenirs, and cigars were only just beginning to invade it, knowing very well that the passengers would hardly be back before nightfall. There were always the same faces. Donadieu recognized them, and they recognized him and did not try to sell him anything, smiling at him in a knowing way, as though their jobs and his were somehow similar.

Whether the ship was in port or out at sea, the captain's day did not vary in the slightest, and no one had ever seen him go ashore. After the siesta Donadieu heard him pacing the bridge for his health the way he himself did, because a sailor must do some walking, too.

He felt he should go to the captain and say:

"We must do something. . . . The three of them are there in the cabin, living apart from the rest of the people on the boat, apart from the real world, and imagining things. . . . At any moment—today, tomorrow—something bad will happen. . . ."

The captain would not even have answered. It was not his job. Only Donadieu believed he was God the Father. The captain's job was to keep the boat running and observe the rules. Donadieu knew that there would be a few sentences in the orders that evening asking the officers to wear their wool uniforms, because it was traditional to dress in blue after Tenerife.

Even if the captain agreed, what could he do for Huret? Allow him to eat in first class? That was no longer possible. Give him money? He had none too much himself. Advice?

Bad-tempered as he was, Huret would not listen to advice.

And Donadieu was tempted to go back to his cabin and smoke a few more pipes so that he would recover the luxurious indifference he had felt the night before and once again believe that in nature some loss is unavoidable. Out of three hundred Chinese, four had already died. Well, so much the better for the others! Out of the two hundred white passengers, there was one madman with a boil; Huret, for whom life in the colony had not worked out; and finally the woman with pale skin who had believed she was suffering from appendicitis and who would not be reassured until the day a surgeon operated on her just to please her. Wasn't that a pretty fair average?

As for Lachaux, he had not more than two years left to live— Donadieu was sure of it. The civil servant with the parchment skin had maybe ten years, because he took such precautions in the way he lived.

But Huret's case was stupid! For Donadieu it had become a personal matter. He was now enraged by the closed door. It maddened him that three human beings were behind that door stewing in their own juices. In the end their thoughts would ferment.

He walked up and down the gangway ten times, and when he went back up on deck, their visit was ending, the lights of Tenerife were being lit, Barbarin and his companions were drinking their last Pernod to the accompaniment of Hungarian gypsy music, and small boats were setting out for the ship one by one.

Donadieu's patient, the one he had asked to undress, was carrying a Spanish shawl that her husband had haggled over for half an hour and bought at the same time as a box of fake Havana cigars. She wore it to dinner and was annoyed to see three or four similar shawls on other women. Afterward, over coffee on the bar terrace, the question was, which woman had paid least for her shawl.

The Hurets had still not appeared. They were stuck there in the ship like a foreign object lodged in someone's body. They no longer took part in the communal life. Did they even know that the anchor had just been raised, and that in four days they would be in Bordeaux? Did they know that the weather reports had been good and that the captain had promised they would arrive without any difficulties, in spite of the list? Did they know that in Europe it was already the end of the season, that as they sailed by Royan they would see the lights of the casino and make out men in tuxedos in the baccarat room, lovers walking on the beach in front of the garlands of light, and floods of taxis? Sometimes you could hear a taxi horn as the ship went past, a sound that was already a breath of city life.

The ship slowly left the port. Donadieu walked along the deck past the groups of people and studied Madame Bassot's beaming face as he went by. She was quite capable of having gone and found a new lover in the city. In any case, she had come back on board with her lieutenant.

"Too bad for them!" he muttered.

That applied to the Hurets just as much as to the other people. His hangover made him sad and pessimistic. He leaned his elbows on the railing and studied the dark second-class deck, where all you could see was the lighted windows of the saloon.

He thought he could make out a form, the form of a man in pajamas, thin and blond like Huret, threading his way among the capstans and the crates of bananas.

As precipitantly as a hunter, he left the first-class deck and ran down the stairway.

Eleven

Because of the contrast between the light and the darkness, Donadieu wandered around like a blind man for a while. He was familiar with every corner of the boat, and yet he kept bumping into things and at one point nearly stepped on two bodies—a couple of sailors who were lying on their backs chatting as they looked at the stars.

As if it had been waiting for just that moment, the phonograph in first class started playing a Hawaiian waltz that Madame Bassot had requested from the purser.

The lights on the island were no longer visible. The only light that could be seen was a torch trembling on a sailboat. The boat must have been out fishing, because when the searchlight illuminated it for a moment, its mast was completely bare, like a fishbone.

Huret had moved. Donadieu looked for him, or, rather, for the dim form of the pajamas that he had seen before.

He did not know what he was going to say. It didn't matter. He would simply talk. In the softness of the night, against the exotic background of the Hawaiian music, he would break down the barrier of mistrust that that maddened imbecile had raised between them. He would help him to be brave; at least he would keep the drama from taking place on board ship.

Darkness lay all around the saloon, which stood by itself in the middle of the quarter-deck. A yellow glow came from its windows. Up above, on the promenade deck, the first-class passengers were enjoying the cool air, wandering around in groups, and leaning on the railing. Two couples were dancing.

As he continued to walk, Donadieu suddenly saw vague faces and forms that were drowned in darkness. He nearly called out, "Huret!"

But just then he saw the young man walking rapidly away from him, like someone who is afraid but does not want to look as though he is running away.

The doctor said nothing but walked more quickly. Huret quickened his pace, too, making his way among the banana crates, which were as high as his head.

Donadieu no longer thought about what he was going to do. It had become a personal matter between Huret and him. He had to catch up with him! He had to talk to him! In order to do this, he who was always so calm was willing to run if he had to.

He almost did. The hold was open. Two sailors were looking for a trunk that Lachaux had demanded because it contained his tuxedo, and several passengers had been in evening dress that night.

The open hold formed a dimly lit square. For a moment Donadieu thought that if he continued to follow on Huret's heels, Huret might fall into the illumined hole.

Always this obsession with playing God the Father! He was only five or six meters behind Huret. He was going to corner him in the stern of the boat, and if the imbecile tried to jump overboard, he would be there in time to stop him.

The record was over, but the flip side was another Hawaiian piece with a languorous melody. The doctor must have been visible from above because of his white cap.

He quickened his pace. Huret lost his head and started to walk faster, too.

"Listen! . . ."

He said it without thinking. This was no longer real life; it was a nightmare, and all the more unpleasant because the doctor realized it was a nightmare.

Instead of stopping, instead of turning around, Huret ran straight ahead now, filled with panic.

Why did Donadieu look up toward the first-class deck? He recognized Madame Dassonville, who was out in the fresh air, her elbows on the railing, her chin in her hands.

He started running, too, heard a strange sound, a dull sound, the sound of one hard body knocking into another, then a slight metallic noise, immediately followed by someone cursing.

It had happened so fast that for an instant Donadieu could not say whether it was he or Huret who had bumped into something.

It hadn't been him! The form he was chasing had disappeared. In its place there was a spot of darkness moving on the iron deck.

And a moment later the doctor leaned over and murmured awkwardly:

"Did you hurt yourself?"

A pale, tense face stared up at him. Then the doctor looked around with the peaceful feeling that it was over, that all the danger had been averted, that he had won the game.

As he was running, Huret had bumped into a fixed block and fallen in such a way that he had broken his thigh bone.

From now on he would not count any more! He was no longer a man, but a patient. After a moment of emptiness, of hesitation, voices began calling back and forth on the first-class deck, there were hurried footsteps, orders were given, and a searchlight halfway up the mast was turned on.

Shadows swarmed in the dust of the overwhelming white light, while Huret stared angrily at the sky.

Madame Dassonville, who was shivering a little because it was colder on the quarter-deck, looked at the injured man without saying anything. The lieutenant took advantage of this moment to caress Madame Bassot's lips. People came out of the second-class saloon. It was impossible to recognize "Marianne," dressed as she was like everyone else and with her hair smoothed down.

Three men from above leaned over to see and cupped their hands around their mouths, asking:

"Who is it?"

Lachaux was standing in the middle, with Barbarin on his left and Grenier on his right.

"Tell Mathias to bring the stretcher. . . ."

Donadieu bustled around, afraid of letting his joy show. It was he who laid Huret on the stretcher, with Mathias's assistance, and he nearly helped carry it himself.

He followed the procession the way he would have followed at a child's baptism.

He had done it! A good leg had been broken, and he was pleased!

Huret did not cry out; he suppressed his groans, clenching his fists every time he was jostled, and in spite of everything examined the faces around him.

Aren't the faces that surround a man when he is hurt always kind and friendly?

"Put him in the infirmary. . . ."

"The Chinaman is there," Mathias whispered.

"In your cabin, then."

Donadieu had won! The three of them were no longer shut up in the cabin together, dwelling on gloomy thoughts.

Now things would work out. Madame Huret would not be able to scold a prostrated man. Huret did not need to walk around furtively at night on the second-class deck to get some fresh air without being seen.

He did not need to avoid Madame Dassonville, or Lachaux, or anyone. . . .

Donadieu watched him as though the younger man were his own little fledgling.

"Bring another mattress. . . ."

The curiosity seekers had left. Madame Huret had not been told yet. There was no need: first the leg had to be set, and Donadieu lovingly prepared to do it.

"Now you're all better, aren't you!" he could not stop himself from murmuring to the patient, though hoping that he would not hear.

Huret did hear him, widened his eyes, and did not understand.

And the doctor was the more embarrassed of the two.

They actually did see the Royan casino and the lights of the promenade as they went by. An hour later they struck the tidal wave, and at that point Lachaux would have had his moment of triumph at last, if he had not been asleep.

The *Aquitaine* touched bottom with such force and listed so far over that the captain telegraphed to Bordeaux for a tugboat.

No one noticed, even though these were the most difficult hours of all for the ship's officers. The ship was really in danger, and the crew prepared to launch the lifeboats.

The air was soft and rather fresh. The humidity of the September night left pearly drops of water on the deck and the railings.

Nevertheless, at seven o'clock, when customs opened, the *Aquitaine*, towed by its tugboat, dropped anchor before the dock, and the passengers burst out of their cabins.

About a hundred people were waiting on land to meet friends and relatives. There was also an ambulance for the madman, and that morning Madame Bassot had put on her black dress again and was looking mournful.

Lastly, there were the company agents.

But Huret, who could not settle his account at the bar, was still in bed nursing his broken leg. For the last four days, his wife had been bustling back and forth between him and the child.

"We have to watch out for complications," Donadieu had said, with a strange smile.

He was lying. The fracture was a simple one, very simple. But he wanted to go on playing the role of God the Father.

It had worked, hadn't it? He had brought both of them safely to Bordeaux, all three of them really, since the baby was still alive, pursing its soft lips around the rubber nipple.

If Huret owed several hundred francs to the bar, they would give him time to pay. Madame Dassonville was no longer there to notice him, nor even Lachaux, who was disembarking with all the dignity of an Asian potentate.

And what about the stolen wallet? . . .

No one was ever sure, although Grenier was arrested two years later for the same sort of theft, in a large hotel in Deauville.

At that time the Hurets were leading an uneventful life. Huret was the second-ranking accountant in an insurance company in Meaux.

As for Donadieu, he was traveling the Indies route again; he would spot passengers who were in search of thrills, and on certain evenings he would introduce them to opium in his cabin. But the rumor was that he never made a profit from it.